RENDEZVOUS WITH THE ROCK

A Novel by
EDITH V. BUCK

Star Song
PUBLISHING GROUP

Nashville

365346

Star Song Contemporary Classics is committed to publishing titles that address real life issues in a dramatic and memorable fashion and are as edifying as they are entertaining.

Star Song Publishing Group, a division of Jubilee Communications, Inc. 2325 Crestmoor, Nashville, Tennessee 37215.
Printed in the United States of America.

First Printing, May 1993

Library of Congress Cataloging-in-Publication Data

Buck, Edith, 1919–
    Rendezvous with the rock / by Edith Buck.—1st ed.
        p.   cm.
    ISBN 1-56233-045-4 : $9.95
    1. Women reporters—Rocky Mountains Region—Fiction. 2. Cults—Rocky Mountains Region—Fiction. 3. Rocky Mountains Region—Fiction. I. Title.
PS3552.U3326R46   1993
813.54—dc20   93-4289
                                                                    CIP

1 2 3 4 5 6 7 8 9 10 — 99 98 97 96 95 94 93

RENDEZVOUS WITH THE ROCK

ONE

Misty Morrow maneuvered her black Porsche in and out of traffic scarcely thinking what she was doing. Near the center of the city she turned into a quiet park, where Syracuse's impressive Oglethorpe Museum of Art stood surrounded with bushes and shrubs boasting the swelling buds of spring.

She stopped her car precisely in the middle of a slot of the museum's parking area and sat without moving. For long moments she stared at, but did not see, the ornate building that bore no resemblance whatsoever to the stark brick home of *The Global News,* where she had just left a desk piled high with notes. Because Lewis Talbot, the director of the museum, had called her to come see him, she had left her desk without completing the story she was writing.

Misty always enjoyed meeting with Lewis, a friend of her father's. Now she was eager to know what he wanted. But her thoughts had not been on him as she hurried across town. From the moment she had left her desk, her thoughts had been on Lance Myers. When he had been talking politics with Hal Peterson last evening, she had overheard Lance mention *The Global* as possible support for his coming campaign for representative to the state legislature. Remembering this, she knew she had to find out what it meant. Something about that comment bothered her. Is it me he wants, she asked herself, or Dad's support and the newspaper's backing?

She was glad she was going away, glad her editor-dad was sending her west to write a series of stories about the camp for terminally ill children that had been built with the fortune of the late Martha Cross. Her syndicated column "Sketches" was usually about art and artists; writing about sick children would be challenging. In all her twenty-five years she had not been around any children that much, let alone sick ones. Syndicated, the stories with her by-line, Mary Alice Morrow, would reach across the nation. It's a great career opportunity, she thought, a chance to broaden myself as a journalist.

Halting her reverie, Misty turned off the ignition. Lewis would be wondering where she was, and she was anxious to find out if his wanting to see her had to do with last evening's reception. It might be something she could use in her column.

She hurried across the parking lot and into a side door of the building. Inside the elevator she pushed the button, then felt herself being gently whisked up four stories to the suite of offices on the top floor. Her heels on the black and white tiles heralded her coming as she walked quickly to the oak door at the end of the hall. DIRECTOR. The single word painted in gold winked in the light as she turned the knob.

The young woman at the reception desk looked up. "Well, hi there! I wondered if you'd make it over here before lunch. How's everything?"

"Hi, Jan." Misty laid her attache case on Jan's desk as she slipped off her coat. "Everything's super. You should've been there last night!"

"Did everything go OK? You went with Lance, of course."

"Of course. Yes, everything was great. I even had a good time in spite of being a reporter at work. But Flora Nasby never showed. Can you feature that? The guest of honor and an up-and-coming artist who wants to become well-known. But we managed without her."

"What are you going to write about her, if she wasn't there to interview?"

"Two of her paintings were there. Lovely pastels. I'll write something about them, and I'll say something about her not being there— you know, build her up as a mystery artist. I'll be kind, but I'll whet my readers' appetites. Who knows? It might be to the woman's advantage."

"But what will the other writers say? They might come down a bit hard. Was the new feature writer for the entertainment section in *The Sun* there?"

"Oh, my de-ah, yes—she was there." Misty brushed her honey-colored hair from her left temple with her right hand arching her arm over her head in imitation. Putting her weight on one leg she thrust her hip out to one side.

"I wish I'd been able to go." Jan's gray eyes danced as she reached for the intercom. "Lewis is expecting you. I'll tell—"

"Jan!" A tall young woman had come unnoticed out of the door marked CURATOR. Dressed in a fashionable brown suit that blended with the deep russet tones of her hair, the woman looked every inch the business executive. "Will you make two copies of each of these and see that the originals get into this afternoon's mail?"

Theba Peterson spoke crisply as she handed several papers to Jan. "Do you have a problem?" she asked Misty referring to the pose Misty had just abandoned.

"No more of a one than usual," came the saucy reply.

A bit of ironic amusement played around Theba's severe mouth as she studied the blond young woman. Then she turned and walked back into her office.

"As I was saying, I'll tell Lewis you're here," said Jan suppressing a smile at the laughter in her friend's eyes.

But his door was already open. From his desk Lewis had seen Theba as she paused in the shadows listening and waiting for the right moment to hand the letters to Jan. And he had seen Misty's brief but expressive pantomime. Now he stood framed in the doorway.

"Misty! Good of you to come so promptly." Lewis Talbot's voice was deep and musical.

Pushing her hair back into place, Misty smiled. She felt comfortable with this tall, well-built man who had given her so much support. She picked up her attache case and gave a little laugh. "It's always good to get out of the office for a bit."

"I guess you know who was the bright light last evening," Lewis said to Jan. Then, turning to Misty, "Come in, and I'll tell you why I called you over."

Lewis followed Misty into the office he had occupied for the last seven years and motioned to a chair near his desk.

Misty sat back in the leather chair and watched as Lewis pulled a newspaper clipping from a folder on his desk.

"Denison Elbert. Does that name ring a bell?"

Misty tilted her head to one side. "Denison Elbert? No, I can't say that the name means anything to me."

"When I was in Denver recently," explained Lewis, "I saw two of his paintings and I was impressed. Evidently he's a new, budding artist. I found this in *The Post*." Lewis handed the clipping to Misty.

"That's a good review," said Misty, handing the article back after a quick scanning of it.

"Yes, it is. I made arrangements for this painting of an eagle to be sent to us for our September showing." Lewis handed Misty a snapshot. "You can see it is—or was—a magnificent piece of work showing the power of the eagle and the natural backdrop of mountains. Every detail was perfect. Just perfect."

"I see that," said Misty then looked at Lewis questioningly wondering why he said *was*.

"I was going to recommend it for the $10,000 prize the National Arts Council is awarding to the best American-born artist. The awards will be made at our September showing," Lewis continued. "We're expecting something like twenty entries. We already have one of Flora Nasby's, and in a letter I had from her recently she promised at least one more. Her painting is great—you saw that last night. Too bad she wasn't there. Someday I'm going to meet that woman." Lewis tapped his pencil thoughtfully. Then he went on, "Good as her paintings are, I still feel confident Denison Elbert would have been the winner. It would be a great encouragement to the young artist."

Lewis stopped talking, and Misty sat up straight on the edge of the chair waiting for what more was to come.

"The painting came directly from him yesterday," Lewis went on. "Theba was here when it arrived, and she had it set up for me when I came in this morning. Come look at it."

As Lewis spoke, he walked over to a table where a gold-framed canvas lay. He tilted it into an upright position and studied it critically—with Misty beside him. She looked silently at the snapshot then at the bird on the canvas. She gasped. While its magnificent wings were spread wide as the bird spiraled upward between jagged mountains, its strong claws, curved as if holding a catch, were empty.

"There should be a fish!" said Misty incredulously as if Lewis didn't know. She looked again at the snapshot then back at the painting trying to reassure herself. She stared at the birds claws and could barely see that paint had been applied to block out the fish the bird was carrying. Neither claw had been disfigured.

"It's been tampered with!" Lewis' voice was tinged with both anger and disappointment as he returned to his desk. Misty again sat in the chair across from him, waiting.

After a few moments of thoughtful silence Lewis spoke, "Your dad tells me he's sending you out to Colorado. To a place in the mountains called Pommel to write a series about Martha Cross."

"About the camp she left her money for," corrected Misty. "Besides that he wants me to look for a long-lost cousin he used to play with. I'm really excited about all of this."

"Camp?" Lewis seemed not to hear what else Misty said.

"A respite camp for terminally ill children. Dad wants a series done on that. Human interest, you know."

Lewis picked up a pencil and tapped it on his desk. Laying it down again, he got up and walked to the window. "I've an assignment for you, too, while you're out there in those mountains."

He turned now and looked directly at the girl. In a dark maroon suit that accentuated her ivory skin Misty looked delicate, almost fragile. Her blue eyes seemed larger than usual.

"Denison Elbert just might be in that same area."

"In that area?" repeated Misty. "Isn't he in Denver?

"No. I called Denver this morning and he's gone. Left a week ago for somewhere in the mountains. I want you to try to find him. Then maybe we'll know what's going on. Surely he doesn't even know about this." He motioned towards the canvas lying on the table.

"You want me to play detective? There are lots of mountains, you know—the Rockies, the San Juans—'In the mountains' could be many different places!"

"I realize that. I'm probably asking the impossible, but I would like you to look around. How long do you expect to be there?"

"For as long as it takes. Three—maybe four months. The camp is just about to open so it should be going full swing when I get there. Dad wants me to be involved with it, if possible, and write from the inside out. But they aren't to know I'm from a newspaper. He's afraid they'll put up a front and things won't be natural. So I'm going incognito, I guess you could say."

"Good!" claimed Lewis with a sudden burst of enthusiasm. "A couple of months will give you plenty of time to look around. You should meet lots of people, and surely someone will know of this fellow."

You know I won't be going for several weeks yet, but I'll do what I can." Misty consulted her watch and stood. "If there's nothing more, I think I'll check with Jan for lunch, then I'd best get back to the office."

She walked to the door then turned with a slight frown, her hand resting on the knob. "Lewis?"

"Yes?" His pencil paused in mid-air and his gray eyebrows went up.

"Do you really want me to look for that artist?"

"I sure do. Why?"

"I was thinking—maybe Theba—"

"Theba? Oh, no. Exploring mountains would hardly be for her," answered Lewis. "It sounds like you're going to have a busy time. Try to have some fun, too, and see the country. You'll be there in the off-season so you shouldn't have too hard a time finding a place to stay."

"That's all been arranged. I have a cabin waiting for me. Oh, don't worry. There'll be fun mixed in with my work. Well—," feeling a slight tug on the doorknob from the other side, she held it securely while she said, "thanks for the vote of confidence in my sleuthing! What was his name again? Denison _____?"

"Elbert," finished the museum's director. "Denison Elbert."

"I'll try my best. Just for you. Would you like me to close the door?"

"Please. I've some phoning to do."

As Misty came out of Lewis' office, Theba Peterson stepped back from the door eyeing Misty with something akin to suspicion.

"I just saw Denison Elbert's painting you unpacked." Misty was intimidated by Theba's cold poise.

"A shame, isn't it," was the detached reply as Theba started for the door Misty had just closed.

"Lewis is busy on the phone," Misty said crisply, "and doesn't want to be disturbed. By anyone."

Theba shrugged her shoulders and turned into her own office. Misty watched until the door closed. Theba might be Hal Peterson's wife, and Hal was Lance's friend, but there was something about the woman Misty did not like—something cold and hostile. She was always angry. Why hadn't she shown more emotion over the defaced painting? Surely she had felt upset and disappointed even as Lewis had. Why hadn't she said more about it?

Misty frowned as she thought again of what she had seen—a painting that could have been worth thousands of dollars defaced and ruined. Did the artist know? Was he himself in some way responsible? Is that why he had disappeared? But no artist would do a thing like that! A thrill of suspense ran through Misty. Now she knew definitely she would do her best to find this man and unravel this mystery.

She crossed the hall to the reception desk. "Jan, how about lunch?"

Jan glanced up from her typing. "Sure. Do you want to go now? Why don't I call the Copper Kettle and have them save us a table, then we can walk over."

"Great," said Misty. "I'm starved."

TWO

Once out of the museum the women began to walk briskly. The cold wind whipped around them while a few splatters of almost-snow landed on Misty's slightly turned-up nose.

"And I thought spring was coming," she said as she bent her head against the cold.

"Cheer up," comforted Jan, "it is. B-r-r. I'm glad we have only two blocks to go."

Their brisk walk turned into a trot leaving both girls breathless when they reached the small brick building sandwiched between towers of concrete.

"Oooh, this feels good," said Jan stepping through the door and feeling the warm air envelope her. "Hello, Gloria," she said to the hostess with the familiarity of one who comes often. "Here we are. I called for a table for two."

"I always like to come here." Misty took a place at the corner table reserved for them and looked around the small restaurant. The baskets of ferns hanging from the rafters accentuated the green in the checkered tablecloths and curtains and were reflected in the copper kettles that hung against the papered walls. "The noon crowd's gone. Good." She picked up the menu and read through it quickly. "Guess I'll by-pass the salad bar and have hot chili and a small green salad. And coffee."

"I'm for the split pea soup on a day like this. They know how to make it here." Jan smiled at the waitress who came to take their orders.

"Chili and a small green salad for Misty and split pea soup and a small salad for me. And two coffees, please."

"You are very efficient, Miss White." Misty teased. "No wonder Lewis keeps you on as receptionist, secretary, office manager, coffee maker and custodian." Warm and comfortable and feeling good about being where she was, Misty smiled at her friend.

Jan stirred her coffee thoughtfully then looked at Misty with the quizzical look that always shone in her gray eyes when she was puzzled. "What do you think about that painting, Misty? Lewis is really upset. You should have heard him when he first saw it!"

"I don't wonder. It's a strange thing."

Jan waited for the waitress to set their steaming hot bowls in front of them then, before Misty could say more, she closed her eyes and reverently bowed her head. Misty, always sensitive to Jan's cues, quickly imitated her friend and waited for her to break the silence.

"He was so excited when he walked into his office this morning and saw it," Jan said after a whispered "Amen."

She took a sip of soup before continuing. "When he really looked at the painting and realized it had been altered, he let out a roar that shook the windows!"

Misty crumbled a cracker into her chili. "Maybe the artist wanted to change the picture, like taking out the fish, and he botched it. Then he went into hiding. But then he wouldn't have sent the painting to Lewis. Not with 10,000 dollars and his reputation at stake."

"I suppose someone else could have sent the painting without being aware it was changed. I just don't believe it was altered when it left the artist," Jan insisted.

Misty looked up at Jan waiting for her to continue.

"Someone else did it. Perhaps the one who crated it. Don't ask me why. Jealousy, maybe. Or possibly it was an accident. Paint was spilled on it and then whoever did it tried to clean it off is my guess. But you're the detective, not me."

"Detective!" Misty gave a little laugh. "You know Lewis asked me to look for this Denison Elbert while I'm out west, don't you? But Jan, I haven't a clue as to where to start or what to look for, and detectives have to have clues. Besides, my real reason for going is to write a series of human interest stories on this respite camp for terminally ill kids."

"It's Martha Cross's fortune that's making this possible, isn't it. I've read her name somewhere."

"She's been in the news—one of the wealthiest women in the state of Colorado. Her husband made his fortune in gold and silver. When she died, she divided it between her heirs and this camp."

"You're going to have yourself a time, aren't you! A gold mine, terminally ill kids and a missing artist. What a challenge!"

"And a long-lost cousin Dad's asked me to watch for. But it's going to be a vacation in a way. I sure need one, I've been so tired lately. And do you know—"

Jan waited.

"I'm going to get to be me. I'm not sure you'll understand this, but—well, last night at the reception I was introduced to oh, at least two dozen people."

"That's bad?"

"I was introduced as the daughter of Will Morrow, the daughter of the editor of *The Global News*. Period."

"So? You are your dad's daughter. That's something to be proud of."

"Of course it is." Misty's voice had a note of impatience. "I *am* proud of it. Dad's a great editor and a great man. He's come a long way in spite of his handicap. But I write "Sketches," and so many people think Dad gave me that position just because I'm his daughter! You'd be surprised how much flak we both get about that. Sometime I'd like to be introduced as just me. That's one appealing thing about this assignment. Nobody is to know I'm from *Global News,* so everyone will know me for me. That should be interesting!"

Misty looked closely at her friend. "You don't think it's cricket, do you, Jan, my going there unannounced or without permission to do a story."

"No, I definitely don't!" Jan pushed her soup bowl to one side. "That's being deceitful, Misty. It's out and out lying."

"Oh, we won't print a word until we have revealed my identity and have let them read everything. That'll make it OK, won't it?" Misty smiled a dimpled smile.

"Being deceitful is only going to get you into trouble. And besides, you'll be hurting others." After putting some change on the table, Jan stood, put on her coat and changed the subject. "What does Lance say about your going? You might lose him, you know. He's pretty desirable, and lots of women would give their eye teeth to have him."

"Present company?" teased Misty.

"Excepted!" Jan made a face. "No, not for me, thanks. But there are others."

"I'm not worried." Then, suddenly, "Jan, I've an idea! I'm going to be roughing it in Colorado. I won't be in a city, you know, but in a small, almost ghost town in the mountains. I'll be living a simple life and doing lots of hiking and biking. I've got to start getting into shape. Will you go bicycling with me this Saturday, if the weather's decent? How about some sessions at the gym, too, one or two nights a week?"

"Next thing you'll be asking me to go west with you," laughed Jan as she stepped out the door.

The two young women, their coat collars pulled up close around their chins, walked the two blocks in silence, for any words would have been whisked away by the wind. They fairly ran across the open park, ducking under trees and laughing as they rounded the corner of the museum to the side entrance.

"Have you got a few minutes?" Jan shivered as she unbuttoned her coat. "I'd like to show you the exhibit room in the west wing. The men are finished with the redecorating and it's beautiful."

"I'd love to see it."

The two ran down the stairs to the lower level. Skirting behind the four exhibit rooms where different types of sculpture were being displayed during this month of March, they came to the smaller room in the west wing. This, Misty knew, was the room where the September showing would be. In spite of the odor of fresh paint that greeted the girls as they stepped into the darkened room, a solemn mustiness hovered in the corners. Jan flipped on the lights, and Misty found herself looking at blank walls, but in her mind's eye they were already filled with paintings by the artists Lewis had contacted for the fall exhibit.

"Did Lewis show you Flora Nasby's painting he has in his office?" asked Jan.

Misty shook her head.

"It's done in soft pastels like her other ones. I think they all would look well here, but someone should check these fixtures." Jan glanced at the lights that were to be directed on the paintings.

"And Eric Teasley's work would show to good advantage right

here. He uses such bold, angular lines. Do you think his painting should be next to the pastels or would that be too close?"

"Too close." Misty stepped back and studied the space. "The two would detract from one another."

"They do need something to ease them into each other," agreed Jan.

"What about the eagle? After I have found the artist and the painting's repaired and all is forgiven, it will be just the one to hang here," joked Misty. And then she fell silent.

In the brief time she had seen the painting, Misty had been deeply impressed. In spite of the obvious flaw, the painting had a gripping majesty about it; the rich colors and exquisite detail gave it a depth that was hard to explain. She would like to see it again. How would it look hanging here? No, it would demand more space with no distractions—nothing to hinder the viewer's grasping the power it expressed.

"Well, darling, are you still here? Is *The Global* managing all right without you?"

Jarred from her reverie, Misty gave a little start. She looked up at Theba, who had replaced her suit jacket with a paint-smeared smock.

Without waiting for an answer from Misty the taller young woman turned to Jan. "I laid some articles on your desk I'd like researched." She clipped off her words as if cutting them apart with sharp scissors. "This room is not ready for viewing yet. I don't think it would do to mention it in your column," she spoke pointedly to Misty. "Or the painting in Lewis' office either. If you ladies are quite through here, I'll turn off the lights."

"We'll be coming in a minute," said Jan gently.

The slender white hand, aimed at the light switch, dropped.

"Don't forget the articles, Jan. This afternoon, maybe? And when I need to discuss what paintings to hang where for a showing, I'll be sure to consult you." Raising her eyebrows ever so slightly, Theba turned and walked away.

Misty relaxed her hands that were clenched in her coat pockets. She looked at Jan, who only smiled and shook her head as she whispered, "I really don't have the right to say where paintings should be hung. I'll tell her I'm sorry."

"Oh, Jan, come on! Honestly! You've got a right to your opinion. What's her problem this time?"

"I think it's Lewis' asking you to look for Denison Elbert. Theba would probably like to do that herself."

"Oh, for goodness sakes! If it wasn't that, it would be something else."

They were in the upper hall now about to go their separate ways. Jan paused on her way to her desk as she changed the subject. "Do you want to go jogging this afternoon? I could meet you at four-thirty."

But Misty shook her head. "I'd better not. I have a date with Lance at six-thirty. Dinner, then the symphony. I may have to work up until the last minute after taking this extra lunch time."

"And you wonder why you're tired!" chided Jan in good humor. "Let me know what day you want to start shaping up."

✃❦✄

It was well after five when Misty let herself into her apartment. "Whew! I'm bushed!" she said to her reflection in the bathroom mirror. The short walk from the garage had made her cheeks rosy. She ran her fingers through her long hair before she brushed it vigorously. "A hot shower and a cup of tea, and then I'll get dressed," she promised herself.

Warm and refreshed after her shower she put on her plush robe. Then on impulse she went to her desk and found a large map. Carefully, she smoothed out the creases as she spread it on the small table in the dining alcove. While she sipped her tea, she studied Colorado and noted the bordering states. She traced around the mountain state with one finger then sighed and turned away. "If I'm not ready when Lance comes," she chided herself, "he won't be in a good mood."

She chose a royal blue chiffon dress with gathered three quarter length sleeves and a soft rounded neckline. Tiny covered buttons from the neckline to the waist held the bodice snugly while the skirt, knee length in front, dipped loosely behind her legs almost touching her ankles. She smoothed the skirt over her small hips then turned in front of her mirror checking herself from all angles. She swept her long hair up and off her shoulders and turned again in front of the mirror, first this way, then that. Lance liked her hair up so she piled it high on her head, fastening it with sapphire-edged combs leaving soft curls over her temples and forehead. After adding a silver necklace around her white throat, she slipped her feet into blue sandals just as the doorbell rang.

"Hi," she said as she opened the door.

Lance, impeccably dressed for the evening in his tuxedo, gave Misty a quick smile and kiss. His black hair, expertly styled and shaped, shone in the lamplight. Misty caught the fragrance of the cologne mixed with his self-importance and confidence as he stepped into the room. A handsome man except for his deep-set, black eyes that were too small for the rest of his face, he stood just a smidgen under six feet.

He looked at Misty critically. "Is that what you're wearing?"

"Well, yes it is. Is there anything wrong with it?" Misty smoothed the dress while she studied it closely. Then she looked up expectantly.

"No, not really. I just thought you'd wear your black dress with the shiny things on the skirt. Are you ready?"

"This dress is fine," Misty assured him as she checked once more in the mirror. Then, after a moment, "I'm ready." She gave a little twirl away from the mirror, her eyes dancing. "I'll get my cape."

"What's the map for?" Lance called to her as she went into her bedroom.

"I just wanted to make sure Colorado is where it used to be. That's where I'm going, you know." She stood beside him now and looked again at the map.

"No, I didn't know." Lance took her cape from her and draped the soft cashmere around her shoulders. "Colorado?"

"Dad's sending me out there on an assignment, and I'm going to do some sleuthing for Lewis, too."

"You're what?"

Misty gave a little lilting laugh. "Come on. I'll explain over the prime rib."

※❦❀

The prime rib was done to perfection. The salad dressing was a delicious house dressing of vingear and oil blended with cheeses. The lights were low and the music soft. Misty could see Lance was relaxed, even enjoying himself as he listened to her with an amused smile.

"If I didn't know you better, Mary Alice," he always used her given name when he was either highly amused or irritated, "I'd think you were nuts."

"Why?"

"To go out there in those mountains by yourself, for one thing. To stay for an indefinite time, for another. And to even think you could find a missing artist that Lewis Talbot is looking for! Missing cousin, maybe. But a missing artist? No. Why doesn't Lewis send Theba? She has a husband who would probably go with her." Lance shook his head. "If I didn't know you better, I'd say you are weird!"

"Well, you don't know me better, and I'm not weird or nuts and *don't* call me Mary Alice."

"Be sensible then. Let your dad get someone else to go or at least send someone with you. And tell Lewis to find his own man. You'd never in all this world make a detective."

"Let's not spoil the evening by arguing." Misty drank slowly until she had drained her glass. Then, crunching a piece of ice between her teeth, she added, "Besides, it's getting late. We'd better go."

✖✖✖

Misty settled herself for an evening of her favorites, Tschaikowsky and Brahms with a Vivaldi number for contrast. She nodded and waved to several other couples before the lights dimmed then slipped an arm through Lance's as she waited expectantly for the orchestra to begin. Feeling no response from the man beside her, she withdrew her arm and gave him a side-long glance without turning her head. He glanced at her with a slight half smile and taking her hand returned her arm back through his.

The music washed over Misty and touched depths within her she seldom explored. She tried to ignore the old familiar longing that rose to the surface as she closed her eyes and listened to the harmonies of Tschaikowsky. Sometimes in church the same emotion drenched her; sometimes on the snowy slopes. There had even been times when she sat alone in her apartment—times when she had been gripped by the intensity of a universal longing for peace and assurance, a longing to belong. Tears slid out from under her eyelashes and would have coursed their way down her cheeks except that she stopped them with the fingers of her free hand. She risked another glance at Lance, hoping he had not noticed. He just might not understand such emotion.

When the last number had been played and the ovations received, the music had left its imprint on Misty.

"Hey, Lance!"

Struggling to take her place in reality, Misty looked in the direction of the greeting aimed at Lance. She recognized Hal Peterson's voice and gave a little tug to Lance's arm. "Let's go this way." She pointed to another aisle. Seeing tall, willowy Theba three times in one day would be too much.

But Lance chose not to notice the impatient signal. Instead he answered, "Hal! Great to see you." After all, Hal, the son of Peterson and Son Engineering Firm, was not only a good friend, but a friend with political influence and good advice. Lance did not ignore such friends.

Misty pressed against Lance trying to make herself less obvious, but her efforts succeeded only in making her honey-colored hair and blue dress look all the more lovely against his dark suit.

"Mary Alice! Misty!" Misty stiffened as she looked into Theba's veiled eyes. "You look simply stunning in that dress!"

Lance looked at the woman beside him and beamed.

"Why don't you join us?" Misty was aware that Theba was speaking to Lance but with a quick you-too-of-course-darling look in her direction. "We're going to Chi-Chi's for supper. Tom and Linda and the Scotts are coming. We want you to come, too." Theba smiled at her then, and Misty stiffened still more.

Two-faced! she thought as she remembered the two encounters earlier in the day.

"That sounds like a good way to end the evening," said Lance. "We'll be there in twenty minutes."

Lance and Misty worked their way through the crowd to the gaily lit marquee while Misty, her heart still edged with a bit of the longing the music had created, tried vainly to feel pleased with Theba's invitation. But this time she could not even fake pleasure. If she had not seen the woman at the museum, if she had not heard her speak to Jan the way she had—but she had seen and she had heard.

Feeling the fresh air of the street cool on her burning cheeks, she looked up at Lance. "I'd rather not go to Chi-Chi's. I—don't feel— that I can."

"Do you have a headache?"

"No, I don't have a headache. But my feet hurt! Besides I'm awfully tired. Why don't you take me home, then you go? I don't want
you to miss it. I just wouldn't be any fun. Besides, you and Hal will
get involved in more politics."

"Your feet hurt?" Lance raised his eyebrows as he looked at Misty.
"Is that what you want me to tell Theba?"

"Sure. Tell her my feet hurt. It's true. And I am tired."

"If you insist," said Lance without any argument. "You'll miss a
good time," he added as he closed the car door.

"Hopefully there'll be other better times without that witch,"
murmured Misty to herself.

She sat close to Lance as they drove to her apartment, but neither
spoke.

"Don't bother coming in," she said when they reached her door.
"I know you want to be with the others. Thanks for the evening. It
was super."

Lance looked down at her. "That dress is OK. Theba seemed to
like it. I hope your—er, feet will be better in the morning. Go take
something for them and get to bed." He leaned over and kissed her
lightly. "I'll call you tomorrow evening."

Misty let herself into her apartment, closed the door and leaned
against it for a moment. She kicked off first one shoe and then the
other. Catching her cape with one hand as it slid off her shoulders, she
carelessly dragged it behind her as she walked across the room.

She stopped at the table where the map lay and picking up a pencil
drew a circle around Colorado. Pulling the combs out of her hair so it
hung free and loose around her face, she leaned over the map and studied it even more closely. She found Denver and a series of little upside
down V's around and to the west of that city.

"Mountains!" breathed Misty. "Pommel must be just about
there," and she put the point of the pencil on a spot in the midst of
the mountains. "I guess it's too small to put on this map. No, there
it is! Right by this river." She drew another circle around the small print
that was the name of the town.

"That's where Dad lived. I wonder—" Against her will she
thought of Theba Peterson. "I wonder if Theba's family lived anywhere near there. Seems like she mentioned something about living in
Colorado as a child. Maybe that's why she wants Lewis to send her to

look for that artist. Maybe she wants to see Pommel, too. Hmm. Oh, well. That's her problem."

With her eyes Misty measured the distance from Syracuse to the spot she had just circled. Then going into her bedroom, she took off her dress and started to hang it up, but instead dropped it on her bed. Opening the bottom drawer of a chest in the back of her closet, she pulled out a pair of faded jeans and a flannel shirt. She took them out where there was more light and held them up for inspection before she put them on and examined her reflection in her full-length mirror.

"They're just perfect," she said. "I'm sure glad I kept them. New ones wouldn't be faded enough. I've got two more pair in there and a couple more shirts. I'll find some cotton skirts somewhere and blouses and I'll have my Pommel wardrobe. Oh," she held her hair back from her face with one hand. "I should have a bandana and another pair of jogging shoes then I'll be all set. And some cheap sandals to wear with a skirt."

She looked at herself again in the mirror and smiled. "You can do it! No matter what Lance says, you can do it!" Then she picked up the blue chiffon and hung it in the closet. She pulled out the skirt of the black dress that hung next to it and looked at the sequins sparkling in the light. "I wonder if Theba likes this one, too. She's seen both of them before, but of course she had to say something in front of Lance. I know she called me Mary Alice just to impress him. Wouldn't it be awful if Lewis should decide to send her with me? Oh, but he wouldn't do that. He just wouldn't!"

Misty eased her feet into her lamb's wool slippers. Still wearing her jeans and flannel shirt, she picked up an atlas her mother had loaned her. It was an old atlas that had been in the family for years and Misty rubbed her hand over the cover enjoying the feel of the rough texture as she had when a child. She used to hide pictures in the book, pictures and paper dolls pretending she was traveling to the different states far from home. She opened it now to Colorado. Two paper dolls cut from a Sears Roebuck catalog of sixteen years before slid to the floor along with three other pieces of paper. Tucking the dolls back into place she curiously turned the papers over in her hand.

One was a theatre program of a little more than a year ago. It had been her third date with Lance, and she had been so impressed with him that even the next day the memory of the program was all fuzzy.

She had borrowed the atlas when they wanted to go skiing in Maine shortly after and for some reason she had tucked the program in the big book.

The second paper was an invitation to a bridal shower, the herald of a marriage that had blossomed into a family of four, it had been that long ago. The third was a church bulletin for Easter dated ten years earlier. She remembered she had sung in the youth choir.

Misty started to put all three momentoes farther back in the book, leaving them to once again be forgotten when she saw another folded paper caught in the binding. Gently she pulled the brittle paper free and, careful not to tear it, she smoothed it open on her lap.

It had been part of the atlas for as long as she could remember, and many were the times she had spread it on her lap just as she was doing now, wondering and imagining. She bent closer to study the faded crayon drawing. There were the jagged lines across the top, which even as a child, she knew were mountains. And there was a cabin labeled "our Home," set in among more jagged lines which bore the name Rockies. It was this that had claimed Misty's childish imagination. A cabin? In the mountains? She had always caught her breath with wonder and excitement when she thought about it.

Her dad had often told Misty stories about the gold mine where the precious nuggets were sluiced from the gravel by running water over the gravel and washing it away. What was the mine like now? Were any of the buildings still standing?

Three stick figures stood in front of the cabin. The name Willie in bright red under the first figure identified her father while his cousins, Matty and Ruby, boasted purple names. I used to love to pretend the cousins were my age and lived nearby, she thought, someone to play with.

Underneath the picture were scrawled the words, "Happy birthday to my dearest cousin Willie from Ruby Wade."

Misty looked at the picture again before gently folding and placing it back in the atlas. Ruby had died some time ago, but Misty's father had no idea what had happened to Matty. It had been forty-five, maybe forty-seven years. Was she still in the mountains? Trying to trace her would be interesting.

Misty closed the atlas and pursed her lips. Matty—Denison Elbert; a lost cousin and a missing artist! What am I getting myself into, anyway? she wondered. It would make it a lot easier, if they could be lumped together. Well, all I can do is try my best to please my dad and Lewis Talbot, two of my favorite people.

She looked at the map on the table once more, then folded it and put it in her desk. Tomorrow would be a busy day, and she was tired.

THREE

"Alice, my dear, you've done yourself proud again." Lewis smiled at his hostess as he touched his mouth with his napkin. "These au gratin potatoes are great. Really great."

"Misty fixed them. She came over early before church and had them in the oven in no time flat."

"Out of a box?" asked Lance stopping his fork halfway to his mouth.

"No, not out of a box!" Misty's smile softened her answer. "I pared everyone of them, so there. And grated the cheese."

"A woman of many talents," murmured Lance, and he winked at Misty across from him.

Misty felt the comfortable warmth that always spread over her when Lance looked at her the way he was doing now. She smiled back and enjoyed still more the appraisal of his look. Moments like this made her forget the doubts which had been nagging her.

"It was good to see you in church." Will, Misty's father, looked at Lance. "It's been a while."

"Yes—well, I've been attending some of the meetings at the Learning Center over on Ridge Avenue. Interesting concepts there. Love, power, developing your inner self-strength to solve problems, and the like."

"I see," said Will. "You'll have to tell us about it sometime. How did you like the sermon?" He turned to his friend Lewis.

"Great, if you like political sermons," was the reply. "Personally, I don't. I can get all I want of politics from the media."

"I thought it rather good," objected Lance. "Since I've decided to run for the position of state representative next term, I'm tuned in even more than I have been to anything political. Even sermons."

"Well, now. So that's what is going on!" Lewis turned to the younger man. "That *is* an announcement!"

"May I quote you?" asked Will with the keen look of an editor who never lets a story escape his scrutiny.

"Not yet, Will. I'm not ready to declare my candidacy just yet. But I do agree with Lewis that the media give good coverage. Especially the press. *The Global News* has always excelled." Lance smiled the pleased smile of one who has aimed well and hit a target.

Misty laid down her fork and searched Lance's face for a trace of what she had seen there only a few minutes before, his love for her. As she looked, the same awareness of something unpleasant crept over her once again. She saw his smile was determined, almost hard, and the lines about his mouth seemed to deepen even as she watched. Only the cleft in his chin remained unchanged.

Misty casually picked up the basket of rolls and passed them to her father while she searched frantically for something to change the subject. "I missed Mr. Hunter this morning," she said not speaking to anyone in particular.

"Eighty-nine's a good age," answered Will. "That's a long life well spent. He will be missed by everybody, very much so. When are the services?" He looked at his wife for the answer.

"Tuesday. And we should go. Poor Henrietta will be devastated without him. Sixty-three years together."

"Well, the old fellow's at peace," said Lewis. "Anyone as faithful to the Lord as he has been is surely in heaven receiving his rewards."

Lance gave a short laugh. "I wonder if he's collecting rewards like he used to collect the offering. He'd stand and wait so a person had to put something in the plate whether he intended to or not."

Pleased with the chuckle his remark drew from Lewis, Lance added, "Can't you just hear old George saying, 'Dig a little deeper, St. Peter'? And there's St. Peter digging deeper into his pockets for more rewards and smiling while he does it."

Uncomfortable, Misty studied her plate and maneuvered a piece of potato on to her fork. She wished Lance wouldn't joke that way. Not about Mr. Hunter anyway. Or was it his joking about that elderly gentleman that bothered her? No, not really. About St. Peter then? No, not him either. St. Peter, she was sure, could take care of himself in the face of Lance's jokes. It was as if—as if he were joking about something real and dear to herself, and she wanted to protect it—whatever it was. That familiar but uncomfortable longing welled up again just as it had at the symphony and again when she listened to the organ prelude this morning. She had the same difficulty swallowing.

Her mother's voice, as Alice briefly summed up the life of George Hunter, drew Misty's thoughts back to the table. "He was a dear," Alice was saying, and Misty wondered if her mother ever had the same longing that she herself had just experienced.

The five, seated around the table with the ecru lace cloth, ate on in a silence punctuated only by the clinking of silver on china and such hostess-pleasing remarks as, "Please pass the potatoes," or "May I have some more chicken?" or "This is delicious."

"Misty, did you say your plane reservations are for the 25th?" It was Lewis who broke the silence.

"For May 25th, not April," she answered, glad for the change in the tone of the conversation.

"April is much too early to go into the Colorado mountains." Alice smiled knowingly. "Even the end of May could be too early. The snow and cold will still be there."

"Mother! What do you think people do who go there to ski? Wait for the spring flowers?"

"They stay in condos and heated lodges," said Alice in a practical voice. "They don't stay in unfinished camps and search for missing artists."

Lance smiled at Misty. The way the light was shining on her, her ruffled pink blouse complimented her honey-colored hair and soft ivory complexion more than ever. "Maybe there'll be a big blizzard and she can't go," he said hopefully.

"In May? Thanks a lot." Misty wrinkled her nose at him and warmed again under his smile.

"I'm not anxious for you to go, fair lady, but it seems there are two against one. Your dad and Lewis are plotting against me. Only God or a blizzard will keep you home. Even your mother's no help."

"This is going to be a wonderful experience for her," defended Will. "And she'll be getting terrific stories about what the charity of that philanthropist, Martha Cross, accomplished. My gal's got her grandmother's spunk and determination. Always has had it. Put your blizzard away, boy. The time will go by fast. Did I hear you say something about lemon meringue pie, Mother?"

"Misty, let's let our pie wait and go for a short drive." Lance suggested as he pushed his chair away from the table. "There's something I want to show you."

Alice Morrow caught her husband's eye and widened her own ever so slightly. Will answered her unspoken question with a sly wink and glanced at Lewis who gave a nod that was hardly discernible.

"Help me take these dishes off the table and get the pie ready for the folks, and I will go." Misty began carrying plates into the kitchen.

"You two get going," said Lewis. "I can bus the dishes and bring the pie in here. Alice can cut it right at the table. Be off with you!"

"Come on, Misty," urged Lance, "We don't want to make Lewis feel bad," he joked. "He may not want to come again."

❧❦❧

"Where are we going?" Misty looked at Lance's profile as they pulled away from the curb.

"You'll see. Not too far."

Distracted by a crystalline cube on a gold cord swinging from the car mirror, Misty was more intent on watching the rainbow reflections of the cube rather than the beautifully landscaped houses they were passing. "I've been attending some of the meetings at the Learning Center over on Ridge Avenue. Interesting concepts. Love, power— your inner self-strength—" Lance had said that at dinner, and the words repeated in Misty's mind as she watched the cube.

She glanced again at the man beside her. Handsome, intelligent and ambitious he was the picture of one who knew what he wanted out of life and who would go about getting it in his own way, in his own strength. She was aware that the only crutches Lance wanted were the few well-chosen people he could use to his best advantage. Am I one of those people, she wondered. Of course I can see why he thinks he must depend on his own inner strength, a strength he has to develop. But is he right? And what if someone or thing is in his way? Will he either brush that person or thing to one side or crush it? How long has he been attending this Learning Center?

She thought back to when he had suddenly been busy Sunday afternoons and Thursday evenings. It had been for at least six months, maybe longer. Whatever, he was becoming deeply entrenched and was obviously intent on developing his personal powers so he could attain his political goals. Maybe I should attend a meeting with him, she thought, to find out something about my inner self. I certainly need some kind of spiritual strengthening.

She turned back to the cube, almost mesmerized by its swinging. After a few more moments of fascination she started to ask, "What does this—?" when Lance interrupted with, "There! See that?"

"All I see is a house that isn't finished," answered Misty taking her eyes off the cube.

"Let's get out and look at it. I meant to get the key so we could go in, but didn't. We can look through the windows though."

Lance put his hand under Misty's elbow as they walked up the stairs to a wide veranda. Then, still holding her arm, he walked to the large picture window that looked out over the roofs of other houses on to a park with tennis courts and the bridle paths she and Lance had ridden together many times. Dropping her arm so he could better shade his face, he pressed his nose against the pane as a little boy might do. "This is sure a spacious living room."

"That's a beautiful fireplace." Misty's breath made a little cloud of steam on the window. "Are you thinking of buying this?"

"Don't you think I should? It'll be great for when I'm state representative."

You'll rattle around in it. Look at how long that hallway is and that spiral stairway. Gracious!"

Lance stood back from the window then and turned her around to face him. "Don't be so naive. It's for us."

"Us?"

"Yes. Us." Lance took her chin in his hand. "You are going to marry me, aren't you?"

Misty searched his face without saying a word. Strange, she mused, I don't feel like I thought I would when this moment came. Then rising to the occasion, she said aloud, "I don't know. You've never asked."

Lance drew her to him. "You know I want you to be Mrs. Lance Myers." He leaned down and put his mouth on hers. His kiss was long and hard.

The roughness of his top coat rubbed her cheek as she rested against him. She felt the rise and fall of his chest against her as he breathed deep, controlled breaths. Struggling to be at ease, the same unpleasant thought she had had at dinner came back without warning. Try as she would she could not suppress it.

"Lance." She broke from his grasp and stepped back so she could see his face. "How long have you been planning on running for state representative?"

"How long?" Lance reached for her hand and held it tightly. "I've wanted to get into politics for years, but I made this my first goal two years ago. You will share it with me, won't you? With your dad's help there will be no problem."

With my dad's help? Misty thought, no problem with my dad's help—no indeed! She put her head down to hide her face.

"For months I've been visualizing it," Lance hurried on, "you, my wife; us, this house—my political career. It will all happen. It has to. Will you Misty? Will you marry me?"

There were tears in her eyes when she looked up, and Lance took them for the tears of joy of a girl who has just been asked the question of her dreams. "We can be married by the end of the month. You can throw a wedding together by then. For our honeymoon we'll go to Colorado first, if you like, then to California and on to Hawaii." He gathered her to him again.

Misty stood very still until his embrace relaxed.

"I'm going to Colorado on an assignment from the editor of *The Global News*. It's my job. I don't take it lightly, Lance, just because the editor is my dad. I can't just walk off and get married." She looked up into his face. She could "walk off and get married." She knew that. She knew her dad would give his blessing. She was stalling for time and she knew Lance knew it. Even so the anger in his eyes startled her.

"I'll—give you my answer when I come home," she added almost apologetically.

"That may be too late."

"If my answer isn't worth waiting for—" she began slowly.

"No, no. That's not it at all." He answered a little too quickly. "It's just that something might happen to you."

"Nothing's going to happen to me."

"You might change, and I want you just the way you are." He studied her face thoughtfully before he kissed her again. Then he led her back down the steps to the car.

Lewis and Will were in the living room when Misty and Lance went back to the house. The men stopped their earnest discussion and looked up at the couple expectantly. Alice came in from the kitchen, dish towel in hand.

"We're back," said Misty avoiding their eyes.

The older people looked from Lance to Misty but when she asked, "Is there any pie left or did you eat it all?" Will shifted in his chair and answered lightly, "We left a piece or two." And he turned back to Lewis.

Misty dropped her coat on a chair and followed her mother into the kitchen. Lance watched Misty disappear through the door then sat in an over-stuffed chair opposite Will and cleared his throat. "We just drove around some of the building that's going on on Beacon Street. A good sign of a good economy."

"Ah, yes, you might say so," commented Will noticing the dark look in Lance's eyes. "Lewis and I were just discussing the president's budget plans. I was saying that—"

When Misty entered the kitchen, Alice went on with what she was doing without saying a word. She watched her daughter cut two wedges of pie and place them on the fine china plates. "Mom," said Misty licking a bit of meringue off a finger, "Did you know for sure that you were in love with Dad before you married him?"

"I knew for sure. Misty, don't ever marry without being sure that you are in love. Some girls think that love will come, or they are in love with the idea of being in love. A marriage based on anything but true love will end in a shambles. I suppose there are exceptions just as there are exceptions to almost any rule, but it would have to take two exceptional people to make the exception! Married life isn't easy. It takes all of the support you can give it, and the first support is true love."

"You and Dad have surely been a wonderful example," answered

Misty, and putting the two plates on a tray with two cups of coffee, she pushed through the door into the living room.

It was dark when Lewis went home, and Lance rose to leave shortly after. "No point in asking if I may take you to your apartment. You have your car here, don't you?"

"Yes, I do. But I'm not ready to go yet anyway."

"I'll call you later. About ten? Bye until then." Lance seldom if ever kissed her in front of anyone, but tonight he took Misty's face in his hands and kissed her gently. Then he was gone.

"Quite an ambitious young man," said Will as he stretched before he sat down again and picked up the Sunday *New York Times*. "Politically, that is," and he winked at Misty. "It will be interesting to see just what his stand is. Right now he doesn't seem too clear on a few particulars."

"Would you support him even if I—even if he didn't know me?" Misty curled up in the chair Lance had been sitting in.

Will lowered his paper and looked at his daughter. "I never compromise, Misty, no matter what. If I don't agree with him, I'll not support him regardless."

Misty looked at the ivory-headed cane that rested against her father's chair. She was suddenly aware of its being separate from her father, something he should not have when all of her life it had seemed to be as much a part of him as his arms and legs. She looked from the cane to the leg that could never keep up with the other one.

"Dad?"

"Hmm?" Will looked over the top of his paper.

"Your cousin Ruby, the one who died—was she older or younger than Matty?"

Will looked at his daughter with narrowed eyes. Drawing his lame leg closer to the chair, he turned to watch the fire. "She was Matty's younger sister," he said almost inaudibly. "Their dad was your grandmother's brother, you know. Jerry Wade. He married Rose Tucker. They've been gone a long time, and Ruby's been gone quite a while. But Matty—I don't know. I haven't heard from her since Ruby died."

"Did Grandfather and Grandmother Morrow live close by the Wades?"

"Nearly a hundred miles apart, but we often stayed with the Wades at their mine when we went across the Divide. Many were the times I played with Ruby and Matty." He moved his cane closer. "The sluice box collapsed when we were playing under it one day. Why, I never did know but it came down on Ruby and me—pinned us both by the legs. Matty screamed for help." Will paused as he remembered. "It took a lot to get us out from under that thing. My one leg was crushed," he paused again and drew his leg closer, "but both of Ruby's were. She was in a wheelchair the rest of her life. I'd give anything—anything if it hadn't happened."

"I'm sure it was a terrible experience," said Misty as she listened to a story she had heard often. She sensed the agony it was causing her father even now. "Terrible," she repeated. There being nothing more to say, she contented herself with watching the fire.

※※

March blew into April and April became May, a time of new life and hopes. As each day passed Misty became more and more excited. She planned every detail of her trip over and over again and read the brochures and maps the travel agency had provided until she had them memorized. And she made lists of topics her stories should cover and thought of what strategies she could use to get involved with the respite camp. While she prepared, she remembered what Jan had said that day in the restaurant. "That's being deceitful—It's lying—Being deceitful will only get you into trouble." She stared at the list thoughtfully for a minute then gave a little laugh.

"Nonsense. It'll be fine. How else could I get good stories?" And she went on with her list and her plans. It would be fun to dress in jeans and jogging shoes and pose as a—pose as a what? An artist? No, not that. She would pose as a tourist. No, not that either. She would pose as just a person who was passing through and needed temporary work. There must be lots of transients in the mountains; she would be one of them. That should be simple. Different, too. It would give her a chance to really discover herself away from all that was familiar.

She thought of Matty Wade. Would she be able to find her? Watching her dad and thinking of what he had said, Matty seemed even more important now than Denison Elbert, although she knew she would keep her word to Lewis and try to locate that man.

Another thought dominated the others. I will have this time and space to evaluate my true feelings for Lance. But more importantly, his feelings for me. She thought of how she had tried to unravel the strand of unrest and disappointment that marred her feelings towards the man. She admitted to herself it had begun as a tiny thread many months ago. Now it was as if her planning to go west had given the thread permission to grow for it had tied itself securely around her heart. She heard Lance saying, "With your dad's help there will be no problem" over and over again.

But Lance, as attentive as any man would be when the girl whom he loved was leaving for an indefinite time, treated Misty as though she had accepted his proposal of marriage and everything was settled. He called her at work; he came unannounced to her office to take her out to lunch, something he had not done before.

There were farewell dinners and parties. "But I'm not going to be gone long," Misty remonstrated. "It's not like I was moving away or—anything."

"But we love parties," crooned Theba at one of the first dinners. She eyed Misty with her intense look. "And you make such a good excuse to have one! To think you are going to be writing stories and looking for a missing man. What else do you plan on doing, or will you have any free time?"

"Oh, I'll manage that," rejoined Misty.

"I'm sure you will." Theba smiled knowingly. "Take plenty of pictures so we can see what that place looks like. And the people."

"One thing I plan on doing in my spare time," murmured Misty, "is to have a good time." And then she smiled up at the tall young woman with the short russet-brown hair and wondered, as always, at the way the penciled brows arched over the hazel eyes and blended into the fine lines on Theba's forehead.

I won't have to see Theba again for a while, she thought to herself and felt wickedly peaceful while she smiled her saucy smile.

When Lance came for her the evening that would be their last together for goodness knows how long, Misty found herself dreading it. The day had gone so well and been so beautiful that she did not want to mar it with the unrest her conflicting emotions were sure to bring.

"I'll pick you up at eight in the morning," he said as he drew her to him when he was ready to leave. "But I'll be waiting for that day when I go to meet your plane instead of take you to one."

Misty clung to him with a moment of longing. Maybe—maybe it is for real, she thought. Maybe he does want me just for myself. I could be happy with him. I was sure he loved me until this thing, this suspicion reared its ugly head. She raised her face expectantly, hopefully, for his kiss, and confusion swept over her again for his kiss was hard and practical. There was no longing in it.

Once the door closed behind him, Misty tried to dismiss Lance from her mind. She was not going to let the thought of him bother her. She began to busy herself with last minute odds and ends, making sure she had packed everything she wanted to take—a suitcase of city clothes should she go to Denver, her Pommel suitcase and backpack, and, of course, her typewriter and new palmtop computer.

She was checking the items a final time when the telephone rang. Both irritation and expectancy tingled down her spine. Lance was in the habit of calling her after he left in the evenings, but tonight? Had he something more to say? Something that would reassure her?

"Hello? Oh, Jan!"

Misty allowed her body to slump against the cushion on the chair while she listened to her friend. "No, it's not too late. Sure. I'd love to have you come over. See you when you get here."

She fixed a plate of fruit and cheese for the two of them to share while they talked. And talk they did—of the parties there had been, of their lunches together and of what Jan would do without Misty. They talked of the summer that was to come and of when Misty would be returning.

They talked of Denison Elbert, and Misty tried to conjure up an image of the man. "I see him as tall and heavyset. He's got a beard and a mustache. And he's quiet—never says a word. He's not very good-looking. He struts around all of the time with a paint brush behind his ear and he keeps eagles in a cage."

Both women laughed at the verbal picture, and then they talked of Lance. "He's going to be really lost without you," said Jan. "What will he do with all of his free time?"

"I'm sure he'll manage. He'll find a way to spend it."

"Hey!" Jan took another piece of cheese and looked at Misty more closely. "You sound just a teeny bit sarcastic. Do you have anyone in particular in mind?"

"I'm thinking of my dad."

"Your dad? I don't understand."

Misty was on her knees repacking a suitcase. Holding a T-shirt in her hand she sat on the floor and looked up at Jan. "Lance wants to impress Dad."

Jan waited.

"He's planning on running for a political office, and I'm sure he wants Dad's backing. You know, the backing only *The Global News* could give."

"That's the way politicians operate, isn't it?"

"Lance doesn't love me, Jan. It's all a big front. He thinks that if I married him, he'd have an in with Dad. So—he doesn't want me for me, for myself. He wants me for what he can gain for himself. See what I mean? I'm glad I'm going away!"

"Misty," Jan's voice was gentle. "You are hurt because you think Lance is deceiving you. Now you know how deceit can hurt—not only you but many, many others."

Misty stared at her friend in silence, but chose not to discuss her plans to go incognito to Colorado. "I'm not going to have any time to worry about him!" Closing her canvas bag with a determined zip she smiled, trying to hide her hurt and confusion.

FOUR

Flying was nothing new for Misty. Even so, every flight was an adventure. This one was no exception; it held the same wonder and excitement as had her first flight—the awesome oneness with the universe, far above and beyond the reach of all that was commonplace. As the plane climbed quickly and became a silver streak in the heavens, she looked down through the 35,000 feet of atmosphere seeing only pin pricks of life held together by a network of tiny ribbons—twisting highways and thread-like rivers that criss-crossed the green and brown earth with the dot of a lake here and there. Once again Misty, caught up in the extraordinary, experienced the never-to-be-forgotten sensation of freedom.

When a blanket of clouds covered the earth, she adjusted her seat and settled back. Closing her eyes, she gave herself up to the motion of the plane, each vibration of the jets reminding her that everything she depended on, everything familiar, was behind her. Only the unknown lay ahead waiting. Her thoughts turned to the future. Hidden somewhere in those jagged mountains I have dreamed about for years are the answers to the riddles that are dancing in my head. I have an important rendezvous with those rocks—I am going to find myself there. In anticipation, she took a deep breath clenching her fists while she curled her toes inside of her shoes. Then she willed herself to relax and remember the morning and the farewells.

Lance had been as affectionate and self-confident as always when he called to take her to the airport. They had said little on the drive from the apartment. To break the silence Misty asked, "What is that thing?" as she watched the crystal swinging as rhythmically as before.

"A crystal." Lance's patronizing voice was such she sensed he would like to have added, "Stupid."

"I can see that. Why—?"

"I'll tell you about it when you come home." And Lance had said little more. In fact, his only real comment had been when he saw Misty's two suitcases, typewriter and backpack.

"Is this all?" His amazement at the luggage was unconcealed, as was his disapproval of Misty's appearance. In her dark corduroy slacks and loose-fitting sweater, her hair hanging loose over her shoulders, she looked completely unsophisticated.

"That's it except for my tiny computer," and she patted her totebag.

"You took four big bags and a garment bag to go to Bermuda for only three weeks. And you were dressed differently."

"That was then and this is now," was her brief explanation as she walked on ahead to the car. "I'm going to a different environment under different conditions."

They had all stood around in a little huddle at the airport, Jan clutching a tissue-wrapped package. Alice and Will with Lewis were beside her, but Lance had stationed himself a little to one side with Theba who was hiding behind her frozen smile.

Misty gave a little laugh. "This is some send-off for a gal who's just going on an assignment!"

"You may be gone for quite a while," reminded her father. "And don't forget, young lady, this is to be part of your vacation, too! If you can work it in," and he smiled.

When passengers with seats from row 24 on back were asked to board, Misty put her arms around her mother. "That's me—way in the back. Bye, Mom. Don't worry now, will you?"

"Goodbye, honey. No, of course I won't worry, and I will write often. Here, I've a note for you already!" Alice tucked an envelope into her daughter's hand.

Misty put the envelope into her pocket while her father put his arms around her. "Bye, Dad," she whispered as he enveloped her in a bear hug.

Lewis gave her a gentle peck on her cheek. "If you have time when you're in Denver, you might call Hal Wright at *The Post* and ask if he has any more info about Denison Elbert," he said as he tucked a box under her arm.

Then it was Lance's turn. "Goodbye, darling," he said simply. "Don't forget to write. I'll check the mailbox every day." He took her face in his hands and kissed her with a kiss that was almost lingering. Misty felt her heart lurch as it had the first time he kissed her. She looked into his eyes for the briefest moment and then turned to the others.

"Bye-bye, everyone."

Before breaking away, Misty looked at Theba who, as if prodded into action, put an arm around her and pressed a cool cheek against Misty's flushed one. "Darling, do take care. We'll miss you."

Jan broke in on the awkward moment. "Be good, you hear?" And she handed Misty the package.

※※※

Once settled, with her packages tucked under the seat in front of her with her backpack, Misty retrieved Jan's gift and carefully opened it. Inside were two books. One, a paperback, had the title *Survival in the Wilderness*. The other was a Bible.

A note slipped out and fell into Misty's lap. "I wish you the best in all that you are going to do, but I will surely miss you. I'll be praying for you—praying that you have a rewarding experience in that camp, and that you find all you're looking for including yourself. Lewis is certainly anxious about Denison Elbert. God bless you, my friend. Take care. Jan. P.S. Maybe I should pray for Denison?" A smiling face was beside the question mark.

Misty bit her lip as she looked out the window. Jan is praying for me, she thought. She looked down at the note again. "I'll be praying for you." The same old discomfort and embarrassment that always surged up in her when Jan mentioned praying did not forsake her now. Why should I feel uncomfortable, she wondered. I pray at church, I always say a little prayer at night before I go to sleep and Dad says grace before dinner—I'm not embarrassed at those times. Then why did she feel this way when Jan mentioned praying, especially now when Jan wasn't even here? She shifted her position as if that would make it easier, but it didn't. Well, and she looked at the note again, all she had to do was put those words inside of the book and shut it and she'd feel better.

After opening the small flashlight with spare batteries Lewis had given her, Misty pulled the envelope from her mother out of her pocket. She looked at it for a second before opening it. Probably full of advice, Misty thought. Her mother had said she would not worry, but then, worrying was a mother's perogative. Especially when her only child took off on such an assignment as Misty was assuming. But all the note said was, "Here's an extra fifty dollars in case you need it. Write as soon as you can. Much love. Mom." Misty laughed softly and thought, my wonderful mom, she's sure trying to turn loose of me gracefully. I wonder if I'll do as well when I'm a mother.

Misty leaned back and thought of her father. Ruby and Matty Wade. If I can't find them, I should at least learn something about them, she promised herself. Someone should know.

She closed her eyes. It would be good to just let go and not think of anything in particular. But instead of relaxing, Misty stiffened at the memory of Theba as she had stood there at the airport.

Strange that she came. One thought led to another. Or was it? It couldn't have been she wanted to be nice to me 'cause I know there's something about me she doesn't like. Maybe Hal told her to be there because of Lance—politics and all that. Or she thought she'd better impress Lewis. Whatever, there she was in all her glory.

Misty felt again the cool cheek against her hot one. I'll ask Mom to have her and Hal over for dinner sometime when Lewis and Lance and I are there, she decided. That should be interesting. If anyone can break through the crust, it's Mom.

Thirty-five minutes after the routine landing in Chicago, Misty, seated in another jet, was on the last lap of her flight heading southwest. She smiled at the red-headed young woman who took the seat next to her after stowing a bag in the overhead compartment.

"Hi," the woman smiled back. "Going to Denver?" She settled herself and fastened her seat belt.

"For a starter," said Misty. "I'm really going on into the mountains. What about you?"

"Denver. I live there. I've been in Chicago on business. What about you?"

"I live in Syracuse. I work for a newspaper there. By the way, my name's Misty."

"And mine's Chris," answered the woman. "I work for a newspaper, too. Isn't that a coincidence? *The Denver Post.* Clerical work," she added.

"It's good to know you." Misty acknowledged the introduction. "*The Post?* That *is* a coincidence!" Misty looked at Chris while she tried to remember who it was Lewis had suggested she call. After a moment she smiled apologetically. "I'm trying to remember the name of someone at *The Post* the director of a museum gave to me. Someone in the art department."

"That's my department," answered Chris. "I know the people there pretty well."

"Do you happen to know anything about an artist named Denison Elbert?"

"He's been in the office, but I didn't get to meet him."

"You don't happen to know where I could find him, do you?"

"Not really. All I know is he left Denver for somewhere in the mountains. He's a ranger, I believe."

"Oh," said Misty. Then, "Do you go to the mountains often?"

"Pretty often. I love to ski in Vail and Breckenridge."

"Have you ever been to a place called Pommel?"

"Once, on a fishing trip."

"What's it like?" asked Misty.

"It's in a gulley along the Spruce River—an old mining town. There's not too much there. Some developers are trying to revive it. They want to make it like every other place in the mountains—you know, cater to skiing enthusiasts in the winter and horseback riders in the summer. There's already a ranch farther up the gulley. And I think some kind of a children's camp is going in near there. But other than that, there's not much. Why, are you going there?"

"That's where I'm headed." Hesitant to say more, Misty turned to her book.

Chris also read until they were nearing Denver, then she leaned across Misty to see out the window better. "We seem to be circling to the west of Denver now. I'd say that Pommel could possibly be right below us."

Misty looked down to where the prevailing winds of the Continental Divide were slowly doing away with the beauty of winter's handiwork. Snow still clung to some of the higher peaks while others, submitting to the winds, exposed bare patches of ground. "All I see are rocks and trees," she said feeling slight disappointment. Everything looked so cold and forbidding—should she really be doing this crazy thing?

※✿※

Far, far below a burly man in the trees stood beside an old blue pickup, shaded his eyes, and looked up at the jet. He watched for a moment, then turned to his truck, and began unloading his shovels and axes.

"Angelo?" came a bird-like voice from the cabin that stood nearby. "Come!"

"Comin'," answered the man. "Stopped at the other cabin," he explained as he strode toward the voice. "The curtains look nice, Mama. She's s'posed to be here tomorrow."

The man paused again and looked up at the sky. The jet was out of sight, but he stood staring at the blue overhead. "She's comin'," he whispered as he rubbed his bearded chin. "Our imaging is taking shape; she's comin'." He spoke as if the words were delicious on his tongue. "Tomorrow." Then he went into the cabin.

※✿※

"Ladies and gentlemen, we are making our final approach to Stapleton International Airport." The captain's words prompted Misty to fasten her seat belt. As she watched, the Rockies in their rugged beauty seemed to reach up to the plane as it glided over a ridge of glistening white peaks. Suddenly, there was Denver with the mountains sheltering its western side and the great plains stretching east.

Misty glanced at her watch. Ten till three. There was a four o'clock bus for Frisco which she should be able to catch, if all went well. From there, on to Pommel.

Slipping on her backpack, she pressed into the aisle and took her turn deplaning. "Good luck to you," she called to Chris, who was already heading toward the exit. "Take care."

Juggling her luggage, she took an a shuttle to downtown Denver, then a cab to the bus station. Finally settled into a seat of the large interstate bus, she gave a sigh of relief. Tired, she laid her head back and watched while other passengers boarded and settled themselves.

Colorado! Was all of this for real? The mountains no longer looked cold and forbidding with snow still capping the highest ones and frosting their sides; they had become the beginning of an adventure. In a short time, she would be crossing those mountains over passes that up to now had been just names: Mosquito, Loveland, Hoosier—all as deep in the history of mining and settling of the west as they had been in wintertime snow. And she would be intruding into the mysterious silence of at least one remote, little-traveled valley creased between the mountain peaks.

The bus ran along the edges of the city; once out in the open it began to climb. Soon the suburbs gave way to deep valleys where old, old mining towns trying to keep up with the present were making the transition from winter to spring. Before long the bus entered a long tunnel that led from one side of the Continental Divide to the other. When it emerged into the daylight, Misty knew they were at a higher elevation.

It was only a two-hour trip to Frisco, but it was nearly dark when the bus stopped. Misty was glad she had made arrangements to stay overnight at a mountaineers' lodge.

When she stepped from the bus, a man climbed out of a waiting jeep parked close by. "Misty Morrow?" he asked in a friendly voice. "I'm Tom Reed from the Summit Lodge. Just climb aboard. We'll be there in nothing flat."

Picking up her suitcases, Tom took great strides back to his jeep with Misty hurrying to catch up. Her breath came in short gasps, and a light-headed feeling she had never felt before unsettled her.

"You OK?" Tom stopped and looked back at the wobbly Misty, who was trying to get her bearings.

"I—I think so." Misty took a deep breath to steady herself.

"It's the altitude," Tom reassured her. "It gets newcomers every time. Just take it easy and you'll be fine."

A quick ride took them to the edge of town and up a steep hill where the friendly lights of a log building winked in the cold dark. The warm air of the lodge rushed over Misty as she stepped inside. At one end of the room was a stone fireplace with a group of young people sitting around it. They looked up as she entered.

The man set her bags down and, taking a key off a hook, said, "Room 29. Right up the stairs and to your left. Just follow me."

"Breakfast is at seven in the dining room," he said setting her suitcases on the floor in front of her room. "Come down and join us now, if you like. We're having a social hour."

After a quick look around the sparsely furnished room, Misty pulled a pair of jeans, a flannel shirt and pullover sweater from her suitcase. She changed quickly then brushed her hair vigorously before going downstairs. Stopping briefly on the top step, she studied the scene below her: a man plucking a guitar; others, some on chairs, some on the floor in front of the fire, munching on popcorn.

Tom stood up as she approached the group. "Sit here," he said in a friendly voice. "Would you like some hot cider and popcorn?"

Misty smiled. The spontaneous friendliness warmed her even more than the fire did. "I sure would, thanks," she said.

"Welcome." A girl in a red plaid shirt moved over to make room for her. "Are you part of our mountaineer group?"

Misty shook her head. "I'm here just for overnight. I'm going to Pommel in the morning."

"You're going to Pommel? That's a neat place, what there is of it. Going to the horse ranch?"

"I hope to sometime. I'm not sure when. I have a cabin out of town aways."

"A cabin? Out of town? I don't think you have too much choice in or out of town. There are a few old cabins, period. And most of them are pretty decrepit. Oh, there are some decent ones owned by summer people but not for rent. No apartments or condos yet. Tourists are beginning to go there, though. You'll like it. Are you by any chance with that children's camp that's being built in that area?"

"I hope to be," smiled Misty. "Did you say, 'Being built?' I thought it was finished."

"I understand they've been delayed—they're just starting. All those people with the camp live in trailers or campers. If you're very far away, you'll want a jeep or a horse. There's no way to get any place otherwise."

"How about a bike? I didn't bring mine, but maybe I can get one here before I leave tomorrow. There is a bicycle shop, isn't there?"

"A bike?" The girl raised her eyebrows and smiled. "Have you ever pedaled up hill at this altitude? It's pretty rough. We're high and you'll be even higher. But if you want one, maybe Tom can accommodate you."

"How long are you going to be there?" asked Tom who had overheard.

"Oh, maybe a month," answered Misty.

"No problem. We'll fix you up in the morning."

Misty was up as daylight began to break. Excitement goaded her until she was dressed and ready to go. Stepping out on to a little porch that faced the west, she caught her breath at the spectacle unfolding before her. The highest snow-covered peak catching the first rays of the sun, not yet fully risen across the valley, became a sparkling pink jewel against an aquamarine sky. One by one the lesser peaks were set on fire with the same glow. The rosy lustre spread slowly down the snowy slopes. Even as Misty watched, the hue changed to gold, and the darkened trees at the edge of timberline took on shape and form, coming alive under the magic touch.

The pageant took a half-hour to unfold. Misty watched unmindful of the cold. Nor was she aware of anyone stepping on to the porch beside her until she heard Tom say, "The alpenglow. Have you ever seen anything like it?"

Misty only shook her head not wanting the scene to change. These were the very mountains her father had lived in as a child. The thought that he had surely witnessed the same glory made the mountains suddenly close and personal. It was as if she were, at the very moment, sharing the same breath-taking splendor with not only little Will, but with Ruby and Matty, too. Surely no words could ever describe what all of them had witnessed.

The spell was still upon her when Tom took Misty, her bags and a mountain bike he had rented to her to the service station where a weather-beaten Army jeep stood next to the gas pumps. A stocky blond man in khaki coveralls was filling the jeep with gas.

"Misty's your only passenger today?" Tom greeted the man.

"Looks as though," grinned the driver.

"Steve will get you there in short order," Tom said as he transferred her bags. "Have a good summer."

As Tom drove away, Misty turned to Steve who was fastening the mountain bike in the back of the jeep along with her luggage. "So this is the Pommel bus," she said for lack of anything better to say.

"Yeah, I guess you could call it that. I make the trip twice a day." The man checked his watch. "Eleven straight up. We'd better leave."

"So far, so good," said Misty as she climbed in. Steve looked at her questioningly, so she added, "When's your next trip?"

"Two o'clock from Pommel. Nine and two from there, eleven and three from here. All set?"

"All set," echoed Misty.

"Then we're off," said Steve and the jeep lurched forward.

FIVE

The gulley widened into a green valley as it stretched back into the hills. A first view gave Misty the impression there were no trees, but looking closer she could see aspen groves interspersed with pine and spruce huddled against the foothills; early spring crocuses and Johnny-jump-ups splashed brightly amongst them. Misty wondered how any man had dared to make his way between the peaks of the distant snow-whitened mountains that were surely as treacherous as they were beautiful.

The jeep rattled across the bright orange bridge that spanned the river and passed a half-dozen buildings before it stopped in front of a silver mobile home. The wide blue stripe girding it and flag flying over its gleaming roof set it apart from other buildings.

"Here you are!" said Steve with a grin.

"This is Pommel?" Misty looked at the few buildings before she opened the jeep door.

"This is it," Steve assured her. "And this is the post office. I'll wait for you while you check with Lillian."

Misty climbed the metal steps and opened the hinged door to be greeted by a large, gray-haired woman poised behind the counter. Steel blue eyes magnified by thick spectacles studied the newcomer as she stepped inside.

"Hi," said Misty. "I'm looking for Lillian Watson."

"I'm Lillian, the postmistress." A smile broke the severity of the older woman's appraising look. "You must be Misty Morrow! I saw you get out of Steve's jeep." Without waiting for a reply she opened a drawer and pulled out a piece of paper.

"You had a good trip?" She held the paper firmly as if she wanted to verify the good trip before she relinquished her hold.

"Yes, a very good trip," repeated Misty.

"Welcome to Pommel," the woman said as though Misty would not have been welcome had the trip been a bad one. "Your cabin's ready for you." She spoke briskly skipping over any further amenities. "The name of the owner is Angelo Giannelli." She handed Misty the piece of paper with his name written on it. "Steve knows where it is. He'll take you there. Angelo is probably waiting for you since I told him I expected you today. You'll know him when you see him. He's a big man with long black hair. You can't miss him. But then, Steve knows him."

"Thank you so much for all of the trouble you've gone to to find me a cabin. I'm looking forward to having an interesting summer here in Pommel."

"You should have," agreed the woman. "There are quite a few things to do—jeep rides in the mountains, fishing, hiking. There's a horse ranch up at the end of the valley you'll have to visit. There's to be an art workshop there to open the season. If you'd gotten here sooner and were interested in art, you might have wanted to take that in. You'll find Angelo's a good landlord. His mother's with him, and she keeps him in line." Lillian Watson gave a little chuckle. Then, catching herself, she asked in her best business-like voice, "You do want a post office box, don't you?"

"Oh, yes, of course."

"Number 23. A dollar and a half for one month, please."

After filling out the necessary form, Misty laid the money on the counter in exchange for the key which she put in her pocket. "Now I think I'm all set," she smiled. "I'll see you again soon." She started to turn away then asked, "You said 'art workshop'?"

"Up at the horse ranch. Silver Ranch they named it," only they should've named it Gold Ranch since it lies right over a gold vein they used to dredge," answered Lillian. "You can still see the tailing piles there. But it's Silver Ranch, and that's where they have these workshops. The one I mentioned will be featuring the paintings of Denison Elbert.''

The look of keen interest on the face of her listener as she took a step closer to the counter to hear better went unnoticed by the postmistress. "A writing workshop, too," she continued, "but not until August. Lots of people think they want to write or paint or do something like that. The mountains seem to inspire them. Pommel's coming to life.''

"You said 'Denison—'' Misty began but was cut off by another customer coming in.

"Elbert,'' supplied Lillian Watson. "Denison Elbert. Oh, hello, there.'' The postmistress obviously was finished with Misty and shifted her attention.

"Thank you,'' Misty threw over her shoulder as she walked away. There would be another time to ask more questions. At least she knew she was on the right track. She half glanced at a lone painting on the wall as she walked towards the door, her thoughts already on the cabin she was heading for.

"See you again,'' Lillian Watson called after her. Then, doling out stamps to the person at the counter, the postmistress spoke as if she were reopening a topic that was familiar to the two of them. "She's another one. Artists' workshop I'll bet. Denison Elbert's paintings are quite a drawing card. This town will be jumping with paint brushes and easels.''

"I'm ready," Misty told Steve as she climbed back into the jeep.

Steve's "OK" blended with the jeep's lurching ahead.

Misty made a mental note of the few cabins they passed, then turned her attention to where the jeep was taking her. Back across the bridge and leaving the cluster of buildings behind, the road followed along the river for two miles before it turned west towards the foothills that buffered the east winds. Here and there, dotting the valley as so many pockmarks, were the remains of a cabin or shed, relics of early mining days. To the south lay a cattle ranch.

Near the hill towards which they were heading Misty could see the framework of buildings under construction. She nudged Steve and pointed towards the only sign of progress in the meadow.

"A camp for kids," he yelled above the wind.

So, thought Misty, that was the camp—under construction. "Isn't it finished?" she called out to Steve above the wind.

He shook his head. "Not yet," his lips formed.

Misty felt disappointed. What she had heard at the mountaineers' lodge was so. She had planned on the camp being completed with children there, but—what would be would be. It would work out.

The jeep turned off the highway onto a dirt road that climbed the side of a curving foothill. It went up the gentle slope and wound past a large rock partially hidden among ferns, then around a bend to a small clearing where a little rough log cabin stood beside an icy stream.

An old battered blue truck stood in front of the cabin. A man in stocking feet, wearing a red and black plaid jacket hanging loose over blue bib overalls tight across his massive belly, waited on the porch. Seeing the jeep, he pulled his tattered red felt hat down tighter over his black hair, stray strands still managing to escape.

"Hi, Angelo," called Steve. "Brought you the lady you've been waiting for, the one to rent your cabin." Then turning to Misty, "This is the end of the line. If you need anything, you can get in touch through Lillian." Wasting no time, he set her bags and the bicycle on the ground, then with a nod of his head turned the jeep and started back down the dirt road.

Suddenly engulfed by her aloneness and the strange situation, Misty took a hesitant step towards the jeep and held out a hand as if to stop it, but it was already lost in the shadows. She turned toward the man on the porch, noticing his run-down boots sitting precariously on the edge.

Angelo's big hands hung loosely at his sides. "You're the lady to rent my cabin." The black eyes above the heavy beard and mustache, penetrating eyes that were almost hidden under heavy, bushy brows, took in Misty's every feature.

"The cabin's not much," apologized the big man averting his eyes from the slight girl who was hesitating on the bottom step. "But Mama and I cleaned it up and Mama, she put up the curtains and put some dishes and things in for you. The mattress is clean and she washed the blankets. I'll show you." He pushed the door open, started to walk in, then remembering himself, stood slightly to one side but only far enough so Misty brushed against him as she walked in slowly, hesitantly.

Stepping into the kitchen, the largest of three sparsley furnished rooms, Misty's heart sank. This was the cabin Lillian Watson had found for her? She stared at a sink which seemed to squat rather than stand under the single window graced with faded yellow curtains—a sink with one lone faucet. At right angles to the sink was an old cook stove with rust spots here and there that had refused to be rubbed away. A brisk fire crackled in the stove sending a comforting warmth into the forlorn cabin. Misty walked over to it and held out her cold hands rubbing them together. Probably left over from the mining days, she thought.

An apartment-sized refrigerator and the electric plate on top of it, both with second-hand store price tags still obvious, looked comfortably familiar and yet strangely out of place. Even at first glance Misty could see the cover on the table in the center of the room was vinyl with faded flowers that matched the curtains. Here and there worn spots that would show up even more under the light of the single light bulb swinging from a cord over the table, added testimony to its aging. A bouquet of blue and white crocuses in a pint jar lent intended elegance to the table.

Misty followed Angelo to the bedroom and caught her reflection in the cracked mirror that hung over the chipped chest of drawers. Her cheeks were flushed and her eyes bright. Wisps of hair hung loosely about her face. "Oh, my," she whispered as she automatically tucked the wisps into place before she examined the iron bedstead standing in a corner with a chair beside it. A window with curtains that matched the ones in the kitchen was close beside the bed; a cheap rag rug lay on the floor.

"This is a good tub." Clumsily Angelo turned on another swinging light bulb in a small room just off the bedroom and pointed to the claw-footed iron bathtub. "It holds water if you push the stopper in real tight," and he held up a hard rubber disk. "Sink's good too. The faucet's a mite rusty and drips, but no matter." With misgivings Misty eyed the sink supported with iron pipes, its rusty faucet dripping rhythmically. A just-as-rusty old toilet with a cracked lid completed the windowless bathroom.

"Water comes from the creek," Angelo was saying. "All you want. The stove heats it. It runs through coils," and he waved his hand in the air to demonstrate.

Coils? in the cook stove? thought Misty. Even she could understand that whether or not the water got hot depended on whether or
not there was a fire in the stove. And it dawned on her the fire would
depend solely on her.

She tested the mattress and felt some comfort in its firmness. She
looked at the cotton blankets on the bed. Satisfied that they were indeed clean, she followed Angelo into the kitchen again and tried not
to notice the unpainted walls and the rough floor boards showing
around the edges of the cracked linoleum. She ran her hand over the
vinyl cloth on the table before she opened the refrigerator door. It
smelled musty and unused.

Catching her lower lip between her teeth, Misty turned to Angelo.
"How much?"

"Thirty-five dollars a month." The big man narrowed his black
eyes as he watched for his tenant's reaction to his price. "And fifteen
dollars for the canned stuff we put in the cupboard."

Misty hesitated. She knew she had no choice but to take the
cabin—for now, anyway. She would check with Lillian Watson again;
perhaps there was something better available. And there was the horse
ranch, she remembered hopefully. Maybe she could find a cabin there
even though it was ten miles up the valley. But for now this would
have to do. If she lost some money on it, it was no big deal.

"That's fine," she said finally without smiling. Drawing her wallet
out of her backpack she counted out the exact amount and laid it on
the faded vinyl table cover. "I'm not sure how long I'll be here. This
is enough for one month—and for the canned stuff."

Slowly Angelo counted the bills before he pocketed them. He
soft-footed his way to the door. "If there's anything you need, I have
my truck. Mama and I go to town once a week. Not much food there,"
he pointed to the food in the lone cupboard above the sink, "so you'll
need something soon."

"Mama will like you," he added with a shy smile. "You will see.
She'll be glad to have you close." He stopped on the porch to put on
his boots. "Oh, I almost forgot. I fixed a garden spot for you. Out
here." He motioned toward the side of the cabin. "Just like Mama's,"
he added. Then he left.

Alone, Misty walked aimlessly around the cabin testing the iron
faucets and opening then closing cupboard doors. She shivered. Had

she done the right thing coming here and especially alone? If Jan were here, they would make a joke out of all this, but Jan wasn't here.

The evening shadows touched the cabin early, and Misty watched the lonely light bulb cast its own shadows as she opened a can of beans in preparation for her supper. She sat near the stove for some warmth as she ate, rinsed off her dishes in cold water, then because there was nothing else to do and she was tired, she got ready for bed.

Pulling the clammy sheet and thin blankets around her chin, she shivered again. Dear God, she began to pray silently, then stopped, wondering why she had come on this assignment. He's got to hear me, she thought, but maybe He's not listening. So she tried again. Dear God—maybe Jan's praying for me—I hope so. Oh, Lord, why did I come here?

Sleep did come eventually, but not until Misty had gotten up twice to make sure the door was securely locked and to check out what sounded like running water. Inspecting the faucets she found a small drizzle coming from one. Try as hard as she could, she could not turn it off. Opening the stove, she saw the fire was out. Well, she would build another but not till morning. With an exasperated "Oh, brother!" she crawled back into bed. The warmth was relaxing; she fell into a restless sleep.

❦

Mama had her chance to either approve or disapprove of the tenant the next morning. There had been a slight powdering of snow during the night, and the air was cold. Misty looked at the old stove and shivered. "Paper," she said. "It's got to be first." But what paper? Taking a few sheets of typing paper, she crumpled them, then placed them in the firebox. "Now kindling's what we always put on a campfire." Finding some Angelo had left for her, she laid two sticks on the paper. Matches were there too, so she struck one and watched while the paper burned and the kindling only charred. "Oh, rats!" She tried again with the same result. After the third try she kicked at the stove in desperation. "There's got to be a better cabin. I'll go see the postmistress and find a place to eat as soon as I write some letters." Putting on her jacket for warmth, she set up her typewriter and began to type.

A timid knock startled her. "Now what?" she asked the typewriter as she walked to the door.

"Well, hi." Misty's eyes opened wide at the sight of the very small woman who stood on the porch leaning against the doorjamb, her breath coming in quick, short gasps. "You must be Mrs. Giannelli."

"Call me Maria, if you please," said the woman.

The shy smile was the only thing that identified this tiny bird-like person with Angelo. Coming only to Misty's shoulder, she had gray hair streaked with a few remaining black strands. Long wisps were straying from the bun on the back of her head, the pins hitchhiking on the collar of a faded tan blouse almost the same color as the woman's skin. The blouse, partially tucked into a long quilted and equally faded skirt, had two buttons missing showing a dingy undershirt. The scuffed toes of worn boots peeked out from under the long skirt; an old green scarf completed the woman's outfit.

Soberly the woman appraised the young woman in front of her while she stooped as if to remove her boots. Straightening, she muttered, "No need. No spirit here yet," so instead she stomped the heavy boots to rid them of any dirt before she crossed the floor; then she sat down in a chair beside the table with obvious relief. She waited a few moments, catching her breath before she said, "I brought bread." She held out a package wrapped in a newspaper and dared to smile again never taking her eyes off Misty's face. "I brought seeds. For your garden." She laid several packets on the table.

"Why, thank you," said Misty picking up one of the packets, then laying it down again. "And homemade bread!" she exclaimed. "What a treat! Would you like some tea?"

"Herb tea, please," said Maria wiping her forehead with the sleeve of her blouse.

Misty checked the cupboard. "Here's some mint tea," and she took the box down, "and here's coffee if you'd rather have that."

"Oh, coffee. Angelo and me—alone, we drink it. It's fine."

"Then coffee it is," agreed Misty pleasantly.

She filled the enamel coffee pot and set it on the electric plate. "It'll be ready in a few minutes." She hoped she sounded hospitable.

"No fire?" queried Maria looking at the cold stove, its door still gaping. With quick understanding she took the newspaper the bread had been wrapped in, laid it in the stove with a half dozen sticks of kindling, and struck a match. In a few seconds the fire was roaring. "Now a bigger piece" sent Misty obediently to the wood piled on the porch. Warmth soon flooded the kitchen, and Misty, feeling almost cheerful, poured coffee for the two of them.

"She's such an interesting little person," Misty wrote to her parents after Maria left, "and I do mean little. Her hands are bird-like, and her big, heavy shoes seem to weigh her down! Her skin is brown as brown can be, and there are dark circles under her eyes. She stayed quite a while. I think she was glad to just sit and rest. I'll venture up the hill to their cabin soon and see what it's like. Dad, they're such fascinating characters I think I'll write some stories about them while I'm waiting for the camp to open; maybe make a collection for a book on mountain people. How does that sound?"

⚜

When Misty had finished her letters, it was too late to go to town to mail them. "I may as well scout around," she decided after putting more wood in the stove and standing on the porch to look at the distant mountains whose peaks she could see through the trees. "It is beautiful here," she admitted to herself, admiring the view. The snow had melted, and the fragrance of spring filled the air.

Slipping and sliding down the rocky hill, following the stream that flowed gently past her cabin, she came to the meadow and pond. Pausing there to listen to a meadowlark, faint sounds of electric saws mingled with birds' songs. The camp. Down behind the trees. Tomorrow she would venture there to see what was going on. Maybe they needed help; maybe she could get work. Doing what, she didn't know, but something might open up.

Climbing back up the hill proved much, much harder and slower than going down. After stopping to pick more crocuses and scooping up a bit of snow hiding under a bush to throw at a tree, she scrambled over the rest of the rocks and sat on a stump to rest. "I've never heard it so quiet," she said to herself. "There is absolutely no sound except an occasional bird song. Even the sound of the saws has faded. I could learn to like this, I think. Jan would say the peace of God is here. I've always wanted a cabin in the mountains, but this one? And Angelo— I don't trust him. I've *got* to find another place."

She knew Angelo and Maria had done their best to make her comfortable—the wood piled on the porch, the "canned stuff" in the cupboard—she would have had no food without it, but she laughed out loud when she saw the boxed-in garden spot next to the cabin. "Just like Mama's," Angelo had said. Now Misty laughed again. "A garden? Me? Plant a garden?"

"Why not?" she asked herself after studying the spot for a few minutes. "It might be fun."

The sun was not yet ready to dip below the trees; there was still time. She went into the cabin to get the packets of seeds Maria had left. Poking tiny holes into the ground with a pencil, she began to place a seed in each one. "Hey, this is a real challenge. There you go." And she poured the carrot seeds into a little furrow.

Covering the seeds, she straightened and put her hand in the small of her back while she flexed her shoulders. Then she turned her face up to the late western sun. Closing her eyes for a moment, she reveled in the sun's warmth as it penetrated her faded flannel shirt and jeans. Opening her eyes, she saw an old toad hop out from under a rock and eye her suspiciously.

"I did it!" she exclaimed with only the toad to hear her. "I've planted a garden. First thing in the morning I'll go to town. Maybe Lillian Watson can tell me who to talk to about getting a job at the camp; it should be interesting to be in on the construction. And maybe this time I'll get a chance to ask her about Denison Elbert." So saying she went into the house, added more wood to the fire and opened a can of baked beans. It would be a long evening, but she would do her best.

❧❦☙

Coasting down the hill in the crisp morning air was pure joy, a feeling of freedom and abandonment before pedaling along the highway. She stopped where she could see the camp, trying to make something out of the activity that was going on. Two house trailers and a mobile home stood to one side, all else were unfinished buildings.

Perhaps she should ride over there now. It was only about a half mile off the highway. "Talk to the postmistress first," she instructed herself as she headed for the bridge. "Stop on the way back."

Misty went directly to her mail box when she stepped into the post office; both the camp and Denison Elbert were suddenly less important than news from home. Anyway Lillian Watson was busy on the phone.

She smiled as she tore open the letter from Lance. Her heart skipped a beat as she began to read, but her smile soon turned into a slight frown. He had such a persuasive way of writing, and she still was not ready to be persuaded. The house was finished now—"their house" on Beacon Street. "Their house?" Beacon Street? It was in another world.

She stared unseeing at the letter for a few moments. Lance smiled at her from between the lines, and as she thought of his ambitions, the old unsettled feeling pressed in on her once again. Pursing her lips, she deliberately folded the letter and tucked it back into the envelope. She would have to face making a decision in a couple of months, but for now she had other things to think about.

"Both Lewis and Theba are as eager as little kids for news from the mountains," Jan wrote. "Theba's planning a trip alone. I think she's going west, maybe to some mountains. I don't know for sure; I wish I did so I could tell you. I guess she's hoping there will be news of the missing artist before she leaves."

Misty tucked the letters, including one from her mom which she would enjoy later, into her pocket and stepped up to the counter. While she waited for the postmistress she studied the painting on the wall. It was a picture of Spruce River and the valley in the fall, well done in soft greens and yellows. The details were clear even to the jagged rocks and quivering aspen along the edge of the river.

"May I help you?" Lillian Watson turned from hanging up the phone. Recognizing Misty she added, "How's everything going?"

"Frankly," confessed Misty in her straight-forward way, "I don't like the cabin. It's too—too primitive. Do you know of any other? Surely there's something better available."

Lillian shook her head. "That's the only one with indoor plumbing available right now. In the fall when summer people leave— But they're beginning to come now, so that's all there is."

"What about Silver Ranch?" persisted Misty. "Would there be anything there?"

"I doubt it." Again the postmistress shook her head. "That's ten miles away, remember. Quite a trip on a bike at this altitude if you should want to come into town."

Misty pursed her lips. "I'll go to the workshop. In two weeks? I can wait that long I guess. Maybe I can find out then. I can handle ten miles on that mountain bike."

"Oh, the workshop happens to be filled," said Lillian. "That's why I said 'if you'd come sooner.' You may be able to get in for the following weekend. There would be no workshop, but it would be a nice way to spend a weekend. Would you like to try? Glenn Fisher, the ranch director, was in just yesterday and left a bunch of summer brochures. Here, have one." Lillian handed Misty a shiny, colorful folder with a picture of a ranch nestled at the foot of mountains.

Misty frowned. The workshop full? Still, if she went the weekend after, she might be able to learn something about Denison Elbert and at the same time find a better place to stay. She could spend this week getting acquainted with Pommel and the camp. "Yes," she said finally, "I'd like that. Should I write for a reservation?"

"I'll call for you." Lillian dialed before Misty could answer. "Glenn? Lillian here. Do you have a vacancy for the weekend after the workshop? I have someone here who's interested." A pause then Lillian nodded to Misty and covered the mouthpiece with her hand at the same time. "It's eighty dollars a night. Is that all right?"

"Fine."

"She wants the room," said Lillian into the phone. "Morrow. Misty Morrow. Misty. M-i-s-t-y. That's right. Thanks, Glenn."

"Thank you for that," smiled Misty, her spirit righting itself. "Now I'd like a roll of stamps, please, and could you tell me who painted that picture?"

Even though she saw the painting every day, Lillian leaned over the counter to get a better look. "That was painted by Denison Elbert. Isn't it lovely? We all enjoy it, it's so realistic. He died four years ago, you know. He was really something. There are more of his pictures at the ranch. When you go there, you'll see them."

"Dead?" Misty's voice cracked ever so slightly. "Dead?" she repeated, unbelieving. "If he's dead, how come they're having a workshop featuring his paintings?"

"To commemorate his birthday. He's a native son, so to speak, and this area is very proud of him."

"But he can't be dead," protested Misty. "I saw one of his paint-ings—" she stopped short, not sure how to go on. "I saw one of his paintings," she began again, "not too long ago—a new painting, re-cently done. Of mountains, and—and an eagle—with a fish—suppos-edly." She added the last word as an afterthought then was quiet, trying to collect her thoughts over tumbling questions. If Denison Elbert were no longer living, what about the article in *The Denver Post* Lewis had shown her? And the girl on the plane who worked for the *Post?* She knew about him. Could both of them and Lewis himself have been mistaken or misled? Was someone else using the name Denison Elbert?

"Could be his grandson's," the postmistress was saying, "but I wouldn't know. Everyone thinks that young man will come into his own one of these days. There will be a different speaker at the work-shop each day; the grandson will be one."

"Is his name Denison Elbert, the grandson's name?" Misty ventured.

"Yes, he's named for his grandfather. Do you need anything else?"

"Oh," breathed Misty, relieved. "One more thing. Could you tell me who is in charge of the children's camp that's being built nearby?"

"Why, yes—Karyl Cross. Fred Barlow is foreman and her assistant. Either one or both of them are over there every day."

"I think I'll stop by there now. I guess that's all. Thanks again for your help, and if you should hear of another cabin, a better one, let me know, will you?" Misty asked as she left.

"Sure thing," Lillian promised as Misty waved and closed the door. "Ellen?" Lillian spoke to a clerk who was busy sorting mail in the back of the room. "You don't know of another cabin, do you?"

Ellen turned around to face Lillian. "There's the McNeil place up the river. I understand they're going to Europe and won't be up until late summer, possibly fall."

Lillian watched Misty through the window as she mounted her bike. "I thought of that," she admitted, "but—no, I don't think so. They'd probably ask too much, more than she could afford. And yet—" Lillian's voice trailed off.

"Yet what?" Ellen had finished her sorting and stepped up to the counter to watch with Lillian.

"I was just wondering—about her." Lillian gestured towards the window. "She wrote me oh, I think it was about the first of January—

yes, it was just after the first of the year saying she wanted to come here and do some research and could I direct her to a real estate agency, she wanted to rent a cabin. As I remember, it was a well-typed letter. Done on a computer. I have it here." She opened a drawer in a filing cabinet and drew out a neatly folded paper. "See? It's perfectly written, very business-like. I think that young lady is something other than what she appears—wanting to go to the workshop, not balking at the price of a room at the ranch for the weekend, and—oh, several things about her. Maybe she could pay what the McNeils would ask. You didn't get a look at her hands. They haven't seen hard work recently, if ever. Why would she be interested in the camp? You don't suppose she wants to work there, do you?"

Without giving Ellen a chance to answer, Lillian went on breathlessly. "And where did she see that painting she mentioned? It doesn't add up. If it's research, what kind would she be involved in? I'll have to ask Karyl Cross what she thinks after the girl talks to her."

"Well-l—" said Ellen thoughtfully, "I suppose it could be any number of things, but it does all sound strange. Do you think you ought to tell her about the McNeil place?"

"I could drop a note to the McNeils and find out if they're interested in renting. I don't like to see this girl get mixed up with Angelo and his crowd. I understand he's getting a bunch together to live out at the old mine. They have their strange beliefs, at least I think they're strange, but lots of people are going for that occult stuff now. Angelo and Maria—they're something else. From what he's told me, they've been visualizing—whatever that is—for a girl for him, and I think they believe this Misty Morrow is the one. Visualizing—channeling—spirits. I sure don't understand any of it. Karyl Cross's camp is just the opposite with their belief in God and Jesus. Misty Morrow could sure get mixed up if she gets involved with Angelo's crowd and works at Cross's camp at the same time!"

"I don't think they'd take her on at the camp if she were mixed up with that occult business," reminded Ellen.

Lillian merely shrugged her shoulders in answer and turned to her desk leaving Ellen to take care of the counter.

Misty pedaled slowly until she came to the one little store Pommel boasted, a typical country store that carried something of everything. "I should take Maria a little gift in return for the bread," the girl thought to herself. "I wonder what I can find in here."

The store intrigued her, and she spent longer than she had intended going up one aisle and down another looking at this and that. At last an inexpensive pin caught her eye. It was a small ceramic rainbow in a gold-like setting. "Maybe she'll like this," thought Misty innocently as she turned the pin over in her hand. "A rainbow—a sign from God. Even if she doesn't wear it, she'll know I was thinking of her."

Misty made her purchase, and tucking the small package into her pocket, she again began to pedal towards the orange bridge, her mind made up to stop at the camp. She wasn't sure just what she would say or do. Perhaps she could find out when they expected the construction to be completed and when the children would be coming. She would ask for work, anything to fill in her time while she waited for the children. She had come to write about them, certainly not about a camp under construction. And of course to look for that artist and her dad's cousins. Where, oh where to begin?

"Karyl Cross or Fred Barlow." She repeated the names to herself. "Karyl Cross is surely Martha Cross's daughter. It will be good to get to know her. I hope I don't slip and give myself away."

She had not gone very far when she stopped suddenly and, balancing herself with one foot, watched a tall woman walking down the opposite side of the street. She was not so far away; Misty could have called to her, or had the woman turned, she would have seen Misty and wondered at the way she was staring. There was nothing unusual about her jeans and sport jacket; they were quite modish, and her wavy hair shone in the sunlight.

"Theba!" Misty whispered the name to herself while a mixture of anger, disappointment, and disgust swept over her. She continued to stare as the woman got into a red and white pickup truck. A man was behind the wheel.

"Wouldn't you know! She did come! Jan said she was planning a trip and here she is. Guess Jan had no idea it was going to be so soon, or that she was actually coming here. Now what am I going to do? If she sees me, she'll spoil everything. She must have come on her own. Sure she did! Oh, that witch! She couldn't stand my being here looking for an artist! That's her thing. If I meet her face to face, I'll sure give her a piece of my mind!"

The red and white pickup turned in front of her and started down the very road that led out of town. Keeping her eyes on the pickup as she pedaled along the highway, Misty saw a mammoth truck come out of the road that led to the camp. The pickup stopped as if to give the big truck room to turn, then it headed towards the camp. The girl on the bicycle ducked her head. "Forget the camp," she muttered, "go back to the cabin and think this over. How can I manage to meet Theba alone?"

⚜

Loaded with a huge yellow bulldozer the truck's progress was slow. Misty could have closed the gap between them had she wanted to, but she preferred to keep her distance and watch. She saw the truck turn on the dirt road that led up the hill to her cabin, but instead of continuing up the hill, it nosed its way into the privacy of the trees hiding the bit of meadow and its pond from the highway. There the truck stopped, and Misty pedaled a bit faster. At the foot of the hill she got off her bike and pushed it until she came to the large rock. Out of breath, she sat among the ferns, separating them so she could watch.

The driver of the truck slid out of the cab. He was a tall man in a brown shirt and trousers and a yellow hard hat that oddly enough matched the bulldozer. He walked a few steps, looked up at the tall trees, walked on a bit farther, then turned and came back to the truck.

As if drawn by the power of the gaze directed at him from the rock, the man looked up, pushing his hard hat to the back of his head. "Hi, there. Do you live around here?" His voice was deep and resonant.

Misty could see that the man was young, three or maybe four years older than she and reasonably handsome. Even from where she sat she could see his shoulders were broad and his body tapered down to a narrow waist and hips. Unconsciously she straightened her bandana and tucked a stray wisp of hair into place before she called back, "Not too far away. What are you going to do here with that bulldozer?"

"Cut a road. We're building a camp over there," and the man pointed in the direction of the meadow from where the building sounds were floating on the still air. "A children's camp," the man explained further. "For sick kids. Sick kids and handicapped kids. And this in here," he indicated the smaller bit of meadow and the pond, "is going to be part of it."

"I saw the building that's going on." Misty's words floated down to the man. "You're going to have to knock down some trees, aren't you?"

"A few." The man turned and began to lower the ramp of the truck. Then he climbed onto the seat of the bulldozer and started its engine.

Misty watched in fascination as the 'dozer inched its way down the ramp on to solid ground. She continued to watch as the man maneuvered the machine around the truck and headed it into the trees. Ruthlessly it went on its preliminary kill; the scent of crushed pine and damp earth wafted up to her.

When the machine was lost to sight, the girl continued on her way, her face rosy from the effort in the warm afternoon sun. She put the bike against the cabin and started for the path that led to the other cabin farther up the hill. She would take the pin to Maria before it got any later and talk to her about the truck and bulldozer.

Misty walked quickly; as she climbed higher, the sound of the 'dozer grew faint. She stopped at the edge of the trees that surrounded Angelo's homestead making a mental note of what she saw. It was obvious the man was trying to eke a living from land that was ungiving and as foreign to him as the mountains could be to one from the Bronx. A half-dozen goats milled around in a pen behind the cabin. In another pen beside them a flock of scrawny chickens scratched futilely in loose gravel. The boxed-in garden filled with soil from the valley was the only fertile spot on the rocky hillside.

As Misty watched Maria kneeling on the newly turned earth digging partly with her sharp little spade, partly with her bare brown hands, she found herself praying, "Lord, don't let that man be home. I don't like him. I don't want to see him. Please, Lord, don't let him be here."

Maria moved rhythmically as she worked her way across her garden spot. "Dig a hole—drop a potato—dig a hole—drop a potato—dig—

drop." She was whispering to each potato even as she had whispered to her herbs when she and her son lived in the tiny apartment over his shoe repair shop in New York.

Continuing to stand quietly in the shade of the trees for some minutes, Misty took in every detail of what lay before her, spellbound by the natural earthiness. Unaware of her audience Maria kept on, her gray hair falling loose from its moorings as was its wont. The little woman seemed to blend in with the soil—warm, friendly, and brown.

The door of the old house opened, and the huge hulk of a man, stocking-footed, stepped out into the sun with the fragrance of the herbs that were crowded on the table and the window sills in the cabin clinging to him. Lemon verbena, lavender, sweet basil, marjoram, thyme—

Misty caught a waft of their mingling as she looked at the man whose jet black hair, free from the confines of his red felt hat, hung in luxurious waves to his collar. The sun's rays caught his beard and flecks of red answered back. Here and there a premature fleck of white stood out in contrast. Misty stifled a gasp at the unique, rugged beauty, but no—she did not want to see him. She would wait for another time when she knew Angelo was not home to bring the pin to Maria. She prepared to turn and run, to retrace her steps unseen.

"Misty!" The man caught sight of the woman. "How's everything? You went to town?"

Misty froze in her steps then looked at Angelo. How did he know she had gone to town? But of course—he had driven by her cabin and noticed her bike was gone.

"Hi." Cautiously, she stepped out from under the trees and crossed to the house walking over the hard-packed dirt where clumps of wild grass and pine needles and cones were indiscriminately scattered.

Maria straightened herself on her knees and waved a greeting with her spade then bent again to her digging.

"Do you know what's going on down at the foot of the hill?" Misty looked up at Angelo who was sipping a mug of coffee, the steam wreathing his face and veiling the look in his black eyes. Now that he was here she had to talk to him.

"Down at the foot of the hill?" Angelo sat down on the top step and rested his mug on his knee. He shook his head. "Afraid not. What's going on?"

"I saw a bulldozer being unloaded, and I talked to the man who is operating it. It seems they are going to build in the meadow. They are going to add to the camp they've already started." Misty seated herself on a step while she talked.

Angelo nodded. "It was written up in the Leadville News some time ago. I'll get it for you to read." The man went into the house and came out with a torn piece of newspaper in his hand. "See here. It says 'Further construction on Martha's Camp, a respite camp for handicapped and terminally ill children, will begin this week. Karyl Cross, director of the camp, who shuns the press and is not willing to be interviewed, admitted that much. Cross also admitted that the camp, which is to be located in the Hill Meadow south of Pommel, is being built with funds bequeathed by her mother, the late Martha Cross who died last August. The camp was begun last September, but further construction has been delayed because of labor problems. Additional buildings and landscaping are to be completed within two to three months. The camp, Cross says, will be open and ready to go by late summer.' So. They have started the addition." Angelo held the piece of paper out for Misty to read for herself.

Misty read quickly then started to hand the paper back to Angelo when something on the back caught her eye. "Elbert, ar—" She looked again at the fragments of paper. "Do you have the rest of this?" she asked the big man hopefully.

Angelo took the torn piece and creased it between his thumb and forefinger while he shook his head. "Just this," he said. "We use newspapers to start the fire."

"Do you know anything about an artist named Denison Elbert?" She pointed to the back of the clipping.

Angelo read the unfinished words then shook his head. "Can't say's I do."

Misty shrugged. "I just saw one man." She brought the conversation back to what she had seen at the foot of the hill. "He brought the bulldozer in and unloaded it and began cutting through the trees."

Maria left her planting and joined the two.

"Hear that, Mama? They are making the camp in the meadow bigger. Just like the paper says. They're beginning to cut a road at the foot of the hill. Misty just saw it."

"Oh, mama mia, what next?" The little brown speck of a woman sat down next to her son. "Soon they take this hill. I get Misty coffee and cookies." She stood with a muffled sigh and, slipping off her shoes, disappeared into the house.

Misty accepted the mug Maria offered her and chose a cookie from the plateful the little woman set down. Remembering the pin, Misty reached into her pocket. "Maria! I have something for you. I brought you this from town. I hope you like it."

The little brown fingers eagerly tore at the paper sack. Maria looked intently at the pin then held it up for Angelo to see. The two of them exchanged a meaningful look, then Maria turned to Misty. "From you," she said simply. "It is beautiful. It means much, no, Angelo?"

But Angelo said nothing. Instead he shifted his position, and Misty felt his leg against her shoulder. Involuntarily the girl clutched the coffee mug a bit tighter and moved away to the end of the step. Together the three sipped in silence and stared at the thick wall of evergreen trees that shielded Angelo's spot from the valley. They strained their ears for sounds of the bulldozer but heard only the faint stirring of branches. Maria glanced at her son, who was watching Misty with his eyes half shut. The older woman smiled a crooked smile and nodded ever so slightly.

"Here, Old Lady. Come here, Old Lady." Angelo's voice broke the silence. Misty turned her face curiously towards the coop of red hens that stood near Maria's garden.

In answer to Angelo's call one hen cocked her head and listened. "Come on, Old Lady," encouraged the man. "Coffee time. Come and get it."

With that invitation the hen separated herself from the others and made an awkward flight to the top of the fence. She perched there waiting for one more coax.

"Come on, Old Lady," repeated Angelo while Misty watched.

Cocking her head to one side, the hen fluttered to the ground and flapped over to the porch. With no more hesitation she came to rest beside Angelo and waited expectantly. Carefully the man broke his last bite of cookie into the bit of coffee still in his mug and set it beside Old Lady. With prim precision the hen thrust her head into the mug and carefully consumed the soggy treat. Then she hopped off the porch and fluttered her way back into the coop.

Misty laughed. "Does she do that every time you call her?"

"Every time," answered Maria. "You like some chicks maybe? Angelo fix you some."

"The goat first. Yes, Mama?" asked Angelo.

"Chickens?" Misty made no attempt to keep the surprise out of her voice. "A goat? No thanks. Not for me."

Angelo stood and stretched. "Come see the goat," he said, ignoring her refusal. "And if Mama says you are to have chickens, you will have chickens."

Curious, Misty followed around the house past the garden and chicken coop to the pen where the six white goats were still butting one another, feeling the vigor and playfulness of their nature. Misty laughed in spite of herself.

"This one." Angelo entered the pen and laid his hand on a little Nubian, a white goat with a black spot on her face and another on her rump. "Come here, Gretchen," he said as he gently separated her from the others.

"She is pretty, I guess," breathed Misty who knew nothing about goats or chickens except that she did not want any.

She looked at first the little woman and then at her son. Both had their dark eyes fastened on her, waiting for her to say what they wanted her to say. Irritation gripped her. "No!" she spoke emphatically. "No, I definitely do not want her. Thank you anyway."

Angelo's eyes narrowed. "I need more grass for the goats. I'm going to put Gretchen in the pen by your cabin and stake her out under the trees."

Misty's irritation shifted from the two in front of her to herself—she felt powerless to keep her glance from falling under Angelo's penetrating look. "If that's what you want to do," she muttered through stiff lips, "it's your cabin and your goat, but I'm not interested. I'll have nothing to do with it."

"We are the same, you and Mama and me. We like rainbows, you like rainbows. We like the earth, you will. You will like the goat, too. We belong here, and we must stick together."

"Oh, is that a fact?" Misty could not keep the sarcasm out of her voice. She bent quickly, pretending to pet the goat so she would not have to look at Angelo.

"I'll bring Gretchen tomorrow," said the man as he gently pushed the animal back into the pen. "I'll fix the pen for her. I'll be there early. Real early. Maybe before you're up." And he laughed.

※❦※

"She will come around, Mama." Angelo and Maria together watched the retreating figure disappear down the hill. "She gave you a rainbow bridge pin. You know, I know—the rainbow bridge that goes from your lower self to your higher self, from my lower self to my higher self—to our God self. They call it what? The an-tah-ka-ra-na. It's hard to say, but Misty, she knows. Why else she give it to you? She must be one of us. The goats. She will like them."

Maria only sighed then walked painfully into the house.

SIX

Misty awoke with a vague feeling of foreboding. She tried to bring the elusive cause to her conscious mind as she sifted through the dream she had had of Lance and bulldozers and falling trees. Was it Lance's letter she had read a third time just before she went to bed? "I love you, you know." No foreboding there. She had felt warmed—almost convinced by his words. "I drove by the house—our house—yesterday. The landscaping is nearly finished. You will love it."

The house. Misty closed her eyes and smiled as she saw herself not walking, but floating down the spiral staircase and standing by the huge stone fireplace. There was a large thick rug on the floor. Oriental, of course. And a light mauve velvet sofa with soft rose wing chairs flanking the fireplace. And there were plants. A fig tree in one corner of the room, a hoya climbing over the fireplace, and—

Opening her eyes to the bleakness of the poverty-stricken cabin, she raised up on one elbow and studied her surroundings. What would Lance say, if he could see where she was now? The old bedstead, the rusted stove, the chipped chest of drawers. She could get a plant or two. A couple of ferns and perhaps an ivy would add much to the little place, but he still would never accept her being there. Misty reached for his letter and read it again.

"I saw Theba and Hal and the rest of the crowd last evening." His handwriting was well-formed and precise. "Theba hasn't said yet where she's going, but she has a trip planned. To Denver, I think."

Of course Theba had not told Lance where she was going. Did anyone know? The nerve of that woman! She probably intended to spoil Misty's plans of going to the camp incognito; that's why she'd come here. Why, oh why did this have to happen? "I just *have* to find a way to meet her when she's alone," Misty decided. "Maybe then I can get her to promise to keep her mouth shut, to not let on she knows me."

Misty turned back to Lance's letter in an effort to dismiss Theba from her mind, at the same time wondering where she was that minute. "Things at my office are shaping up and look hopeful. I'm sure the position I want is mine. We'll celebrate that and other things when you come home. Make it soon, darling. Hurry."

Celebrate his promotion? He would doubtless get that coveted position with the firm, for Lance did have a persistent way of getting what he wanted, Misty admitted to herself.

She stared off into space. She had begun a letter to him the evening before but had put it to one side uncertain just what she should say. She still did not know.

❧❧

With a shake of her head she brought herself back to the present. It was not her dream or the letters that had teased her with foreboding when she woke up. It was—oh, yes. She had it now. It was Angelo and his goat.

She set her lips in a firm line as she swung her feet out of bed. Cautiously, she peered out of the window. Angelo had said he would come early. "Real early." Those were his very words. "Maybe before you're up." And he had laughed a laugh she could not forget.

There was no sign or sound of him yet, thank goodness. She dressed quickly, pulling on her jeans and a plain, navy blue sweat shirt, then built the fire. After brushing her hair, she made it tight in one long braid that hung down her back, tied a blue bandana over her hair, and slipped on a short jacket.

Nibbling on a piece of bread and jam, the woman stood on the porch of the little cabin breathing deeply of the spring air so fresh and pungent. For the first time she noticed the broken-down fence and dilapidated shed across the road from the cabin. That must be the pen

Angelo had mentioned. Well, what he did with it was up to him. She wanted nothing to do with him or the goat. If she were gone while he was there, there would be no chance of her being involved in any way.

Her first priority was to go down to the camp. She understood now, from the article Angelo had read in the paper, that construction at the camp had been delayed because of labor problems—that's why it wasn't ready as she had expected it to be. Well, labor problems—all the more reason to try for a job. Then she would see even more of the camp than she had planned. She understood, too, why her dad had not wanted her to identify herself. Karyl Cross did not like the press, and since Misty's column was syndicated, Karyl would be suspicious if she heard the name Mary Alice Morrow. And, of course, she had her own reasons for keeping her identity hidden—to learn what it was like to be just Misty.

Now there was the matter of Theba. Misty could not risk meeting her in front of others. "Why Misty Morrow," she imagined Theba would say, "Mary Alice, dear. How nice to see you. And you look so stunning in that get-up."

Involuntarily, Misty looked at her jeans and jogging shoes. Then she imagined herself standing with her hands on her hips, looking Theba squarely in the eyes while she asked in her hardest voice, "What do you think you're doing here? You've got a lot of nerve, spoiling my plans. Please leave. Now!"

Coming out of her reverie, Misty comforted herself. "I'll go to town and watch for her. She's sure to come to the post office or store. Hopefully, I'll meet her alone."

The trilling notes of a flute-like whistle came through the trees, and Misty knew it was Angelo. Looking up the sheltered path she could see the man with the little goat behind him. For a moment she watched the animal dancing, winding the rope around Angelo, then she went into the cabin, closed the door and locked it.

Pouring herself a mug of coffee, Misty watched out the window as Angelo unwound himself and tied the goat to a tree. She saw him straighten a leaning fence post then begin on a second. When he began on the third, she decided she had seen enough—she would go to town. With only a wave to the man for greeting, she mounted the bike and began coasting through the trees, only to have to pull into the brush halfway down to let a battered van, laboring up the hill, pass her. Two men and a woman were bunched together in front returning Misty's stares as they chugged by.

At the foot of the hill she stopped at the camp road. There were building sounds, but Misty saw no one. A blue Volkswagon turned into the camp site, paused while the driver looked at her, then went on.

The altitude still bothered Misty some, so she pedaled slowly into town keeping her eyes open for the red and white pickup; Theba just might be in it. But the truck was nowhere to be seen; there was no sign of Theba on the street or in the store.

"I'll try the post office." Misty was getting frustrated. "While I'm there, I'll ask Lillian if she knows anything about the Wade family. I should've asked her the other day, but it slipped my mind. I'll ask her now while I check for Theba."

But Lillian was away until late afternoon, and the clerk had never heard of the Wades. Misty checked her mailbox, but there was nothing. Disheartened as well as frustrated, and feeling she was accomplishing nothing, she headed back to the cabin. She paused again at the camp's road, sure this time she saw Theba talking to one of the men. Half tempted to go to the camp regardless, she decided against it. She simply must see Theba alone first!

The yellow van stood under the trees. The two men and woman apparently had been helping Angelo. A quick look showed Misty they had finished their work—sturdy posts and taut wire fenced in the bewildered goat.

"Misty!" Angelo caught sight of her before she could escape into the cabin. "Come see Gretchen."

Reluctantly, Misty walked over to the pen, the four watching her as she crossed the yard. "Hi," she smiled at her appraising audience.

Angelo made no attempt to introduce his helpers, but Misty gave them a quick survey—the two men, one tall as Angelo, the other short, were both wiry, clean and unshaven. The woman, large and dark-haired, was dressed much the same as Misty was dressed.

In spite of herself the girl bent and petted the goat's soft curved nose only to have her hand caught in a mouth that was warm and wet. When the little animal dropped Misty's hand, she emitted a single pitiful "Baa."

"She's lonesome. She misses her brothers and sisters," said the shorter of the two men.

"That she does," agreed Angelo. "I'll have to bring another to keep her company. Goats are like people. They need another one with them. A companion." He looked at Misty and smiled a smile that was lost in the heavy mustache.

Angelo walked to a stump and sat down wiping perspiration from his forehead with the sleeve of his shirt while the others began picking up tools and putting them in the van. He had taken off his old red felt hat and hung it on a nearby tree branch leaving his long black hair free, shining like a raven's wing in the sunlight.

"Gretchen needs lots of water. Good fresh water." He gave Misty a sidelong glance as he spoke.

"So?" queried Misty. "Don't look at me."

Ignoring the interruption Angelo went on, "She's finicky about that. And grain and grass. I'll stake her out over there," he indicated a green patch, "for a starter." He walked over to the goat and, fastening the rope around her neck as before, led her to the patch of grass.

"Make it snappy, Angelo," called one man. "We haven't got all day."

Looking in the direction of the voice, Angelo tied the free end of the rope carelessly around a tree. "I'll bring another to keep her company in a day or so," he called as if Misty were interested. "I have some wood to finish cutting. I'd better go now and get with it. But I'll bring one of Gretchen's sisters soon."

"Remember, they're your animals, not mine," Misty reminded the man as she walked on to the cabin porch.

Picking up his tools Angelo paused and checked a fence post one more time. Then he climbed into the van with the others. "Come see Mama," he called once more to Misty, undaunted by her coolness. "She has some herb plants she forgot to give you yesterday."

Misty did not bother to watch the van go up the hill to Angelo's. She was just glad it was gone. In a few days she would climb the hill to get the herb plants that Angelo could have brought to her today. And to see Maria again and ask about her garden.

Glancing at her clock she saw it was not three yet—plenty of time to go back to the post office; Lillian must be there by now. She filled the stove with wood, put more water in the kettle, then went back outdoors. Pausing by her bike she looked over at the goat. "How're you doing, Gretchen?" she called. But the goat only continued to graze, working her way further across the grassy patch. In her eagerness to reach the tender new shoots on a nearby bush, she strained hard on the rope pulling it loose from the tree.

"Hey," said Misty noticing the rope. "You're supposed to be tied." Instinctively, she ran toward the goat intent on retying it. As if suddenly wound up, the goat sprang into the air and bounded off while Misty made a lunge for the rope that was snaking across the ground. Missing it, she tripped on a root and fell flat.

"Oh, you!" she called and then scrambled to her feet brushing at the wet dirt that coated the front of her jeans and shirt. "Go ahead and have fun. I'll tell Angelo you ran away soon's I get back from the post office."

Concerned in spite of herself, Misty scanned the brush that covered the hillside and spilled over the edge to the meadow. "Gretchen?"

As if in answer to her call, Misty saw a flash of white leap into the air its ears flopping and rounded nose sniffing. Then it disappeared under the scraggly bushes only to reappear again farther down the hillside the rope still dangling from her neck.

"The rope," Misty spoke out loud. "It could get caught on the brush or rocks and maybe choke her. That would be awful. I guess I'd better go after her myself."

She began her descent of the hillside although with not quite the same ease and grace as the goat. She slipped on wet grass, then stopped to free herself from brush that caught at her hair and clothing. She tripped and slid on loose shale and fell twice as she picked her way to the edge of the meadow. Then she stopped.

The bulldozer. She had forgotten about the thing, but there it stood directly in front of her. Quiet, but still threatening. Cautiously Misty took a step and looked towards the pond. The big yellow monster had eaten its way to the edge of the water, leaving a brownish ribbon of wet slippery clay that was outlined with bruised and fallen trees.

A man's jacket on the bulldozer hood lay so Misty could make out the initials "D.Q." on a tape stitched inside. Looking around self-consciously, she saw no one. "Whew," she whistled. "I wouldn't want anyone to see me like this." Probably the day's work was over, and whoever owned the jacket had gone home without it.

"Gretchen!" she called with authority. "Come here! Now!"

A jack rabbit ran out from under the brush and a plaintive bleating accompanied a scampering of tiny hoofs. In the same instant a blur of white again flashed through the air with the little goat this time landing on top of the jacket.

"We meet again!" Conscious of Gretchen on her perch and of her own muddy self, Misty could only stare at the man who stepped from behind the bulldozer,

"That's yours?" The man motioned toward the goat.

"Well, no—but, yes—" It was too difficult to explain right then.

"Will she come, if you call her?" He looked at Misty and suppressed a laugh.

"I—I don't know. Gretchen, come here! Please?" Misty took a step closer.

The little goat gave another spring and landed higher yet—on top of the cab of the bulldozer. "Gretchen?" repeated the man his eyes twinkling. "She doesn't want to come, does she?"

"Come on, you!" Misty put a hand on the bulldozer and looked up at the goat. "Right now!" she commanded.

"I'll get her for you," and, looking up at Gretchen, her would-be rescuer began to climb up to her pinnacle.

But Gretchen had ideas of her own. She watched from her high spot apparently waiting for the exact right moment. Perhaps it was the bright yellow hard hat that attracted her. Perhaps she wanted to save the man the trouble of climbing all of the way up. Whatever went on in the goat's mind was her business, but just as the man's fingers reached for the end of the rope that barely hung over the edge of the cab roof, Gretchen jumped. Horrified, Misty watched as a mixture of white goat, yellow hard hat and brown shirt and trousers connected with the soft wet clay.

"Oh, dear!" The woman's hands went to her face. "Oh, I am sorry!"

The man, disentangling himself from both the goat and the rope, stood and looked at Misty with a triumphant grin. "Got her!" He gathered the goat in his arms and looked from it back to the woman.

"How are you going to get this home?" he asked.

"Walk," said Misty. Then she looked at the hillside behind her. Leading Gretchen over that slippery shale and through the brush was out of the question. And carry her she could not. "Up the road," she added knowing that meant sloshing through the slippery wet clay for at least a quarter of a mile before she came to the road that led up the hill to her cabin.

"I'll drive you," said the man who was still cradling Gretchen in his arms. The little head hung over his muddy arm, the ears hanging limply over her eyes and nose. She was completely relaxed in her innocence.

Even though embarrassed, Misty could not help smiling at the animal. "We can walk," she repeated.

Gretchen's rescuer turned towards a jeep that was parked nearby. "Gretchen wants to ride," he said, "so you'd better come, too." He opened the jeep door. "You get in, and I'll give her to you."

Misty settled herself and held out her arms for the goat. "You! Look at the mess you got me into," she whispered as the man walked around to the driver's seat. "Next time I'll just let you go!"

"I'm really awfully sorry." Misty took a good look at the man as he climbed in beside her. Mud caked his face and hands as well as his shirt and trousers, but his brown eyes were laughing. He had replaced his hard hat at a rakish angle, and he looked for all the world like a mischievous schoolboy out to enjoy himself.

"No problem. It's all in a day's work. I know the goat is Gretchen. I'm Del Quinn. You are—" He looked at Misty to finish his sentence.

"Misty," she said simply.

"Misty? I like that. Just Misty?"

"Misty Morrow."

Del grinned. "One moisty morning Misty met a man clothed all in mud."

They both laughed.

"How far up the hill do I go?" asked Del as the jeep came to the end of the clay ribbon and turned up the rough road that wound up the hill.

"About half a mile. Around the curve up there," replied Misty then she fell silent. "This is it," she said when her cabin came into sight.

"Can you manage?" Del leaned across her and opened the jeep door.

"Sure." Misty, still holding the rope, slid out of the jeep after the goat jumped to the ground. "I'll put her in her pen. She's probably half starved by now."

Del's eyes took in the clearing with the cabin and the neatly stacked wood and the goat pen across the way. "Quite a place you have here. Did you and your husband build this?"

"Husband? Oh, I'm not married. Angelo and his mother live— OK, OK, Gretchen!" Misty pulled tighter on the rope. "I'd better get her over there." She smiled at the man in the jeep. "Thanks loads. I'm sorry for all the trouble."

"Not at all." Del took one last look not only at the rough cabin but at the woods and clearing and the road going on up the hill. Then he turned his jeep while Misty struggled with the gate to the pen and pushed the goat through it. When the jeep was out of sight, she belatedly raised her hand with a little wave before she went into the cabin.

❧❦❧

"What do you think, Darby?" The four sat on the steps of Angelo's cabin waiting for Maria to shuffle out with steaming mugs of herb tea.

"Hmm. Fiesty little thing." The shorter of the two men answered Angelo's question.

"I mean the girl, not the goat," reminded Angelo.

"And I mean the girl," replied his friend. "She's pretty, just like you said. But so small. And fiesty."

"She's what Mama and I have been visualizing. We've worked hard at it for over a year, ever since we came here. When Mrs. Watson asked me if I'd rent this cabin to a young lady from the east, I knew—I just knew it was working."

Maria came on to the porch, passed the mugs around then settled her tired body on a rickety chair. She said nothing.

"Are you sure she's one of us?" Jess, the taller man, asked.

"Well, she gave Mama a rainbow pin, and she's planted the garden I fixed for her. I checked and it's growing. Sure, lots of people plant gardens, but I don't think she would have, if she wasn't one of us. She is a bit fiesty, but she'll come around. The goats will help. She'll get attached to them. Wait and see."

"Where in the east is she from?"

"New York state," Angelo answered the woman called Prescott. "As a matter of fact, Mama and me are from New York. It seems as though she was sent to us. I think it's great." He slapped his knee for emphasis.

"We'll work with her, and she'll come around." Prescott reassured Angelo. "Keep on visualizing."

The five sat sipping their tea while they thought of Misty, then Darby spoke. "How're things coming at the mine? When do you think we will be able to move in?"

"I'm a-workin' at it." It was a point of contention between them. "The one cabin's about ready. I'll need help to put up two more."

"We can all live in one until the others are ready." This was Jess's idea. "We'll stock it real good with food and water. We'll be ready for whatever comes."

"There'll be lots of others coming this summer. Some of them might get homesick and freak out. Better have some sedatives on hand," advised Prescott.

"Misty won't freak out," countered Angelo. "I'll take care of that."

"I didn't say she would." Prescott spoke testily. "I just meant some would—or might. There's always some. Want to go back home to their families or their church."

"Are you going to marry her?" Darby asked to smooth Angelo's ruffled feelings.

"I'm going to marry her if that's what the Master wants, and I think it is," assured Angelo.

Maria nodded. "We channeled," she said simply.

"Let's have a session now," said Prescott. So the four of them, Prescott, Jess, Darby and Angelo followed shuffling Maria into the cabin. Four of them sat on the floor while Maria, after pulling the curtains to darken the room, sat in a chair to complete the circle. The men and Maria looked at Prescott then followed her example of sitting perfectly straight with their hands in their laps. When she closed her eyes, the others closed theirs.

Prescott spoke. "Relax and be at peace in the presence of God."

A few moments of silence followed while she waited for each one to try to relax. Angelo's labored breathing betrayed him; he was struggling. Jess sighed and Darby shifted to be more erect. When she was satisfied all were ready, Prescott spoke again. "Image a ray of light coming from the sun. It is shining on you. Now slowly take a deep breath. A ray of light is emerging out the top of your head; it is opening your energy nerve center, your chakra near your heart."

Again Prescott paused before she continued with a short prayer. "Oh, Master of Light, Master of Love, we come to you for wisdom and for guidance." She waited before giving further directions to the other four: "Imagine yourselves seated in the garden of the soul, a beautiful garden which will open us to our higher selves and enable us to receive from the Master."

Another few moments of complete silence were followed by, "We invite the presence and the energy of our beloved Master, Ralah. We are honored with your presence. Thank you for your dedication and love. Share your wisdom through us, beloved Master. What would you have us do in regards to this person Misty?"

All was quiet, not even Angelo's labored breathing could be heard. When Prescott spoke again, her voice was changed to one soft and melodious, even sensuous—not Prescott's voice at all. "I have brought this beautiful girl to Angelo to be his mate. He must love her, and she will learn to love him. Remember, love is the greatest force in the universe. Love everything around you and that includes Misty. She will learn to love you."

Outside a goat bleated plaintively. The wind stirred little bits of dust. Prescottt's voice was normal when she said, "Beloved Ralah, give us wisdom about the camp you would have us build."

More silence, then in the soft, musical voice, "Be patient. Build not a camp but a center for learning at the mine called the Jerose Mine. It will become a place of beauty and will please me greatly. Many will come from all over to learn and help you build our new world of peace and love. I am leaving you now. Peace."

It was over. Prescott exhaled audibly and her shoulders slumped. "You heard the Master?" she asked the others looking at each one in turn.

"We heard," said Darby and the others nodded in agreement.

"Misty already knows about the bridge to God," said Angelo

pointing to the rainbow pin on Maria's chest. "She will learn more from our classes. Like we heard Ralah say, I am to marry her."

"And we are to really build a camp," said Jess.

"A learning center," corrected Prescott. "And it will be beautiful with many flowers and trees."

Jess shook himself as if to get rid of the spell, then stood. "We'd better get going, it's getting late. Angelo, are you going to take another goat down to fatten up? So we can use either one of them—later?" he asked as they all walked out to the porch.

Angelo nodded. "Yeah. They'll be fatter, in better shape than any here in the pen," and he waved his hand towards the area behind the cabin. "Don't any of you talk to Misty or bother her," he warned his friends. "I'll take care of her."

"OK, OK, don't get your fire up," Darby said, "Remember, love— we all love each other. And peace. That's what we want. When are we meeting again for another channeling session?"

"Tomorrow night after dark," said Angelo. "Come here. Bring candles, ours are almost gone."

Jess, Darby and Prescott climbed into the van leaving Maria sitting in the rickety chair with Angelo leaning against the doorjamb.

SEVEN

Karyl Cross stood watching the men unload the lumber. The two weeks since Del had come had been a time of unsuppressed excitement for her. She had been even more excited than when they started the camp last fall. That day in September, the day when her mother's dream had begun to take shape, had been a red-letter day. Karyl could still remember the look on Del's face as he turned the first shovelful of dirt. She had an idea of the struggle he had been through, so she was elated to see him his old self—relaxed and cheerful, even joking. "He's evidently reconciled to being a ranger," she confided to Fred, "and given up his other ideas except as a hobby. But a good ranger he will be."

The groundwork for the camp had been begun before her mother's sudden death last August and Karyl, working beside her mother, had caught the spirit of her dream. Much had been done in the fall, but there had followed that difficult time when the Christian standards of the camp had caused unrest and problems with the workers. Those workers had deliberately ignored the Christian principles, bringing in their crystals and rainbows and other occultic symbols. Construction was stopped, of course, until these few were dismissed, the standards reviewed, and new commitments made. All of this had delayed the opening of the camp which should have been ready by now, and Karyl, striving to remember God's promise that all things work for good for them that love Him, had fought exasperation. Now she was encouraged. These past weeks there had been more bulldozing, the cutting of the road to the lower meadow by the pond, then the pouring of two more foundations. And today the lumber.

Karyl smiled. Fred, a natural-born foreman, was helping Del unload and stack the fragrant pine boards, the two working without speaking in perfect harmony and rhythm. Other men were busily framing in what was to be the main building of the camp. They had decided to put it here in this meadow where it would be near the lake, and Karyl was glad. The children would enjoy both the building and the lake so much more. The new barrack and the chapel would be close by.

Thankfulness and affection surged over Karyl as she watched the men. She knew how pleased her mother would have been. Martha Cross had watched these young fellows grow up; she would have been satisfied that they were as committed to the respite camp and what it stood for as her standards demanded.

A slight breeze that ruffled Karyl's short brown hair went on to tease a corner of the blueprint stretched out on the hood of the red and white pickup truck. Karyl smoothed the blueprint and held it firmly while she studied it. She felt Fred's presence beside her. "As soon as we get the main building and the barrack finished, we can open, can't we? We can wait for the house and chapel." She looked up with a smile as she spoke.

Fred took off his cap and ran his fingers through his thick, blond hair, then he, too, his arm around Karyl's shoulders, leaned over the blueprint. Karyl moved to one side to make room for Del who joined them.

Del gave a short laugh. "You are eager to get things underway, aren't you."

"You know I am," answered Karyl. "This was a dream of Mom's for years. Thirteen, to be exact—ever since I was eighteen. And you know I've shared it with her; if only she'd been able to see it materialize." Karyl was silent for a moment, remembering.

Controlling her emotions she continued, "The money she left is plenty to do just what she wanted." She paused again watching Del's face. Satisfied there was no sign of bitterness, she went on. "Martha's Camp, a camp for handicapped and terminally ill children. 'A respite for them and their parents' was what she said so many times. Those kids need this, Del. Their parents need it. Look at Cindy, struggling with little Dillon's illness day and night, Karyl shifted her position so she could see Fred better. "Your sister is a wonderful, caring mother, but she needs a rest, a chance to get away. I'm glad we started this last fall. We've just got to have this camp ready this summer!"

Del placed his finger on the blueprint. "The edge of the pond will be here as soon as we get it dredged out and widened. Only then it will be a little lake."

"And get the ducks and swans on it," added Karyl. "How long do you think it will take?"

"To get the ducks and swans? About an hour."

"Be serious! To get the main building and the barrack ready!"

"How long do you estimate, Fred?" asked Del.

Fred rubbed his chin thoughtfully. "If the fellows really push it and if we don't have any more accidents, both buildings could be ready by the first of July."

"Poor Todd." Karyl rolled the blueprint and put a band around it.

"He's doing all right," consoled Fred. "That board fell on his ankle with a lot of force. Call it a hazard of the profession. Fortunately, the break isn't too bad. He'll be out of commission for several weeks, but he'll be back."

"We're going to have to manage without him, I guess." Karyl looked wistfully at Del. "You're going to have to leave too, aren't you?"

"It looks that way, but I'll be back in the fall, if not before. Everything will roll right along without me. You've got Roy and Drew. But I do think you should get someone to take Todd's place until he can come back. You need someone to run errands and to be a gofer."

Karyl laughed. "I think Todd got tired of hearing 'go for this and go for that.' Maybe we can find someone to take his place, but I don't know who. There are a lot of new people in Pommel, but I'm afraid of getting involved with some like we had last fall. We can't ask either Drew or Roy to be a gofer, that's for sure! They'll have to work doubly hard as it is to get this place anywhere near ready by July."

"Whoa!" Fred gave a deep laugh. "We're not obligated to be ready by then. I just said that if all goes well and the men push it, it could be."

"Oh, but we've got to be ready by then. I'm thinking of the parents and of the kids who are waiting to come. They might have been here by now if things had worked out better. Maybe," Karyl paused as a new thought came to her, "maybe now that the weather's decent, I can bring a couple of them out to watch the building. Dillon would love that, wouldn't he?"

"Would he ever!" said Fred. "He'd love to be here right now, helping."

"Tell you what," said Del. "If I can get down for a couple of days when the weather's warm, I'll put the shell on the pickup and Dillon and I can camp here overnight. Do you s'pose Cindy would let him do that, Fred?"

"You know you won't get away in the warm weather," Karyl interrupted before Fred had a chance to answer. "You probably won't get back here until the snow drives you down with the elk."

"One never knows. I certainly want to come for the dedication. Well," and he turned to look over the meadow, "there's work to be done. I'm going to skirt around the pond and get the layout."

"I've got to check some things with Drew," said Fred starting toward a tall, heavyset man who was filling the air with the buzz of a power saw. "I'll give you a whistle when the next load comes in," he called over his shoulder.

Del turned to the pond. He was caught up in the vision and the excitement of the project. No one could be around Karyl for long and not be. He pushed his hat to the back of his head and looked around, but he wasn't really seeing the pond and the rocks. Instead he saw the mosaic pattern of events that over the past year had led him to where he was. Oh, not all of the choices had been his. Martha Cross's death had been a blow. He had felt cut loose from all ties and anchors, and for a time he had drifted. In his despair and bitterness he had railed against God, demanding to know why, oh why had He taken a woman so full of life and vitality with still so much to offer. And why had she apparently forgotten him in her will? The same taste of gall rose in his throat even now as he thought of it. Karyl, stable and patient in spite of her own grief, had seen him through much. And he had clung to her without realizing it.

Del had known of Martha's dreams prompted by her own handicapped sister. He had known a large part of her fortune would go to Karyl and to her sister who had been out of touch with the family for several years. Her share was being held for her in a Denver bank until she could be located; the rest had gone to the camp.

But he and Martha had been so close. "Del," she had encouraged him, "Karyl's sister isn't the only one who has Grandfather Cross's talent; you have, too. You are more patient than she is, more persistent. You can go a long ways, if you work at it. Don't give up." With those words ringing in his memory, hadn't he had a right to expect her to help more than she did?

Angry with himself for the envious thoughts that persisted he kicked at a clump of grass. Shouldn't I be a bit thankful, he reasoned? If Martha had willed me enough to carry out my plans for more study, I'd still be in the city and I wouldn't have all of this. He looked again at his beloved mountains and their valleys. "This will be my classroom," he whispered as he set his jaw with determination. " 'I will lift up my eyes to the hills, from whence comes my help.' "

A heron flapping in for a landing on the pond brought his thoughts back to the camp. He watched the big bird for a moment, then balancing himself on a rock, imagined what the pond would be like as a lake with a smooth lawn between it and the barrack. There would be children—some on crutches or in wheelchairs, some too fat and others too thin. Fred's six-year-old nephew, red-headed Dillon, who meant almost as much to Del and to Karyl, as he did to Fred would be one of them.

Del thought of the suffering that would be eased here in this place. The new environment, new friends, distracting activities—all could make anyone's pain more bearable if not almost forgotten. Why, he could almost hear Dillon laughing again. Satisfied with his vision and with what he saw before him, Del turned toward the bulldozer. He would begin now to widen the pond.

"Meew, meew." Del stopped and listened. He knew the sound well—the kittenish cry of a fawn. Searching the underbrush he soon found the little spotted creature huddled close to where he was standing. Stepping carefully, he stooped to examine the fawn. Small and undernourished, it looked at Del with large eyes full of fright. Trying to stand, it sank back on the grass shivering.

"Where's your mother?" Del ran his hand gently over the thin body. "Did she go off and leave you?" He looked at the young deer thoughtfully. The mother had perhaps been frightened by the bulldozer and, being unable to distract the machine like she would a dog or other animal, she had abandoned her baby. Or perhaps she was still hiding, hoping to lure the big monster away. Maybe she had been hit by a car on the highway.

"There are two sides to everything," muttered Del to himself as he thought of the camp and the good that was intended and of the devastation of the woods in contrast. "If only little guys like you didn't have to suffer. Guess you'd better come with me." The man slipped his hands expertly under the small form and lifted it holding it against his chest. "Easy now. No one's going to hurt you." The stiff little legs began to relax as the warmth of the man flowed over the rigid body.

"I've got your first customer." Karyl looked over her shoulder at the sound of Del's voice.

"What? Oh, for goodness sakes. It's so tiny! And it looks so sad!"

"It needs lots of TLC and some milk. It's half-starved. We've got to feed it."

"With what? Coffee? A doughnut? Where shall we put it?"

Del laid the fawn on a tarp in the back of the pickup and gently stroked him. "We've got to do something right away."

"I could go into town," suggested Karyl, "and get a baby bottle and some milk. Or maybe some baby formula would be better. But what will we do with it after we've fed it? I don't have much room, and we can't leave it here overnight. It'll have to be fed every few hours."

"I've got it!" Del exclaimed. "We'll take Sorrowful up to Misty."

" 'Sorrowful'? Well, the name suits it, I guess. But Misty. Who in the world is that?"

"She's a young woman who lives up on the hill over there with her goat."

"Is she the one you met that day you fell in the mud? You said something about rescuing a 'maiden and her goat.' " Karyl looked at Del, her finely arched eyebrows raised high.

"The same," said Del. "Now we'll take her Sorrowful. Hurry! Take the jeep so we won't have to disturb the fawn."

Karyl paused to pat the fawn then gave Del a mock salute. "Yes, sir," she said as she climbed into the driver's seat.

"Tell Fred where I've gone and why," she called as the jeep began to bounce over the rough ground. The little monkey that hung from the mirror by a cord danced rakishly with each bounce. The free end of a blue bandana that was tied to the mirror and braided into the monkey's cord waved in the breeze.

No more than half an hour had passed before Karyl was back. "Two bottles complete with nipples and five pounds of powdered milk," she triumphantly announced. "And a can of Simlac. If I may say so, this is some way to build a camp. I hope we don't find many Sorrowfuls."

"There's only one," said Del as he tenderly wrapped the tarp around the deer and picked up the bundle. "Besides, you know what your mother always said, 'First things first.' We can't neglect this little one, camp or no camp. It's probably because of us it doesn't have a mother. You'll have to help me take it up Misty's mountain. You drive and I'll hold it." He called to the men who looked up from their work, "We won't be gone long."

❧❦❧

Misty carefully searched the pockets of her rain jacket. "My bandana must have caught on the bushes when I went after Gretchen the other day," she said out loud as she searched a second time. "I can't find it anywhere. Maybe tomorrow I'll go look, but I don't relish going down that shale bank again."

The sound of a whistle caught her attention. "That's Angelo." She walked to the kitchen window. "He must be bringing the other goat."

The big man shouted a greeting even without seeing the girl. "Misty? Here's Gertrude like I promised."

"I don't want to get involved," Misty told herself. "He's sure determined to make a country girl out of me."

"Misty!" called the man again. "Come see Gertrude." He tied the goat and started toward the cabin.

"He knows I'm here. I may as well answer him," she muttered.

"Good morning," she said formally from the safe distance of the porch. "I see Gertrude. Wherever do you get those names?"

"Mama names them. She said Gertrude should go with Gretchen. Gertie here had twins, but we've taken them away from her."

The goat stood quietly chewing grass she had pulled on the way down the path. Her udders hung full.

"You know how to milk?" Angelo asked.

Misty shook her head and stifled a laugh. Milk? A goat? "Are you kidding?" she asked under her breath wanting to chuckle at her own pun. Out loud she said with all the firmness she could muster, "Angelo, I told you—they're your animals. I'm not interested."

"I know you don't have a bucket so I brought one." Without smiling Angelo held the pail for her to see.

"Angelo! I said—"

"I'm going to put Gertrude on the porch so she's up a little higher. I want to milk her. Maybe you'd like to learn how to do it. It's OK, Gretchen." Ignoring Misty, who was clenching her fists and gritting her teeth, he spoke to the bleating goat in the pen. "It's OK. Gertrude's coming in a little bit."

"It's my cabin," he reminded Misty as he lifted Gertrude on to the porch. The pail in place, Angelo began to set a stream of milk pinging against its side just as the sound of a vehicle came through the trees. Misty tensed even more. Was it the yellow van coming again? It had gone by twice since those people had helped Angelo with the pen. If that's who it was, they would stop, and she didn't want to talk to them. She had spoken to them once, and while the woman was friendly enough, Misty preferred to not meet the men. About to go back into the cabin and shut the door, she saw it was a jeep coming out from under the trees. Del Quinn? He was coming up here again? What could he possibly want? Maybe he had found her bandana and was returning it! Or maybe he was coming just to see her? Misty's curiosity was aroused even more when she saw a woman sitting beside him.

"Here, Gertrude!" Angelo's voice brought Misty's attention back to the goat in time to see her kick over the pail. Automatically, the girl leaned over and righted the pail, straightening to see Del get out of the jeep holding a bundle in his arms.

"Hi, there. We brought you another friend! It looks like we're just in time." Del walked to the porch with long steps.

"A fawn," breathed Misty forgetting the goat and Angelo. "Isn't it beautiful? Is it an orphan?"

"Apparently," said Del holding the tarp away from the animal. "We brought it to you to take care of until it's big enough to go on its own." The man's eyes met Misty's for the briefest second while he stood the fawn on the porch. Then he turned to Angelo.

"We've got the milk all right." Angelo began again to send a stream into the pail.

"And now you've got bottles." Karyl had walked up unnoticed. "Hi, Angelo," she said as she placed her package on the porch.

Misty looked up from the fawn and froze. Her mouth went dry as she looked at the tall young woman standing by Del. She had the short wavy brown hair, the finely arched eyebrows, and yes, the smile; but she showed no recognition of the girl in the jeans and T-shirt who was staring so rudely. She can't possibly be Theba, or she'd say something, Misty thought and shuddered to think what Theba would say if she saw her in the position she was in. Instinctively, she stepped off the porch to separate herself from Angelo and the goat.

Closer, Misty dared to get a better look at Karyl. A quick glance showed hands that were work-roughened, and a single diamond, not a wedding set like Theba's.

"It's hungry, isn't it." Struggling to regain her composure, Misty gently touched the fawn Del had placed on the porch and was supporting with one hand.

"It's half-starved," answered Del. "How about filling a bottle and trying your luck? Or try putting it on the goat." He gently pushed the fawn over closer for the goat to sniff.

"Here, baby." Angelo held the deer next to the goat's dripping udders. "Good, eh?" A drop fell on the fawn's lips, and he began to search for more.

"Look at that," said Karyl softly as the fawn first nuzzled the goat then began awkwardly pulling and sucking as Angelo directed his muzzle. The goat protested at first by kicking then settled down to the comfort of being nursed.

"That's right, Sorrowful." Del gave a low chuckle. The little group watched in silence until the fawn at last had its fill and turned away.

"OK, she's all milked. Here, you take her and put her in the pen," Angelo held the rope out to Misty. "I'll make a bed for this one." He touched the fawn lightly. "It's best to keep it away from Gretchen for a while. Be sure to go into the pen with it when you take it to Gertrude. Gretchen could get rough until she gets used to it."

Misty stood tall. "*You* be sure when *you* go into the pen," she said forcibly. "Remember, it's *your* goat," she added as she stalked off away from the animals.

The group around the cabin stood silent as the trees until Karyl, taking hold of the situation, walked over to the jeep. "We have another package of powdered milk here, in case you need it. And some baby formula just in case." She held the package out to Misty. "It might come in handy," she said with a smile.

While Misty walked over to take the package, Del turned to the man still sitting on the porch. "You are her neighbor. Right?"

Angelo smiled as he watched Misty. "Neighbor today, yes." He fell quiet watching her before he went on. "She is beautiful," he confided softly. "We get along well. And Mama." The man paused. "Mama loves her like her own. The three of us—we'll make a happy family."

Del studied the man intently, but Angelo did not notice.

"She will learn." The man rubbed his hands together as he spoke in an undertone. "Beautiful," he said again. Then he laughed and spat on the ground.

"We'd better go," Del said suddenly. "Keep the bottles, Misty." Turning on his heel, he started for the jeep. "They're in case you need to use the powdered milk for Sorrowful."

"Angelo will take care of Sorrowful along with his goats." Misty looked at Del almost pleadingly, hoping she had successfully disassociated herself in his eyes from both the man and the animals.

"Whichever, I'm sure Sorrowful's in good hands," Del said without smiling, and Misty vaguely wondered what had upset him. He had been so sparkly, so full of fun that day he brought her and Gertrude home. And he had been quite jovial when he had driven up just a few minutes ago; something had happened in this short time and she was puzzled.

Before the jeep started down the hill, Karyl leaned across Del to speak to Misty, and because Karyl was crowding him, Del put an arm across her shoulders. Misty scarcely heard Karyl's words, "You come see us" while Del gave Angelo a farewell salute as they drove away.

❧❦

"Misty didn't introduce me," Del complained as the overhanging trees brushed the jeep.

"She probably didn't think of it," explained Karyl. "But you should know him. That's Angelo Giannelli, the fellow who holds a lease on the old Jerose mine. If you can call what he's doing 'working the mine,' then that's what he's doing—working the mine. Speaking of introductions, why didn't you introduce me to her?''

"I didn't think of it," echoed Del. Then, "So that's Giannelli."

"That's who he is all right."

They drove in silence for a few moments, then Del blurted out, "How can she stand being engaged to him?"

"What makes you think they're engaged?"

"He as much as told me. 'Neighbor today,' he said. Then something about the three of them making a happy family."

"Three of them?"

"His mother's number three."

"Sounds cozy," said Karyl. "Everyone to her own taste. I'd say off-hand," she added, "he has his hands full, and I don't mean with just the goats and fawn."

They were at the bottom of the hill before she spoke again. "There's something about her—something I want to check out. When I go to Denver I'll bring back some pictures."

"Pictures? What pictures?" Del asked.

"You'll see. Didn't she remind you of someone?"

"Hmm, no, can't say that she did," Del admitted. "How long will you be gone?"

"Oh, not very long—four maybe five days."

"You won't hire someone to take Todd's place before you go?"

"There won't be time. I'll take care of that soon's I get back."

※❦※

Misty stood watching until the jeep disappeared from sight, then biting her lower lip, her eyes smoldering, she turned towards the cabin where Angelo still stood watching her.

EIGHT

Knowing now that it was not Theba she had seen, Misty felt buoyed. She was eager to get on with what she had come to do, so with keen anticipation she cycled to the camp twice the next week only to be disappointed when told by one of the workers that the director, who could do no hiring herself but would have to meet with the camp board to consider any application, was not there. If Misty were sincerely interested, could she come back in five days?

Returning from the camp after her second try, Misty stopped to ask Lillian Watson about the Wade family. "Wade?" queried Lillian Watson. "Wade? I can't say that I've heard of them. You see, I've been here in Pommel only two years, and I really don't know anything about the old-timers. When you go to Frisco sometime, maybe you could go to the little library there, or even the newspaper might have some information. Sorry." And she looked at Misty quizzically.

Frustration nagged at Misty. Nothing, but nothing was going right. Well, she would try to make the most of her time while she waited to see the camp director. Goodness knows when she would be going to Frisco, so researching the Wades was out, at least for now. And as for finding Denison Elbert—getting in at the camp first seemed to be her best bet. If she couldn't get on at the camp, well—she'd face that later. While she waited, she would write the stories she had assigned herself to write about Angelo and Maria, and possibly even Angelo's friends.

So she wrote about the escaping goat and the bulldozer, about the old hen that drank coffee. And now that she could look at the incident of Del with the fawn and the woman with him from the distance of time, she could better ignore the anger and embarrassment that had crowded in on her and see the humor in the situation and the colorful narrative it made.

During breaks from typing she watched the fawn. Nourished by the goat's milk, it was developing fast. She had seen deer in the zoo, of course, but never before a wild one. The little animal fascinated her until she finally took a real interest in it. Every day its spindly legs seemed to have stretched out and become stronger. Soon it gambolled about the pen as if it had always been there.

"One of these days you will jump the fence and be gone," Misty told it as she dared to rub its velvet nose. "You've got to eat and grow strong so you can take care of yourself out there in that world."

Every morning that week at exactly nine o'clock, Angelo rumbled down the road in his truck heading for the old mine. Twice after he had coaxed the old pickup home up the hill, he walked back down, whistling. "To check on Sorrowful and the goats," was his excuse.

Both visits left Misty feeling a little more wary, a little more defensive, for the way the man looked at her grew more intense. She could not ignore his attempts to get her attention, and she found herself wishing he would not come, even dreading the sound of his whistle. When she heard his truck on the hill, she willed that it would not stop. Twice the yellow van lumbered by her cabin with not just three but five, maybe six or more passengers—they were so packed in it was difficult to count them watching from behind the faded yellow curtains. The van would stay at Angelo's for several hours then rumble back down again bringing with it an aroma of roasted meat.

The week went by fast, Friday came with a burst of sunshine and warmth, and Misty looked with satisfaction at the stories she had written. She hoped her editor-dad would like them as well. Standing to stretch, she opened the door to the sun and saw Maria plodding down the hill clutching a pot of something in one hand, a little kitten in the other. The little woman in her tan blouse and quilted skirt paused by the pen to watch the animals, laughing at the fawn's antics before she sat on the porch to rest. "Basil," she said holding the pot out to Misty. "It is good fresh or dried. Take good care of it. The kitty's for you, too. You like it?" She stroked the kitten's black fur then set it on the porch."

"He's adorable," said Misty reaching down to pet the newcomer. Then, "May I get you something to drink?"

"No, no coffee today. I must get back." And the little woman stood to retrace her steps. Misty, hoping to hear another story about Italy or early New York, decided to walk back up the hill with her.

They followed the shadowy path under the trees, the one young and eager, the other gray and slow both stooping to pick the tiny red strawberries mixed with the wild flowers on the hillside.

Noticing how very difficult it was for Maria, who had grown so frail in such a short time—frail and wispy as a brown leaf—Misty sat on a rock and invited the older woman to sit on a stump close by. To make conversation and to give the woman time to rest, Misty told Maria happenings from her childhood hoping they would stimulate Maria, and she would open up and talk as she had at other times.

But Maria's eyes had a far away look in them. She's not the least bit interested in what I'm saying, thought Misty as she watched the stiffened, claw-like fingers pick nervously at the faded skirt. When she saw the woman's lips begin to move, Misty leaned closer to catch every scratchy word.

"Angelo," the woman began with an effort, "he is good and kind. And strong. Very strong." She waited as if for Misty to digest these words before she went on. Then, "We understand each other. But a mother is a mother. He needs a wife. A good wife who likes what he likes. He make her a good husband." She sighed then added, almost inaudibly, "There so little time."

With the relief of one who has said all that can be said, Maria coughed and slowly started up the hill again using a piece of broken limb for a cane.

Misty resented the implication in Maria's words, but she said nothing until they could see Maria's garden through the trees. "You're tired," Misty said then. "Surely you'd like some coffee now. Let me make you some."

"It's almost time for the Old Lady's afternoon treat. This one and the one in the pen over there." Maria gave a cackly laugh at her own little joke. "Here comes Angelo. He knows it's coffee time."

"So what do you think of Misty's herd, Mama?" Misty grew tense at the sound of the man's voice. If she had known he were home, she would not have come all the way with Maria. She fought the desire to turn and run, to get as far away as she could in the shortest time possible.

"Some herd," Maria was saying. "Two goats and a deer. The little fawn looks fat." The woman sat down wearily. "Ah, Misty—we had a good visit. See?" She held up her little plastic pail. "We picked strawberries. They are early this year. And we talked." She glanced sharply at her son, a glance that did not go unnoticed by Misty who read meaningful unspoken words between the two. The blue of the girl's eyes deepened like the center of a hot low-burning fire. She set her lips in a firm straight line.

"So—you talked," answered Angelo softly, lowering his eyes from his mother's and avoiding Misty's. "Sit down, Misty." He looked at her then. "I will call the Old Lady."

"No thanks." Misty backed away from the porch step where she had sat before. "I—I must take care of these berries right away. Thanks anyway. Some other time."

"You sure you don't want coffee?" Maria desperately wanted the woman to stay. There was so little time.

"No thanks. I'll see you soon," and Misty walked deliberately into the shadows of the trees. Once beyond the lowest branches she began to run.

"What did you say, Mama? It was too much maybe. You scared her off." Maria winced at the brittle tone in her son's voice as she watched the shadows swallow the woman's retreating form.

"I will pay him no mind," she murmured to herself. Then louder, "I just told her how strong and fine you are. She needs to know, but she is like a young doe. Skittish. Shy. It takes time. Don't hurry her. She will be good for you." The woman sat silent studying her brown hands. "Some coffee, then I lie down."

"Yes, Mama," said Angelo obediently. He ran his hand over his face then turned from watching the trees where Misty had disappeared and went into the cabin.

Part way down the hill Misty slowed to a brisk walk. I see what's going on now, she thought furiously. Oh, how stupid I've been! I never trusted Angelo, but what I thought was friendly concern and neighborliness on Maria's part seems to be well-planned plotting.

Mother and son not only talk about me, they are trying to surround me with themselves and bend me to their will. Maria has betrayed me; she is behind it all; she obviously rules not only her son's actions, but his thoughts as well. What was it Lillian Watson said that first day when I stopped at the post office? "His mother keeps him in check," and then the she laughed. She knew! Why didn't she warn me?

The woman kicked at a rock in the path, then picked up another and threw it into the bushes. She clattered noisily into the cabin and set the pail of berries down on the table with a thud. Lance is right, she thought, I am naive. Stupid too! The garden—the goats—the herbs. What am I being caught up in anyway? Oh! Those two. What a pair! Well, they can't spin their web around me.

She turned from the mirror and walked restlessly to the open door. Seeing the deer stretched out on a pile of straw in a corner of the shed sleeping peacefully, she went out to the pen where she could see him better, and she remembered how Del had stood by her porch with the little fellow's funny face peering out from under the tarp. Now, rising from the ashes of her anger, that old, old longing she had become accustomed to glowed once again.

She had met Del only casually, but she had to admit she had liked him. Then there was that woman who looked so much like Theba— polished, poised, sure of herself. Apparently she belonged to Del. "Know what?" Misty spoke to the sleeping fawn. "I've placed myself on the fringe, on the fringe of society where Angelo and Maria are. I walked into their lives, and they are trying to pull me deeper into their circle. I want out."

She rested her chin on a fence post and watched the rhythmic breathing of the deer. "Silver Ranch," she said suddenly. "I'll be there for two days, and surely, surely I'll find another place to stay and learn something about Denison Elbert besides. Perhaps even meet him." The thought was like a bit of harmony in her suddenly discordant life.

Feeling more cheerful, she turned back to the cabin. "I'll go to town," she said with sudden decision. "I'll mail my stories and get a new bandana and some other things I might need for the ranch."

After washing her face with cold water she brushed her hair furiously and re-braided it so a honey-colored pigtail hung neatly over each shoulder. A clean pink and white checked shirt donned, the loose dirt brushed off her jeans and she was ready.

"Stop it!" she scolded the freckled face looking back at her from the mirror as the thought that maybe she would run into Del crossed her mind.

She put her coin purse in her pocket and stomped out to her bicycle. The breeze on her face as she coasted down the hill refreshed her. She heard the throb of the machinery in the meadow along with the pounding of hammers and the buzz of saws. Wondering if the director was back yet, she only glanced down the well-graveled road that had replaced the slippery clay ribbon.

She pedaled slowly down the lone street of the town, stopping first to mail her stories and to exchange a few pleasantries with Lillian. Then she went on until she came to the combination grocery and general store she was getting to know so well.

When she stepped inside, the aroma of cotton, leather and oil mixed with that of coffee and spices greeted her. Intrigued as before, she wandered up one aisle and down another again looking at and pricing everything. Overalls, shirts, suspenders, tobacco pipes, sweaters, nails, pencils, underwear. Finally in a far corner piled in with the socks and handkerchiefs were the bandanas. After choosing another blue one, she walked over to the bakery goods. She stood for a long moment. Then, taking out her coin purse, she counted the bit of change she had brought with her. Satisfied she had just enough for two doughnuts besides the bandana, she chose a doughnut with colored sprinkles on it and one with chocolate frosting.

Rolling the bandana into a sweatband and fastening it around her head, she started to put the doughnuts in her backpack when she heard a voice beside her. "Hello. I didn't recognize you at first, but it is Misty, isn't it?"

Misty looked up into the brown eyes of Karyl Cross. "Hi," she said defensively. "Yes, I'm Misty."

"And I'm Karyl. I don't think we've really met. How's Sorrowful?"

"Fine, thank you." Misty kept her voice cool and level. Then, feeling more was expected of her she added, "Gretchen and Gertrude think he belongs to them now."

Karyl smiled. "Gretchen and Gertrude! Maybe you should name the fawn Glen?"

"The name it has suits it fine," was the brief, crisp answer.

"You haven't been down to the camp. Do you hear us up on your hill?"

"I—" began Misty hesitantly, "I've been down twice."

"I've been away this week," said Karyl, "but I'm on my way there now. Why not stop in on your way to your cab—er, house. You'll be interested to see what's going on. After all, we are your neighbors."

"I suppose I could," said Misty studying the face in front of her that was so strikingly like Theba's.

"I'll be watching for you." Karyl eyed the faded jeans and the backpack with the two doughnuts. She had seen the purchase and the thin coin purse. She shifted her full package from the bakery and smiled again. "Bye for now," and she walked on down the street.

Misty watched the retreating back of the tall, slender young woman in designer jeans. Her boots were shiny and her lavendar sport shirt was complimented with a harmonizing triangular scarf around her shoulders. She walked gracefully to a red and white pickup truck. Getting in, she drove off heading out of town.

"Hmm." Misty's thoughts followed the truck down Main Street. "That's the same truck I saw following the bulldozer. She has to be Karyl Cross, the camp director. She's back. I guess I'd better stop in. This is as good a time as any."

But Misty did not hurry. If she had, she would have missed Prescott and her companion who were crossing the street coming towards her. "Hi there, Misty. Wait up, will you?"

"It's good to see you." Prescott, smiling, spoke sincerely. "I want you to meet our good friend Gwen."

Even though Prescott was a friend of Angelo's, Misty was glad to see her as long as he wasn't with her; she liked her for her warmth and friendliness. So she returned her smile. "Gwen's just come from Erraid," Prescott was saying, "an island in Scotland. She's here to open one of her workshops. You'll want to come, won't you?"

"A workshop?" queried Misty. "Well, I don't know—what's it on?"

"It's about developing your inner self," explained Gwen. "I've had great success with these workshops not only in Scotland, but in England and Germany as well."

"Developing my inner self?" Misty was curious.

"That's right. How to seek the source in yourself. You have the strength to solve all your problems, you know, by getting closer to this source. The aim of the workshops is to teach our own how to do this—how to get closer."

"You will come, won't you, Misty?" asked Prescott. "You know we all love you and want the best for you—we want you to know how to seek your source and have true happiness. We'll let you know more about the workshops soon. But now we've got to go."

Prescott gave Misty a quick hug, then with a smile she and Gwen continued on their way leaving a somewhat bewildered young woman sitting on her bike.

After watching the two for a full minute, Misty pedaled out to the street. She took her time, not wanting to get to the camp too soon. She would think about what Prescott and Gwen had said later. Right now she was a bit apprehensive, not so much about seeing the camp, but who was there. If Del were there, and he surely must be—what would it be like to see him again? She gripped the handlebars of the bike a bit harder.

The shadows were lengthening when Misty finally reached the freshly graveled road. She rode slowly toward the camp, but heard nothing. Everyone had probably gone home by now, she assured herself. Surely no one would be working after hours. Well, she would go all the way down. Maybe even Karyl had gone, she herself had delayed so. If no one were there, she could go back tomorrow.

She stopped when she saw Karyl's pickup. The jeep stood close by. She had no chance to change her mind even if she wanted to. She had already been seen.

"Misty!" Karyl was waving to her from the steps of one of the unfinished buildings. "I'm here. Come on over."

Slowly Misty pedaled across the grass.

"Everyone else has left so it's pretty quiet. Come in and see what we've done." Karyl walked into the skeleton of a building as she spoke. The air was filled with the scent of freshly cut pine, and Misty breathed deeply of the fragrance as she followed.

"This is the dining area." Karyl's enthusiasm was evident. "See? The window looks out on the pond. Only it's a lake now."

Misty looked in amazement at the large body of water that had taken the place of the small pond. Piles of freshly dredged mud outlined the edges and the ground looked soggy and marshy. But the little stream that fed the lake from off the hill could be seen, and there was a wall of rocks for the water to run over making a miniature waterfall.

"Isn't it nice?" asked Karyl. "Del did it. There will be trees and shrubs along the banks, and water lilies and ducks and swans."

"The blue herons loved the pond," said Misty almost accusingly.

"They're still there. And there'll be more to watch—lots of children. The barrack where they will stay is over there."

Karyl led the way into the kitchen. "I wish Del could have stayed until it was all finished." She ran her hand lovingly over a smooth counter top.

"He's gone?" Misty ventured while examining a window sill very closely.

Karyl studied the young woman for a moment before she answered. Misty, standing framed in the window, had a fineness about her that her jeans and checkered shirt could not disguise. "He's on his way back to the ranger station in Stillwater National Forest," Karyl said finally, deciding not to go into details. "Have you ever been there?"

Misty shook her head. "No," she said briefly.

"Del loves it. But he'll be here for the camp's dedication later this summer. He promised. The cook's office is that room over there, and this is my office."

Misty followed Karyl into the one room that was finished. Facing north towards the mountains, it was light and airy and already amply furnished. Everything was neat and spoke of efficiency. A large map hung on one wall and on the other was a large oil painting. Misty looked at it casually, but from where she stood it was impossible to see the picture well, certainly not the artist's signature.

Karyl was saying, "Come see the view. Nothing but trees and mountains. That's where Del's going, away up there." She pointed to the high peaks and Misty stood beside her to look.

The two young women wandered back to the porch. Karyl tucked her pencil behind her ear and ran her hand through her short brown hair. She looked at Misty thoughtfully.

"One of our men had an accident last week—broke his ankle and will be laid up for however long it takes. We're looking for someone to take his place of being a gofer—just a short-term job of running errands. We're a Christian camp so the person must be a Christian." Karyl paused, then remembering the thin coin purse, asked, "What about you? Are you a Christian? Are you interested in the job?"

"Well, yes—yes, I'm a Christian. And the job is what I came to see about when you were gone—to see if you need some more help."

"Have you ever driven a pickup?"

"I drive," Misty answered evasively.

"The errands and jobs around the grounds that require a pickup just aren't getting done. We need all of the help we can get to keep things rolling. I know Fred will be glad I've found someone, if you're interested and want the job. We would want you here by eight in the morning."

"I—I think I could handle it." Misty had not expected it to be this easy. Driving a pickup around the grounds? Going on errands? Getting to know the other workers? She would be involved in the camp after all, and she could write, from the inside out as her editor-dad wanted. And she would be doing something totally different. It would be a wonderful chance to prove herself.

"We really need you. I'm glad you stopped by. Be sure to bring a sack lunch. We furnish tea and coffee."

"I'm glad I stopped by, too." Misty smiled. Maybe someday she would be able to tell Karyl just how glad she was.

She knew Karyl was watching as she rode away, so she turned once and waved then began to think about what she might be getting herself into. She had never driven a pickup—it was probably a stick shift. But she could do it. Oh, how Jan and the others would laugh. The very thought made Misty laugh out loud.

She would be working for Karyl Cross, she reminded herself. She would try not to resent Karyl. After all it was just because she looked like Theba. But Misty sensed Karyl was questioning her in some way. Did she think Misty was not her equal? Not her equal? Well! Then Misty remembered Karyl and Del bringing the fawn. They had seen Angelo milking the goat, the run-down little log cabin, herself in her faded jeans—Misty could easily imagine what the scene must have looked like to them.

She looked down at herself now. She was dressed the same way, and Karyl had seen her few purchases. Of course, that was it. Karyl thought she was poverty-stricken, a poverty-stricken gal from nowhere. And Karyl was working with all of that money left by Martha Cross.

Irritation ruffled Misty as she gave a little "Huh." It certainly would be a new experience for her to be shunned because of apparent poverty or because of a different life-style! But—and a smile broke over her face. "Really it's great," she reassured herself. "I asked for it, and it's just great. No one will ever guess who I am! And," her enthusiasm increased, "someone there will surely know about Denison Elbert, and I'll bet I can get a lead on the Wade family, too. But I wonder—what about the board that was supposed to meet and do the hiring? Everyone they hire is supposed to come up to the camp's standards. What standards? Being a Christian, that's what. Well, I qualify. Don't I go to church almost every Sunday? I'll go down in the morning for sure."

What a challenge this could be! And there was always the chance that Del—Misty shook her head at this thought. Karyl was between them. No chance. Besides, she was going to be at the camp for only a short time, and he wouldn't be there again until late in the summer. She would probably never see him again.

In the quiet of the evening she opened her journal on the kitchen table to record the day's happenings. She thought of Prescott and Gwen, of the source of the inner strength they said she had—a strength that could solve all her problems. Could that be possible?

Her eyes rested on the Bible Jan had given her when she left home. Maybe the answer was in that. She hadn't looked at it since unpacking, but she would, if not tonight then tomorrow for sure. And she would write about this to Jan, for her friend was well-informed; she knew about such things.

And then Misty thought of Lance. He had said something that Sunday that seemed so long ago, about going to a Learning Center and—what was it he had heard there? Something about love and power. And yes, something about strengthening or developing his inner self. How strange that he would have mentioned practically the same thing Prescott and Gwen spoke about. "I guess," Misty decided, "I will go to those workshops. Then I will know what Lance is talking about when I see him. Maybe that crystal in his car has some connection with this. Well, I'll think about that later."

Smoothing the page of her journal, she began to write. She had put down only two sentences when she heard the truck coming up the hill. Laying down her pen, she walked to the door and locked it.

NINE

"So you're really going to leave us." It was not a question but a statement, and Drew Swanson made it as he rolled down the window of the little blue Volkswagon. He wrinkled his nose as he detected an acrid scent on the warm breeze. Testing the breeze again with several short sniffs he commented, "Sure smells like smoke." Then, "When do you plan on leaving, Roy?"

"Not until the first of August. I need a change. Something everyone needs occasionally."

"You're going to give California a try?"

"My older brother has started a printing business and wants me to come help. Yeah, I've decided to give it a try. It's a lot different from carpentry, but—"

"I know. Change." And the older man gave a little laugh. "Things won't be the same without you either on the project or the camp board. Del will surely miss you."

"He's not here that much," answered Roy. "I'll miss him, but we've gone our different ways before, and we always seem to get back together somewhere."

"Are you sure this is what you want to do? Maybe there'll be more gals out there, huh, fella?" and Drew gave Roy a playful punch on the shoulder.

"No, not sure. But I'm going to do it." Roy chose to ignore Drew's last remark. "The building here will be over the hump by then so you can all survive without O'Brien, and as for the camp board—I'll keep in touch and I just might come back. Say, that does smell like smoke, doesn't it. See anything?"

The two drove on in silence while Drew scanned the horizon he knew so well. "It's pretty hazy over those hills," he indicated the mountains to the west. "Too early in the season for lightning so it must be an old smoldering tree that's finally burst out. No sweat. The fellows at the ranger stations will watch that it doesn't get out of limits."

"Where are we going?" Drew turned from scanning the horizon as, instead of turning in at the camp, the little car kept on until it came to the road that led up the hill.

"I've wanted to go up this road ever since we started working on this part of the camp, and there's no time like the present." Roy braked the car and looked up the hill, then shifting gears, began a slow ascent. "I know that big fella we see driving a blue truck lives up here somewhere and I'm just curious. The other day I saw a girl with him in the store. He was loading her stuff into his truck, but it looked like she was riding a bike."

"That big fellow is Giannelli," said Drew. "He and his mother are quite a pair. Harmless, but strange. They're into the occult, believe in reincarnation and all that. Even animal sacrifices. He's the guy who's working the Jerose mine."

"Hey, look at this," said Roy as Misty's garden nestled against the poverty-stricken cabin and the goat pen across the way came into full view. "Looks kind of sad. Neat, though. Doesn't seem to be anyone around. Oh, yes there is. Over there behind that tree," he directed. "He sure doesn't want to be seen, does he?"

"That's Giannelli all right," said Drew as he saw the man. "Let's go. I don't feel too welcome."

"Say," Roy turned the car and headed down the hill, "this is the place where Del brought that fawn he was talking about! There it is over there in the pen. Then this must be the place where the gal lives. Maybe they all live here. Oh, well. What time is it anyway?"

"That little fawn fell into good hands when Del found him," said Drew as he consulted his watch. "It's five to eight. We'd better get going."

He was silent until they reached the bottom of the hill and turned toward the camp. "We're going to have to work doubly hard to make up for Todd's not being here," he said thoughtfully. "Maybe Karyl's hired someone else."

"Oh, she wouldn't do that without consulting the board; we'd all have to agree the person came up to the camp's standards. We haven't heard a word. At least I haven't. Not having Todd will slow us down, but we'll manage. Who's that Fred is talking to?"

As Roy parked the Volkswagon under the trees, he looked intently at the two who were talking together. Lunch buckets in hand, he and Drew walked slowly, both taking note of the girl dressed in faded jeans and a simple T-shirt. A blue bandana tied over her hair did not conceal the honey-colored wisps escaping around the edges, but not until he walked around beside Fred could Roy see she had large blue eyes. He recognized her at once as the girl he had seen with Angelo Giannelli.

"Morning, fellows," said Fred. "We have a new truck driver, Misty Morrow. Misty, this is Drew Swanson and Roy O'Brien."

Misty smiled at the two men, quietly appraising them and liking what she saw—large, compact Drew with his thick thatch of blond hair; slim Roy, straight as a lodgepole pine, his close-cropped hair shining copper red in the bright sun.

Drew smiled a warm accepting smile as he shook Misty's hand with his large rough one. "Welcome to the crew," he said heartily.

"Hi." Holding himself erect and appearing to be more than his five foot eight, Roy's hazel eyes above his reddish mustache were serious as he appraised Misty. A new worker? And no board meeting?

The sound of a truck coming into the camp grounds broke into the moment. The red and white pickup drew up alongside the jeep half-hidden under the trees and stopped with what seemed to Misty to be a flourish. She watched with an involuntary tightening of her muscles while Karyl, wearing new stone-washed jeans topped with a denim shirt open at the throat slid easily to the ground. "Morning everybody! Misty! I see you've already met the gang."

Karyl walked quickly to where the four were standing. Misty could not help but notice the expression on the men's faces. It was obvious they were glad to see this woman even though the eyes of the one with the copper hair were still scowling. Karyl must have noticed the scowl, too, for she made a point of saying, "How are you, Roy?" in a friendly voice even though she turned to Misty a little too quickly.

"Did Fred tell you he's your supervisor? You're responsible to him and he will tell you what to do. If you have any questions, just ask him. I'll be in my office, if anyone wants me." With that, and without looking at Roy or Drew again, Karyl broke away from the group and walked towards the building. "I left the keys in the truck," she called over her shoulder.

"Roy," said Fred, "you and Drew load the pickup with the lumber for the dock, then our new driver and I'll take it down to the lake. Be right with you, Misty," and he followed Karyl to go over the plans for the day.

Roy gave Fred a quick questioning look. After giving Misty one more unspoken appraisal, he followed Drew.

Fred, with a wide grin on his face, pushed the door of Karyl's office open. "How's my gal this morning? You look pretty sharp, if I may say so."

"You may say so," laughed Karyl returning his embrace. Then, breaking away she asked seriously, "Are they disturbed?"

"Roy is."

"Fred, I prayed about this last night, and I feel I've done the right thing. Maybe I was impetuous, but I told her this is a Christian camp and asked her if she were one and she said she is. All I didn't do was consult the board, and I'm sure they would agree she needs us. She has no money, and if she's involved with that Giannelli, she needs rescuing." Karyl opened her purse and drew out a faded snapshot. "Look at this. I told you I knew I had a picture somewhere. I found it in with some of mother's things."

Fred took the picture of a young girl with long hair that looked to be light, possibly honey-colored. Her eyes were wide and smiling. Walking to the window, he studied the picture closely.

"There is a resemblance, isn't there," he said after a few minutes. "But what about her involvement with Giannelli? Just because she says she's a Christian doesn't necessarily mean she is. Have you forgotten about the ones we dismissed just because of beliefs like his?"

Karyl shook her head. "No, I haven't forgotten, but I—well, I just felt this is the right thing to do, Fred. That's all. Like I said, she needs us. I know this will be all right. After all it's only until Todd is able to come back. It's not as if it were a permanent thing. I don't think Drew minds, and Roy will come around. And Del—he'll understand when he hears about it. You understand, don't you?" She looked anxiously at Fred as he handed the picture back.

For answer he only smiled.

※❀※

Outside the two men worked quickly, neither one saying a word. One—two—five—ten—fifteen. Soon there were two dozen long rough boards in the bed of the pickup.

"There you go." Drew smiled at Misty. "It's all yours, but you'd better wait for Fred. Here he comes now. See you later."

Misty caught her breath. This truck? She had envisioned a beat-up one like Angelo's. But the red and white pickup? She curled her toes in her shoes and rubbed the palms of her hands on her jeans. Out the corner of her eye she saw Roy walk away without a comment of any kind. She turned at the sound of Fred's voice.

"OK, let's get started." Fred climbed into the bed of the truck. Sitting on the edge, he braced himself against the stacked lumber. His "Let's go!" rang out loud and clear.

Biting her lower lip and feeling her mouth go suddenly dry, Misty turned the ignition and started the engine with a roar. She stepped on the clutch and, fumbling, put the stick shift into reverse. The truck jerked backwards. Confused, Misty hunted for the brake, missed it and stepped on the accelerator.

Fred, hanging on so tightly his knuckles were white, yelled "Look out!" as a sturdy tree loomed in the way.

The truck met the tree a split second before Misty found the brake. A slight crunch of metal mingled with a groan from Fred. The girl bit her lip even harder as she found the clutch and managed to shift into neutral. "Oh, brother!" she muttered to herself, "now what have I done?" She leaned out of the window to see Fred jump to the ground.

"No real damage," he said after a quick inspection. "More noise than anything." He took one look at Misty's face. "It's OK, it's OK," he added quickly.

"Here, let me show you the gears." Fred climbed into the cab and began a quick rehearsal. "Low down here, second, high. This is reverse up here. Get it? Low, second, high, reverse. Atta girl. You're too short;

you need a pillow. Try this." The man took off his jacket and rolling it tightly, tucked it behind her. "Better?"

Misty nodded.

"Now, let's go that way," and Fred pointed ahead.

Carefully, Misty pushed in the clutch, and with a hand that trembled ever so slightly, she put the gear into low. Slowly, she pressed the accelerator as she let out the clutch, and the truck inched forward.

"Good girl," praised Fred. "There's the pond over there. Don't forget to stop when you get close to it."

Misty relaxed as they both laughed.

❀❀❀

"She made it!" Karyl gave a little clap as she watched from the window with Roy and Drew looking over her shoulder.

"Right on target all right," said Drew as the pickup stopped. "Where did you find her, Karyl? She's a cute little thing."

"Actually, Del found her."

"He did, did he?" questioned Drew. "Where 'bouts? Does he know she's working here? Hey, she's willing, too. Look at her helping Fred unload those boards. How about that!"

"She lives up on the hill over there, doesn't she?" Roy asked.

"No, Del doesn't know about her being here. Yes, she lives up on the hill over there. Del thinks she's engaged to the Giannelli man."

"I thought that's who she is," said Roy flatly, remembering the plain little cabin and the man peeking from behind a tree. "If she is engaged to Giannelli, and if he's into the occult like Drew says he is, then she must be into it too. We definitely do not want any of that around here. What are you thinking of, Karyl?"

"Roy, she hasn't been here long. It still might be possible to save her, to get her away from Giannelli and his influence. She said she's a Christian; we must help her regardless," Karyl went on patiently. "She needs money. Look at her clothes. I saw her in the bakery yesterday buying two little doughnuts. That's all. Just two little doughnuts. She could stand some new jeans and shoes, and a shirt."

"Let Giannelli take care of her." Roy watched Misty as he spoke. He had noticed how faded the jeans were and the T-shirt.

Drew asked, "Has she tried to find a job any place else? Probably not."

"A job? In Pommel? Drew! Frankly, I was drawn to the girl when I saw her in town yesterday. I've seen where she lives, I know her circumstances, and it's sad. We must reach out to her, show her Christ's love no matter who or what she is. You know, we could be entertaining an angel unaware."

"Hiring an angel unaware," corrected Roy wryly. He laid down his hammer and looked at Karyl accusingly. "What about the board meeting we're supposed to have before hiring anyone so we can question them? Do you know for sure she's a Christian? How could she be and be engaged to that—that guy! Personally, Karyl, I don't agree with you all the way. Christ's love, yes but—well, it's your money," he added almost bitterly without waiting for an answer. He turned back to his work of making cupboards. "You're the boss."

"What are you paying her?" asked Drew hoping to deflect any real argument.

"The minimum. Is that all right?"

"Sounds good to me. Like Roy says, it's your money."

Karyl turned so she could talk to both men. Her voice was low and smooth. She smiled as she spoke patiently. "No, not my money. The camp's money. And as for my being the boss—before mother died, we formed a corporation and you two are part of it with her approval and blessing. You know that. She named me executrix or director—whatever—with Del and Fred as co-whatever. I took this responsibility only because mother left it to me. I've tried to include everyone in all decision making, and now that this one time I've gone ahead of you, you're critical and bitter." Aware she must clear the air at once, or the problem would grow, she looked at Roy.

"I just want to use the money the way it should be used," she went on gently. "I want to be a good steward of it. And reaching out to others is part of the stewardship as well as the purpose of the camp."

Roy walked over to Karyl. "You're right. It is the camp's money, and Drew and I are part of the organization. That's why I'm wondering how come you hired a little Miss Nobody we know nothing about just on the spur of the moment. Sure, the purpose of the camp is to reach out to others—to sick kids and to anybody who comes to Pommel. I'm not angry, Karyl. Just curious and concerned that you didn't include all of us in making the decision."

Karyl smiled as she spoke deliberately. "I feel the Lord has brought her to us for a special reason. And we do need someone to fill in for Todd."

"Her lifestyle is something else," Roy argued. "I saw the cabin where she lives. It looks zilch to me. And that big bozo—If she's here, he'll be hanging around too. Do you want that kind of a person around Martha's Camp?"

"Let her work as messenger or driver until Todd gets back," Drew interrupted. "Then you can let her go."

"Roy," Karyl spoke seriously, emphasizing her words. "*She said she is a Christian*. And don't you see? She needs us and the camp, and what we stand for. She needs us for friends."

Karyl stood quietly looking at the two men.

"You say we should reach out to others." Roy's eyes did not leave Karyl's. "Then why did you let those others go? We should've reached out to them, too. What's the difference between her and them? Some of them said they were Christians."

Karyl frowned. "I—we—should have reached out more to the others, I know, but I wasn't as aware then of their needs as I am now. The Lord would have us show His love to anyone He brings across our path. We will show love to Misty while we can. Remember, she is only here until Todd comes back—short-term. And we'll try to reach Angelo."

"You're right, I s'pose." Roy tapped a nail into position then turned and spoke sincerely, " 'Love' is our byword. Todd may be back sooner than we think; we'll have to work fast."

Roy turned to his hammering, filling the air with loud blows. After a few moments he walked over to Karyl. "I'm sorry. I'll help all I can to reach out to her and maybe she is an angel in jeans." He looked out of the window. "A cute angel at that." He turned back to Karyl and smiled, then kissed her lightly on the cheek.

"Thank you, Roy." Karyl looked at both men earnestly. "I'm sure everything will work out. If Angelo is a bother, well—we'll face that when it comes. But we'll try to reach him too. All right?"

"I'm with you," said Drew, "and so's Roy, aren't you, boy?"

"It's fine with me," said Roy good naturedly, "to just let it ride and see what happens—until Todd comes back."

"I've a suggestion to make." Drew lay down his hammer. "We can still have a board meeting. Keep Misty on until Todd's back then decide whether to keep her or not. Kids will be coming, and we'll need more help with them. We will have had the advantage of observing her and getting to know her in the meantime."

"Great!" agreed both Roy and Karyl in a single breath. "That's a tremendous idea, Drew. I know Fred will go for it," added Karyl.

"Here comes the crew to work on the barrack." Roy glanced at his watch. "They're late, but at least they're here."

"There's one thing more." Karyl held up her hand to stop the men from leaving.

"Such as?" asked Drew.

"Let's not pry. Pass the word around that nobody is to ask her any questions. I wouldn't want to embarrass her or maybe drive her away. OK?"

"Right. We'll alert the others."

❧❦

As the morning wore on, the air was full of sounds of progress, and Misty was caught up in the middle of it. After two trial runs with Fred at her side she graduated to soloing to the lake and back, bending the tall grass into a road.

As she began to relax and take her driving easily, she watched. She watched the bulldozer smoothing the banks of the pond, and she thought briefly of Del. She watched gravel trucks following the bulldozer their spilling contents clearly outlining not the pond anymore, but the lake. She watched carpenters scurrying like busy ants. She watched Roy as he literally ran from one area of the grounds to another. She watched Drew. And she watched Fred.

"Here I am," she told herself proudly. "Inside of the camp and so far so good. Now to keep my eyes and ears open. They all seem like people who are in touch with what's going on. Dad will be pleased with the way things are working out!"

"It's lunch time, Misty," said Fred after her tenth, or was it her eleventh trip? She had lost count. "Did you bring yours?"

Misty nodded. "It's in my pack on my bike."

"We all eat together in the dining area. Get yours and come on in."

"How's it going?" Karyl smiled at Misty as she walked into the dining area clutching her paper sack. Misty looked around the unfinished room casually. About a dozen men, all with lunch sacks or boxes open beside them, were there some sitting on the floor and some on piles of lumber. And she, Misty Morrow, felt suddenly shy. She had walked into banquet halls where there were men in black ties, and she had not felt this way.

"Sit anywhere," invited Karyl. Misty chose a spot next to Roy, sat with her legs curled under her, and drew a single sandwich out of her sack. Roy moved to give her a little more room and casually looked at the woman with the few freckles on her nose.

"Fred," Karyl asked quietly, "will you return thanks, please?"

Misty took a quick look around the circle at the men, wondering what she had gotten herself into now. Then she, too, bowed her head and stared at the floor in front of her while she reminded herself she was thankful she had even the one sandwich and doughnut. She was really hungry!

She felt more comfortable and at ease when everyone began eating and talking—comfortable and included. "Here, Misty, have some carrot sticks." "Help yourself to the grapes, Misty." "Have some peanuts?"

"There's plenty of coffee and tea. Sadie makes it by the gallon," said Fred as a rosy-cheeked woman walked over to the group.

"Can I get you something to drink?" The woman's round cheeks dimpled as she smiled down at Misty. A bright blue plaid apron covered her ample figure. Beads of perspiration outlined her upper lip and plastered gray strands of hair to her forehead.

"A cup of tea would taste good, thanks." Misty liked the woman immediately.

"You're taking Todd's place," smiled Sadie as she returned with the tea. "It's good to have you with us. If you ever feel the need to get away from all of this," and she playfully scowled at Roy, "you're welcome to hide out in the kitchen." With that Sadie began picking up empty cups and cookie plates.

"Sadie's going to be our kitchen engineer," said Roy. He had decided to say something to this little Miss Nobody, and Sadie gave him what he was looking for.

"Kitchen engineer?" asked Misty.

"That's another title for cook," laughed Roy. "She can't wait for her domain to be finished, so she comes out every morning she can and tells us what to do, and keeps the coffee pot going."

"Quite a few people seem to work here." It was Misty's turn now to try to make conversation.

"There's a crew of twelve today," said Roy. "Sometimes not so many, sometimes more. We're anxious to get the camp ready, so some of the guys work for as many as twelve hours. Now that the days are longer, they can work well into the evenings."

"I know. I've been hearing saws and the bulldozer when it's almost dark." Misty ate her sandwich slowly to make it last.

"Here, have some." Roy pushed a bag of potato chips closer. "Great guns! Just one thin sandwich? That's hardly enough to keep a truck driver going. Don't be bashful; take a handful."

"Yes, sir," one of the men was saying, "we'll be able to have kids here by early July."

"Shall we set the dedication for then?" asked Karyl.

"When will Del be able to come?" asked Roy.

"I don't know for sure. I have to take the jeep up to him when he sends for it. I can ask him then. Let's not set a date until we know his schedule. Summer is a bad time. Especially this summer. Have you ever seen it this dry so early in the year? If we don't get some rain soon, he may not get down at all!"

"You can say that again," agreed Roy. "We smelled smoke this morning on the way to work, didn't we, Drew?"

"We sure did, but it's gotta be a prescribed fire up near the timberline. Let's let Del set the date for the dedication. We can be flexible. Well, back to work." Drew snapped his lunch bucket closed and stood up. "Sadie, those cookies are super. You're going to have us all spoiled. You know what we'll expect when you have your kitchen around you!"

Sadie laughed good-naturedly. "I've got to keep you happy, so you'll get it finished." She carried the leftover cookies to a cupboard. "I'll leave these here for your afternoon break. I'm going now."

"See you tomorrow," Drew said, "if you can make it. Roy, did you bring another gallon of Formica adhesive?"

"I thought you did," said Roy as he, too, stood and prepared to go back to his carpentry.

"I guess we both forgot it. Misty, how would you like to go to the store and get some?"

"Sure," answered Misty, who had been watching Sadie. "I'll be glad to. Now?"

Fred nodded his approval. "Here, I'll give you a purchase order so you'll have no problems."

Misty drove carefully down the camp road and turned on to the highway. It was good to have four wheels under her again, and it was strangely satisfying to know she had proven herself to these people in just this short half day. Even though Karyl resembled Theba as closely as she did, she certainly did not act like her. Misty shuddered when she thought of what Theba would have said about her backing into a tree. Or Lance, for that matter. He would have ridiculed her, put her down. But Karyl had said nothing. She had not even bothered to inspect the slight damage to the truck. She reacted the way Jan would have. And Fred had been really casual about the incident.

Now Misty was driving on the highway alone. She smiled to herself, and her smile broadened with a little chuckle added. It beat riding the bike, and there would be no problem parking in front of the one store. Of that she was sure.

There was no problem finding the adhesive either. It was in the corner where the nails were. "We keep things on hand just for those folks," the storekeeper told Misty. "They're good customers. They have quite a project there."

Driving back to the camp as if she had been doing it forever, Misty remembered following the bulldozer on the big truck, and she thought of Del. He must be a special person the way everyone talks about him. Why, they won't even plan a date for the camp's dedication until he can be here. Early in July maybe, they say. And Karyl is going to take his jeep to him when he's ready for it.

Karyl is lucky to have Del, as Misty thought of him, a wistfulness came over her like a cloud. Why can't I feel this way when I think of Lance? I want to see Del again. But that's silly; I don't really know him. It's probably because I know I won't get to see him again. I'll be gone by the first of July, if all goes well with my series of stories. And he isn't coming until later that month. Well, and she shrugged, that's the way it is. But I can remember; the memory will be my souvenir of my time in Colorado.

She wasn't very comforted by the thought of Del as just a souvenir, but as she saw the camp in front of her, Misty tucked her thoughts of Del away. At the same time she allowed herself the joy of being important even in a small way to these people who accepted her without any questions. She laughed out loud, pleased with what she had done. Everything was working out so well! And in three more days she would be going to Silver Ranch for the weekend where there was the chance of learning something about Denison Elbert. I better think of him instead of Del Quinn, she reprimanded herself.

As she drove into the yard, Misty waved to Roy who was carrying a ladder and, for once, not running. He gave her the victory sign in return, and grinned.

TEN

The rest of the week passed without mishap. By Friday Misty felt as much at home behind the wheel of the pickup as she did behind the wheel of her Porsche. She reveled in the warmth and friendliness of the people at the camp and could not help but notice Roy O'Brien managed to sit by her everyday at lunch. But she did not object. She enjoyed his easy-going banter and joking.

It was Roy who explained a prescribed fire to her. The subject came up often as the haze on the horizon lingered day after day. "It's a fire started by nature, usually lightning." Misty listened with intense interest watching Roy so closely he stirred uncomfortably.

"It seems," he kept his gaze on the hazy horizon, "that lightning causes a fire just about once every decade—it has for millions of years. But since there hasn't been any lightning yet this season, the one up there is more likely from a tree that's been smoldering for several years. They do that, then they finally burst open and cause a fire. Fire's nature's way of burning the old rotten stuff out of the forests.

"It seems like such a waste," commented Misty. "Does it do any other good besides burn the rotten stuff, as you call it?"

"Oh, yes. Somebody discovered that fire's necessary to release seeds from certain hard cones that will not open otherwise. That's the way new trees are started. So when these fires begin on government land, they are allowed to burn within their limits. But believe me, they are carefully monitored and managed. They don't do any harm unless they get out of bounds like what happened in Yellowstone a few years ago."

Misty looked where Roy pointed; an orange haze coated the hills. But the fire was well within its limits, Roy assured her, and was near the subalpine area far from Silver Ranch. No need for concern.

※❦※

The forty-five minute ride to Silver Ranch allowed Misty to gather her thoughts. She had checked her mailbox before she boarded the Silver Ranch Wagon, a silver-colored van that transported guests from Frisco and stopped in Pommel for her. There had been another letter from Lance. "I'm counting the days, my sweet," he wrote after the usual social news items. Misty crammed the letter into her pocket when the driver of the van called out, "OK, folks. Let's go." She would read the letter again later. For now she wanted only to watch the river flowing westward while the van followed it upstream.

Bordering on a curve of the river where a glacial stream made a sudden appearance from out of a narrow, rocky ravine, the ranch lay nestled in the foothills just like in the picture on the brochure. Stepping into the lodge, a rambling log ranch house in true western style, Misty was intrigued by the living room with its huge stone fireplace, exposed beam ceiling and knotty pine paneling. Pole furniture completed the room. Beyond lay the airy dining area with its crisp curtains and color-ful table cloths. The joy of adventure and anticipation surged through Misty.

From her room she could see the barns and corrals with their rustic rail fences. A dozen or more horses—quarter horses for the most part with a few appaloosas and Arabians mixed in—grazed in an adjoining pasture. She had already signed up with the group that would ride the seven-mile trail up the narrow ravine following the river.

Only eight gathered at the big, red barn after breakfast the next morning. Dressed mostly in Western garb, they stood around com-menting on the haze and laughing among themselves.

Some of the riders were anticipating their first experience on a horse's back, but not Misty. She easily mounted the chestnut quarter horse that was brought to her thinking of the times she and Lance had ridden together at the stables in the hills north of Syracuse. But those rides had been in well-groomed parks along smooth grassy trails, nothing like the trail that wound up the mountain side. Reigning in the impatient horse, Misty looked at the sheer walls of rock on either side of the ravine and wished the haze that seemed to be getting more dense by the moment would go away.

"Everybody ready?" The guide, a man in his early forties, studied the group in front of him. "The haze is from the fire up in Stillwater National Forest," he explained. "It's far enough away to be of no concern to us. It's at the subalpine level, which means it's approximately 11,000 feet up—3,000 feet higher than we are here in the foothills. The smoke is drifting down and is caught in this ravine, but there's no danger. We'll line up and stay in that formation. Our ride is seven miles up the ravine for those who have ridden before. For you beginners we have a three mile limit. Jed here," a young blond man with a red bandana around his neck took off his cowboy hat and waved it in the air at mention of his name, "will bring you three-milers back. We all will be back in time for lunch." The group applauded and then fell silent to listen to what more the guide had to say.

"Now. How many of you have ridden before? Four of you," he counted. "We're half and half. Ok, those who are inexperienced will fall in behind three of the old hands and one of you more experienced riders bring up the rear behind the youngsters. You," and the man indicated Misty. "Will you bring up the rear?"

For answer Misty gave a mock salute wishing she had thought to buy a cowboy hat to wear instead of her bandana. She eased her horse into position patting his neck to reassure him while she waited for the starting signal from the guide.

"Ride on!" he called out, his voice echoing from the hills. One by one the horses started pacing themselves to follow each other. The man called Jed rode alongside the group to better keep his eye on the first-timers.

Misty rode easily, keeping a comfortable distance between herself and the horse in front of her. At the end of the line she felt almost as if she were riding alone and, save for an occasional joking exchange with Jed who would drop back to speak with her, she gave herself up entirely to the ride. She noted the variety of berry shrubs along the way—the low-growing currant and gooseberry bushes mixed in with the wild grapes, and the snowberry with its pinkish flowers and white berries.

Over all towered the hackberry bushes with their cherry-like fruit. There were lodgepole pines and quivering aspen with sturdy, obstinate spruce growing out of the shale of the canyon walls.

She recognized the blue harebells remembering the ones Maria had pointed out to her on one of their walks. And the forget-me-nots and mountain daisies. Goldenrod thrust their yellow spears up towards the sky; purple cinquefoil grew in colorful clumps. It was a new world for Misty. Different even from where the camp was; different from where her cabin stood. And she loved it.

The three miles seemed to pass quickly, but the weary newcomers were ready to turn back when Jed gave the signal. "I'm glad we're going back," a young woman confided to Misty. "I don't like this haze. It seems to get thicker every minute. I think everyone should go back."

Misty only smiled in response, but she looked at the tops of the trees and tried to see up the ravine. The far end was obscured by what seemed to be a cloud, but she knew it was smoke. She looked at the guide questioningly, but he didn't seem to notice. When he called out, "Ride on!" Misty fell in behind the other three as they began to continue up the trail. She did not want to miss any of this ride, for when would she have another opportunity?

The trail was marked off into miles by a white line painted on trees. Misty noticed that when they passsed the first mile. Two miles. Three miles. Just before the fourth mile the trail split. One arm of it curved around and went through brush back downstream towards the camp. The other arm of the trail continued up the ravine. The guide spoke to the man riding closest to him, then to the other two. Assuming Misty would follow, the guide raised his arm in a salute to her. She returned with a friendly wave and reached into her pocket for a tissue. When she drew the tissue out, her small cosmetic bag came with it and fell to the ground spilling its contents. Stopping her horse, she slid off and knelt to retrieve the bag and gather what lay scattered about.

Mounting again, Misty continued up the stream at a leisurely pace. Her eyes were smarting now, but she urged the horse on, certain the others were just ahead. Surely, she thought to herself, that guide knows what he's doing. He probably wants us all to get our money's worth and will go on for all seven miles. It's not much farther. I passed mile six a bit ago so mile seven must be close. She ended her thoughts with a sneeze and longed for a drink, her throat and mouth were so dry.

"I'll bet you'd like a drink, too, wouldn't you, old boy," and she patted the horse's neck. "Here, let's stop. The others will be on their way back in a minute; we can wait here for them. It's OK," she assured the animal whose nervous whinnying and pawing of the ground echoed in the ominously silent forest.

Holding the reins lightly, Misty stretched out on her stomach to reach over the rocks for a drink of the icy cold water. Suddenly she felt the reins jerked from her hand as the horse reared and took off down the trail. A small but glowing branch had bounced off the horse's rump and landed in the stream. A wave of panic swept over her. At almost the same instant she heard a low growling echoing down the ravine. Stunned and at first unable to move, Misty looked up. The anemic white smoke she had seen from the ranch had turned dark brown.

Behind the column of smoke flickered an orange light—a strange translucent light—and far up the ravine glowed what she knew to be flames. A smoke column, bending with the wind, spiraled towards her. The wind had sent the flaming branch to brush the horse, leaving Misty alone.

Fear spurred the young woman to action. Without a second thought she began running down the trail, sensing she would have to travel fast to keep ahead of the fire whose awful roar seemed to be getting closer with each breath. She must get to the ranch. It was straight down the river. But where were the other riders? They must have turned back at the fork in the trail. The guide knew the danger and headed for the ranch thinking she was following. "Why, oh why did I stop to get that silly cosmetic kit?" she panted to herself. "That's when I lost them. Oh, God! Please get me out of this."

She ran on thankful it was downhill, thankful she had done so much running with Jan before she left home. She dared to stop after she had gone a mile and, panting as much from tension as from exertion, she looked cautiously over her shoulder as she might look for a pursuer who was about to overtake her. The dark smoke continued drifting through the trees; a slight orange cast to the sky was still visible behind the screening branches.

Misty looked at the river flowing on as though nothing could ever disturb its peace. Her throat was parched. Dared she take the time to scoop up another drink? She found a low spot on the bank and once more lowered herself onto her stomach and leaned out over the rocks.

A dozen or so of what looked like little black worms floated by. One came up in the handful of water she cupped to drink, but she could see it was not a worm; it was a pine needle burned crispy black. As she dumped it back into the flowing stream, Misty saw how many of the blackened curlicues there were. And here in the unprotected shale ravine, the roaring of the fire sounded almost as loud as it had before. Not waiting to fully quench her thirst she took two quick sips and then splashed a handful of the cold water on her hot face before she scrambled back onto her feet and began running again.

She had run for a good ten minutes without stopping before she was conscious of another sound coming towards her—a pounding of the hard-packed earth. A horse? It couldn't be her horse, it must be another. Then she was not alone in these terrifying woods.

"Whoa, Gus." A man in a ranger uniform looked down at her from the back of his spotted appaloosa. "Hi, there. Are you the gal from the ranch, or are you another stray I haven't heard about?"

He leaned down and reached a hand out to her. "Put your foot in the stirrup and climb on behind me," he instructed without waiting for her answer. "You're going to be OK."

Misty grabbed the man's hand and swinging her leg in a wide arc, she hoisted herself to the rump of the horse.

"Good girl," praised her rescuer. "Now hang on. Put your arms around my waist," he instructed as Misty hesitated a brief moment. The man turned his head slightly to talk to her over his shoulder, and Misty found herself staring at a thick, light brown sideburn. "I've got to make a stop at my cabin over here in the woods and report on the fire, then I'll take you back to the ranch. You are the one from there I'm looking for, aren't you?"

"I—I guess so," admitted Misty. "I was riding with the group and got separated from them. A burning branch hit my horse while I was getting a drink and he took off."

"Yeah. Well—" The ranger knew this was no time to lecture the young woman hugging his waist about the perils of getting separated from a group when riding up the ravine so, instead of saying what he had a mind to say, he merely grumped "Well" again and then added, "don't worry, we'll have you back in time for the evening square dance."

They rode on with only the scrunching of the horse's hooves on dry, brittle sticks and needles breaking the eerie silence. Soon they branched off on the trail that veered away from the original trail and curved back towards the ranch. A quarter of a mile into the woods there was still another trail that climbed the steep side of the hill, going up and up. "Hang on," the man called as he felt Misty's grip tighten. "This goes up pretty straight."

The trees thinned to where there were almost no trees at all and scarcely any shrubs. A wide expanse of meadow stretched ahead of them. On the edge was a small cabin, its newly oiled log walls shining in the haze. The man dropped the reins as the horse came to a stop underneath a lone blue spruce. "This is as far as we go this trip," he said as he slid to the ground. "I have to make some reports to the fire-management office before I can take you to the ranch. Won't take long, but you'd better come inside and relax while you're waiting." He held up his arms for Misty, and without hesitating she slid off the horse's rump and allowed the ranger to catch her.

Leaving the woman to herself, the man strode a few yards to what looked like a white metal post in the ground. He knelt down beside it and checked the connecting instruments, at the same time making notations on a little pad he pulled out of his pocket. Seeing Misty watching him, he offered a brief explanation. "A lightning detector. Just checking to see if there have been any strikes. Freda here," and he waved his arm towards the haze, "is from a smoldering tree, but we keep check on lightning regardless. We really get zapped up here at times. Have to keep everything well-grounded."

"Is the fire all right? Is it—what do you say?—contained?" asked Misty anxiously.

"The wind has shifted, so the fire's heading back the other way. It's still within limits, so yeah, it's OK. It sounds worse in the ravine than it really is—sounds closer and noisier because the air currents suck the sound down the hollow canyon, and it bounces off the shale walls. You weren't really as bad off as you probably thought. Still one never knows which direction the wind's going to take. It's part of my job to go out on the trails and find people like you and get them back away from any danger."

"Is that what you do mainly? Look for lost people or those in trouble?"

"Well, no, not mainly but managing people is one of our biggest jobs," he went on to say as he fastened a bag of oats on the horse's muzzle. "Manage people up to a point, that is. We have our ethics here in the wilderness and one is 'You're on your own.' If people can't read signs and follow regulations, that's tough. But we do try to keep them informed and protect them as much as possible."

"I don't think everyone who hikes or camps realizes what all you do. It's good to know there are fellows like you here."

"We're always on the lookout, and we carry walkie-talkies. Come on inside while I enter this info on the computer and call the office. You'll notice everything's grounded inside. Like I said, we really get zapped here at times." He led the way into the cabin. "Here," he said as he walked over to the small stove, "I'll put the tea kettle on and you can make some tea while I do my thing at the computer. You're probably starved. There's bread and peanut butter and jelly. Make several while you're at it. I could use some."

While waiting for the computer, the ranger turned to Misty and with the first smile he had offered said, "Go ahead and make yourself at home," and he pointed to a door that opened off the airy room that served as kitchen, dining and sleeping space.

Grateful for the ranger's thoughtfulness Misty went into the bathroom. Taking out her cosmetic kit she found her comb, shook her hair free, combed it thoroughly then replaced her bandana. As a last touch she smoothed her eyebrows carefully.

She stood for a moment in the doorway of the large room. Wires were everywhere, attached to all the furnishings. "Oh, that's what he means by everything being grounded, I'll bet," she said to herself. Satisfied with her own answer, she went to the kitchen end of the large room to make the tea.

From her spot by the stove she cast stealthy glances at the man at the computer. He had taken off his hat, and Misty could see that he was bald except for a thin covering of light brown hair that grew into the thick sideburns. He was not tall. She had noticed that when she got off the horse. Nor was he of stocky build. Her arms had gone around his waist quite easily. "Rather wispy," would have been her description of him. He appeared to be about forty, although with his thinning hair, it was hard to say. He could perhaps be in his late thirties.

After she had made her mental notes of the man's physical features so she could relay them to Jan when she shared this experience with her friend, Misty again let her gaze wander around the room. What was that she saw standing next to the dining table? Was it an easel? And were those canvases on the table? And brushes? And oils? Curious, Misty walked over and picked up a picture. It was an oil painting of a fox. Or was it a dog? No, the shape of the muzzle, the setting of the eyes and the reddish coat, a poor attempt at painting fur—all bespoke of a fox. The animal was peering from behind a bush of some description, and from the looks of him, he was daring a hunter to identify him rather than to stalk him. In the lower right hand corner of the painting were the initials "D. E."

Pursing her lips ever so slightly and opening her blue eyes wide, Misty picked up another painting—a meadow full of yellow blooms of no definite description enclosed by a fence of various sized rails. Like the painting of the fox this one also bore the initials "D. E." A half dozen paintings, all of animals or of nature in its different seasons, lay on the table. Carefully, she drew one that lay half hidden under the others to where she could see it better and gave a little gasp. It was a rough sketch of the same painting of the eagle that lay in Lewis's office. There were the mountains, there was the great bird, a bit shaky perhaps but still the great bird, but this one had a fish in its claws. The letters "D.E." were bold.

Misty looked from the painting to the straight back of the man submerged in his work. Why, he was Denison Elbert! Who else? To think she'd found him so easily, and just by chance. Wouldn't Lewis be pleased? These simple, crude paintings were easily explained—they were merely quick sketches of the masterpieces that were to come.

What an opportunity! She finished making the tea and quietly placed a steaming cup along with two sandwiches by the computer. Sipping her own tea, she stood staring out of the window at a mother quail with half a dozen tiny ones in the meadow near the spruce tree. A jack rabbit appeared from nowhere, scattering the little family, while overhead a blue jay flew raucously from one tree limb to another.

While the girl waited, she half listened to the artist-ranger as he completed his radio report. "Wind has shifted from northwest to southeast and is blowing Freda back into her limits. Yup, one. From Silver Ranch. No campers on the trail. Right-o. I'll call back at twenty."

When he shut off his radio and Misty saw he was through with his work and ready to eat, she stood beside him, the sketch of the eagle painting in her hand. "I'd like to talk to you about this." Misty held the picture out to the ranger. "I saw the finished painting." She paused, letting the words sink in.

"You? You saw the finished painting?" The ranger set his cup down. "You couldn't have."

"But I did." Misty hesitated, not sure how far to go. "In a museum in Syracuse."

"That painting's not in any museum," assured the ranger.

"You're Denison Elbert, aren't you?" Misty kept her voice casual.

The man squinted from the steam of the hot tea as he put the cup to his lips, so Misty could not see the expression in his eyes. Taking a quick, shallow sip he answered with a question. "How long have you been at Silver Ranch?"

"I came yesterday," she said. Then getting the point of his query she gave a little laugh. "If I'd been there last week for the artists' workshop, I'd know you were Denison Elbert and wouldn't have to ask. Right?"

"Right," agreed the man taking another sip of tea. "You wouldn't have to ask."

Misty bit her lip. She wanted to say more; she wanted to tell him the fish was missing from the painting she saw; she wanted to tell him that he had a good chance of getting the $10,000 if the painting were repaired. But instead of saying any of these things, she laid the sketch down and walked over to still another finished canvas propped against the wall next to a day bed.

"Oh, this is nice. Really nice." It was of the fox, beautifully done. The features were distinct and the fur so realistic Misty touched it with the tip of her finger. "Nice," she repeated. "Very nice. Lewis would like this one too."

"I beg your pardon?" The ranger walked over and took the painting from her.

"Lewis Talbot, director of the museum. He's a friend of mine. Have you shown this painting in any exhibit?"

"Shown this painting?" repeated the ranger still holding the picture. "Perhaps I'll show it some day." He leaned over to pick up his hat. "It's getting late, and before I take you back to the ranch, I've got to go over the ridge to Sawtooth Gulch and check on a fellow at the old Jerose Mine. You can stay here, and I'll come back and get you, or you can come with me. Maybe," he looked at the paintings on the table then turned the finished picture of the fox away from Misty's gaze, "you'd best come with me. It'll save time going back to the ranch. Ready?"

Misty cast a searching glance at other canvases on the table, one with a brush beside it as if just re-touched. Then, with the distinct feeling the ranger did not trust her or want her to see any more, she followed him to a waiting jeep.

At first Misty could see no road, the terrain looked unbroken. But as they bounced along and headed up the side of the mountain, she could see tracks that proved the jeep had been that way before. She wanted to think about what she would write to Lewis and how pleased he would be. It was best, she decided, she say no more to Denison Elbert. It was for Lewis to tell him about the defaced painting and the possible prize. She had done her part and right now she wanted to dwell on the satisfaction she felt, but hanging on to keep from being thrown out of the open jeep, it was impossible to think of anything but her own survival.

The ranger looked at her out of the corner of his eye. The wind was whipping her hair out from under her bandana and around her face, already a rosy pink. The man grinned and stepped on the accelerator a bit harder; Misty gripped the side of the jeep tighter.

The view from the top of the ridge was breathtaking. For miles in all directions jagged windswept peaks, some with patches of snow still on them, some completely bare and treeless, reached to the sky. Above timberline now, the bitter wind cut through Misty's clothing. But there was no haze, no smoke to remind them of the fire—nothing but a few clumps of stubborn grass and sagebrush trying to grow in the rocky ground.

"Are you frozen?" shouted the ranger turning his head so he could be heard above the wind.

"N-no. I'll be OK."

"We're almost there." And the jeep began to follow a path that led down the other side of the mountain into a sheltered gulley. They were halfway down the slope when Misty spotted the decaying remains of a mine. A ribbon-like stream meandered down the hillside. Beside the stream, poles supported the remains of an old sluice box while further down, shambles of broken, weathered boards marked where the rest of the box had collapsed.

Misty looked intently at the mine with growing interest. Tumbled shacks, victims of relentless snows and winds, lay in hopeless neglect; but set apart stood a cabin that appeared to be intact. A plume of smoke drifted skyward from the chimney. Beside the cabin stood the old blue pickup so frighteningly familiar to her. It evidently had come over the narrow road leading from the mine, down the gulley to the highway.

The ranger drew up next to the truck. "Better come in and warm up. Angelo won't mind."

Misty's throat tightened. She hesitated, but she was cold so she followed the ranger.

"He's probably back up the gulley." The ranger's words reassured Misty as she stepped into the empty cabin. "Soak up some of that heat, then we'll take off. No need to see the guy. I just wanted to make sure everything was OK, and it is. No signs of Freda around here."

While Misty rubbed her hands over the stove and felt the warmth drifting up to her wind-bitten face, she took in the details of the cabin. From where she stood she could see three other rooms, all sparsely furnished with only the necessities. Was he intending to live here, to leave his cabin on the hill? Could such a good thing happen to her? She rubbed her hands harder.

"If you're warm enough, we'd best go."

"I'm ready." Misty took a last look around the bare kitchen.

Following the ranger outside, she paused on the porch. To steady herself on the rickety steps, she put her hand on a post that supported the sagging roof and felt the imprint of knife cuts in it. Someone had at one time carved something in the pine wood and Misty was curious. She could barely make out the crude heart that had defied time and weather. The letters "M. W. loves D. C." were barely discernible.

There was so much to think about! But Misty tucked what she had seen into the back of her mind and concentrated on the ride back to the ranger's cabin. It was rough and fast, but the wind was behind them and not nearly so biting.

The horseback ride to Silver Ranch with Misty once again mounted behind the ranger, took the better part of an hour; but it was not yet dusk when she slid off the horse's rump. "Thank you so much, Mr.

Elbert," she said sincerely. "Thank you for rescuing me and for letting me see your paintings. I'm going to write to Lewis right away. He'll be contacting you."

The slight ranger did not smile. "Contacting me?" Misty detected a note of alarm in his voice.

Misty looked up towards the ravine. "The fire doesn't look so menacing from here," she wanted to detain Denison Elbert just a bit longer, "but it looks bad enough. I think I'll stay out of the ravine for the duration. Have you ever done a painting of a fire? The colors could be magnificent."

"No, I never have. One thing at a time. Enjoy the rest of your stay at the ranch," and the ranger started to wheel his horse.

"Wait!" said Misty. "Can we meet again and really talk?"

"I doubt it," answered the ranger. "I sure don't want to rescue you again." Giving a slight nod, he prodded Gus into a gallop, leaving little spurts of dust and a bewildered Misty behind him.

�✿

The hot shower Misty enjoyed chased the chill and remaining tension out of her body. While she leisurely soaped herself, she thought of all that had happened in the past few hours; there had been so much. She pictured Denison Elbert again. She chuckled as she remembered the image she and Jan had conjured up—a fat man with paint brushes behind his ear and a cage full of eagles. No, it wasn't his appearance; there was something about the artist she had not expected to find—a coldness, an air of detachment. It was almost as if he didn't like me, thought Misty. Maybe he thought I was too nosy. He sure isn't ready to be friends. Maybe if he knew who I am, what I can do for him. I've got to manage to see him again and ask some more questions, if he'll talk to me. What a story!

With that decision she deliberately dismissed the artist from her mind and with a ripple of excitement thought of the mine. M. W. and D. C. Who were they? Whoever they were, they loved one another in those years gone by. What was it the ranger had called the mine? Jerose. That was it. The Jerose mine. And that was where Angelo went!

There was too much to think about now; she would tuck it aside until she went to bed. Right now she barely had time to get ready for dinner, and she was hungry!

Dressed in her long brown skirt with little yellow flowers in a border around the hem and a matching blouse with long sleeves, she looked pretty and appealing. She had fixed her hair in a single braid that hung down her back, leaving little tendrils across her forehead and framing her face. Her appearance of that of a young schoolgirl invited the other guests to make much over her. They sympathized over her experience of the day and showered her with questions about being in the ravine so near to the fire. When she was able to tell them about the lightning-detector systems and about the remote weather sensors and high-altitude scanners, they were amazed at her knowledge. She pretended a casual reaction to what she had gone through, intimating that there really had been no occasion for alarm.

After the evening meal of lasagna and crisp salad complete with apple pie à la mode Misty found a chance to wander through some of the long halls of the ranch house and to study the pictures and artifacts that were hanging there. She stopped in front of a painting of the alpenglow touching the peaks of the mountains that were easily seen from the camp site. The pastel shadings of the mountains were exquisite, and Misty studied the painting closely before she looked for the artist's signature. In the lower right hand corner of the painting, small but clear, was the name Flora Nasby.

"Beautiful, isn't it." The manager of the ranch, on his way to start calling the evening square dance, stopped and admired the painting with Misty.

"Do you know her?" asked Misty.

"No, I don't. She sent us this painting for our opening. I understand she was raised in these mountains, but other than that no one seems to know a thing about her."

"Oh," said Misty, not taking her eyes off the painting. Then, "I met Denison Elbert today."

"Oh, did you?" The manager looked at her questioningly. "He was supposed to be at the workshop here last week to talk about his grandfather's techniques, but he couldn't make it. I'm surprised he was on the trail!" The manager studied Misty for a moment then tapped the painting again. "Magnificent, isn't it?"

He started to walk away but paused to ask, "Are you coming to the square dance?"

She looked up with the expression of one whose thoughts are far away. "I'll be there in just a few minutes," she answered automatically.

Alone in front of the painting Misty thought again of the ranger she had met. Her cheeks crimsoned as she remembered his remark, "You wouldn't have to ask." Why had he led her to believe he had been at the workshop? He was, really, a strange person—but many artists were temperamental.

After looking at the painting of the alpenglow one last time, she turned towards the recreational hall where she could hear the others gathering to the call of, "Choose your partners, ladies and gentlemen!"

ELEVEN

The atmosphere was heavy. The same unnatural stillness Misty had noticed at Silver Ranch lay over Pommel and the valley. She knew it was because of the fire, but there was no need to be concerned—the fire was within its limits.

Reluctantly, Misty returned to the little cabin on the hill. The aura of the time at the ranch stayed with her; she savored it as she would the taste of something delectable, not wanting it to leave her. But she would be going back. She had to—to see Denison Elbert again. To go to Silver Ranch was the logical thing to do, for his cabin was not far from there. Surely she could find it. He had certainly seemed eager to get her off his hands, but that didn't bother her. She had been rebuffed before. She simply had to see him again—soon. Of course she would write Lewis immediately all that she knew, but he would want more details and an address so he could contact the artist. And there was her column.

Yes, interviewing Denison Elbert was important—very important, but she had today to think about, and right now she was driving to the store to get the paint Fred had sent her for. "Misty," he had said, "I think you would be good at painting. Come here and see what I have for you to do." She had followed him questioningly. He wanted her to paint? There in the kitchen was her answer—cupboards, clean and new, waiting for the painter's brush.

"Well, here you are," she told herself as she got back in the truck with her purchase, "getting ready to paint cupboards. And Fred thinks you'll be good at it."

At first Misty didn't see Angelo draw up beside her. When he got out of his truck, their eyes met for a brief moment, but neither spoke. In that time she saw he looked tired and yes, angry. Maybe it was the way the light was shining in his eyes, but he looked almost sinister.

"Huh," she whispered to herself as she drove away, "he's probably wondering what I'm doing here. Well, I'll tell him. I wonder if he's been spying on me?" She clutched the steering wheel a bit tighter as she pulled out onto the highway and checked in the rear view mirror to make sure he wasn't following her. "I'll tell him," she repeated, "and what's more I'll ask him about that cabin at the mine. Why does he have things in it? He'll be surprised I know about that!"

Her first day of painting completed, the sun was dipping behind the trees when a tired Misty pedaled up the hill. When she saw Angelo sitting on her porch, his huge hairy arms folded on his knees, she stopped under the trees and watched. Even the old red hat was drooping. There was something forlorn and desolate about the whole picture, and Misty noted every detail. But she was wary. Why was he there? As she watched, she was even more aware of the stillness. Everything was quiet—deathly quiet. Hot. Dry. Still. A little lizard inched through the dust as if it, too, felt the oppressiveness of the dry heat.

Filled with her looking, Misty scuffed up some dust with her toe. She turned to retrace her steps without him seeing her, but a disturbed rock made a ping against the wheel of her bike.

The man's big body jerked with surprise. "I didn't hear you coming," he said. While he looked at the girl, he drank in all there was about her.

"How's Maria?" asked Misty, trying to appear nonchalant while at the same time hoping she could divert his attention from herself.

"I've been busy. I'm a working lady now, you know."

"You drive the truck that belongs to that camp," he said accusingly. "How come?"

"I sure do. Why not? I drive the truck sometimes, and I paint sometimes. It's great."

"Paint?"

"Cupboards, mostly."

"You get paid?"

"Certainly I get paid. What do you think?"

"Mama will teach you how to grow herbs, and you can sell them in town. You can make money that way."

Misty studied the man silently. "I must build my fire," she said after a few moments. "I have some berries for you to take to Maria." She leaned the bike against the cabin then stepped around the man into the doorway.

Angelo stood and followed her. "Mama. I think she's sick." He watched Misty's quick sure movements as she started her fire, crumpling the paper and laying the kindling just so. Her cheeks were rosy, and the freckles on her nose stood out even more. The few dabs of paint on her forehead made a ridiculous patttern.

"Sick?" Misty struck a match before she looked up at Angelo. She remembered how frail Maria had looked the last time she saw her. It had been difficult for her to get out of the old rocking chair, and when Misty had protested that maybe she should just sit until she felt strong again, she had answered, "I'm old, Misty, but I love the earth. I'd rather die putting seeds into the ground than doing anything else." And she had waved her pointed trowel and shuffled out towards her garden.

"She might die," Angelo caught his breath. "The spirit said he might take her."

"Spirit?" repeated Misty. She stood by the stove and looked at the big man, visibly afraid for Mama for all of his hulk.

"Mama's spirit out there," explained Angelo as he waved his hand in the air. "She's been with it before, and now it's calling her back."

Misty shuddered but said nothing. Not daring to turn her back, she pretended to busy herself at the sink.

Angelo walked around to where he could face her, and Misty inched away. "You have paint on your forehead," he said after a moment of staring.

Misty, glad for the change of subject, rubbed her sleeve near her hairline. "I'm not surprised. We're working hard to get the main building ready. Then the kids can come." She added more wood to the crackling fire then filled her tea kettle.

Angelo continued to stare, and whenever Misty took a step, he took one too so he could see her face.

"Misty." He took a step closer to her, then stopped.

"Here are the berries." Misty kept her voice steady. "They're wild grapes." She held the jar out to Angelo.

"Misty," began the man again ignoring the jar. "I want you. I want you to come with me."

"Come with you?" Misty tensed. "I'll come see Maria in a day or so. I'm pretty busy right now. You tell her that." She felt her throat tighten and the palms of her hands grew moist.

"No, no. Not just to see Mama. Come with me. To live. I want you."

"Oh." Misty set the jar of berries on the table. "No, Angelo. I won't come with you."

"To be my wife. That's what I mean. You and me. And Mama, of course. She doesn't feel very good right now, but she will feel better if you will come. She would be so happy."

"I'm sure Mama would," said Misty wryly. She shook her head. "I don't love you, Angelo. Two people who marry must love one another, and *I do not love you*." She spoke emphatically.

"I'll teach you to," persisted the man. "I'll teach you to love me." She stepped back until she felt the hard sink resisting her. Angelo reached out a hand and took her by the arm pulling her to him with a strength that frightened her.

"No, Angelo!" Misty pushed against his expansive belly. "No!"

The man leaned down and kissed the top of her head, his heavy beard mingling with her hair. "Misty, Misty," he whispered. "My Misty."

Misty was smothered by the closeness of the man. A terror she had never known before almost paralyzed her, but she managed to slowly raise one arm to his shoulder. As he released her head, she tipped it back and looked into his face. Forcing herself to be gentle, she placed her hand on his beard and said soothingly, "Angelo? What would Mama say? She wouldn't want you to hurt me, would she?"

The man's arms slowly relaxed. Taking advantage of the moment, Misty gave another sudden push on his stomach and managed to step away from him.

Angelo stood looking at her, his breath still coming hot and quick. "You're not ready now, but someday." His voice trembled ever so slightly. "Someday real soon because Mama doesn't feel very well, and we want to make her happy while there's still time, don't we?"

He picked up the berries. "I'll wait." He smiled a tremulous smile and walked to the door, perspiration glistening on his forehead. Then he turned and added, "She'll be OK. I'll talk to her spirit tonight."

Misty closed the door and sat down, trembling violently. She pressed her hands against her cheeks and stifled the desire to scream. Her fear of Angelo, which had been only instinct, had surfaced and become terrifyingly real. What would he have done if I had not discovered his weak spot, she wondered frantically. Would he have hurt me? Undoubtedly. She knew of a girl who had been raped; just the thought gagged her. Would I be able to survive, if something like that happened to me? But my reminding him of Mama worked magic. Like a simple boy he didn't want to do anything to displease her.

Hugging herself with one arm as if she were cold, Misty wiped the sudden tears away with the other hand while she walked to the door and locked it. As if that wasn't enough she tipped a chair under the knob.

She flung herself face down on her bed and willed that her body relax. As the tension slowly drained away, she thought of Maria. Maybe she isn't really ill. Maybe Angelo just said that to lure me up there. Could be he and Maria have a plan, and this is part of their plotting. I'll have to be more careful, she advised herself. I can't ever, ever really relax here. Who knows what either one of them might do? Oh, if I could only find another place to stay! I'm scared, she admitted to herself, I'm really scared.

Trying to reassure herself by being practical, she checked the fire. It was burning briskly. The water would be warm enough for a good bath before too long. She wished it would be really hot, then maybe she could relax some. She was tense and keyed up from Angelo's visit, and her muscles ached from the stretching to high cupboards all day. She needed to relax and get a new hold on herself for she suddenly felt as though she were wasting time. While she waited for the water to get hot she re-read a letter from her dad.

"Keep up the good work." She read the encouraging words hungrily. She knew he meant the camp stories she had written even though the children hadn't come yet, and by now he had her letter about finding Denison Elbert. That should be a big plus, she reassured herself as she relived the horror of the forest fire and the ranger's rescuing her.

What a story there was in that! But she wasn't satisfied—she needed to talk more with him, to find out about that ruined canvas.

Thoughtfully, she read on. "Lance keeps in touch. We had him over for dinner with Lewis last week. Senator Appleby and his daughter Sharon finished out the party. Sharon's about your age and according to your mother is quite a socialite. You'll meet her when you come home."

There was more hometown news that Misty read through quickly. The letter ended with the plea, "Write soon, honey. We're anxious to hear everything."

Misty knew her dad hoped for news of the Wades. She laid the letter down and stared straight ahead trying to think if there was any-thing—anything at all. The only possible clue was the old mine with its tumbled down shacks and sluice box. And the heart with the ini-tials. What was the name of the mine? The Jerose?

That sluice box was collapsed, and Misty remembered her dad and his cousin Ruby had been injured by a sluice box that fell on them. She had to go back! Even if Angelo should be there. When she went to see Denison Elbert again, somehow she would get over the Divide to that gulley. Maybe the ranger-artist would take her; possibly he knew something about the mine.

Misty filled the tub with almost-hot water and stirred in some bub-ble bath that foamed around her as she lay back. Her thoughts shifted to Del. Where was he in those mountains, where in relation to Saw-tooth Gulch and the mine and the fire? Was he out riding trails like Denison Elbert, looking for people who needed to be warned?

Misty had overheard Karyl telling Drew once that Del didn't want to take a woman up in those mountains with him, that no woman would be happy there. How were they going to arrange their marriage then? Would she stay in town and he would come down every so often? Misty was sure that if she were Karyl, she would be climbing the highest peak with Del.

Dressed in clean jeans and a fresh blouse, she removed the chair from under the doorknob and unlocked the door. She paused on the porch listening carefully while she looked up the road that climbed the hill. Satisfied she was alone, she looked across to the goat pen where the goats and the deer were busily nuzzling their feed Angelo had left earlier. While she watched, the rosy sky faded to a deep purple, and one by one the stars began punctuating the sky with their brightness. There were no clouds. The evening was as warm as the day had been in spite of the soft breeze that sprang up.

Misty sat on the step staring at the star-studded sky. Were the stars shining at home like that? Would she be watching them with Lance?

With a tiny sigh she went into the cabin. Tomorrow would be another busy day. After carefully locking the door, she put the chair back under the doorknob. She glanced at the papers on the vinyl cloth-covered table. She should do some typing, but she was tired. That could wait.

❄❄❄

It seemed to Misty that she had just fallen asleep when the sound of a motor wove itself into her dream. She was in the red and white pickup driving towards the lake and couldn't stop. Something kept hitting the truck. There were loud noises as if rocks were banging around in the back of the truck. She was afraid.

"Misty! Misty! Wake up! It's me! It's Angelo! Open the door!"

Misty lay perfectly still trying to reconcile the noise with her dream. Then as reality woke her, she began to tremble.

"Misty! Wake up! It's me. I need you!"

Misty shivered more and drew the blanket tighter. "Oh, Lord, please! Make him go away!" She peeked out from under the cover ever so cautiously to make sure the chair was still under the doorknob.

She heard the man stomp off the porch, but then he was tapping on her window with a tap that became louder as he called, "Misty! Misty! Wake up! It's Mama!"

She threw the blanket back and pulling on her jeans, put a blouse on over her brief nightshirt. "I hear you," she called. She picked up the stove poker as the thought went through her mind it could be a trick to get her to open the door. But if Maria really did need help—

She opened the door a crack to the night air and to the man who was again standing on her porch. "What is it?" The poker was cold and cut into her hand as she clutched it behind her.

"It's Mama. She can't breathe. I'm taking her to the doctor, but I need help. Can you come? She hurts bad."

Misty looked beyond the man into the dark. She could barely make out the outline of Maria slumped against the truck window. "I've got to dress," she said closing the door and locking it.

In a matter of minutes Misty was climbing in beside the woman. Carefully, she put an arm around the frail body and drew her close so the gray head rested on her shoulder.

"She hurts," Angelo said again and the truck lumbered off into the night.

Misty heard the rasping breath and the rattling in Maria's chest. In the dim light she could see how tightly the skin was drawn over the face. Once brown, it was now gray and beaded with perspiration. Little moans escaped from the blue lips that were parted slightly. Misty wanted to shrink away. She wanted to escape, but she couldn't. So she held Maria and was frightened.

The ten-mile drive seemed like an eternity. Down the rough hill to the highway, across the river into Pommel and on down the valley until finally the small, white clinic, that served Pommel and the surrounding area of farms and mines, stood commanding in the midst of the night.

Angelo blasted the horn as he drove into the driveway, and seconds later lights came on in the adjoining house, then in the clinic. A large man in slippers, tucking his shirt into his trousers, appeared on the porch. A woman was at his elbow. Misty was aware the rasping in the spent body she was holding was fainter, but she said nothing.

Taking in the situation, the doctor was at the truck door helping Angelo with Maria, carrying her gently inside and laying her on an examination table. Deftly the doctor checked the withered body, then fastened oxygen tubes into her nose. It was as if she were shut off from the two who watched while the oxygen began to flow into the pinched nostrils. But it was too late. Maria's body was empty now like a dried, once-brown pod from which the seed had fallen.

"Mama!" Angelo cried out.

Misty looked at Angelo and fought her own emotions. First the little woman's quiet, empty body and now tears running down the big man's face into his beard. It was too much. Abruptly, she left the room. Better to stand on the porch of the clinic and look out over the quiet, dark valley. In a few hours the sun would be coming up. And the sun would be warm.

After a time had passed, Angelo stood beside Misty. He blew his nose noisily. "She's gone." Fresh tears began to course down his cheeks. "She's gone," he repeated. "Mama's dead."

"I'm sorry, Angelo. Very sorry. I wish I'd gone to see her again." There seemed to be nothing else to say.

"She will come back." The man dabbed at his eyes. "She's not really dead. Not really." His voice choked again with his denial. "I'll sacrifice—to her spirit. She'll come back. She liked the berries. She took just one taste, that's all she could eat, but she said they were good." Angelo smiled faintly.

The doctor's wife, coming onto the porch behind them, said softly, "If you folks would like some coffee, I have some in the kitchen."

Together Misty and Angelo followed and soon sat across from each other, neither one saying a word. Misty stared into her mug. She thought of all that had taken place during the afternoon and now. She looked at Angelo's hands warming themselves on his hot mug. Worn hands, but big and strong. She remembered the strength in them and how he had held her.

"I'll have to make arrangements in the morning," said the man finally. "Mama has to be—" He paused as he searched for the right word, the word he knew Mama would want him to use. "Planted. Like a seed," he explained huskily.

They drove away from the clinic, back through the still sleeping valley, back past Pommel, across the bridge, down the highway and up the hill. Misty had left a light on in her cabin, and the rays from it shown on the goat pen and on the pine trees. They were friendly rays; she was glad to see them. She was glad to get out of the truck away from Angelo, away from his grief. Without waiting for him to go up the hill, she locked the door and put the chair under the knob. Then she crawled back into bed.

She lay staring into the darkness, for sleep would not come. She thought of Angelo going back to his house with his mama's things there, mute and cold and useless. Misty felt a sudden pity for him. Death didn't care who or what it took—a flower, a bird, a child—a mother. She drew the covers closer around herself and felt relief that she was not really involved in Angelo's grief, that death had not touched her.

But stronger than any pity was her fear of him. Would he come back?

Finally she dozed. The sun pouring through the window awakened her; she revelled in the warmth that disspelled all thoughts of coldness. It was a new day. She was alive. She had work to do. What had happened during the night seemed like a bad dream. She thought briefly about Angelo. No, she could not hold out a hand of sympathy; sharing his grief might give him the wrong idea.

The others were already on the job when Misty leaned her bike in its usual place. Roy caught sight of her as she walked towards the building. He grinned broadly. "Hi there, Miss Misty. Missed you!" And he laughed.

Misty waved as she turned towards Karyl's office where she found both Karyl and Fred leaning over papers spread out on the desk. "I'm sorry I'm late," Misty apologized. "Angelo's mother had a heart attack and we had to take her to the clinic. She died."

"I'm so sorry to hear that." Karyl straightened and looked at Misty closely noticing the tiredness in her eyes. "Wouldn't you like the day off, to help Angelo?"

Misty shook her head. "There's no need for that. He can do all that needs to be done."

Karyl's eyes widened. "When is the funeral to be?" she asked after a moment of stunned silence.

Again Misty shook her head. "I don't know yet. I suppose Angelo will make the arrangements today. I'll want to go to the funeral, if it's all right with you." She looked at Fred.

"Of course. If any of us can be of any help, let us know. If Angelo needs anything."

"I imagine he'll ask you himself if he needs your help," said Misty. "Well, I'll go get to work now."

"Work is good therapy," Fred encouraged. "You've had a hard experience, but working can ease the pain."

"I'll go finish the cupboard I started yesterday." Misty turned to go then paused, her head almost brushing the painting on the wall. "Angelo thinks that she's going to come back again. I know that isn't so." She looked from Karyl to Fred.

"No, Misty," said Fred kindly, "it isn't so. Everyone dies, but only once."

"I know he's wrong. He can't accept she's gone." Misty answered.

"Pastor Rubeck, our camp pastor, will be glad to help if your friend wants," Karyl suggested.

Misty smiled. "I don't know if Angelo would be interested or not. I doubt it."

As she turned to go, she looked again at the painting on the wall. The signature Flora Nasby in the lower corner of the painting caught her eye. She hesitated a brief moment. Flora Nasby? Here? She glanced at Karyl, tempted to ask her, but instead walked to the door and closed it after her.

TWELVE

Graveside services were held for Maria. The morning was hot and sultry as every morning this week had been. Misty had accepted Angelo's offer for a ride to the cemetery, but now she lingered behind as he walked across the brittle grass to where his friends were sitting in a circle under a tall spruce tree. Angelo took his place between Prescott and Gwen; like the others he sat up straight and tall letting his hands lay palms up in his lap.

Curious, Misty walked slowly until she was within hearing distance. Each one in the circle sat with eyes closed; only Prescott was speaking. "Oh, Ralah, come. Give us directions for this time."

Not a sound could be heard, not even a bird until Prescott spoke again—only this time, as when she had channeled before in Angelo's cabin, she spoke not in her own natural voice but in a low, sensuous tone that was quite unbecoming to her.

"Commit this one to me," the voice said. "I have been waiting for her; I will prepare her for her next life."

"What would you have her son do? Angelo? What would you have him do now he is free from his mother?" Prescott's voice was her own, and then it changed again as Ralah spoke through her.

"Angelo must marry as I have instructed. And he, with your help, must build the camp. It will be a beautiful spot that will become a learning center with gardens and cabins and meditation centers.

Now commit this one who has left her earthly body to me for I must leave."

Misty felt rooted to the spot as a mixture of fear and bewilderment crept over her. Oh, dear God, what is this? What have I heard? Are these people for real? She wanted to run, to get away, but she could not. The channeling finished, Prescott was talking softly to Gwen and Angelo, and Misty knew the service for Maria was about to begin. So instead of running she stood quietly apart, watching. I'm going to see this through to the finish, she promised herself.

Gwen, dressed in a white gossamery gown and holding a lighted candle, stood at the head of the casket. One by one each of the others approached her, lighted a candle from the flame of hers, then took their place by the casket until they encircled it. When everyone was in place, Gwen began a chant. Without any prompting each of the others took up the chant as they swayed in rhythmic unison. The candle flames flickered gently in the breeze while their voices blended musically repeating over and over:

"Spirit, Spirit, take her soul;
Master Spirit, make her whole;
Lead her, guide her through the dark
'Til on another life she does embark."

After what seemed an endless time Gwen signaled the others to be quiet. "It is done," Prescott spoke. "Our dear Maria has gone to be with the Master Spirit. He is preparing her for her next life as he said he would. We may see her again; we may not. But we must go on in this life loving and waiting knowing that our turn will come to prove ourselves. We now commit our dear one's body to the ground." And the lowering of the casket was begun.

Out of the corner of her eye Misty saw a lone man standing under the trees watching as she had been doing. She turned her head ever so slightly, and the man acknowledged her with a faint smile. When the ceremony was finished, he walked over to her.

"I'm Pastor Rubeck from the camp. I'm truly sorry. Only God can give peace."

Misty hesitated and studied the pastor's face intently, but she answered with only a shy smile before she continued to the truck.

"Misty, wait."

Turning to see Prescott coming toward her, Misty drew in her breath sharply.

Prescott put her arms around Misty, hugging her tightly. "We're so sorry for Angelo, but Maria will be all right. And you—we love you, you know. We're so glad you were here! Next time we channel you must join us. We love you very much—all of us."

Misty stood perfectly still neither resisting nor returning Prescott's embrace. "We love you." It was good to hear those words again. Here in this unfamiliar place, where she had been struggling to keep up a false identity, where no one seemed concerned, it was good to hear that expression of love. Angelo's friends were not pretending or lying to each other; she did not understand what they believed, but they were sincere and—they loved one another.

Uncertainly, Misty gave Prescott a slight hug in return and smiled at the others who had gathered around the two. "Thanks, Prescott," she said huskily, "it's good of you to say so. I must go now. Angelo's waiting."

✠

"It's over," Angelo said as he started the motor. They drove in silence through town, but as they neared the road to the hill the big man spoke again. "I need you, Misty. The house is so empty." His voice choked, and Misty's heart skipped a beat.

"I'm sorry, Angelo. I'm sorry Maria is gone and you're alone." She laid a hand on the big arm feeling it quiver under her touch. "But I just can't."

"You're not ready maybe," Angelo reassured her. "Mama said it takes time. 'Go slow,' she said."

A wave of anger teased Misty then quickly subsided.

"Mama liked you," Angelo was saying. "She said you could maybe be the daughter she never had."

The little brown leaf of a woman was beside Misty again as she remembered the visits they had had. Angelo was so close to his mother, Misty reminded herself. Of course he was crushed now. He would be lonely and confused, for he had no one to give him the support and guidance he needed. No one to direct his approaches or to tell him what to say. Neither had he anyone to restrain him. And a cold shiver went down Misty's spine at the thought. The word "Mama" would surely have lost its power once the shock of grief was past.

"Let me off here," she said when they reached the road that turned into the camp. "I'm not going to the cabin. They are expecting me to come work. You go work, too. That will help." She closed the truck door and without another word turned and began to walk briskly, glad to get away from him, glad to be alone and to let the fresh breeze blow away what of death still clung to her—and glad to be able to think of Prescott and what she had said. It was all so strange. Should she join them another time?

She paused on the edge of the camp trying to repress the wispy uncomfortableness that was becoming too common. What was it? A barrier between herself and the camp? She gave herself a little shake. These people were her friends. Or were they? She wasn't involved with them to the point of sharing her deeper thoughts, so she couldn't really call them friends. But none of them had yet asked her any questions that would encourage her to share herself. Not Fred or Drew, or Karyl—not even Sadi. And she had volunteered nothing, nor asked them any questions. She came closer to sharing herself with Roy than with any of them. Oh, if I only dared tell him about Angelo and my fear of the man! Misty fretted. But I can't do even that without revealing my identity. Is that why I feel uncomfortable? I don't know, I just don't know. Perhaps they don't care. But I know they do care; they show their concern in so many ways, seeing to every need I have revealed to them. I am uncomfortable, she decided, because they have something I don't have—a peace, a joy—and I want it.

Prescott cares too, Misty changed the direction of her thoughts. Didn't she say she loved me? I need to be included, to be part of a group, but not a part of Prescott's group. It is too chilling, and there is Angelo.

No one said anything when Misty entered the building. She went right to the cupboard she was to paint and began covering the counter top underneath it with protective newspapers. Roy gave her a faint smile and a mock salute then busied himself with his hammer. Because of the frown and worried look on her face, all respected the grief that must surely be hers.

"Del called last night." Karyl's words broke the silence like pebbles being tossed into a still lake. Misty stole a look over her shoulder to see to whom Karyl was talking. It was Fred.

"He wants his jeep," Karyl went on as the two of them walked past. "He's back down from the tower now and needs it. I did tell him when he left someone would bring it to him. Shall we take it up at the end of the week?"

Their voices faded as they walked into Karyl's office so Misty could not hear Fred reply, "You know I want to. I'd love to have a weekend with just you and Del, but I've promised Cindy I'd help her move some things. Why not take Misty with you?"

"Misty?"

"Sure. She could drive the pickup."

"I'm really disappointed you can't go. I'd forgotten you promised to help Cindy. I was hoping you could talk over some of these projects with Del."

"We'll get a chance later. This would be a good time for you to get to know Misty better. And it would get her away from what's-his-name and all that's going on right now. I think she needs that."

"Angelo," supplied Karyl. "If she'll go," she agreed thoughtfully. "We'd be gone at least two days. That's an idea," she added brightly. "I'll ask her."

Karyl watched and waited while the afternoon wore on. The other workers had left when she went to the kitchen where Misty was still working. "It's quitting time. Are you going to stay all night?" she asked lightly.

I don't want to go up there on the hill. I'm afraid of Angelo. He's alone now. The thoughts burned in Misty's mind, but instead of telling the truth, she said, "I thought I'd make up for the time I took off today." She dipped her brush into the paint.

"That's not necessary." answered Karyl warmly. "You must be tired. There's one thing I do want to ask you. Why don't you put your things away first?"

"Oh, all right." Misty gave a little laugh and jumped down off her perch. Quickly she cleaned the brush and put the lid on the paint can. She began to scoop up the paint-splattered copies of the *Denver Post,* then stopped. There was her article "Sketches." One she had written before she even left home.

She stooped to read her own writing, and Karyl came to look over her shoulder. "Oh, I want that!" she exclaimed. "I save these for Del. I didn't mean for that to get in the discard pile!" She quickly began tearing out the copy of "Sketches." "I'll just run into the office with this and be right back."

Misty stood staring at the door of Karyl's office. She's saving my column for Del? He's reading my articles? The ranger I met, Denison Elbert, might be interested, but Del?

She thought about the little game she was playing, the role she had created for herself. I've gone past the point of no return now. I can't very well say to Karyl, "I wrote that. I'm not at all what you think. I'm really a journalist, and I'm here to write stories about your camp." She looked down at her jeans and her jogging shoes that had splatterings of green paint on them. No, I can't identify myself now. Who would believe me? I will have to play my little game out until it's finished. I'll be leaving Pommel soon, and maybe these people need never know. Still, if Del—oh, why did I get myself into this? She gave an audible sniff as Karyl came back into the kitchen.

"You're tired, Misty. You've had a rough day. You shouldn't have come to work."

"I'm fine," said Misty. "What was it you wanted to ask me?"

Karyl looked at the tired face for a long moment, deliberating before she spoke. "Del wants me to bring his jeep up to him," she said finally. "I need someone to drive the pickup so I'll have a way back. Can you go? It will take two days."

Misty's heart gave a little lurch. She turned to crumple up the newspaper more tightly so Karyl would not see her expression. See Del? Should she do this?

"Sure." She didn't trust herself to think further. She turned and looked squarely at Karyl, determined not to feel guilty. "I'd like that."

"Great. If we go Friday and come back Saturday, we'll miss only one day of work. And you won't be away from your home long. Is that all right with you?"

"Any day's fine," said Misty wishing with all her heart they could go this minute, so she could escape the possibility of seeing Angelo.

"I'll get a message to Del tonight, so he'll be sure to be at his cabin. Get a good night's rest. See you tomorrow."

As Misty pushed her bike up the hill, she tried to sort out her thoughts and emotions. I'm going to see Del once more. Probably for the last time, a bonus I didn't expect. Karyl had asked her and she, Misty, had felt—well, maybe a tiny bit guilty in spite of her trying not to when she answered, "I'd like that." Del and Karyl belong to each other, she reminded herself. I just wanted to see the man. Surely there's was nothing wrong with that.

Then there was this other thing about Del reading "Sketches." Thank goodness her by-line was "Mary Alice Morrow" and not "Misty"! She thought of the material she had sent in. Then she smiled. The stories of the camp wouldn't be published for at least another four or six months and all of this would be behind her. Karyl and all the others would know the truth about her, but they would forgive her because of what she wrote. Perhaps she would come visit the camp again next summer; come in style, and they would laugh about this episode.

Friday managed to inch its way into position. Misty was up before the sun bustling about. She was tempted to wear her dark blue corduroy pants outfit and to let her hair fall loose over her shoulders, held back at the temples with clips just as she had when she had flown west. Tempted as she was she could not step out of the character she had created for herself. It would never do to go dressed in her pant outfit and wear makeup, so she pulled on a pair of clean jeans and a sleeveless T-shirt of blue and white diagonal lines. After plaiting her hair into one long braid, she tied her bandana into place and studied her reflection once more, satisfied with what she saw.

"Be good now," she warned the animals, who stood watching her as she walked to her bicycle with her backpack. She had become used to the little creatures, even rather fond of them. Now she took time to scratch Gertrude behind the ears before heading down the hill.

When she pedaled into the campgrounds, she saw Karyl standing by the jeep talking to Fred and Drew. Roy, standing by the truck, greeted her with an appreciative grin. "Good morning, lady. You look all set for a great day. It's going to be mighty quiet around here without you. Is there anything I can do for you while you're gone?"

Misty smiled broadly. "Can't think of a thing, but you're a sweetheart, Roy, for offering." In the exuberance of the moment she reached up and gave him a kiss on the cheek.

Roy's smile faded from his face. He looked at Misty quietly. Deliberately taking her face in his hands, he kissed her gently on the mouth.

Then he laughed. "So there. Turnabout's fair play. Have a good trip and drive carefully."

Misty, feeling the eyes of everyone on her, put her hand up to her mouth where Roy had kissed her. With a slight flush she said, "I'll be careful" then turned and climbed into the truck.

The sky was overcast when the two women drove out of the camp yard, Karyl driving the jeep on to the highway that wound up the mountains west of Pommel. She checked in her mirror to make sure Misty was behind her, gave a little wave to the girl who waved back, then pressed the accelerator to the floor. The monkey and the blue bandana swayed with the movement of the jeep as it began to climb.

※ ❦ ※

Far up in the mountains Del checked his watch. Eight o'clock straight up. Karyl had said they would leave by eight so they must be on their way, she and Misty. They should be at his station by two—possibly as early as half past one. He looked at his face in the mirror and ran his hand over his smooth skin. He would shave again at noon, then he would be sure there was no stubble. No woman must think that because he lived alone high in the mountains he didn't take care of himself!

He smoothed his bed that showed no wrinkles and made sure nothing was left lying around his bedroom. He checked the tiny kitchen and refolded the towel that hung near the stove. Next he took a broom and went into the living room and swept up a dustpan of nothing from the linoleum floor, straightening the braided rug with the toe of his boot. He blew some imaginary dust off his bookshelves and checked his watch again. Eight-thirty. He looked around the room for one last check then walked quickly to the window where an easel and several brushes still lay. "I'd better put these out of sight," he muttered to himself and placed them inside a small storage room where a small cot stood hospitably ready for a guest. Pausing on the threshold, he took time to put the brushes and easel a little further out of sight then pulled the door closed behind him.

He poured himself another cup of coffee and turned on the radio to hear the news. Satisfied, he picked up his transmitter to check with the fellow ranger who was still manning the lookout tower.

"How's everything, Joe?" The transmitter crackled.

"Under control," came the reply. "Saw a grizzly with two cubs about daybreak. Saw several elk yesterday when I checked the supplies in the winter cabin. The elk are moving down now, slow. Everything's much too dry. Pray for rain, boy. Is this the day Karyl's bringing your jeep?"

"She's on her way."

"Roger. Smitty's calling. Talk to you later." Del heard Joe switch his receiver off.

❧❧

Misty drove carefully behind Karyl. Here and there the warm sun broke through the clouds making the grasses and trees along the side of the road brilliant. An occasional chipmunk scurried across the road only to change its mind and scurry back. As the truck climbed, the mountain sides became steeper. Misty looked up and up at the jagged peaks cushioned here and there with snow and glaciers. They were the Fourteenies, the very peaks she saw from the camp, almost all of them over 14,000 feet.

Two and a half hours had passed when the jeep rounded a horseshoe curve with the truck coming confidently behind. Karyl pulled over to a rest area where the road straightened out again. Bits of mist floated in the gorge below them.

"How're you doing?" Karyl asked as the truck pulled alongside of the jeep. "Tired? Let's get out here for a bit and stretch."

"I'm doing fine." Misty slid out of the truck. Walking over to the edge of the road, she looked down at the waters of Saddle Stream swirling far below. Then she turned and watched a cascading waterfall, lost in the feeling of splendor.

"Isn't it beautiful?" asked Karyl simply. "God made it all."

"It's so—so magnificent. I've never seen anything like it." Misty turned again to the gorge.

"I brought some sandwiches," said Karyl after a few moments. "Let's sit here and eat."

Taking a picnic hamper from the jeep, Karyl made her way to a large flat rock and spread out a small cloth. She placed sandwiches, cookies and fruit on paper plates and drew out a thermos of coffee. "Sit here in the warm sun," she invited.

"I should have brought something," apologized Misty as she sat down near Karyl.

"No need. Sadie put up this lunch. Sit over here and enjoy the waterfall."

The two ate in silence, hearing only the cascading water and the call of the mountain birds. A little squirrel came close enough for Karyl to toss him a pinch of bread. He sat on his hind legs and ate greedily. A camp robber swooped down when Misty put crumbs on a rock.

"It's not much farther to Del's. About sixty-five miles," Karyl said finally. She looked at her watch. "We'd better go. Another hour and a half should get us there."

Once again Misty started the truck and swung on to the highway behind the jeep. Slowly they began to climb, passing more waterfalls and glacial streams. Misty had no idea where they were or what would mark the entrance to the forest where they were going, so she watched the miles on the odometer tick off. With each passing one she felt a strange sensation growing in the pit of her stomach, and a tightening of her throat. It's the altitude, she told herself.

Fifty—fifty-one—when fifty-three miles had sloughed away, Karyl put on a turn signal. Misty took a deep breath and followed up the gravel road marked with the sign "Stillwater National Forest." Deep into the dark forest that smelled of crushed pine needles and dry moss they went. The going was slower now, but Misty wished it were slower yet. Almost she wished she had not come, that she was back painting cupboards with Roy whistling nearby.

Around a final curve the log cabin came into view in the full sun, free from the confines of the forest. Misty stared in disbelief. The rail fence, the flag fluttering from a pole—to her it was like a dream.

Del heard the motors and looked out the window. He waited a few seconds before opening the door. While he waited, he ran his hand over his face as if to wipe away any expression that might give his feelings away. Karyl, with her keen discerning ways, must see nothing. He tucked his shirt into his trousers more securely, straightened his collar, and squared his broad shoulders before he opened the door.

"You made it!" he called as Karyl walked up the path to the cabin.

"Surprised?" She held up her face for a kiss. Then she turned to

Misty who was busying herself with something in the truck, not willing to look when Del greeted Karyl.

"Come on, Misty."

Almost reluctantly Misty slid out of the security of the pickup. Slowly she walked up the path. Not until she put her foot on the first step did she dare look at Del.

"Hi, Misty. It's good to see you again." The crinkles around his penetrating brown eyes were the same; his hair even curlier without the hard hat to press it down. And he looked taller, possessing that same definite, indescribable strength.

The man held out his hand in greeting and Misty felt his warm firm grasp close around her own. "H-hi," she stammered, conscious of a warm flush spreading over her neck and face as she smiled up at him.

Del looked at her for a long moment. Then, seeing Karyl looking at him with raised eyebrows, he said, "Come in, both of you. Tell me— how's the camp coming?"

THIRTEEN

The mixed aroma of coffee and bacon drifting into the little room where she had slept soundly caused Misty to stir. She lay half awake, half dozing, listening to Karyl's voice and Del's deep chuckle. While she dozed she re-lived the afternoon and evening before.

The sun was still warm on the cabin and yard when the three of them had hiked up to what Del called his Glory Rock, a rocky shelf that jutted out of the side of the mountain. They scrambled up onto the granite shelf and faced a view Misty would never forget. Del stood with an arm around the shoulders of each woman, the three looking in silence. The rugged, wind-swept peaks were closer now, and Misty thought of her wild ride over them when she visited the mine in the gulley. Remembering the fire, she stared at the cummerbund of haze girding the mountains.

Starting from their barren tops, the sides of the mountains sloped together to form the deep valley, the rocky slopes gathering trees and brush as they went until they ended in the lushness below where the pink of the early wild roses mixed with the pale lavendar mariposa lily, reminders that it was June. Far below, the sparkling waters of Saddle Stream could be seen winding their way around boulders that had tumbled down through the ages.

After a few minutes Del spoke reverently. "I never cease to wonder at what God has created. That's why I call this Glory Rock."

Looking straight up the face of the mountain where they stood,

Misty saw the creases that were gulleys and ravines. A half dozen white figures moving on the rocky slopes caught her eye. "Mountain goats," Del explained.

A bald eagle soared from a tall pine and began circling the valley spiraling down, down, down as he watched for an unwary fish to surface in the river. The brush behind them crackled, and a white-tailed deer cautiously peeked out.

"There's Sorrowful's cousin." Del took his arm from Misty's shoulder to point to the deer, his voice still low. Misty smiled, afraid to speak for fear she would break the spell.

"Do you like it?" Del asked after a few moments, looking at Misty. She nodded. "It's beautiful. I would never get tired of all of this." She studied the scene carefully, etching it on her memory.

"Let's go on up," said Del finally, "and I'll show you the source of Saddle Stream." So they climbed over rocks following deer trails through the scanty brush. Pulling themselves up a steep incline, they came to a place where several trails converged as if the white-tailed animals had come from different parts of the mountain to meet before descending into the valley. Without hesitating Del took the trail that went to the right and wound on farther up the steep incline through fields of shooting stars and forget-me-nots. The sun was warm and the air fragrant with pine. All was so still, so very still.

"There it is," Del said at last, pausing for Karyl and Misty to catch up with him.

Misty looked and saw nothing but a huge boulder spotted with orange fungi. Warm from the exertion of climbing, she walked to where Del waited. "All I see is this rock." She rubbed the soft moss gently.

"There. See that?" and Del, reaching out a hand to help Karyl the rest of the way, pointed with his toe to a small stream bubbling from under the huge boulder.

"That is Saddle Stream?" Misty asked in disbelief.

"That is Saddle Stream," Del answered. "This is the source of that raging river down in the valley. Hard to believe, isn't it?"

Karyl got down on her knees and, cupping her hands to catch the icy water, sipped thirstily. "Mmm, is that ever good. Try some, Misty."

Misty knelt beside Karyl. Two, three times she sipped and looked up at Del laughing while the drops clung around her mouth. "That's delicious."

Holding out a hand to her, Del helped her stand. He held her hand for a breath of a moment then let go to pick up a pebble that lay nearby. He tossed it into the water. "This little stream is fed by many other streams both here on this mountain and on the other side of the valley. Since we're on the east side of the Continental Divide, the river will eventually empty into the Atlantic Ocean."

Karyl picked up a small rock and studied it. "Look at the fool's gold in this," and she held her find for Del to see. Then she handed it to Misty. "Want it for a souvenir of your trip to Saddle Stream?"

The return trip to the cabin was a quick sliding on the slippery pine needles that covered the path. Noticing again the way the deer trails converged, Misty knew it wasn't very far to the cabin. Del led the way along the single trail that wound back down to Glory Rock and then on into the yard.

Supper was a stew Del had prepared the day before. Never, thought Misty, had anything smelled so delicious. The fragrance of the blended vegetables and meat was tantalizing. Both women, hungry from the unaccustomed climb, filled their plates not only with the stew but with the tossed salad and hot biscuits Del made while they sat on stools in the kitchen watching and talking. They ate in front of the fireplace, and Del insisted that Misty sit facing the window so she could see the mountains.

The evening in front of the fire passed all too quickly. Misty vaguely remembered falling asleep watching the flickering flames while Karyl and Del talked in low voices. When Karyl laughingly awakened her, the fire was burning low.

"This couch is my bed, Misty, and I'm tired. You sleep in here," and Karyl had opened the door to the small storage room where the little cot was waiting.

Wide awake now, Misty looked at the bit of fools gold Karyl had given her. She squeezed her eyes tight shut again and pictured Glory Rock and the stream. A tap on her door interrupted her reverie.

"I'm up," she answered and rolled out of the cot, barely missing the corner of the easel that had been hurriedly tucked out of sight. She dressed quickly, knowing Karyl and she would have to get an early start back to Pommel. She wished she could turn the clock back and keep turning it back, so the time to leave would never come.

"I'm sorry I overslept," she apologized as Karyl handed her a glass of juice minutes later.

"This altitude does that to people. Del thinks there's no other place like it."

"Is there?" he challenged Misty.

She shook her head. "There is no other place like it," she assured him. "I could stay here forever."

"Forever's a pretty long time," Del said lightly as he turned to the stove.

Their talk turned to other things. Del began asking Karyl more questions about the camp, and they continued discussing plans and programs they had begun to talk about in the evening.

"Tell Fred I think his ideas are great. I like his plans for the area by the lake."

"Are you going to be able to come down and spend a weekend with Dillon like you thought?" Karyl asked then quickly explained to Misty, "Dillon is a little boy with a brain tumor."

Del shook his head. "I'm afraid not. I wasn't thinking ahead when I said that. Not at this season I can't. Not with Freda still smoldering, even if she is over on the other ridge. I don't like to disappoint the little fellow or his mom. You didn't say anything to either one of them, did you?"

"No, I didn't want to raise his hopes. Don't worry about him," Karyl soothed Del, "he's going to be able to come spend a day at a time now that he's in remission. You'll be able to come to the dedication though, won't you?" she asked Del.

"That I can arrange. I have to come to town to meet with the regional manager sometime in July, so I'll arrange it to coincide with the dedication. Joe and Smitty can take care of things while I'm gone."

Misty ate in silence. It sounded as though the dedication would be in only a few weeks—a short time considering the work to be done.

"I brought you another "Sketches." It's in my bag. Don't let me forget to give it to you. It's about the reception for Flora Nasby, the artist who painted that picture in my office and the portrait of mother. I have no idea who the woman is or how she would have known mother. Nobody seems to know anything about her. This article states she didn't even show up at her own reception. Can you imagine?"

Misty's grip on her coffee mug tightened, but she kept her face expressionless as she watched Del's face for his reaction. She saw his eyes cloud over as he said, "Flora Nasby? I'd give anything to meet her." He was silent a moment then added, "Thanks for the article. I'll be glad to read it. One of us should contact the woman who writes "Sketches" and ask if she knows anything more about Flora. By the way, don't let me forget. I've something for you to take home with you. It's for Endicott. He'll pick it up."

"I'll remind you," answered Karyl, then after a moment, "Do you know what we should do before Misty and I leave? We should stop in at the mine. It's not much out of our way. Let's take the jeep, then we won't have to bring you back. I'd like to check things out there."

"Oh!" She looked at Del and put her fingers over her mouth before she turned to Misty with a hasty explanation. "This is the mine your friend Angelo is working. You don't mind, do you?"

"The mine Angelo is working?" Misty thought quickly. The same mine Denison Elbert had taken her to. This was her chance to go again, but why did Karyl want to go there? Out loud she said, "Why should I mind? Of course not."

A walk around the small yard, a last look at the peaks behind the cabin and across the valley, and it was time to go.

"Well, Misty, can you tear yourself away?" Karyl asked.

Misty flushed and turned from looking. "I'm ready."

"Del and I'll go in the jeep. You follow. OK?"

Back down the winding road away from the cabin and soon out onto the highway, Misty stayed close behind the jeep, as they turned back towards Pommel. She made a note of the mileage. It just might be well to know how far the access road to the mine was from this road that led into Stillwater Forest. She had not noticed any road on the way up the mountain, but the way Karyl spoke it could not be too far.

The road was not marked. Anyone not knowing where it was would have difficulty finding it. There was no access, but tire marks ran across a narrow ditch by the side of the highway and into the sparse woods indicating that vehicles had gone that way before. Misty carefully followed, watching the little jeep lurch as it crossed the ditch and began its way up a fern-lined gulley that lay hidden under the trees. Off to the right, scarcely visible, was a rough, unpainted cabin—the rangers' winter cabin where emergency supplies were stored.

The road began to climb steadily, scarcely visible even a few feet ahead. Ten miles had ticked off before Misty saw what she knew lay at the end—the tumbled shacks and gray cabin of the mine. But something more had been added. Behind the cabin was a foundation for another building. Stacked neatly beside it was lumber. It was evident Angelo had plans for the mine.

Misty parked alongside the jeep and followed Karyl and Del to the cabin porch. "Let's look inside first," said Karyl as Del hesitated. "It's OK to go in. I've got that understanding with Angelo. He's around here. Smoke's coming out of the chimney."

"Hey, look at all of this," Del exclaimed as he stepped inside.

Karyl and Misty stood staring at the furnished room, Maria's old chair by a window as if it had always been there.

"Just when is he planning to move in?" Karyl asked Misty as she peeked into the bedroom.

"How would I know?" Misty was startled by the question.

"Let's get out of here," said Del after a few more moments. "I don't like to intrude into someone else's place. You'll tell him we were here, won't you?" he asked Misty looking at her without smiling.

"I don't—"

"Look at that!" Karyl interrupted her. "I heard he was starting to build here!" She and Del walked over to the new foundation and stacked lumber, obviously unhappy with what they saw.

But Misty lingered behind stopping on the porch steps to examine the carved heart. Satisfied it was as she remembered it, she walked up the slope near the cabin to the pile of dry kindling, all that was left of the old sluice. Looking from the big boulders partly covering the rubble, to the cabin, to Karyl and Del with their obvious concern, Misty pieced it all together. The mine belonged to Karyl. It had been her parents' and the M in the carved heart was for Martha. Of course.

"Quite a mess," commented Del who had joined Misty. "That avalanche pretty much ended the mining here. But I'm sure," he added brightly, "Angelo will have good luck. He'll find some gold eventually in that dumped gravel up the gulley. I hear him up there now." He paused, listening, and Misty too could hear the faint sounds of a motor.

Then, after a moment, "Ready to go, Karyl?"

"We'd best. I don't want to get home too late. Take care, won't you. We'll see you before too awfully long," and Karyl accepted another light kiss from Del. "Bye, bye," she smiled in response.

"Tell Sorrowful and the goats hello." Del opened the truck door for Misty to climb in. "You'll be at the dedication?"

"Of course she will." Karyl answered for Misty. "She's as much a part of the camp as anyone."

Misty opened her mouth to say something, but shut it again.

"See you then," and before he climbed into the jeep and followed at a distance, Del watched the pickup begin to retrace the road over which they had driven.

At the highway Karyl turned the truck towards Pommel and, with a toot of the horn and a wave out the window, saw Del turn the jeep in the opposite direction.

Without looking behind, Del adjusted the blue bandana swinging recklessly from the mirror. Pressing the accelerator to the floor, he climbed the mountain with the speed of someone being pursued.

⁂

"It's good Del's coming down in July," Karyl said finally after she and Misty had driven several miles in silence. "He needs to get off his mountain occasionally."

"You're not going back?" It was a test question.

"Oh, I'll go up for a weekend later on. We're too busy now with registration at camp coming up. That's very soon, you know. Besides, Del's going to be really busy, too, now that campers and hikers have started going into the park. Someone always seems to get lost or hurt. And there's always the danger of people accidently setting forest fires. Especially when it's so dry."

Wondering about Karyl's seeming nonchalance, Misty leaned her head against the window of the door and stared at the aspen trees as the truck sped past row after row of them. In a happier mood she would have appreciated the slender white trunks and the quivering leaves gentle against the blue sky, mountain sentinels standing firmly in the forest floor carpeted with columbines. But in her present mood the trees served only to form a hypnotic glaze over the conflict that raged within. Seeing Del again had disturbed her more than she cared to admit. It's not right, she told herself. I'll fight it. Why is Karyl so casual? How can she be? I wish I could ask her all of these questions about the mine that are bubbling up inside of me, but I can't without identifying myself.

In the silence that lay between them, the pull to tell Karyl who she was, to explain herself, almost overwhelmed Misty. But she would not. She had, she reminded herself, passed the point of no return.

"Do you know anything about working with children?" Karyl's question came as a relief.

"Not really. Why?" Misty shifted her position and looked again at the woman beside her. Why did she always look so neat and well-groomed? And why was she always so calm and in control? She'd just left Del and look at her!

"I was just wondering. Todd will be back soon, but we will need someone to help with the children's program and in the kitchen. Fred and I have been working on the camp program, and we were wondering if you'd like to try."

"I suppose I can try," murmured Misty while her thoughts began to churn. What an opportunity! It would certainly be a new experience for her and there would be more stories.

"By the way, remember I mentioned a child named Dillon? He's Fred's nephew. You'll like him. He's a special six-year-old!"

When the clock on the dash pointed to twelve, they stopped to eat the sandwiches they had made at Del's. A short half hour later, after tossing their crumbs to a chipmunk, they started on their way again. The peak of the trip over, the balloon of excitement deflated, Misty felt drained. Once down out of the mountains she fell under the lull of the sameness of the landscape. Her eyes closed in spite of herself until she heard Karyl's announcement, "We're here!"

Opening her eyes, Misty straightened her bandana. "Ooh, I didn't mean to sleep like that!"

"You were tired. Would you like to come to my place for something to eat before I take you to get your bike?"

Misty hesitated; she resented having to return to the fear of Angelo. But if she went to Karyl's, it would only prolong it. She wouldn't get to her cabin until after dark; that she did not want to do. "No thanks. I think I'd better go right home."

"Some other time then."

"I've really enjoyed this," said Misty when the pickup finally came to a stop in the camp yard. "It's been great."

"It worked out well, didn't it? Thanks for going along. See you Monday."

Alone at the deserted camp Misty slowly pedaled toward her hill. She looked up toward the cabin. Everything seemed so lonely. So quiet.

"Hi, all of you," she said in a stage whisper as she reached the goat pen, hoping her voice did not carry to other ears. "Hi there, Gertrude. Sorrowful. Gretchen? Gretchen?" She called a second time. "Where are you?" Noticing feed had been put out recently, she added, "Guess your tummy's full and you're sleeping it off."

She turned from the pen and tried to whistle nonchalantly as she went to the cabin, but she looked toward the shadowy trees out of the corner of her eye. On the porch was a jar with milk in it—goat's milk. She looked at it for a long moment then carried it in with her.

In minutes she had a fire built. She cut some bread and cheese, and while the tea water heated, she sat at the table. Resting her chin on her hand, she stared out the window sorting out her thoughts.

She remembered all that she had seen during the past two days—the valley, the mountains, Del's cabin. She heard his deep chuckle and saw the crinkles around his eyes that always seemed to deepen when he laughed. She felt again his firm warm clasp around her own small hand and his arm across her shoulders.

She brushed sudden tears from her eyes. This is no time to cry, she silently reprimanded herself, no time to waste on thinking of things that cannot be. He belongs here in the mountains; my home is in the city. His thing is a ranger's jeep; mine, a computer. Besides, there *is* Karyl. And I have Lance.

No, there were other things to think about, like the mine—the crushed pile of wood—the boulders—"An avalanche," Del had said.

If there had been anyone near the sluice when those huge boulders suddenly came down the hill, he could have been injured. Neither Del nor Karyl had mentioned anything about anyone being hurt. Strange, Karyl had not even walked over to the old sluice to look at it. She had probably seen it so many times she knew every stick. "I've got to write to Dad," Misty told herself as she stood up. "I'll tell him I'm going to be working with the little kids and that the dedication of the camp will be in a few weeks. He'll surely want me to write a story about that. And I'll tell him about the mine." Misty looked out the window.

Perhaps if she took a walk, she would be able to stop any more thoughts of Del.

Unlocking the door, she stepped out on the porch. She looked around the clearing then began to walk aimlessly. Finally she started up the hill toward Angelo's house. Even though she knew he was at the mine, she wouldn't go all of the way—just as far as the edge of the trees. She wanted to know if he had really moved to the mine.

A breeze floated down the hill and swayed the tree branches as Misty walked under them. Slowly she walked on until she reached the end of the path, then she stood and stared at the darkened house.

Blowing its gentle way around the hill, the playful breeze rustled softly over the garden where the seeds Maria had lovingly planted had become plants growing into maturity. Not seeing any other signs of life and sensing a strange emptiness, she dared to walk into the yard. There was not only no Maria on her knees pulling at the heavy weeds, but neither was there any Old Lady waiting for her coffee. There was nothing in the goat pen.

An acrid odor of burned flesh and hide hovered over everything. From where she stood Misty could see what must be a pile of ashes with a—yes, it was a metal table of some sort in the midst of them. Her hand flew to her mouth to stifle a scream as realization swept over her. Angelo had taken Gretchen. Oh, he had fed her first along with Gertrude and Sorrowful, then he had tied the rope around her neck and led her out of the pen, just as he had led her down the hill when he first brought her. The trusting little animal had followed him, probably jumping around his feet and playfully winding the rope around his legs as she had done the morning he had brought her to Misty.

Had those two men, Jess and Darby, and Prescott been waiting here at Angelo's cabin? Of course, they had been there. And no doubt Gwen had been with them—and others. Which one of them had killed the little goat? Surely Angelo, who seemed to be so fond of the animals, couldn't do a thing like that! Misty cringed. Oh, they wouldn't have let her suffer, would they? If they were going to kill her, wouldn't they be merciful and do it quickly?

Had the fire been roaring already or did they wait and build it after they killed the goat? Oh, dear God! Misty's horrified mind raced. An animal sacrifice. Maybe they didn't kill her first—maybe they tied her to a stake and then—then—Or maybe they had made an altar. That was it—an altar. That's what the old table was. They had laid her on that—tied her down alive and then—Oh, Gretchen! Poor, poor little Gretchen. I remember chasing you down the hillside, and you jumped on the bulldozer and—it was because of you I met Del!

Daring to go no closer, fearing what else might be there, Misty backed away as she fought to control the nausea that gripped her. She remembered Angelo's words after Maria's death, "I'll sacrifice—to her spirit." She had not given his words much thought; she would never have believed he meant what he said, even Angelo.

An animal sacrifice? In this day and age? Such things happened in pagan days—animals were sacrificed to heathen spirits; I've read about it. And I remember hearing in church that ages ago the Jewish people sacrificed animals. But hadn't they killed them first? They were merciful, and that was before Jesus came. Can it be happening today? With these people I know? Oh, it can't be! I just can't be! But those ashes. They look still warm, and the smell—oh yes, it did happen. And I remember the first time I saw those people coming from Angelo's, the same smell followed the van down the hill. They've done this before! Oh, Lord!

Misty looked at the house, at the chimney, cold and black, overseer of what had happened to Gretchen. Feeling compelled to see if there was any life at all around, she forced herself to walk ever so slowly up the one—two—three steps to the porch, mentally poised and ready to run. Pressing her face against the window, she peered into the darkened kitchen. There was nothing to see. The house was empty.

The breeze blew a leaf across the dry yard and then disappeared into the woods.

Misty did not sleep that night.

FOURTEEN

"Hi!" A small voice floated up from the foot of the ladder.

"Well, hi." Misty smiled down at the upturned face. "I'll bet you're Dillon, aren't you."

"Yup, I'm Dillon. Who are you?"

"I'm Misty."

"Misty?" The boy wrinkled his nose. "That's a funny name. That's what the weather is sometimes when it's wet but not really raining."

Misty finished the spot she was painting. "Can't help it," she said. "That's my name."

"Where did your mother get it?"

"Out of a can of rain, I guess." She tried to joke with the child even though she was exhausted.

"That's not true. Rain doesn't come in cans!"

"You're right, it doesn't. I was teasing you. I just picked up the name 'Misty'."

"Didn't your mom name you? Aren't you anybody?"

"Oh, I think I'm somebody. Everybody's somebody. Look out, I'm coming down. I don't want to drop any of this green paint on that red hair. You'd look like a Christmas tree ornament!"

"It's a long time 'til Christmas," said Dillon as he stepped away from the ladder. "Didn't your mom name you? Really?"

"Can you keep a secret?" Misty whispered as she looked at the boy confidentially.

Dillon nodded.

"My mom named me Mary—" She started to add the Alice but caught herself in time. He just might pass the name along; it would not take too much for Karyl or Fred to put Mary Alice together with Morrow. So she hurried to add, "But I like the name Misty better."

Dillon tilted his head to one side. "Mary?" He tasted the name on the end of his tongue. "I like 'Misty' better, too, for you. It's pretty. It sounds soft and nice like rain. I think I like you. What shall I call you?"

"I'm glad you like me." Misty smiled as a warm feeling flooded over her. "I like you, too. Call me Misty like all of my friends do. Nobody ever calls me Mary, so don't you." She spoke almost emphatically.

"Can I help you, Misty?"

"Help me? Paint?"

"Uh huh."

"Hmm." Misty picked up a small board. "Here. I'll get you a brush and you can paint this."

"Is it important? I want to paint something important."

"Well," said Misty thinking fast, "we'll make it important. It can be your very own board. That makes it very important—it belongs to you."

"I'm going to be a painter when I grow up."

"That will be nice. Then you can paint houses and make them pretty."

"Not houses! Not that kind of painting! Real painting like Grandpa Cross used to do. Uncle Del does it sometimes. Only I never knew him. Grandpa Cross, I mean. He wasn't my real Grandpa anyway. He died."

Misty searched the child's face. Grandpa Cross? Uncle Del? Painting? "Oh?" she asked. "Is Uncle Del your real uncle?"

Dillon shook his head. "No. Just pretend. But he paints sometimes. He paints good."

"Maybe someday you'll be able to paint like that. We'd better get busy, don't you think?"

Every morning after that when Karyl drove in to the camp, Dillon was perched on the edge of the seat in the pickup, for all the world like a little prince surveying his kingdom. He greeted his Uncle Fred with an enthusiastic hug as Fred lifted him out of the truck; then calling, "Misty, Misty, where are you?" he would run to her no matter where she happened to be.

A new warmth pervaded the camp with Dillon there constantly at Misty's side. The little redhead quickly wound his new friend around his finger while he wound himself around her heart strings.

"You two have a thing going for sure," remarked Fred one day at lunch as Dillon sat close to Misty and opened his own lunch pail.

"We certainly have, haven't we, Dillon. We've got a thing going," agreed Misty.

"What does that mean, Uncle Fred?" The boy looked at his uncle questioningly.

"That means you two are good friends."

"Yup," and Dillon nodded. "We sure have a thing going." He cuddled closer to Misty.

❧❦❧

It was easy for Misty to form the habit of having a surprise for Dillon. The first time she brought a pretty rock she found by the stream. The next time it was a tiny tree frog she made comfortable in a jar with grass. When she brought a bird's nest she had found near her garden where it had fallen from a nearby tree, the habit was formed. Seeing the nest, Dillon was beside himself and wanted to know about the bird that had lived in it.

"Was it a mommy bird or a daddy bird?"

"Both," answered Misty. "Mr. and Mrs. Sparrow."

"Mr. and Mrs. Sparrow," repeated Dillon slowly. "Did they have any children?"

"There were three little sparrows—Elmer, Teddy and Wendy."

"Two boys and a girl," said Dillon with satisfaction. "They were a family, weren't they."

"Yes, they were a family."

"I wish we were a family."

"You're a family—you and your mommy and daddy."

"I haven't got a daddy," said Dillon matter-of-factly.

"Oh, I didn't know."

"But I have Uncle Fred. Mommy says he's as good as a daddy."

"I'm sure he is. Uncle Fred is a very nice man."

"Did any of them die?" Dillon asked.

"Did any of whom die?"

"Any of the little sparrows. When the nest fell out of the tree, did any of them die?"

"No, no I'm sure they didn't. They just—well, they just built another home, and they're happy there now."

Some days Misty's treat would be something for the boy to eat with his lunch: raisins in a sandwich bag, a couple of cookies, or some wild berries she had found hiding in the grass near her garden. Once she brought him some goat's milk in a jar.

"Goat's milk?" and he wrinkled up his little nose. "Do I like it?"

"I don't know. Try it and see."

"Look, Uncle Fred, this is milk from a goat." And he wrinkled his nose again.

"Mmm. Let me taste it." Fred took a sample sip. "Hey, that's good. You try it."

"Can I see your goat someday, Misty? This tastes pretty good."

"Someday. Maybe real soon. Now eat your lunch, then it'll be time to rest."

Time rollicked by. Misty not only enjoyed her new friend, but she studied him and spent her evenings writing about him and their adventures of the day. She looked forward to each new day with as much anticipation as did the little redhead.

Her newfound love was boundless but did not prepare her for the day when Dillon was not in his place in the pickup beside Karyl. That was the same day she brought a perfect little Y of a tree limb which she found in the woods. Polishing it carefully and attaching a wide rubber band to the prongs, she fashioned a slingshot that would please any little boy. When she heard the truck drive in, she laid the surprise in plain sight and waited for his usual call, "Misty, Misty, where are you?"

"Didn't Dillon come?" She looked up expectantly as Fred came into the kitchen alone.

"He's not able to make it today," answered the man softly. "His mother called at seven this morning and said he has a severe headache and is nauseated."

"That doesn't sound good. Is it his tumor?"

"Yes, seems that's what it is."

Misty laid down her paint brush and came a few steps down the ladder. "I can't believe that little guy has a brain tumor!"

"It happens that way sometimes," said Fred with a gentle smile. "They discovered it three years ago shortly after his third birthday. They operated, but couldn't get all of it. Months of chemo followed, but that didn't do a thing except make him miserable. We just take one day at a time."

So Misty put the slingshot beside the special board that boasted of many coats of paint of different colors—"A Joseph board," Fred called it—and she went on with her work.

"Kind of quiet around here without that little redhead, isn't it," said Roy when they sat down to a somber lunch.

"I miss him," said Misty simply. "But everyone does. I'm sure Fred is terribly concerned. Dillon told me that Uncle Fred is as good as a daddy!"

"He is that," said Roy glancing at the man who was talking with Drew. "Fred would do anything for the boy. Cindy is Fred's only sister, and it's terribly hard on him to know what she has to go through with Dillon. She nursed Dillon's father until he died, and now this."

Roy was thoughtful for a minute, then he went on. "It's a tough thing, but we'll have to take it as it comes. That's the way their parents and the kids themselves do. I know I could learn a lot from them."

"You know, don't you," Roy continued, "that registration is to be next Monday? The kids, who come from as far away as Denver, will stay for the first session. The others who will be here for the second and third sessions will register by mail." He glanced at his watch. "Look at the time! We'd better get with it, so we'll be ready." With that he closed his lunch pail and stood, giving Misty a little reassuring pat on the top of her head as he walked away.

Registration on Monday? Children and their parents coming from as far away as Denver? Misty continued to sit. She watched Roy walk away without even seeing him while she thought, "A one-hundred mile radius around Pommel!" She had heard Fred say that once and when she gasped, he laughed. "Just sick kids, Misty; not just any kid who wants to go to summer camp. Sick kids and handicapped. But even so there will be quite a few."

Now as she slowly broke a cookie into pieces Misty tried to imagine what Monday would be like. "I could learn a lot from them," Roy had said. Maybe she could too, but she was not as concerned about what she might learn as she was about the stories she would add to the ones she had already written. This was a Christian camp, Karyl had told her. Were all the children who came from Christian families? Probably. She herself was here because she had told Karyl she was a Christian. Well, she was—wasn't she? She still had to be interviewed by the board now that her short term of filling in for Todd was over and this new phase of the camp had begun, but she was ready for that.

"When the children come, I'll do what Karyl asks me to do, help with them or help Sadie." She brushed a few stray crumbs into her hand. She was able to amuse Dillon, so perhaps she could amuse other children, too. But Dillon was special. Maybe she could play a few games and read stories to all of the children. Whatever, she would keep herself detached. No need to get emotionally involved, not even with Dillon. The others would keep her from concentrating on him. If he came back, he would be caught up with the others himself.

"No matter what I do with the kids or in the kitchen," she concluded as she folded her lunch bag, "I'll have to keep my eyes and ears open. There's lots going on here."

❧❦

"Finished, Misty?" It was Sadie who was picking up the empty cups and plates of cookies. "I don't mean to hurry you."

"Sorry I'm so slow. I was just thinking about registration, what it will be like."

Sadie smiled and sat down beside Misty. "Have you ever been around sick children?"

Misty shook her head. "I can't say that I have."

"This camp was started, you know, by Karyl's mother because of her sister who was crippled. She saw how worn out her mother got taking care of a handicapped child, so she came up with the idea of a respite camp. And here it is, simply because the Lord built it. 'Unless the Lord builds the house they labor in vain who build it.' That's what the Bible says."

Misty sat staring at the empty cup she was twisting around and around in her fingers. Martha's sister. Crippled. Martha. Those were her initials carved on the post at the old mine, weren't they?

"My youngest had cystic fibrosis. We had him for six years."

Misty roused herself. "He died? I'm sorry. Do you have other children?"

"Three others. You remind me of Ruthie. She's my youngest living one. She's just about as big as you only her hair is brown. She works at a ski resort. In the gift shop. She acts in a little theatre, too."

"Maybe I'll get to meet her sometime. Does she ever come here?" The question was an idle one in an attempt to show some interest.

"Oh, yes, she comes home when she can. She'll be here in September. That's in between seasons, after the summer tourists and before the ski season. They're going to try to use this camp for skiing in the winter, I think. Will you still be here?"

"It would be fun to be here then. I don't suppose there will be any children?"

"No, no kids after September. But there's so much money poured into this, they can't let it just sit during the winter, so I think Karyl wants to have it used for a ski lodge. For church retreats and like that. I'm glad I don't have all of that money to worry about. Did Karyl ever tell you you look a lot like her aunt?"

Not waiting for an answer, Sadie stood up and began to pick up the cups she had set down. "Well, this isn't getting the kitchen cleaned up or the cheese grated for Monday's pizzas. Registration will be an experience, believe me."

"Sadie," Misty asked, standing to leave, "Do you know anything about a Wade family?"

"Wade? No, no I don't think I do. Do they live around here?"

"They were pioneers. Lived in these mountains a long time ago." Misty searched Sadie's face while she waited.

"I haven't lived here all that long. Sorry. I've never heard of them." And Sadie continued to the kitchen.

※❀※

Sunday, Misty was restless. She caught herself looking up the path towards Angelo's old house. There had been no signs of the big man, and she watched carefully every time she went to town. Not once had she seen him or his truck, so he must be spending all of his time at the mine. It was too pleasant a day to worry about Angelo. Better to go down to the camp and look around.

Slipping and sliding, she took a shortcut down the hill where she and Gretchen had gone that day that now seemed so long ago. Once at the camp she walked slowly across the grounds. Everything was deserted. The meadow was hers again. And the pond that had become a lake.

She paused on the bank of the lake and watched the minnows skimming under the surface. Then she crossed the meadow and picked a few wild roses along its edge before she came to the small white chapel with the stained glass windows depicting Jesus with round-faced, laughing children clustered around him.

Misty hadn't been in the chapel yet. She knew it was almost finished since the pews and organ had just been installed. "There's probably nothing in there that needs painting," she thought wryly, "unless it's the cross." The symbol she had seen Roy working on was leaning against the building ready to be put in place.

Maybe it was because everything was so quiet—no trucks, no people, no hammering or sawing, no movement of any kind. Maybe it was because the sun was shining warmly. Whatever the reason, Misty was relaxed and at peace with herself.

She sat on a rock resting her back against a tree while she let herself think of Del. What would he say when he saw the chapel? She could almost hear his chuckle of approval. Maybe he and Karyl would be married there. It would be an ideal place. And Karyl would stay here while he went back to the mountains.

The sound of a motor brought her back to the present. Looking in the direction of the road, she felt her heart skip a beat when a green jeep came out from under the trees. Could it possibly be Del? Her throat tightened as she watched a man climb out.

The disappointment that stabbed her when she recognized Denison Elbert faded the moment she realized the opportunity before her. The artist here, at the camp! A perfect time to interview him. Be casual, she admonished herself. Don't scare him away.

But the ranger did not see Misty. Without looking to right or left, he walked rapidly to the main building. Letting himself in, he disappeared inside only to reappear a few minutes later with what Misty recognized as the wrapped package Karyl had brought from Del's. Holding it with both hands, he hurried toward his jeep.

"Hi!" called Misty.

The ranger stopped and watched the woman running toward him. He waited until she got close before he spoke. "Oh, it's you!" His voice was crisp, unfriendly. "What are you doing here?"

Taken aback, Misty slowed to a walk. "I work here." She hoped her voice sounded pleasant.

"I'll just bet you do." The man pushed his hat back on his head. "This is Sunday. Nobody else is here, but you. It's ten thirty. Everyone else is in church where they belong. Karyl Cross wouldn't allow anyone to work on a Sunday so don't give me that. Inspecting more paintings?"

Stunned at the implication she was snooping, Misty's blue eyes smoldered. "What are *you* doing here? Why aren't you in church?"

"I'm on duty today," was the ranger's reply.

Misty pointed to the wrapped package remembering Del had said something about it's being for someone named Endicott. "Where are you going with that? It belongs to someone else."

"I really don't believe that concerns you." He climbed into his jeep and secured the package beside him.

"Wait!" Misty walked closer to the jeep. "I'd like to talk to you some more about that painting of the eagle and the fish. Lewis Tal—"

The ranger started the jeep and revved the motor, glowering at the transfixed Misty. "I should tell you that I intend to report your being here to Karyl Cross. I suggest that for your own good, you go back to wherever you came from."

The jeep spit up dust leaving Misty biting her lower lip.

※❀※

"It will be a busy morning," Karyl told Misty about registration when Misty questioned her. "They'll start coming at nine, and the parents will leave right after lunch. Oh—" Karyl hesitated. No, she would not speak to Misty yet about her being on the camp grounds yesterday morning. Had she really been nosing around as Doug said? Maybe she was just enjoying it. After all, Karyl reminded herself, it was her own fault Misty wasn't in church—she had simply forgotten to invite the woman to join them.

Even so, Karyl had spent some bad moments last evening thinking about Misty. She had begun to wonder about her two days ago after talking with Lillian Watson. Lillian had shown her the letter Misty had written requesting a cabin—a professional looking letter. And as Lillian had pointed out, Misty's hands were smooth and well groomed, the hands of someone who perhaps worked in an office. And Karyl had agreed with Lillian it was rather strange that a young woman of Misty's apparent lack of means had gone to Silver Ranch for a weekend.

The frown between Karyl's eyes deepened as she remembered again what Doug had told her the evening before. Why had she been so interested in the paintings in his cabin? And who was this friend of hers she had mentioned to Doug? Someone in a museum, he had said.

And there was what Pastor Rubeck had said. He had told Karyl about the occultic ceremony at Maria Giannelli's funeral and Misty's apparent closeness with Angelo's group. It fit in with what Karyl had heard about Angelo intending to use the mine for an occultic center. That's why she had wanted to check it out. It had been awkward with Misty along, but Karyl had seen for herself that Angelo was getting the place ready for the workshops on the occult Lillian had mentioned. A group was even to live there. Wasn't the foundation for a new cabin evidence of all this? Had Misty come from the east to help set this up? Karyl frowned more; with Misty staying on at the camp, if children weren't lured to the mine, parents could be enticed through the children.

Karyl shook her head slightly as if disagreeing with herself. I like Misty; I don't want to ask her to leave. But there is so much evidence against her. Let it be for now, Karyl advised herself. I told Misty we want her to work with the children, so perhaps she should stay on until after registration, but leave before she has close contact with any of them.

Karyl walked closer to Misty who had proven more than satisfactory in so many ways. "Dillon will be able to come." Karyl's voice betrayed nothing. "He's feeling much, much better. I thought you'd like to know."

Nothing prepared Misty for the children she saw getting out of cars and vans and mini-buses. Some were carried, some were in wheelchairs, and some walked with canes or crutches. Others tried to run with a hop and a skip, laughing at their new experience. She watched for Dillon and smiled when she saw his red head bobbing up and down while he carefully helped push a friend in a wheelchair. Children like these had always been someone else's concern, not hers. They had always been on the other side of the street. Now they surrounded her.

"Look at them come," said Drew. The men had laid down their work and were watching with Misty.

"They look happy," she said with surprise.

"Of course they're happy," agreed Fred, "every kid likes to go to camp. Look at that little guy on crutches over there. Did you ever see such a grin? We have a big responsibility," he went on after a few moments of watching. "They're coming to learn how to live. That's a big order."

"'Learn how to live'?" repeated Misty. "I thought some of them aren't going to make it, aren't going to live very long."

"Nobody can know how to die without knowing how to live," said Fred. "And nobody can know how to live without knowing how to die."

Fred made it sound so simple. "To know how to die, you have to know how to live. And to live, you have to know how to die." Was there really a way to know?

Registration went fast. Soon all fees were paid and all children officially guests of Martha's Camp. Finished with this part of their day, the children with their parents fanned out over the grounds. The green grass became alive with them, their bright colors blending with the flowers that bordered each building and path. The long barrack looked inviting with swings and flower boxes completing its wide porch. The lake, home of a dozen ducks and two swans swimming gracefully among the lily pads, beckoned. The small rowboat, tied to the dock yet to be completed, was tempting as it rocked with the gentle motion of the water.

From Sadie's domain came the aroma of gigantic pizzas ready for hungry mouths. Each pine table in the dining hall had a small vase with a bunch of yellow buttercups in it. Misty had fixed those, stopping to pick the flowers on her way to work that very morning.

Sadie beamed. "Misty, are you going to help serve?"

"I'll help wherever I can, whatever Fred or Karyl wants."

Like everyone else Misty was caught up in the spirit of the day, wanting to be a part of it, eager to help, to touch, to share. And so she served pizzas. She cut them into smaller pieces for hesitant mouths; she tucked bites into drooling mouths, and she wiped chins covered with sauce. She felt a part of all that was happening, and she loved it.

"That's Misty." Hearing Dillon's voice, she turned to see him pointing her out to another child.

She walked over to the boy and put her hand lightly on his shoulder. "Hi, Dillon. I'm glad you're back. I've missed you."

"Missed you, too," said the boy over a mouthful of food.

When at last the parents left, they went quickly, not daring to look back. Misty watched as Karyl and the nurses walked among the children wiping away the tears of those who felt the wrench of being left behind.

"Oh, my, please don't make it rain. It's such a nice sunny day!" The child in a wheelchair stopped crying and stared as Misty spoke to her.

"That's better. We need sunshine. All we can get. Tell me your name."

"Gertrude." The girl drew a deep breath as one last sob escaped her.

"Gertrude?" Misty pretended great surprise as she dropped to the grass beside the girl. "Do you know I have another friend named Gertrude?"

"You have?" The girl gave a sniffle.

"I sure have."

Dillon, who had seen Misty sitting on the ground beside the wheelchair, ran awkwardly from where he was watching and plopped down beside her. A plump little girl on crutches sat on the other side. Misty saw the child had only one leg, but she tried not to notice as she went on talking. "See if any of you can guess what my friend Gertrude is. She's white and she has four legs."

"A cat?" The little girl in the wheelchair smiled.

"Nope, not a cat. I have a black kitten, but Gertrude is white. She does have two black spots on her though. Dillon, what's your guess?"

"A dog. My name's Jenny." The little girl with the crutches interrupted.

"Nope, not a dog, Jenny. I'll have to give you another clue. She stands about this high," and Misty measured Gertrude's height with her hand. "And she has big floppy ears."

"Does she give milk?" asked Dillon knowingly. Other children had joined them, and Misty smiled at the faces that circled her.

"Yes, she gives milk."

"A cow!" shrieked Gertrude and the wheelchair jiggled with excitement.

Misty shook her head slowly and looked serious. "No, not a cow."

"All girl things give milk, Dopey, 'cept birds and snakes and things," and Dillon gave the wheelchair a shake.

Misty put a restraining hand on Dillon's arm while she looked at the other eager faces. "A goat!" exclaimed a pale-faced boy who hugged himself with excitement.

"Right!" Misty clapped her hands to show her delight. "My Gertrude is a goat. She says—who knows what she says?"

A chorus of "Baa"'s deafened her, and Misty put her hands over her ears until the goat cries faded away.

"Who can be a goat? Don't make any sound. My friend Gertrude doesn't talk all of the time. Let's all be quiet goats."

Some of those who could got on all fours and pretended to be eating the grass. Two of them jumped in the air and pushed one another down rolling and laughing. Little Gertrude thought for a minute then began butting the air with her head moving her frail body in unaccustomed exercise. Jenny hopped around stopping every few hops to wave a crutch in the air.

Dillon stood alone, perfectly still, his hands shading his eyes as though he were looking in the distance. Misty watched him for a second then asked, "What are you doing, Dillon-goat?"

"I'm looking," replied the boy. "I'm a mountain goat. I'm strong and well and king of my mountain. I'm looking out over the mountain peaks watching my other goats."

Misty felt her throat tighten as she looked at the thin body poised so rigidly. "Great!" she exclaimed. "Have you seen the goats in the mountains?"

"Uh huh. Uncle Del took me there twice. You know Uncle Del, don't you? He's real nice, don't you think?"

Misty felt a flush spread on her throat for no reason. "Yes," she said, "I know Uncle Del. You're all good goats," and she clapped her hands again to chase away her thoughts. "Sometimes my goat-friend has to be tied to a tree so she can be out of her pen and eat grass. She has to be tied, so she won't run away. Who can be a tree?"

The children stood in different poses. They were mini-statues, some with arms hanging down, others with arms held high or arched over their heads.

"Just look at those beautiful trees! I see a willow and a pine and a—"

"I'm an oak. I have lots of acorns."

"Good, Dillon."

"I don't like to interrupt this growing forest, but it's time for trees and goats and other kids to take a rest." Karyl had been watching from behind Misty. "It's off to the barrack for all of you. Peg and Doris, our nurses, are going to help care for you. They'll take you to your brand new cots where you're going to rest. Think of that!"

The children looked at Karyl, then in their own ways they scrambled to follow the two nurses who had come to get them.

"That was terrific, Misty." Karyl stayed behind the children. "You are a natural with children!" She gave Misty a hug.

"That was fun. I loved doing it," said Misty looking pleased.

"I can see your goat-friend someday, can't I, Misty?" Dillon still lingered. He took hold of Misty's hand and looked into her face with little-boy longing. "You told me I could. Remember?"

Misty looked at Karyl who nodded. "Why not?" she murmured.

"I said you could, so you sure can," Misty answered enthusiastically. "There's a deer, too."

"A real live deer?" Dillon's eyes were wide.

"A real live deer," reassured Misty.

"Can I see him, too?"

"Sorrowful would love to have you come see him. I'll take you real soon. How does that sound?"

"Oh, boy." Dillon lifted Misty's hand and pressed it against his forehead. "I think," he said slowly, "I'd like to lie down now."

Misty let go of Dillon's hand as Peg came and took his free one.

Together the nurse and boy walked toward the barrack with Karyl joining them. Dillon turned once. "Bye, Misty," he called over his shoulder.

"Quite a guy, isn't he." It was Roy, who stood unnoticed beside Misty.

Misty nodded. "Yes he is. I surely hope everything works out for him."

They watched the boy until he went into the barrack then Roy turned toward the lake. "Now that things have quieted down, how about a boat ride. You have some free time, don't you?"

"A boat ride?" Misty followed Roy's look.

"Sure. There's the row boat," and he pointed. "I'm a good rower. How about it?" He grinned at Misty.

"OK, if you think you can handle that vessel." They both laughed and Roy started toward the lake. Misty matched his step jogging with him to the water.

"This is great!" Misty sat opposite Roy as he rowed the small boat away from the dock.

"I can sing, too," and he ran up and down the scale in a clear tenor. Then he began improvising, "There was a maiden fair with long and golden hair—Um, let's see. I'll have to think of some more lines for next time."

Misty laughed. "Everything looks so different from out here, doesn't it. The dining hall looks different, and the barrack—"

"Look at the stream behind you," prompted Roy.

Misty turned and watched the sliver of water spilling down through the brush, falling over rocks into the lake.

"And over here—" taking his eyes off Misty for the moment, Roy maneuvered the boat to the opposite side of the lake, "—is where the stream flows out and down the valley."

A heron rose from the tall grass and flapped over their heads. "They nest here," said Roy.

"And the ducks," added Misty.

"And the frogs." They laughed together.

"Someday let's wear boots and follow the stream down the valley a way and see what we can find."

"Oh, I'd like that." Misty smiled happily, enjoying the ease of Roy's friendship.

"And," Roy went on, "we'll see how the lake is for swimming. It's not very deep." He looked over the side of the boat. "But we could at least go wading. For now, once more around then we'd better go back."

They were both quiet as Roy dipped the oars into the water, and the little boat made the trip around the small lake once more.

Del made this lake, Misty was thinking. Looking at Roy, she wondered what it would be like if it were Del sitting there instead.

"The kids will love a boat ride," she said finally, dragging her fingers in the water and making tiny ripples. "You will take them, won't you? I'm sure Dillon would be excited. And that live wire Jenny, the chubby girl with the one leg."

"Soon as the dock's finished. It's not safe for them the way it is."

Deftly Roy tied the boat to the unfinished dock then stepped out and held his hand for Misty. Putting her hand in his, she sprang lightly to the loose boards.

"That was fun. Thanks." Quickly she withdrew her hand. "Now back to work." Together they trotted back to the main building. "Thanks again." Misty turned to go in the kitchen door.

"See you," said Roy and watched the girl run up the steps and disappear inside.

FIFTEEN

When the camp had settled into a programmed routine, Misty's life took on a new pattern. After lunch each day she found herself telling stories to the children with red-headed Dillon cuddling close.

While the children watched her every movement and hung onto her every word, she probed her memory for stories that would be of special interest. Whether it was about Angelo's hen, Old Lady, or about Sorrowful, or even Spirited and Sprightly, the horses she and Lance rode at the academy north of Syracuse, she never tired of watching the expressions on the children's faces. The day she realized she was really helping these little ones forget their pain and discomfort for at least a short time, she felt rewarded.

The children who clustered around Misty every day were high with excitement during their last week of camp; they would soon be going home and Misty, too, had decided to leave, to go to Denver for a week. In the letter Lewis had written praising her for finding Denison Elbert, he had mentioned that a showing of Flora Nasby's paintings would be held in Denver. The artist would be there. "If you can see your way clear," he had written, "it would be great if you could go."

It didn't take Misty long to decide she would go to Denver for the showing. What a chance to meet the mysterious Flora Nasby, and while she was in the city, she could do some research on the Wade family. Then when she came back to Pommel she would have more to go on.

Before the children left, there would be that exciting time called the dedication. Work had progressed more rapidly than expected; all was in readiness ahead of schedule—it seemed only right the ceremony be held so this first group of campers could take part. Everyone was making elaborate preparations, and although Misty wanted to be a part of it, her mind was made up. The camp could get along without her; she wouldn't be missed. Then she heard Karyl's happy words, "His plans have been changed. His supervisor is coming earlier than expected, so he'll be coming soon. Friday morning at the latest."

Of course. Del was coming.

※❦※

"It's going to be a gala affair," said Sadie hanging her kettles on their hooks.

"I'm sure it will be just that." Misty stopped sorting the silverware to hear better. She looked at Sadie intently as if to say something then began sorting again.

"Everyone's going to wear dresses. All the ladies, that is. The fellows will have on ties. Can you imagine Roy and Drew with ties? And Fred? They'll all be slicked up; I guarantee it." Sadie laughed. "And Karyl will look like a queen. You know there's going to be a wedding, don't you? Won't she be a beautiful bride?"

"I guessed as much," said Misty banging the forks into their holder. Then, "I haven't got a dress," she said in self defense. "Just a cotton skirt and it's not very good. I don't really need to be at the dedication anyway." Perhaps it would be best not to tell Sadie she was going to be gone. She would only want to know where and why. The less said the better, Misty decided.

"Don't need to be at the dedication?" Sadie put her hands on her hips and scowled at Misty. "You most certainly do need to be there, young lady. You've been an important cog in this wheel. It's because of all you've done we're ahead of schedule—well, partly. What size do you wear? Eight? Ten?"

"Eight," answered Misty as she began putting the knives away.

"You wear the same size my Ruthie wears. Her blue dotted swiss is in my closet, and I know she won't mind, if you borrow it." Sadie's eyes fell to Misty's feet and she self-consciously curled her toes inside her scroungy sneakers. "I'll bring the dress tomorrow, and we'll find you a pair of shoes," Sadie said with a finality that should have settled it.

That evening Misty faced herself in the old cracked mirror. "You lied to Sadie, you know," she scolded. "You do have that dress you brought in case you go to Denver; of course it's not what they would expect little Misty to wear—it would be a dead giveaway. There's that long skirt and blouse you wore at the ranch though." She looked at the skirt hanging in the makeshift closet then shook her head. "I'd better start packing."

Misty turned from the mirror and pulled a suitcase out from under her bed. "Three more days and I'm going to Denver!"

"I'll bring Dillon up to see the animals tomorrow right after lunch." She looked out at the goat pen. "Then I'll turn Sorrowful loose. It's time for him to go."

❧❧

Dillon was beside himself with excitement when Misty asked him if he was ready to meet Gertrude.

"Do you mean it?" he asked in disbelief. "Is today really the day?"

"It sure is. It's really the day. I told her you were coming, so we don't want to keep her waiting. I said we'd come right after lunch and that you would have to come back for your rest. How about that? We'll skip story time today. Doris will tell the others a story for me."

"Is Sorrowful there, too?"

"Yes, Sorrowful's there, too. He's waiting with Gertrude. Climb in the truck, and I'll be with you in a jiffy."

"Sadie!" Misty called through the kitchen door. "I'm taking Dillon to see the animals at my place. I've Karyl's permission."

Sadie's ample figure came out of her office. Her face was flushed from the heat, for there seemed to be no breath of air anywhere. The smudge of flour on the end of her nose made a cool contrast to her flaming cheeks. "Wait. I've got the dress. Ruthie wants you to borrow it. I called her last night, and she said that's fine." The woman bustled back into her office only to reappear with a large dress box. "Take it with you now, then you won't have to carry it on your bike."

Misty hesitated a brief second then took the box. She didn't want to say anything that might upset Sadie who already looked like the world itself depended on the cakes she was baking. "Tell Ruthie thanks. I'll take good care of it. You know where I am, if anyone asks. We'll be back in about half an hour."

She glanced at the boy out of the corner of her eye as she drove to her cabin. His bright red hair made his pale face look even paler. There were dark circles under his eyes, and his mouth looked drawn and pinched. He sat watching with solemn eyes as the truck climbed the hill.

"OK, Dillon?" Misty asked gently. "Just a bit more and—here we are!"

Dillon slid to the edge of the seat to see better. "Where are they?" Then before Misty could answer, "Is that your house?"

"That's my house and over there's Gertrude. See Sorrowful? He's in the far corner."

"Can we get out so I can pet them?"

"Sure. Come on."

Together the two walked over to the pen. "I've brought you some company, Gertrude." Misty pulled a handful of grass and handed it to Dillon. "Here, give her this."

But Dillon had eyes only for the deer who was lying stretched out in the sun. "Is he dead?"

"Dead?" repeated Misty. "No, Sorrowful's not dead. He's just asleep."

"I'm going to be dead," said the boy.

"Don't say that, Dillon." A strange chill took hold of Misty.

"Mommy says it doesn't hurt. She says it's just like going to sleep."

Misty squatted down beside the boy. "Dillon. Look, honey— maybe when you're one hundred and twenty years old—" Misty looked deep into the boy's hazel eyes not knowing what else to say.

"It's OK, Misty. I'm not afraid. I'll go to heaven 'cause I believe in Jesus. I'll be with Him and Daddy. Are you sure Sorrowful's only asleep?"

Misty busied herself with more grass. "I'm sure. See? He's moving. He heard us talking. Give some more grass to Gertrude. She's hungry."

Sorrowful kept his distance while Gertrude pulled at the grass making Dillon laugh. Neither Misty nor the little boy spoke as they stood side by side feeding handfuls of grass to the animal and making a pile of it on the ground for her to munch on later. The sun was warm on their backs, and the freshly pulled grass smelled sweet.

"Would you like to see my kitten?" Misty asked after a bit.

For answer Dillon slipped his hand into hers and went with her to the cabin. They found the kitten curled up on the bed. Dillon put his face on the quilt next to the little animal and stroked it gently.

"Where did you get him?"

"A friend gave him to me," answered Misty remembering Maria. "He was lonesome."

"He's singing." Dillon kept stroking the soft fur. "That's a pretty song, kitty. Do you sleep here?" He looked at Misty without raising his head.

"Kitty and I both sleep here."

"Your house isn't very big. Where does your husband sleep?"

"I haven't got a husband. Would you like to go out to the garden and pull a tiny carrot?"

Dillon stayed with his face on the quilt, his arm cradling the kitten. His thoughts seemed to be far away.

"Dillon?" Misty spoke in almost a whisper. "Dillon, does your head hurt?"

The boy roused himself. "A little. I think I'd like to pull a carrot now." He put his hand out as if to steady himself when he stood, then he followed Misty.

"We'll pull a carrot or two, then we'll have to go back to camp. We've been gone too long already."

"Which are the carrots?" Dillon stood looking at the straight rows of the garden.

"These over here. Those are beets, then beans and these are the carrots. You're a carrot top yourself."

"Carrots have green tops!" The boy put his hand on his hair.

"Your top is the color of a carrot, silly." Misty tried to laugh, but it stuck in her throat. "They're not big yet, but here's one to pull."

Dillon leaned against her. "Here, pull it, honey," and she eased the carrot part way out of the ground.

"It's dirty!" he exclaimed.

"We'll wash it then you can eat it on the way back. Want another?"

"Uh, uh." He bent over. "Look it. It's dead." He held a black beetle in the palm of his hand.

"Yes, I guess it is."

"We have to bury it."

"It's OK to just put it down."

"We have to bury it!" he insisted.

"Well, all right," and Misty began scooping a little hole with her fingers feeling the boy's body heavy against her knee.

Dillon placed what was left of the insect in the hole then looked up at the bright sky. "Why's it getting dark, Misty?"

A stab went through the woman. "I think we'd better go back to camp before it gets any darker." She put an arm around the boy's thin shoulder to guide him to the truck.

Dillon took a few steps then reached out. "Misty!" Terror filled his voice. "I can't see very well. It's too dark. My head hurts. I want my mommy!"

Misty scooped the boy into her arms. He trembled against her. She had taken only a few steps when she heard the jeep.

🙞🙜

Minutes after Misty and Dillon had driven away from the camp, Sadie heard a familiar voice behind her asking, "What's to eat, Lady Sadie?" Turning, she saw Del in the doorway laughing at her surprise.

"Del Quinn! You're here! You came early."

"Right you are as always, Sadie McQueen. I'm here two days early. Where is everybody?"

"Karyl and the pastor are with the children. And Fred—there he is out back. Fred!" The woman tapped on the window. "Del's here!"

Soon the kitchen was alive with talk and laughter. "I've got four days in Pommel. Four whole days. Until Sunday night."

"Boy, that's terrific," said Fred. "Let's go get Karyl while Sadie makes some coffee. OK, Sadie?"

So while Misty and Dillon fed the goat and the deer and petted the kitten, Del was listening to Karyl and Fred. "Everything sounds great," he said after he had asked a dozen questions. "I'm going to go take a tour. It's sure different than when I saw it last."

"The best part is the children," said Karyl. "They're resting now, but they'll soon be up! Jennie Stark is here. She's a live wire in spite of having just one leg. And Timmy Yost. Remember Jed Yates? He's here, too. Sadie," Karyl turned from Del, "have Misty and Dillon come back? He should be resting, too."

"No, they haven't. The truck's not out there." Sadie looked at the clock. "They left just before Del got here. About forty-five minutes ago."

Karyl frowned.

"Where are they?" asked Del. "I want to see my friend Dillon."

"Misty took Dillon up to see the animals, but they should be back by now. I'm a little concerned."

"Fred and I can drive up, if that will make you feel any better."

"Would you mind?" asked Karyl. "I'm sure everything's all right. Misty probably doesn't realize how late it's getting, and Dillon's too entranced with the animals."

"Come on, Fred."

Del looked up the hill ahead of him as the jeep nosed its away along the rough road. He gripped the wheel and tried to listen to what Fred was saying about Dillon having a set-back, but doing better lately.

Both men saw Misty with the boy in her arms at the same moment. The anguish on her face was plain even from where the jeep stopped.

Del was beside her in a flash. "He's—he's—he can't see," said Misty. "His head hurts." Her own face was ashen. She stood looking at Del too shaken to wonder at his being there.

"We'll take him. Fred—" Fred held out his arms for his nephew who was quiet now and seemed asleep. Gently Misty gave over her burden, then she stood alone under the trees as the jeep made its way back down the hill.

Automatically, she turned to the truck. She would have to take it back. Remembering the dress box, she carelessly threw it into the cabin.

The jeep was parked in front of the barrack, but as Misty slid out of the truck, she saw Fred's car head out of the yard, the tires spinning tiny swirls of dust. Fred was at the wheel, and Karyl was beside him with Dillon in her arms. Del and Pastor Rubeck were in the back seat.

Misty felt rather than heard Roy coming along the path. He saw her pale face and clenched hands and stood quietly beside her.

"The others are in the chapel praying," he said after a few seconds. "Would you like to come, too?"

Misty shook her head and turned away.

Roy took another look at the girl then went to join the others.

Left alone, Misty walked through the empty dining hall to the kitchen. Four coffee mugs were on the table, but Sadie was in the chapel and everything was quiet. Too quiet.

There was nothing she could do—the children were resting and the nurses were with them. Go pray? No, she couldn't do that. Feeling her aloneness like a dead weight, she walked out to her bicycle. Since her plans for the day were in a shambles and she was left alone, she might as well go to the cabin. Without looking back, she rode out of the camp and up the hill.

The goat was eating the last of the grass she and Dillon had pulled. Sorrowful looked at her quizzically, then flicked his tiny flag of a tail and curled up on the straw.

Misty walked numbly into her cabin. Sitting on the edge of the bed, she put her hand out to the kitten who purred in his sleep. A spider in a corner of the window was wrapping a struggling fly with his fine sticky web.

Misty watched the struggle while she tried to sort out her feelings. Why did I feel so alone? Why should the others have included me in the trip to the hospital? Why should I expect them to include me now in this moment of tragedy and pain? Well, I'm was going to go away in two days. Maybe I'll just go on home from Denver, then none of this will matter! Not really.

Just what is my problem, anyway? Why do I feel this way? Roy offered to be with me so I don't have to be alone. But I refused him. Why? There was an aching void within her. "Del," she whispered. Could he fill the void completely, or was there something more? He had come so suddenly, so unexpectedly just at that horrible moment when she held the unconscious Dillon in her arms. And he would be here until after she left. Misty set her lips in a firm line. Yes, it was Del—partly.

"Oh, God!" she sobbed letting the tears fall unchecked. She cried for Dillon. She cried for herself. She cried for everyone who had pain. She cried until she felt drained, then she walked to the kitchen, kicking the suitcase that was in her path. She built a fire, filled her tea kettle and set it down with a bang.

The kitten walked to the door and mewed. Misty let the kitten out, slammed the door shut, locked it, and put the chair under the knob. The spider was not disturbed. He went on with his web.

SIXTEEN

"Misty, will you pour the punch tomorrow night? You will, won't you?" Misty gave no answer. "We're counting on you." Karyl looked up from the clipboard in her hand and smiled. "Doris and Peg want you to help get the kids dressed, too, and over to the dining hall. They're going to be high with excitement, and you have such a soothing way. Especially with Jenny."

Misty, conscious of Del in the other room talking with Fred, smiled and said only, "She's a live wire, all right."

There was so much going on, and Karyl was so involved; Misty knew it was not a good time to announce she would be going to Denver in the morning. No, she would wait until later that afternoon to tell Karyl.

The whole camp was a whirl of excitement. Misty felt it pulling at her, but she was not about to change her plans to meet Steve in front of the post office by quarter of eleven. The thought of meeting Flora Nasby spurred her on and almost overshadowed the reception.

She would take her luggage to the post office in the truck, bring the truck back to camp, walk to her cabin and get her bike. She would ride the bike to the post office and leave it there. Flawless plans. Yes, everything was ready. Someone else could subdue Jenny and dress her. Someone else could bring the children to the dining hall and pour the punch.

"Cindy brought Dillon home yesterday. I saw him last evening," Karyl was saying.

"Is there any change?" Misty had started for the kitchen, but she stopped, waiting for Karyl's reply.

Karyl shook her head. "No change. He's still in a coma, hanging on. The doctors say he could stay this way for several weeks, or he could go today. Cindy wanted to care for him at home. Wouldn't you like to see him?"

"Oh, yes," answered Misty. "I would like to see him—very much."

"Del's going this afternoon. Aren't you, Del?" Karyl raised her voice so the man in the next room could hear her.

"Aren't I what?" Del called back.

"You're going to see Dillon this afternoon, aren't you?"

"I'm planning on it."

"Misty would like to go along."

"Oh, I—" Misty started to protest as Del walked into the room. "I don't want to be in the way. I can go some other time." She felt her face flush.

Del smiled. "You won't be in the way. Nobody else is going. Let's go at four. How does that sound?"

Misty answered with a soft, "That's fine" then turned abruptly. She tried to be calm and rational, but from that moment nothing seemed to go right for her. Whatever she touched seemed to fall or slip through her fingers, if not disintegrate. She dropped a glass that broke into fragments. She spilled a cup of milk on the floor. Even an old saucepan she was filling suddenly sprang a hole.

She fumbled her way through the morning until Sadie, wiping the beads of perspiration off her forehead, took pity on her. The kitchen was stifling enough without the tension that seemed to float with Misty.

With sudden inspiration Sadie said, "There are some plants on the chapel porch that need to be placed on the platform. Why don't you go fix them?"

Misty finished wiping off the cupboard before she answered. "Maybe I do need a change of scenery. If you'll tell me how Karyl wants them placed, I'll do it now."

"Put the ferns that are there on the risers on the platform. Place them all around, behind and on either side of the pulpit. Then arrange the mums and glads on the floor in front of the ferns. It shouldn't take too long."

"I think I can handle it. I'll see you later."

Misty walked across the lawn slowly, stopping twice to look up at the mountains. Was it normal for prescribed fires to break out again? She sniffed the air then went on to the chapel. Stepping inside as if she were afraid she might disturb the quietness, she stood without moving. The sun filtering through the small stained glass windows made colorful patches on the pews, spilling over onto the floor. Another larger window that framed a cross of red and gold glass all but filled the wall behind the pulpit. Although warm and close, the chapel was a quiet spot set apart from the activity that pulsated in the other building.

After a few moments, Misty picked up a potted fern in each hand and carried them to the platform, placing them on the risers. Too warm, she slipped off the shirt she was wearing, certain no one would see her in the faded tank top she had hurriedly put on under it. Feeling more comfortable, she dropped the shirt on the edge of the platform then carried more plants to their places. It was when she was arranging the plants from behind the risers she heard the chapel door open. Soft words floated up to her.

"Isn't it lovely?" It was Karyl's voice.

"It's all you dreamed it would be, isn't it." Del's voice responded, deep and resonant. Misty stayed motionless, the ferns and pulpit screening her.

"You do want the wedding to be here, don't you?" The third voice was one she had heard only once before.

"We surely do, Pastor." Karyl's voice again.

"Come on. Let's practice. This is as good a time as any." Misty, conscious she was eavesdropping but not wanting to be seen, heard Del begin to sing, "Dum-dum-de-dum."

Karyl interrupted with a laugh, "Oh no, not now, thank you. It won't be long though. September will come all too soon, and there's so much to do!"

"You're going to be a beautiful bride." Del's voice sounded even deeper.

"That she is." Pastor Rubeck was still there.

"Have you decided how many attendants you'll have?" asked Del.

"Two or three. At one time I thought of asking Misty, but—" a slight pause then, "she won't be here."

No one noticed that some of the ferns waved as if a breeze had disturbed them. No one heard a slight gasp behind the risers.

"She's leaving?" Del's voice again, fainter this time because he had taken a step back from Karyl and the pastor. "She's been rather upset ever since the other day when she had Dillon with her. She's a very quiet person."

"I know. She's very fond of Dillon, but I'm afraid I'm going to have to let her go. We do *not* want any more of those occultists here. You saw how the cabin at the mine is fixed up and the foundation for more building! Angelo and his friends are planning on starting a commune there—occult."

"Are you sure?" interrupted Del.

"That's what Lillian Watson told me, and she knows what's going on around town. They're even going to have workshops and bring in other people. We just can't have any of that. Look at the risk we'd be taking with the children. Besides, Doug told me some things I haven't told you yet, things you should know. I'm sorry about all of this. Misty told me she's a Christian—"

"Well, isn't she?" demanded Del.

"She said she is, but I don't know. I was sure she would fit in with the camp. She's a very unusual person. There's something about her I can't quite put my finger on. I wish I'd made more of an effort to get to know her."

Then Karyl's voice changed and became brisk. "I've a zillion things to do by tomorrow, but I did want you to see the chapel before it's full of people. I see there are still some more plants to put in place. Sadie said she'd ask Misty to arrange them, so I know it'll get done."

"I'll come with you and help Fred." Misty was sure Del paused and took one last look. "This is really nice. It will be packed tomorrow night, won't it."

"It should be," answered Karyl brightly. "I'm glad Ben Rubbins can leave his mayoralty in Frisco long enough to be with us. It's going to be nice. I only wish mother could see it."

"She would be pleased." It was the pastor's voice again.

"Come on, Del, if you're coming with me. And don't forget we have a five o'clock appointment. Pastor, are you coming?"

"You two run along. I'll see you both tomorrow night."

Misty heard Del say "Okay," and she knew that he and Karyl had left. But Pastor Rubeck? Misty heard him moving. From behind her fern screen she could see him take a pot of mums in each hand and start down the aisle towards the platform. Taking a deep breath, she braced herself to meet the pastor.

When she heard no more movement, she carefully looked around the pulpit. Leaving the two pots of mums on the edge of the platform, the pastor had retreated to the second pew where he was kneeling, his arms resting on the back of the pew in front of him, his head on his arms.

Stealthily, Misty reached through the plants and managed to grab her shirt. A fern tickled her nose; in spite of herself a soft sneeze punctured the quiet. Pastor Rubeck raised his head.

Misty stood like a statue for a long moment, she and the pastor staring at each other. "I'm sorry," she apologized when the moment passed. "I was fixing the plants and I couldn't help overhearing."

"It's all right." The pastor looked at her, waiting for her to say more.

"I should have let them know I was here, but I didn't." Misty smiled weakly. What more could she say? What more should she say? "It's lovely in here, isn't it. It makes the camp complete, perfect for a wedding."

She paused, embarrassed, then saw the portrait of Martha Cross on the rear wall of the chapel—a welcome change of subject. "I'm sure Martha Cross would be pleased with what has been built in her name. Did you know her?"

"Yes, I knew Martha. I knew the whole family—her parents, Jeremy and Rose Wade, and her sister, Ruby."

"Ruby?"

"Ruby and Martha, only everyone called her Matty."

"Martha? Matty?"

"Yes, Martha—Martha Wade. She married Denison Cross. Ruby was crippled in a mine accident. She died when she was—oh, she must have been thirty, thirty-one."

"Ruby was crippled in a mine accident?" repeated Misty.

"She and Matty and a cousin of theirs were playing around a sluice box," the pastor explained. "Some heavy boulders rolled down from above and crushed the sluice, so it fell on them. Matty—Martha wasn't hurt, but Ruby and her cousin were. After Jeremy died, Rose had to take care of Ruby all by herself and it was too much. Seeing her mother struggle inspired Martha with the idea of a respite camp and Karyl, bless her heart, has faithfully carried it out, building this camp according to the standards her mother insisted on. Her sister hasn't been any help at all."

Only bits of what the pastor said registered in Misty's whirling thoughts. Matty—Martha—Ruby—a sluice box—a cousin. Martha Cross was her father's cousin Matty, Karyl was Matty's daughter, so Karyl was—

Fighting the confusion and shock that gripped her, Misty groped to say something—anything that would sound logical to the pastor. "Then the old mine up Sawtooth Gulch—Karyl's mine is—"

"The old Jerose Mine—Jeremy and Rose's old place. Yes. You've been there?" The pastor asked, narrowing his eyes ever so slightly remembering what Karyl had said about the cabin being fixed up and a commune moving in.

"I've been there twice—once with Karyl and—Del, and once with another ranger," stammered Misty. "I'd like to see it again, but I guess I won't since—well, I heard Karyl say she was going to let me go, so it looks as if I'll be leaving soon."

The pastor smiled to soften his words. "Like I said, Karyl is very careful about keeping the standards her mother set for the camp; She seems to feel you don't measure up."

Leaning against the back of a pew for support her pounding pulse all but choking her, Misty flushed. "When I first talked to Karyl about working here, she asked me if I were a Christian. I am! I go to church; I don't do anything bad. I feel that I've done all I was asked to do here to the best of my ability."

"I'm sure you have," answered Pastor Rubeck gently. "You say you're a Christian, and yet you're involved with the man Angelo Giannelli and his friends. The standards of Martha's Camp emphasize Christian standards based on Jesus Christ, his death, burial and resurrection. These other people, Giannelli and his friends and many, many others like them, believe everyone has their own inner strength. They believe all they have to do to find the source within themselves is meditate on that source; they believe each person is himself a god. Some who believe that way call themselves Christians. But they have nothing to look forward to after this life, Misty. Only those who believe the biblical Christ is the Son of God, and who believe faith in Him is the only way they can come to God, will have eternal life."

Misty nodded. "I know they believe in their own inner strength. There's to be a workshop here on finding your own source. Some woman from Scotland. But I'm *not* involved with Angelo Giannelli and his friends! I rented his cabin because it was the only one available; I don't like it or him. And I do go to church almost every Sunday when I'm," Misty almost said "home" but finished with, "when I'm near one."

Pastor Rubeck rubbed his chin thoughtfully. "Misty, going to church doesn't make one a Christian. It's a personal relationship with Jesus Christ. I suggest you tell Karyl what you have told me. And think about what I've said. If you would like to talk more, I'll be back tomorrow."

He checked his watch. "I must be going. I'm late now." He smiled then said as an afterthought, "You know, you look very much like Ruby."

Left alone, Misty put cold hands on her burning cheeks. It was hard to realize—Karyl Cross, her cousin. Not a close relative, but there was a blood relationship; they came from the same family roots. And it was hard to accept that this—this woman, her cousin, was rejecting her and on religious grounds at that.

Misty was angry, hurt and bewildered by the turn of events. Not knowing whether to laugh or cry, she looked at the cross framed in the window behind the pulpit and muttered, "If You're in here, why don't You speak to me?"

But she didn't want to take time to listen to God or to talk to Him; she wanted to leave—now, this minute. She didn't want to see Del or Karyl or Roy or any of them. She just wanted to leave. She picked up the mums the pastor had placed on the edge of the platform, sorely tempted to throw them. Instead she put them in place, planning how she would tell Karyl she was going before Karyl had a chance to ask her to leave. And when she went to Denver, she would keep on going home. There was no need to come back. Her last assignment was finished—she knew who the Wades were. Indeed she did! But first she would tell Karyl she was not involved with those other people and their way-out beliefs. Involved with Angelo and his friends? What a laugh! If Karyl and the others only knew how afraid she was!

While she was at it, she would tell Karyl who she was, why she was here—the whole thing. It would not be easy, but it was the only thing to do. And she would ask if she could borrow the truck to take her things—all of her things—to the post office in the morning. By this time tomorrow she would be well on her way.

The plants in their places, Misty stood again under the portrait of Martha Cross for a closer look. So that was Matty. In the portrait Martha's hair was snow white, faint lines around her mouth and eyes delicately suggested her age. The portrait must have been done not long before her death, and it must be the painting Del had given Karyl when they were at his cabin. Misty stretched to see the artist's signature. It was as Del had said—Flora Nasby.

❧❀❧

A subdued Misty smiled at the group of children sitting around her on the lawn after lunch. "Tell us the story of the hen who likes coffee. Please?" Jenny had taken Dillon's place in sitting close.

"Do you want to hear about Old Lady again? You probably know it by heart, but here goes. Old Lady was a fluffy red hen," she began. As the story unfolded, Jenny puffed out her cheeks making loud clucking noises until Misty had to lay a quieting hand on her.

"Jenny, you're a good hen. Hey, where are you going?"

"No place." The plump girl started to hop away from the group, but at Misty's question she turned and hopped back. "Can we be ducks tomorrow?"

"And swans," another voice piped up.

"Tomorrow you're going to be ladies and gentlemen," reminded Misty. "Tomorrow is the—"

"Dedication!" shouted the children in unison.

And I'll be gone, thought Misty. Out loud she said, "Right! Now it's nap time. Jenny, you walk beside Michael while I push him. Let's make a train. Michael and Jenny and I will be the engine. The rest of you be the cars in back of us. Jenny! Beside Michael, please."

Misty began watching the clock at quarter to four. Still shaken from her morning encounter, she was reluctant to see Del, but eager to see Dillon. At five minutes to four she casually walked outside.

"We'll take the jeep." Del was already there with his hand on the door.

"Del!" It was Karyl calling from the porch. "Don't forget. Five. I'll be waiting."

Del signaled he heard then held the jeep door open for Misty to climb in. She sat close against the door and folded her hands in her lap—tightly. After they had driven out of the campgrounds, she dared to study the man's rugged profile out of the corner of her eye. She noted the straight lines of his nose and his angular jaw. His hands on the wheel looked strong and cared for. His sleeves were rolled back exposing brown, muscular forearms.

Misty wet her lips with her tongue for they felt strangely dry, and then she stared straight ahead. She thought again of Martha Cross— the Matty of the old faded birthday greeting; she relived her conversation with the pastor and stifled a gasp.

Del glanced at her. "You OK?" he asked.

"Yes," she managed to get out, "I'm OK." Lapsing into silence, she went on with her thoughts.

If Misty had turned to look as they drove past the small lumber yard that stood a mile out of town with its stacks of fragrant fresh-cut boards, she would have seen the blue pickup parked to one side of the road. Perhaps she would have been alarmed if she had seen the look on Angelo's face as he watched the jeep. She might have been even more alarmed if she had seen the pickup turn onto the highway and follow them at a discreet distance. But she was with Del which was, of course, half the reason why the pickup followed them.

But she did not see the pickup. She was too busy staring at a silver Honda parked on a side street. A tall, willowy woman with russet hair was standing by the car looking down the road.

Karyl? thought Misty. But it couldn't be Karyl. They had just left her at the camp and besides, Karyl had no Honda that Misty knew of.

The woman caught sight of the approaching jeep and quickly ducked to get into the car.

Misty glanced at the man beside her again. He was too quiet, too preoccupied. Probably with the fire that was back up in the hills. Perhaps she should say something. "When do you go back to the park?"

"Sunday. I'm fortunate to be here for even a short time and see all of the kids. You know, you have a real talent with children."

"I have?"

"I watched you taking them to the barrack this afternoon."

"Oh."

Misty said nothing more. She noticed for the first time the blue bandana tied in with the monkey dangling from the mirror. She looked at the bandana then back at Del. Was that the one she had lost? Should she ask him about it? She felt she should say something, but rather than mention the bandana she said, "I miss Dillon."

"We all miss him. He's in a coma, you know, so don't be surprised or disappointed that he doesn't respond."

They had driven half way to Frisco before Del stopped in front of a green and white house set in a small yard with a huge blue spruce tree by the gate.

"Here we are," he announced softly, "Hi, Cindy," he waved at a young woman on the porch who looked very much like Fred. She waited for Del and Misty to join her. "Oh, it's good to see you, Del," she said with a smile. "Come on in."

For answer Del gave her a hug. Then he turned to Misty waiting in the doorway. "This is Misty Morrow from the camp."

"I feel that I know you." Cindy held out a hand to Misty. "Dillon speaks of you often. It's good of you to come."

Even in those few seconds Misty wondered at the quiet peace that came from Dillon's mother. She was not sure just what she had really expected. Tears, maybe. Surely despair. Or the hopelessness and coldness she had seen with Maria. Anything but this quiet peace. A strange warmth reached out and touched her. Nothing seemed hopeless, nothing seemed beyond this young mother's love.

Misty and Del followed Cindy to Dillon's room. The late afternoon sun shone through the window making the animals on the colorful bedspread seem almost alive.

Misty stood by the bed and stared at the small form that barely made a lump under the covers. His hair, redder than ever on the pillow, made a flaming halo around his face. His hands lay quiet on top of the spread, his fingers curved ever so slightly. A stuffed dog with a torn ear sat in one corner of the bed keeping an unmoving watch with his button eyes.

"Has there been any change?" Del scarcely whispered.

Cindy shook her head. "No. The doctors say he won't wake up. He will just—slip away." There was a slight catch in her voice. "He's in God's hands," she went on evenly. "In a way it seems that he's already gone home."

"It's been a privilege to know him," Misty whispered not knowing what else to say.

"Thank you," answered Cindy. "He's always been special."

They watched for a few more minutes in silence. "I'll be glad to sit with him, if you'd like to go get some fresh air." Misty sensed the fatigue in Cindy. Too, she wanted to be alone in the room with the boy. Would the warmth still be there? and the peace?

"Really, I'm fine." Cindy seemed reluctant to leave.

"Misty's right, Cindy. You need a break. Let's go take a turn around the yard."

The quietness of the room wrapped itself around Misty as the two went out on the porch. She leaned over the bed. "Dillon," she whispered, "Dillon, can you hear me? It's Misty."

She sat down and smoothed the bedspread as she watched the shallow breathing move the covers ever so slightly. Gently, she took his hand in hers. It was so light. Like a sleeping bird, she thought as she laid it down again.

After a moment she walked over to the window looking up at the sky dotted with fluffy puffs of clouds. "For the angels to sit on," Dillon had said once when all of the children had been lying on the grass watching another cream-puffed sky.

With an unwavering gaze Misty stared beyond the clouds trying to penetrate heaven itself. "Why?" For the second time that day she challenged God. This time her eyes searched the blue. "Why do You do this? I thought You were love. Why are You so cruel?"

Perhaps it was a breeze that had escaped unnoticed from the motionless trees that briefly touched Misty's face. Perhaps it was Someone who wanted to reassure her that He knew of the suffering and He was still there. So He touched her and with the touch was a feeling of peace. The girl stood with her eyes closed as the tension left her body. Then she turned back to the bed. Nothing had changed.

"Thank you." Misty looked up. She had not heard the returning footsteps. "Dillon would be happy to know you stayed with him," said Cindy softly. She smoothed the red hair with one hand.

Del touched Cindy's arm. "We have to go now. If you need any of us, call, will you? I have to go back Sunday morning, but I'll try to see you and Dillon again before I leave." He leaned over the boy and took one of the cold hands in his big warm one, holding it briefly as if he would impart some of his own strength to the child.

Misty was glad Del said nothing as they drove away. But there was nothing to say. Matters of the world had no place with them now. She glanced at him once, then twice, noticing his jaw was set as he studied the sky and mountains in the distance. She was content to just sit quietly beside him.

The campgrounds were alive with activity. It was play time before the evening meal; a game of wheelchair bowling was in full swing. Those who could were playing their own version of badminton while several boys were throwing balls back and forth to one another.

"Pretty lively bunch," remarked Del.

"I guess," agreed Misty trying to bring herself back to the present. "It looks like they all had a good rest. Thanks for taking me with you."

She slid out of the jeep and stood by her bike while she watched Del park next to Karyl's pickup. It was nearly five so Karyl was, of course, waiting for him. Karyl, her cousin—and the thought was a strange one—was in her office where she and Del could be alone. Misty sucked in her breath and caught her lower lip between her teeth. Well, that took care of her talking to Karyl and telling her all, as she had planned. She would come back down to the camp after supper and talk to her then.

"Have they found her yet?" Sadie's strong voice came through the trees to Misty. The woman was standing on the porch of the main building calling to Doris who was coming from behind the barrack.

"Not yet," called the exasperated nurse. "We've looked everywhere."

Misty cupped her hands around her mouth and called to Sadie, "Who are you looking for?"

"That rascal Jenny," Sadie called back. "She just bounced off somewhere on her three legs and no one can find her."

"I'll ride around the grounds and see if I can." Misty jumped on her bike and started off, the wheels making a crunchy sound in the dry dirt.

It was after she had circled behind the rose garden and the dining hall that she headed toward the lake. She remembered Jenny asking, "Can we be ducks tomorrow?" Perhaps she was down there now watching the little feathered creatures.

As Misty rounded the curve from the dining hall, she saw the child. Jenny, ignoring all warnings, had crawled under the ropes that marked the area as out of bounds. Somehow she had gotten herself into the boat that was tied to the unfinished dock.

"Don't let her get on the dock, please," said Misty to herself as she rode fast. "Why, oh why didn't I remind her to stay away from the lake?" But even as she spoke, Misty saw the chubby little figure dressed in shorts and T-shirt crawl on to the loose boards. Expertly, she hopped to the end of one and leaned over. A single mallard drake paddled from under the boards.

After a breathless minute Jenny stood upright. Frantically, she balanced on her one leg waving her crutches wildly in the air. Then the unsupported board began to go down under her weight until, with a scream, she felt the water close around her.

By the time the child had rolled over, Misty was beside her. "You're all right, Jenny," she told the sputtering girl. "The water isn't that deep. You could stand up, if you tried. Hang on and I'll get you out." Misty reached for a tree branch to pull herself and Jenny up on the bank, but the branch slipped out of her grasp, and she fell back into the water. Jenny, arms wrapped around Misty's neck, gave a piercing scream.

"Here, give me your hand." Del had driven to the lake when he saw what was happening.

Gratefully, Misty let Del pull her and the crying Jenny to firm ground. "She wanted to be a duck, I guess." Misty pushed the wet hair out of her eyes. "I don't think she'll try it again."

Misty's clinging clothes dripped into little puddles. "You're soaked," said Del needlessly.

"Sort of," agreed Misty.

"I'll take you to your house after we take Jenny back."

Self-conscious, Misty shook her head. "Just take Jenny. I'll be all right. I'll ride my bike. Besides, Karyl's waiting," and she glanced towards where Karyl stood watching.

"If that's what you want. Come on, Jenny, let's go." Del opened the jeep door and lifted the child in speaking gruffly to her. "Now why did you want to go fall into the lake?"

Misty stood where Del left her, still dripping. She saw the jeep stop, and she saw Del lift Jenny out. She saw Karyl running to the two of them and then stand beside Del. A pang of intense longing went through Misty.

Roy's little blue Volkswagon, on its way out of the camp, slowed to an almost stop at the sight of the bedraggled figure with her bike. He sounded the car's horn, but if Misty heard, she paid no attention. The little car went on its way.

"And she's my cousin," Misty muttered under her breath. "Well, I'm leaving tomorrow even if I don't get to talk to her." She set her lips in a firm line and began to pedal down the road, her shoes making little squishy sounds.

SEVENTEEN

After Misty changed her wet clothes, she went out to the garden to pick lettuce for her supper. The leaf she tasted was bitter, so she dropped the handful she held then pulled a few more stunted carrots. She knelt down staring at the drooping plants. They had started out so bravely; now they were dry and neglected. When she had planted the seeds, life was an exciting adventure, and she hadn't even met Dillon. Now he was dying.

Drawing up her knees, she rested her forehead on them and shut her eyes. What's it like to die? she wondered. Is it really just like going to sleep? Everyone has to some time. And only once. There's no second chance. Do you have to wait until you get to the end of the line and look back at all of your mistakes knowing you can't do a thing about them?

She sifted some dirt through her fingers while her thoughts went back to her home and early spring. George Hunter died, she thought of the old gentleman, so active in their church, had he made many mistakes? He'd done so much good, he must be in heaven. And Maria—I doubt all of that gobbledygook got her anywhere. But Dillon—he's too young to have made mistakes. He said he would be in heaven with Jesus. And he's not afraid.

She opened her eyes then but still sat letting the sifting dirt make a little pile over an ant hole. It would, Misty admitted while she watched an ant tunnel out and begin the work of reconstruction, be good to go to Denver—to be in a luxurious hotel, soak in a hot bubbly bath that didn't smell of rusty pipes, and dress in her three-tiered dress and high heels. The climax would be to meet Flora Nasby. Would she dare ask the artist about the paintings of hers she had seen, especially the portrait of Martha Cross?

I'll stay in Denver only a few days, Misty decided. No need to stay longer, no research on the Wades is necessary now. She reflected again on the turn of events, on her relationship with Karyl. And Karyl has a sister so I have another cousin. I suppose I'll meet her in time, Misty thought. No one seems too concerned about her, so why should I be?

Yes, Misty knew she would go home. She had found out enough about herself—she could do other things, she could get along on her own personality without the crutch of society. I do, she admitted to herself, still have a hollow longing deep down inside, but maybe I won't fill it here after all. I'm ready to call it quits. To be in my apartment again with all of its comforts, to be back at the office with my computer, and with my dad close by, it wild really be great. I'll leave Angelo a note on the door.

Will it be good to be back with Lance? In his letters he says he is still waiting. Jan has seen him with the senator's daughter several times, but that's all right. My thoughts have been wandering too, but I'll forget Del. Well, maybe not forget—just tuck the memory of him away. Can I marry Lance, move into that spacious house with an Oriental rug, and have children? I still don't know.

The sun was touching the tops of the trees when she finally stood. She walked to the animal pen and put her hand on the deer who came to meet her. Slowly she opened the gate so as not to frighten him. Giving him a slight push toward freedom she said, "You can go back to the woods now. Go, fellow, the world is yours." She watched him disappear then went into the cabin and fixed a sandwich.

She would, she decided, go to the camp a bit earlier in the morning than usual and tell Karyl everything. Well, almost everything—she would not tell her of their relationship, not yet. That would come in time. But she would tell her who she was professionally, tell her she was leaving and ask if she could borrow the truck.

The box with the dress caught her eye. Blue dotted swiss! She had almost laughed when Sadie offered it to her and she smiled now. Her mother might have worn the dress of cotton flocked with blue dots when she was a high school freshman going to her first prom.

Curious, she took the dress from between the folds of tissue paper and held it against herself. Sadie's Ruthie probably had worn it in a theatre production. Intrigued, she pulled off her jeans and shirt and felt the satin lining cool against her skin as the dress slipped over her head. She coaxed the zipper up as far as she could reach then stretched her arms to feel the dress's perfect fit. The heart-shaped neckline edged with a fine white lace showed off the whiteness of her throat; little velvet bows held tucks that shaped the sleeveless bodice.

She kicked off her sneakers and began to twirl. The full skirt flared out, the white lace edging making a hoop around her slender legs. Her pony tail fell partially loose with the motion and little tendrils of her still-damp hair escaped, framing her face. She twirled once more then stopped. The sun was dipping behind the trees except for one flagging ray that came through the open door and rested on the girl as she stood there smoothing the dress over her hips. It was a simple unsophisticated dress, quite unlike anything she had ever worn. Lance would not have approved, but he would never see it.

Her thoughts were on nothing more definite than her twirling when she heard the motor of the old blue pickup jolting up the hill and into the clearing. With a gasp she pressed both hands against her face then breathed, "Oh, no! Not him!" She backed away from the door, but not before Angelo saw her.

The spell was broken. Misty locked the door against the summer evening and once again put the chair under the knob. With almost a single motion she pulled on her jeans, slipped the dress off and reached for her shirt. Her hands trembled and she was cold.

The girl remained motionless a few minutes listening. She heard the truck struggle on up the hill, passing her cabin by. Then hearing nothing she opened the door a crack and called softly, "Kitten-cat, where are you?" But instead of the little black kitten there was the deer standing on the porch. "Sorrowful, you're free. Go!" The animal stood with one foot raised. "Go! Scoot!" She gave the fawn a little push and with a bound he was gone, disappearing into the shadows of the trees. "Bye," she called softly. "Take care."

※❦※

Misty awakened from a troubled sleep even before the sun was completely above the horizon. She stirred and stretched then remembered the evening before. But nothing had happened during the night. There had been no knocking, no one calling her name. Nothing. Now it was today, and she was going to Denver, then home to Syracuse.

As she once more went over every step of what she intended to do, the sound she had been subconsciously listening for and dreading even in her sleep came through the trees. Some things that are frightening in the dark never seem so bad in the daylight, but this sound, so completely associated with Angelo, had come to be monstrous even on a summer morning. Every muscle in the girl's body tensed and she held her breath. But the truck went on down the hill. "Oh, thank you," she whispered. "I will never, never, never have to hear that again," she added.

There was time to have a small breakfast before she went to the camp. She would ride her bike as usual then put it in the truck when she drove back to the cabin to get her suitcases. It was too early for Karyl to be at the camp, but Misty was eager to get started. She would wait for Karyl who would listen to her story then let her borrow the truck. It was all very simple. "Just don't let me see Del," she said out loud. It would be easier that way.

She could not help but notice that the smoky film edging the western horizon was darker than it had been yesterday. The prescribed fire that had been smogging the air had burned itself out, or so Roy had said. If so, this haze was something new. Another fire? She stopped once and sniffed the morning breeze that should have been fragrant and fresh but wasn't. Then she hurried on to begin her day.

The truck stood outside the kitchen just where it had been the day before. But of course. Karyl had ridden with Del in the jeep the evening before. Or with Fred which she often did. No need for her to drive the truck home. Misty could hear breakfast sounds in the kitchen; voices were floating out of the barrack windows. Soon the quiet lawn would be alive with the children coming to devour Sadie's cinnamon toast and hot oatmeal and cocoa.

"Sadie?" Misty called through the door, "is Karyl here yet?"

"Not yet," answered Sadie.

"I want to be sure and catch her the minute she gets here." Misty gave no further explanation.

She sat on the steps of the porch watching for the jeep. Where was Karyl anyway? While she waited, Misty went over and over in her mind what she would say; what would Karyl's reaction be? Ten minutes then fifteen passed before she finally saw a car coming. As it got close, she recognized Roy's Volkswagon. He had Drew with him, but where were the others? The unaccustomed tension made the girl both disturbed and irritated.

"Hi, Misty," Roy called out before the car stopped.

"Where is everybody?" she demanded as she stood and walked toward the car. "Where's Karyl?"

"I think Karyl and Fred are with Cindy. Fred said they'd be here by noon. And Del has a meeting with his supervisor."

Misty watched Roy get his tools out of the car. "Do you suppose anyone would mind if I borrowed the truck for a while?" She could, she decided, get it loaded then talk to Karyl.

"I'm sure no one would mind." Roy turned from unloading the car. "There's only one problem."

"Which is?"

"It's not running. Something's gone haywire with the electrical system and won't be fixed for a day or two. They had to send away for a part. You can borrow my car, if that'll help."

Misty looked at the small VW that was loaded with still more tools and boxes. "Thanks, but—that's OK. I've got quite a few things I want to take to town."

"Del will be glad to help out when he gets here, but that probably won't be until this afternoon."

"I'll manage," Misty said crisply and walked to the kitchen.

She would manage, but how? Ideas tumbled in her mind as she helped Sadie. "I'll call Lillian Watson. She can get hold of Steve for me, and maybe he can come to the cabin and pick me up. There's got to be a way," she muttered to herself.

It wasn't until after the oatmeal was dished up and children seated, that Misty had a chance to phone. "Could you have Steve call me when he gets in?" Misty asked Lillian. It would be so much better to ask him herself. He had taken her to the cabin that first day; surely he would be willing to pick her up now.

Watching the clock and knowing when Steve would be arriving from Frisco, Misty listened for the telelphone while forcing herself to go through the same routine as all of the other days. Why, oh why couldn't everything have worked out as easily as she thought it would? The truck not working! It had worked perfectly every other time she used it! Why not now? If Steve didn't call, she would miss the reception for Flora Nasby. On the other hand, if she was going to have to stay at the camp, she could have at least one more story to write. The dedication could be a fitting ending for her series. And if Denison Elbert should come to the dedication, she would have one more chance to discuss that painting of his in Lewis's office. But deep down inside Misty knew she could not face going to the dedication, story or no story.

The day soon swallowed Misty in its activities. The myriad flowers and plants that transformed the dining hall into an indoor garden would take anyone's mind off her worries. Misty arranged and re-arranged the flowers until the last vase of salmon-colored gladioli was in place and Sadie rang the lunch bell. Even the children were subdued by the unusual floral splendor. They ate quietly, anticipating the evening when their parents and friends would be there and a man called "the mayor." Pastor and Mrs. Rubeck were sure to come, too.

"Are you going to wear a dress?" Jenny took a bite from her sandwich as she watched Misty feed Jeremy.

"A dress?" Misty smiled as she wiped the little boy's chin. "Do you think I should?"

"Yes," grinned Jenny. "You'd look pretty in a dress."

"Are there going to be streamers in here?" another small voice asked.

"Uh huh. Streamers and balloons."

"Who's going to put them up?"

"I am as soon as you chicks are fed," Misty replied.

Jenny giggled. "Chicks. We're not chicks."

"I am. I'm Old Lady," and Michael began blowing into his milk.

"Michael, no! Eat nicely, and then you're off to bed." Peg came over to help.

"No story?" asked Jenny.

"Not from Misty," said Peg. "She's got other things to do today and you need extra rest. Maybe Doris will tell you a short one after you're ready for your nap."

Misty watched the last child leave the dining hall. She saw Karyl and Fred come in, but it was much too late now. Steve had not called, and now he was surely gone to pick up his customers.

The gray line along the horizon had shifted and grown rapidly into a wide cummerbund girding the sky, but Misty hardly noticed; she was too torn between wanting to take part in the evening's activities and her determination not to. The children's excitement was contagious, but Misty, knowing Karyl was going to ask her to leave and knowing why, reassured herself she wasn't really wanted.

"Maybe I'll come down later and just peek in," she promised herself.

Karyl picked her way through the clutter of the decorations. "I wonder what's keeping Del."

Misty said nothing. It was hard to face Karyl now, almost too hard to speak.

"I'm rather concerned. See that haze over there?" and Karyl pointed towards the gray horizon. "That's Del's area. I'm sure it's another fire and it's out of bounds."

"I hope it's not serious." Misty knew her words sounded empty. A forest fire was always serious. She remembered all too well the roar in the canyon, the falling black pine needles and the smoke. Sometimes she relived that horror in her dreams. And that fire had been controlled. Karyl thought this one was out of bounds. If it was, and in Del's area, he would probably have to go.

Misty looked at Karyl's tired, pale face and thought, "She really is concerned. There's Dillon and now this. Maybe she's got about all she can handle."

Out loud she said, "Everything's going to be all right, Karyl. Don't worry," and she forced a smile. "You don't want to spoil this evening."

"Oh, I'm not worried. The fire, Del, this evening—everything's in God's hands so I've nothing to worry about. But look what time it's getting to be! There's still much to do. Del will be here any minute. I think instead of helping with supper tonight, you should finish putting up the balloons in the entryway. Is that all right with you?"

"Sure. I'll be glad to. Roy can fill them then float them up to me, and I'll tie them in place. Roy! I need you!" she called.

Misty was on the top rung of the ladder waiting when Roy came and grinned up at her. "For someone who needs me you're kind of out of reach 'way up there," he said lightly.

"Guess this is a good place to be then," countered Misty. "I'm waiting. Fill one and send it up, will you?"

"Catch!" and Roy floated a balloon up to her. And then another and another. Never taking his eyes off the girl, he watched her quick graceful movements as she tied the balloons into rainbow clusters.

"Hey, O'Brien!" It was Drew calling.

"In here," answered Roy. "Gotta go," he called to Misty. "Here's one more." And a bright yellow balloon floated up to the top of the ladder.

"Thanks for your help." The words were scarcely out of her mouth when Misty heard the jeep stop under the trees. She heard Del's step on the porch, but she busied herself making sure the balloons were tied securely.

"Look at this place, will you? It looks great!"

"Karyl's been wondering about you," said Misty without looking down.

"I've been longer than I thought I'd be. We flew over to take a look at the fire that just broke out."

"Is it out of bounds?" Now Misty looked into Del's upturned face.

"Afraid so, but it's not big yet. A small crew is going in to hem it in."

Del reached over and held the ladder as Misty came down. He took her by the elbow and helped her the last few steps. She felt the warmth of his hand on her arm and smiled inwardly as she thought how many times she had run up and down that ladder with no assistance.

"Where is Karyl?"

"In her office, I think." Misty started to carry the ladder, but Del took it from her as he went out.

"Of course he wants *her*," thought Misty with a twinge of jealousy as she watched him go into the office and close the door. She gave a few finishing touches to the room then went through the dining area to see the children while on her way to check with Sadie.

"The punch is in this, Misty." Sadie was lifting a huge kettle from the cupboard. "It'll be in the refrigerator. Help yourself to some supper and then you'd better go so you can be back in time. It's five-thirty and the doings begin at seven-thirty."

Sadie put the kettle of punch in the refrigerator then turned to the stove. "Sit down and I'll dish up some supper for you. You've worked hard all day. You must be tired. Things like this take more energy than a normal day." She set a plate of food in front of Misty as she clucked over her. "Have you tried on the dress?"

"Mm-yes, I tried it on. It fits perfectly. It's so pretty, I don't like to wear it. Something might happen to it."

"Pshaw, nothing's going to happen to it. Ruthie wore it once for a costume, it's nothing special. Now you wear it and enjoy it. You know you've done a lovely job with the decorating around here. It's perfectly beautiful. But I mustn't keep talking or you won't eat, and you've got to run along and get dressed."

"What about you?" asked Misty between bites.

"I'll get there. Don't worry about me. There's a lot of me, but it doesn't take long to dress it. Want some more?"

"No, thanks. Like you say, I haven't much time. I'd better go. Thanks, Sadie."

What would she say if I told her I'm not coming tonight? wondered Misty as she headed away from the camp. They'll get along without me.

She pedaled slowly up the hill. If the truck were running, she'd be in it on her way. No, if the truck were running, she'd be in Denver by now getting ready to go to Flora Nasby's reception.

When she came to the rock where she sat when she first saw Del, she paused and looked back. Although it was not dark yet, the garden lights were on, flickering like so many fireflies through the trees. "I will not go!" she said firmly. "They will wonder where I am—at least Sadie will, but I just cannot go."

She searched the sky where the evening star was already shining. "I wish it would rain!"

It was lonely in the clearing without the deer. Misty stared at the pen then walked a few steps into the woods where she had seen the animal disappear. "Sorrowful?" she called. "Sorrowful, are you in here?"

Hearing the crackle of the dry brush, she stood stock-still. The brown body blended with the trees, so at first she didn't see the deer, but the flick of his flag of a tail gave him away. The quizzical little face seemed to be smiling at her from under an aspen tree.

The animal nuzzled Misty while she put her arms around him. "You stayed! I wish you could talk!" She buried her face in the deer's neck. "You don't have any problems. You're free to go, you know."

The deer trotted beside her as she headed back to the cabin. He went into the pen and sniffed the feed trough.

"No! I won't feed you. You've got to go and learn to take care of yourself. Everything fell apart for me today, but in a day or so I really will be gone, and then you'll be on your own for sure."

She opened the cabin door reluctantly, not noticing the note she had left for Angelo was gone. The bulging suitcases lay where she had left them, mute reminders of her broken plans. Every bit of hominess seemed stripped away from the cabin.

Misty sat on the edge of her bed and looked at her clock. Six thirty. Another hour and it would be time for the service in the chapel to begin. She thought of the children excited and waiting. She thought of Karyl. "I'm counting on you," she had said. She thought of Sadie. "The punch is in here." She thought of Del.

Her hand went to the box where the dress lay in its tissue paper. Then she had another thought, a thought that made her smile a sad little smile. "I couldn't go even if I wanted to. I've no way to get there. No way can I ride my bike in this dress or even walk. I can't carry it on my bike, and I'm not about to walk down and dress there."

The snapping of a branch caused her to look towards the door. "Sorrowful?" she called opening the door and stepping on to the porch.

"Misty?" came the answer.

The big man came out from under the trees. As always he was dressed in bib overalls over a flannel shirt. Only the red felt hat was missing. His hair hung full over his shoulders, but its beauty did not impress Misty this time.

"How long have you been there?" she asked angrily.

"Not very long. I've been away, but I came back to get you. You've changed your mind by now, haven't you? I've given you time like Mama said I should. I've been watching you. You didn't leave today like you said you were going to. You're still here in my cabin. That's a sign you want to stay." He began walking towards Misty.

Misty began to perspire. There was no time to go back into the cabin and lock the door, he was too close. "Uh, Angelo, you're—you're tired and hot. Why don't you sit on the steps and rest?" Hoping to appear casual in spite of the cold dread that was possessing her, Misty stepped off the porch and began to walk in a wide arc around the man.

Her eyes darted around the clearing measuring the distance to the road. She would run down the hill towards the camp, if she could get around him.

He stepped closer. If he was smiling, the smile was lost in his beard. His black eyes under their bushy brows were steely and intent. They never wavered from the girl.

"Angelo," Misty forced her quavering voice to stay even as she inched towards the road. "What would Mama say?" Oh, help! she cried inwardly. Somebody help, please! He's getting closer.

"Mama said I should keep trying. She wanted me to have you for my wife. She will be pleased."

Angelo seized Misty, but she resisted him with all her might. She grabbed a tree branch, but he pulled her loose from it and dragged her toward the cabin. Her feet made grooves in the hard-packed earth.

"Let me go! Turn loose of me! Let me go!" She hit him with her free fist then bent to sink her teeth into his grasping hand.

The sound of a motor drowned her cries. Angelo's face, dripping with perspiration, turned purple as the jeep came into sight. With an oath he dropped Misty and stumbled out of sight.

Misty stood in shock, rubbing her smarting arm.

"Misty! Are you all right?" Del jumped out of the jeep even before the motor had quit running. "Did he hurt you?" He looked intently at the girl for a moment then added, "You're shaking. Can I get you something?" He wanted to hold her, to comfort her.

Misty shook her head. "I'm OK," she managed to choke out.

"We wondered where you were. Karyl sent me to see if you need a ride, but maybe you need to rest instead."

Misty brushed the tears off her cheeks as she shook her head. "I'm OK, really. But I'm not going. I wasn't planning on it. Besides, I've no way to get there in a dress." Another stray tear rolled down her cheek.

"I've come to get you," he explained patiently. "Unless you'd rather stay here with him." And he nodded his head in the direction Angelo had gone.

"Stay with him? Are you kidding? But I'm not going with you." Misty did not seem to be able to move.

"I can see you're not ready. Are you sure you're all right?"

"I'm sure. But I'm not go—oh, I'll hurry." Misty, her resolve completely melted, started for the cabin then paused. "Del, thanks for coming when you did."

"You're sure he didn't hurt you?"

"I'm sure." The girl smiled wanly. "Uh—will you come in?"

"I'll wait out here, thanks."

"I'll hurry."

Del looked around cautiously. He walked across the small clearing, and as he approached the shadow where Angelo was hiding, the big man turned and walked heavily on up the hill toward his old house. "I tried, Mama," he muttered to himself, "but it's no use. Please don't be angry with me." Without going into the house the man got into his truck and started back down the hill.

Hearing the pickup coming, Del stood in the road forcing the glowering Angelo to stop.

"You stay away from that woman." The words burned on Del's tongue, but he only stared at Angelo who stared back. It was a full minute before the heavy man with the long black hair spat in the dust, gunned the old pickup, and fairly sailed down the hill.

❧❧

Misty washed quickly. She bathed her face over and over with cold water and then let her hands rest in hot water to ease the tension out of herself. She was still trembling when she slipped the dress over her head. "Oh, this thing!" she said in exasperation as she tried to close the full-length zipper reaching first over her shoulder then trying to stretch her arm up her back.

Leaving the zipper partly undone, she fixed her hair. There was no time for anything fancy so she brushed it quickly and let it hang loose and shiny.

Slipping on her sandals, she stood in the open doorway. "I'm ready."

"You look—beautiful." Del appraised her from head to toe.

Misty flushed. "Thank you," she said softly. "I'm ready," she reminded him.

"Um—yes, sure. Yes. We'd better go. It is late and I'm supposed to introduce the mayor from Frisco who's probably wondering where I am." Del gave his deep chuckle.

He stood to one side to let Misty go first. "Just a minute. Your zipper. It's not all the way up."

Misty reached over her shoulder. "I know. I can't reach it. I'll ask Sadie."

"I'll zip it," and Del quickly closed the gap in her dress. He put his hands on her shoulders and turned her around to face him. Putting his hand under her chin, he tipped her face up to his. "You're lovely, Misty."

Misty looked deep into the quiet, brown eyes for a long second. Then she stiffened and turned away. "Karyl is waiting," she said coldly.

"What's that got to do with it?" Del caught her arm.

"Everything. You said it was getting late." She pulled her arm free and walked to the jeep.

They rode in silence. It was Del who spoke first. "I was tempted to kick that big guy all the way to Denver. Would you have minded?"

"Minded? Why in the world should I mind? I'd be glad! He's been up at the mine. I didn't know he was anywhere near until just now. He would have hurt me, if you hadn't come along."

Del stole a glance at her silhouette. She was sitting straight and looking directly in front of her. The jeep slowed down.

"You didn't know he was anywhere near?"

"I knew he was gone last week, his house was empty. And you know what we saw—his furniture at the mine. It's a relief to know he's not living in that place up the hill. But he came back—to get me."

"You would've been glad if I'd run him off? You'd be relieved?"

"Of course! How can you ask such a question? Can't you see what he's like?"

"How come you're engaged to him then?"

"Engaged? to Angelo? Me? Karyl thinks I'm involved with him and his crazy religion, and you think I'm engaged to him. Great! Just great!

Whatever gave you that idea?" She studied Del's profile in the twilight.

"He told me his intentions of marrying you the day I brought the fawn to you. I should've known better!"

The jeep stopped and Del put his arm across the back of the seat.

Misty drew herself up straighter yet as she said coldly, "Karyl's waiting."

"That's all right. Karyl's used to waiting for me."

A lump took its place in Misty's stomach. Karyl was used to waiting for him? He always smiled at other women the way he was smiling at her, and Karyl waited for him? She could not have heard correctly.

"She's been taking care of me for years," Del was saying. "You see, my mother died when I was ten and I moved in with Karyl's family. She was fourteen at the time so she's had to look out for me for a long time—she and Theba. And that's involved a lot of waiting."

Misty turned toward him. "Theba? Did you say Theba?"

"Yes, Theba. Her sister. She's pretty much out of touch with the family right now—lives in the east. But she and Karyl took care of me when I was a little guy. Someday I hope I can let her know how much she's meant to me."

Misty struggled to bring her voice under control, to sound casual. "You've lived with her—Karyl and—and Theba—most of your life?"

"Eighteen years, to be exact. Aunt Martha was like my own mother."

"'Aunt Martha'? Karyl's—and Theba's mother?"

"That's right."

"Then—Karyl is—your—cousin?"

"They both are. Who did you think Karyl was?"

"Karyl's engaged to—I thought she was engaged to *you*. You've been talking about the wedding. Yesterday in the chapel I was there and I heard—"

Del tipped his head back and laughed the laugh Misty loved to hear. Then he stopped and looked at her. "You goose," he said softly. "You silly goose. I wish it was lighter so I could really see the expression on your face! Karyl is engaged to Fred! Didn't anyone tell you? How come you didn't know? They aren't very demonstrative, I'll admit, but I would have thought you'd have guessed."

He studied the girl's shadowy face in the soft evening light then took both of her hands in one of his. "Misty," he said quietly, "I have to leave tomorrow, but I'll be back as soon as I can. Probably in three weeks, maybe two. I'd like to know you will still be here. I'd like to think that you're waiting for me to come back and we can go on from here."

Misty felt the warmth of his hand on hers, but she said nothing. She did not trust herself to speak. Taking her silence for "yes" Del cupped his hands around her face and kissed her gently with a wanting kiss. He laughed as he released her and said, "Karyl's waiting." And he drove the jeep on down the hill.

EIGHTEEN

The chapel was full when Del and Misty walked through the door. Others were already on the platform. The soft organ music accompanied the flickering candlelight shadows dancing on the walls while the muted song of the crickets drifted through the open windows.

"I have to go up on the platform with Karyl," Del whispered as he let go of Misty's hand. "You sit up front so I can see you."

Misty slipped into a pew beside Sadie and smiled. The white-haired lady patted Misty's arm, and Karyl, who had watched Misty and Del walk down the aisle hand in hand, raised her eyebrows ever so slightly as she smiled.

Roy did not smile. The young man whose auburn hair shone like burnished copper in the dim light looked at the vision in blue dotted swiss and swallowed hard to rid himself of the lump in his throat. After all, he and Misty would be going their separate ways soon—he didn't have much time left.

When the organ stopped playing, the chapel seemed as quiet as it had been when Misty was in it alone arranging the plants. Except for the crickets that continued to sing. Everyone looked at Del expectantly as he walked to the pulpit to introduce a short, round, baldheaded man whom Misty had never seen before. Her first thought was that the man looked ridiculously out of place beside tall, slender Del. His short stature rising not very high above the ferns on either side of him reminded her of a sawed-off stump growing out of the green, woodsy floor. His loose-fitting brown suit, wrinkled from the heat, was the bark in the process of peeling off.

The man, his bald head shining brightly in the rays from the light over the pulpit, cleared his throat twice and Misty forced herself to listen. "Ladies and gentlemen," he began, "it is indeed my pleasure as mayor of Frisco to take part in this dedication of Martha's Camp, a camp that serves an area within a radius of one hundred miles."

Misty's attention wavered when she felt drawn to look past the mayor at Del who sat next to Karyl. His eyes met hers and a warm flush spread over her neck and face. They would have some time together tomorrow before he had to leave. He would come for her early in the morning, and they would have until two o'clock to get acquainted. He had said he had much to tell her about himself, and she would tell him who she was. She would tell him about her column "Sketches" and that Karyl was her cousin. Not a first cousin, but still a cousin.

Misty sat bolt upright in her chair as if she had been stung. Sadie looked at the girl whose face was suddenly drained of all color, and she patted her arm again. It had been a long, hard day and it was hot.

Misty's eyes were riveted on Del. He's her cousin, too, she thought. She ran her tongue around her suddenly dry lips. Then he and I—maybe we're cousins. Oh, dear God, don't let it be!

She sank back in her seat and closed her eyes until she had control of herself, then with an effort she looked back at the mayor who had finished speaking. It was Pastor Rubeck who was saying, "Let us pray." So Misty bowed her head, glad for the escape. But instead of closing her eyes, she studied her hands. Why this? Why? She thought of all that had taken place in the past hour. She allowed herself to think of Angelo and then of how Del had been sure she was engaged to that man. The image of the long, black hair hanging over the shoulders, the beard so close to her face and the black eyes burning under the bushy brows passed in front of her, and she shuddered.

She stole a look at the ranger through veiled eyes. He was leaning forward, his elbows on his knees with his face buried in his hands, and Misty knew he was praying. When the prayer was over, he would smile down at her again, and she would summon all of her will power to avoid his eyes. For both their sakes she must discourage him until she knew.

She returned to the prayer and closed her eyes trying hard to listen. The pastor was asking for the Lord to bless the camp and to grant continued wisdom to those who were directing and carrying on its activities. Then he said "Amen."

Karyl, in a pale green cotton dress, walked gracefully to the podium. Poised and confident, she began to give a few words of welcome and to talk about her mother's life-long dream. But Misty did not hear.

When Del stood up to present the rest of the camp staff, Misty's heart beat rapidly, but she stared at the back of the head in front of her and did not look up when he mentioned Fred, tall and handsome in his white jacket and dark trousers. Nor did she look when Del mentioned Roy and Drew or the nurses, Peg and Doris.

When Del said, "Our beloved cook, Sadie McQueen," Misty glanced at the woman beside her and saw that she was blushing. But Sadie held herself tall and erect as she took her place on the platform beside Peg and Doris. Her face framed by the white Puritan collar of the lavender dress and her own white hair, the matronly woman was pretty as any picture.

"And last, but by no means least, is our Jill-of-all-trades," Del was saying. "If a cupboard needs painting, she does it. If an errand to town is necessary, she goes willingly. If an extra hand is needed to soothe or dress or feed a child, she is there. She has been Karyl's right hand assistant, Fred's partner, Roy's apprentice and Sadie's kitchen crew from the beginning. And she has endeared herself to the children with her ability to tell stories and help them forget for a time each day the harsh realities of their lives. I'm pleased to introduce Misty Morrow."

Misty wanted to escape. Instead, she momentarily pressed the palms of her hands against her hot cheeks then stood reluctantly midst the applause. She had to look at Karyl who smiled encouragingly and at Del who beckoned her to come to the platform. Holding herself rigid she took her place beside him and the others. Del's sleeve brushed her arm, and she moved a step closer to Roy, at the same time directing a forced smile to the up-turned faces of the parents. What should have been a happy, fulfilling time, a fairy-tale ending to her experience in the mountains where she had proved herself to herself, was pure torture for Misty.

The organist began to play then and everyone, children and parents alike, began to sing. Misty could not help but listen to Del's bass and

Roy's fine tenor. She knew that she would never, never forget that song as long as she lived. "Fairest Lord Jesus, Ruler of all nature—"

Misty tried to follow Sadie to the dining room, but she was stopped by first one set of parents and then another, all eager to talk about their child and the camp. The children themselves pressed against her clamoring to get her attention, proud to show her to their parents and to show their affection for her. Finally freeing herself, she began to walk quickly when she heard a voice behind her. "There you are. May I get you some punch, Miss?" Roy slipped an arm through hers while he teased, "I do know you, don't I?"

"We've met," said Misty with something that resembled a smile, glad Roy was beside her. "I'd better get over to the punch bowl and help Sadie."

Roy dropped his arm and took Misty's hand loosely into his as they made their way through the crowd.

"Here, Sadie, I'll do that now." Misty gently pushed herself between the woman and the bowl.

"Do you know this lady?" Sadie asked Roy teasingly as she let Misty have her place. Then she said with enthusiasm, "You are gorgeous, absolutely gorgeous." And she turned away nodding her head and smiling to herself.

Roy stationed himself next to Misty and began handing out the cups of punch as she filled them. He saw Del come into the room and look anxiously around. Roy saw his friend's face light up suddenly; he watched Del begin to make his way across the room.

"I thought I'd lost you already," Del said when he got close enough for Misty to hear. "I see Roy's taking care of you for me. Thanks, fellow."

Misty looked down at the cup in her hand, but not before Roy caught the expression in her eyes. He glanced from Misty to Del then swallowed hard before he stammered, "Oh, I see someone I need to talk to. Here!" The punch in the cup he was holding sloshed over the sides as he put the cup in Del's hand.

But Misty put a restraining hand on Roy's arm while she smiled at him. "Don't go. I'm going to need some fresh air in a few minutes, it's so stifling in here. Del, why don't you take a cup of punch to Karyl? She looks like she could use one." The girl dared to look at the ranger then and saw his jaw was set in a firm, hard line.

More visiting with children and parents plus pouring endless cups of punch wore the evening away. When the last car had driven out of the camp yard, Misty stood on the porch with Roy and saw Del talking seriously with Karyl and Fred. Pastor Rubeck was with them. A telephone jangled in the distance, and Drew called, "Del? Telephone."

"I must go help Sadie," Misty told Roy finally, and she went into the kitchen with Roy following. Sadie already was busying herself with the inevitable cleaning-up. Tying an immense white dish towel over her dress and making herself look smaller yet, Misty began helping with what had to be done.

She looked up when Karyl came into the kitchen with Fred beside her, but she did not smile.

"Dillon died this evening," said Karyl quietly.

"Dillon—died?" Misty stood still in the middle of the kitchen, her hands full of spoons.

"This evening," said Karyl again. "About an hour ago."

"Bless his dear heart," said Sadie. "Now he won't have to suffer any more."

"Fred and I are going to Cindy now." Karyl paused and looked at Misty, then she and Fred started to walk out.

Del put a restraining hand on his cousin's arm. "That was Dick on the phone. The fire's out of control and I have to go. Tell Cindy, will you? Tell her I'll come as soon as I can."

Karyl said nothing, but Fred gave Del an understanding clap on the shoulder. "Take care," he said and they were gone.

Misty began putting the spoons in the sink and felt rather than saw Del cross the kitchen to her side.

"The fire's spreading fast," he spoke as to a child who did not understand. "I have to go. I'm flying in with some smoke jumpers tonight."

"Shouldn't you wait until daylight?" Misty kept on putting the spoons away.

"There's plenty of light from the fire," replied Del. "I'm to be at the field in forty-five minutes. I'd like to take you home first, if I may."

"Go ahead, honey," encouraged Sadie. "I can handle what needs to be done. The rest can wait until morning."

"Roy can take me." Misty looked at Roy who was smashing paper plates into a garbage can.

"No." Del spoke with authority. "I will take you. We need to go right now."

Without another word Misty untied the towel from around herself and followed Del, not daring to look at Roy. Neither one spoke during the drive up the hill.

Whatever am I going to tell him? thought Misty as they rounded the curve to the cabin. He's got enough on his mind. She tried to imagine how he felt, what his thoughts were knowing he would soon be jumping into the fire. She stole a glance at the man and saw the same determined look.

He walked with her to the porch of the cabin. Scanning the clearing with a penetrating gaze, he listened intently for several moments. Then, putting his hand under her chin, he tipped her head back and searched her face in the dim light.

"I don't know what's happened, Misty, but something is bothering you. You get a good night's sleep and don't worry about it, whatever it is. Everything's going to be fine. You know, God can make all things happen for the good." He smiled at her then. "I'll be back as soon as I possibly can. This shouldn't take too long. Hopefully, we will have tomorrow to talk. You'll be OK."

"Del, there's something you should—" she began, but he placed a finger on her lips.

"Not now," he said. "Tomorrow." Then he kissed her gently on the forehead and walked away looking into the shadows as he went.

Misty took a step as if she would stop him, then she stood perfectly still and watched as he got into the jeep and turned back down the hill. She stood moments without moving, no longer watching where Del had gone, but watching the shadows of the trees. A branch crackled and she caught her breath. What was it? She looked intently into the dark shadows again. Only a deer. Was it? Only a deer?

She reached behind herself to the door and without turning, backed into the cabin. Closing the door quietly, she locked it, put the chair under the knob, and this time pulled the kitchen table up close as an added barrier. What if Angelo is out there? she asked herself. What if he saw Del leave and he knows I'm here alone? True, he left when Del came to get me, but he could have come back while we were at the camp. Oh, please, please don't let him be anywhere around!

Not daring to turn on the light, she felt her way around in the dark. Hanging the dress in the closet, she pulled on her shirt and jeans then stumbled to the kitchen. Feeling her way, she found the tea kettle, put some water in it, fumbled for the lone electric plate and put the kettle on. After three tries she found the jar of instant coffee, made a strong cup of the brew, then stood by the sink drinking it slowly while listening for any suspicious noise. Every rustle of a leaf, every scurrying of a mouse, every soft ping of a pine needle dropping on the roof was magnified a thousand times and added to her terror. She sipped the coffee slowly. There has been so much today, she thought, too much— Angelo, Del, the dedication, Dillon. I have been on an emotional roller coaster all day, and it isn't over. Too much. But I must not sleep. I am exhausted, but I must not sleep.Her eyes were accustomed now to the dark, so while she sipped, she wandered from window to window looking, watching.

Three cups of coffee and an hour later she crawled into bed, jeans and all, but she did not close her eyes. Staring at the ceiling, she re-lived the minutes when Angelo had tried to pull her into the cabin. She felt again his hand on her wrist, was again aware of his closeness to her and of his tremendous strength. The memory wrenched a sob from her. I know Angelo isn't going to give up; he may be out there now waiting until he is sure I am asleep. She kept staring into the dark. He may try to get in at any minute. Oh, Del, Del! Please hurry back! Why did you have to go so suddenly? But even if you hadn't gone to the fire, I would have had to come back and be here in this cabin all by myself. Or maybe you would have stayed and made sure I was safe. You would have camped outside and watched for that man, and everything would have been all right. But you left. If only I weren't alone. Why didn't I stay at the camp? Why didn't I tell Del how dangerous Angelo really is? Will morning ever come?

She thought of Roy. Del knew the possibility of Angelo coming back, so maybe he had asked his friend to come watch. Misty crawled out of bed and peeked again out the window hoping she would see Roy on the porch, or maybe see the camp truck parked under the trees. But there was nothing.

≈

Del was not one to be afraid. What lay before him was part of his work, something every ranger knows can happen. Each one of the five summers that he had been a ranger he had been engaged in a scrimmage with fires of different sizes. And he had been expecting tonight's alert. Any other time he would have almost anticipated the excitement, but this time he regretted having to go.

It was Misty. Something had happened during the evening; something was wrong. She did, he reminded himself, have something about herself to tell him. What could it be that made her change so suddenly? Surely it wasn't Roy. He pictured her standing alone on her porch of the cabin when he left her. The unwelcome image of Angelo crossed his mind so he said out loud, "Take care of her, Father."

He joined the other men already assembled at the field. His friend Smitty, round and bearish in his asbestos suit, was one of them. Quiet words of greeting were exchanged—no laughter, no joking. Only solemn anticipation of sharing a dangerous mission together.

Airborne, Del looked down at the lights twinkling below him. He could make out the camp nestled close to the hill where he knew Misty was. He prayed again, silently this time. "See us safely through this, Lord, and remember—take care of her." Then he looked at the fire that lay ahead.

While Misty stood sipping her strong coffee and listening, the small plane was skirting the acres of forest that had become an inferno. The firefighters who were already there could be seen on the south side. Some were chopping and cutting trees and brush. Others were digging trenches. All in a desperate effort to cheat the hungry flames.

"We'll go to the west of it," announced the pilot, "then you guys can jump."

To the west. Del looked beyond the fire to where Stillwater Springs lay. Beyond the springs was Saddle Stream separating his cabin from the fire. The winter cabin lay in a hollow protected by Saddle Stream and a smaller stream that forked surrounding the cabin on three sides. Just across the gulley was the old Jerose Mine.

It was while he was looking beyond the fire to where the cabins were safe that Del felt the suction of down draft rocking the plane. It jerked violently and bobbed like an uncontrolled boat on a stormy sea. At a signal from the pilot to eject, and without further thought, Del opened the door. He stood to one side making room for the other men to go before him. "Out!" he yelled. "Everybody out!"

With two crouching figures silhouetted in the doorway, the plane gave one more lurch before it was sucked into the midst of blazing trees.

❦

Misty could not return to her bed. She sat where she could see out the window. There was nobody, nothing outside for hours—nothing but darkness. Then suddenly she saw something. Yes, there was something—a pink line along the eastern horizon. Morning had come. And Del had said "Not now. Tomorrow." Tomorrow was today. He would be back soon, and she could tell him how long the night had been and how afraid she was.

Even in the faint light Misty could see the air was heavier with smoke than it had been; she could smell it inside the cabin. She fought a new fear, then shook herself. Del had said he'd be back soon. Why should she worry? She encouraged herself by remembering what Roy had said: the fire that had been coating the air with smoke was contained. The air would soon clear.

NINETEEN

The haze stung her eyes when Misty went to the camp at the usual time. She paused on the way and looked towards the mountains. Was Del still over there? No, he must be back by now, dirty and completely exhausted. Misty steeled herself for when she would see him.

Sadie was dishing up bowls of cereal when Misty walked into the kitchen. "Karyl wants to see you," the older woman said keeping her eyes on the bowl in her hand. "She's in the office."

The woman's voice did not have its usual lilt, and as Misty looked at Sadie, she could see her mouth was set in a firm, unsmiling line. Something more was wrong. When Misty walked into Karyl's office and saw Karyl standing by the window with Fred, her hands began to perspire.

"You wanted to see me?"

"Misty," Karyl searched the girl's face hoping to find something there that would help her say what she had to say. She spoke bluntly. "The plane crashed. Del and the pilot are missing."

It took Misty a second to grasp what Karyl was saying. "The plane? You mean Del's plane?"

Karyl nodded.

"It couldn't have crashed," protested Misty. "He said everything would be all right and he'd come right back."

"They crashed near the fire, Misty. Evidently a down draft," said Fred gently. "The other jumpers all got out. Del insisted on staying with Brian. He insisted on being the last one to jump, which was just like him. Then it was too late."

"How do you know?" Misty clutched the edge of Karyl's desk.

"I got word from his supervisor at four this morning," said Karyl softly. "The other jumpers all checked in. They can't find Del or Brian."

"They will," insisted Misty.

"The other men are sure both are lost."

Misty stared at first Karyl and then at Fred. She refused to believe what she was hearing. She shook her head. "No, they're wrong. Not Del. He said he'd be back."

She felt numb as she closed the door to Karyl's office. She wanted nothing more than to be alone, to be completely away from others.

"Hi, Misty." A little voice called to her from the dining hall.

Misty paused then forced herself to answer, "Hi, Jenny."

"Come here." Jenny motioned as she smiled a smile that was circled with toast crumbs.

Misty walked into the dining hall slowly. The plants that had made the room so festive the night before looked out of place in the morning light, as if they were making a desperate effort at keeping up a pretense. But the children were chattering happily, oblivious to the shadow that hung over the camp.

Misty stood beside Jenny. "I'm going home today. Mom and Daddy are coming to get me in one hour." The child held up one buttery finger.

Words were beyond Misty right now, so she smiled a thin smile.

"Come over here, Misty." It was Jeremy this time who beckoned and again Misty responded. From one to the other she went, allowing herself to be momentarily drawn away from her shell of pain into the circle of life these stricken children created.

❧❦

And so the morning ground away. When the children were gone and the camp was deserted except for a few of the staff, Misty turned her steps away from the buildings to the solitude of the lake. The afternoon sun filtered through the trees and cast shadows on her as she sat on a log that had been pushed back and half hidden from the casual eye among the bushes near the tumbling creek. She was back again to her pond and her meadow. She watched a heron light gracefully before her and wished dully that with the sweep of his wings the bird would clear away all that had happened, so she could truly be as she had been. In the midst of her numbness Misty wanted to go back to when she had first come to Pommel and to the hill. She wanted once again to be able to explore life, to be able to seek it without being stung by what she found.

Misty didn't hear Roy as he walked along the path that led around the lake on his way to inspect the work that was being done on the dock. It was when he straightened from kneeling on the boards that he saw Misty half hidden by the bushes. He did not call out with his usual greeting but walked slowly along the path until he came to her.

"Mind if I sit too?" he asked.

Misty said nothing but moved to make more room.

"It hurts, doesn't it," the man ventured gently. He did not look at Misty but at the horizon that could barely be seen through the haze. "He loved it over there. He would have rather died fighting for those mountains than anything. But he would have given his life for whatever he believed in."

"He didn't have a chance to fight," was her bitter reply.

"Nobody knows what happened after the others jumped. But we do know he was willing to take a risk so others could live. He was willing to stay behind so the other fellows could get out. They're over there searching now. Maybe—just maybe—" Roy's voice choked.

"We were in junior high when a fire broke out in the school." He went on after a few minutes. "The smoke was really pouring into our classroom. Del saw it first, and he had everyone marching in order while he came last making sure everyone was out." Roy gave a little laugh as he remembered. "He got a citation for that, but he never talked about it. That's just the way he was—others before himself."

"He loved animals," said Misty thinking of Sorrowful.

"You can say that again. He used to have three or four injured birds or cats or dogs in the backyard. He and Karyl's mother were a lot alike that way. She practically raised him, you know."

"He told me."

"Yes, he loved animals and beauty. And he was always painting pictures of what he saw. Art came to be his first love when he was about fourteen. He won a prize for the best painting of the mountains and that really motivated him. He studied art in college and then went to an art school for a couple of winters. He was planning on going to Paris to study this winter. You didn't have time to know Del, did you," probed Roy.

Misty was quiet, watching a duck paddling by. "I thought he was engaged to Karyl," she said after a moment, "and he thought I—well, he thought I was engaged to Angelo. But I'm not."

Roy looked at the profile beside him and noticed the crease between her eyebrows. "Karyl's his cousin."

Misty nodded. "I know. He told me."

"Did he tell you his real name? It's Denison Elbert. He's named after his grandfather. Karyl's mother coined the name 'Del' to tell them apart. His grandfather was an artist, you know."

At first Misty seemed not to hear, then Roy's words penetrated. She sat bolt upright. "He's Denison Elbert? He's the artist, the one who paints pictures of mountains and eagles and animals?"

"That's Del." Roy smiled. "He's been pretty secretive lately about his painting, ever since he had an exhibit in Denver. I think he sent a painting back east to enter a contest. In fact, I got the impression the director of a museum asked for it. There was to be a prize—something like $10,000. I don't believe he ever heard whether or not it was accepted. If he sent the painting I think he sent, it was the best thing he had ever done. If he'd won that prize, I'm sure he would have used it to go on to school. You see, he'd given most of his inheritance to Cindy to help with Dillon's expenses, and he had practically nothing left. He didn't know what was going to happen; he just kept saying it would work out. 'All things work together for good' was one of his favorite quotes."

Misty squeezed her hands together. "He is Denison Elbert!" she repeated as if in a dream. Then a belated ray of hope shone through. "You said he was named after his grandfather. Then Karyl's mother— was she really his aunt?"

"Only by marriage. Del's mother Nola was a sister of Karyl's father, Denny Cross. Nola Cross Quinn died when Del was about three." Roy looked at the girl beside him who had buried her face in her arms across her knees.

He wasn't my cousin after all. He wasn't my cousin. He wasn't, the thought went round and round like a broken record.

"It's rough," sympathized Roy. "But Del's safe, you know. He's in heaven."

"He's dead."

"Dillon and Del were pals. They're together now. Del died fearlessly; he wasn't afraid. Ever since I've known him, he has lived fearlessly because he wasn't afraid to die. It was the same with Dillon; he faced his sickness like a trooper."

Roy picked up a handful of small stones and tossed them into the water watching the rings they made spread out. "Those rings go on and on and blend into the lake just like our lives blend into eternity."

The two sat together united in their common grief. For one there was peace. For the other an intense longing. Misty, free now to love Del, allowed the pain of loss to seep through her. The words Roy had said, that Del could live because he wasn't afraid to die and he could die because he wasn't afraid to live, were the same words she had heard Fred say about the children who came to camp. Could she, Misty Morrow, weave all of that into her own life?

"What did you do before you came here?" Roy tossed more pebbles as he broke the silence that lay heavy between them.

"I work for a newspaper in Syracuse." Misty weighed her words carefully. Karyl should be the first one to know all she had to tell so she would say nothing more.

Roy watched a tear slip down the girl's cheek. "You loved Del, didn't you." Then after another moment, "I'm sorry. I wish I could help."

"He was your friend," said Misty responding to the warmth of the man beside her. "You miss him, too."

"A good friend for twenty years—ever since we came to know Jesus." Suddenly Roy stood. "This is no good, Misty, sitting here. Have you had anything to eat?"

"I'm not hungry."

"Sadie's gone so there's nothing here to eat. She looked for you after the kids were gone. I guess she thought she could help you through this. If anybody could, it would be Sadie. But nobody could find you. She finally went home since the camp's closed until Monday. I'd like to take you into town for a bite to eat. You're hungrier than you think. Come on." Roy held out his hand to the girl who took it without further protest.

It was late when they returned from town and finally stopped in front of the little cabin on the hill.

"You'll be OK?" Roy asked anxiously looking around the lonesome clearing.

"I'll be fine. I'm tired, so I know I'll sleep."

"Would you like to go to church in the morning?"

"No, no I think not. Thanks anyway. I want to be alone."

"Were you going to leave the other day when you wanted to use the truck?" Roy asked impulsively.

"Yes. I was going to go to Denver and then home. It was a pretty sudden decision. I was going to tell Karyl and ask—"

"You're still planning on leaving?" he interrupted.

"Maybe Tuesday. I'd like to wait until—until they're sure—but—"
She looked away from Roy.

"I know. I'm leaving Monday for the coast and I'd like to wait, too."

"You're leaving? Monday?"

"After Dillon's funeral. I have another job waiting in California. We have to go on living, you know. Cindy asked me to sing at the funeral." He paused and their minds met at the junction of pain: the little boy's funeral and Del.

"I'm sorry, Misty." Roy fought to control his voice. "I can't tell you how sorry. Believe me, I know how you're hurting."

Misty forced a smile, but her lips trembled. She started to put out her hand then let it drop to her side. She wanted, oh how she wanted to reach out to Roy and touch him, but she could not.

"You're sure you'll be all right?" He looked around the clearing again unconsciously putting off leaving, knowing this might be the last time they would have together.

"I'm sure. Thanks, Roy, for everything. You're a dear."

She watched him get into his car and gave a little wave before she turned and went inside.

The blue dress still hung where she had left it. She fingered it for a moment then quickly folded it, put it in the box and slid it under the bed.

Misty was tired—more tired than she had ever been, but sleep did not come easily. She lay staring into the dark trying to detach herself from all that had happened and knowing that she never could, that it would always be a part of her. Her thoughts went back to the evening before, and she relived every moment, the emotions she had experienced learning that Del was Karyl's cousin and knowing he might be hers, too, and that she would not be free to love him. And then learning the truth from Roy.

Roy. The two of them had said little while they sat in the small restaurant. Both were lost in their thoughts, willing to trade the present to erase the last twenty-four hours, if it would bring Del back. Both were feeling comfort in the other's company—finding relief in being silent and in the simple necessary act of eating.

It was Roy who broke the silence by telling her something about the work that was waiting for him on the coast. He watched Misty anxiously as he talked, but a nagging thought had begun drawing Misty's attention. She listened politely to what Roy was saying, and as he talked, she knew what she wanted to do. She wanted to go up to the mountains again before she went home. She wanted to see Del's cabin once more. She wanted to see where he had lived, to see his mountains and Saddle Stream one final time. Then she would be able to leave.

Picturing Del's cabin now that she was alone in the quiet dark, she folded her arms under her head on the pillow and made her plans.

Monday was Dillon's funeral. At eleven. She would leave for Stillwater Park right afterwards. Surely there would be no problem with borrowing the truck this time. It would be late when she got to the ranger cabin, but she would stay overnight, come back early Tuesday morning in time to have Steve take her to Frisco.

With her plans giving her comfort, Misty's tense body finally relaxed and sleep enfolded her. She slept the night through.

❦❧

Monday morning she pedaled down to the camp as if it were any other Monday. But it wasn't any other Monday. It was this Monday, the third day after and no word of triumph had come from the men searching on the mountainside. Even though this pall hung over her, the trees were the same, the grasses were the same. The sky, the lake with the ducks and swans—all the same as they had been. Why, she wondered vaguely, does life go on seemingly unchanged when a big hole has been unmercifully torn in my life? How can nature be so unperturbed, and how can it be business-as-usual over there in the little town when there is suffering so close by—Cindy in her bereavement and Fred and Karyl hurting, and me. Who is God, anyway, that there can be sunshine under one of His hands and darkness under the other?

She stood on the steps of the main building looking out over the grounds. By noon the lawns would again be alive with children, new children strange and afraid and homesick. She almost regretted that she would not be telling the story of Old Lady drinking coffee to these newcomers. It would give a sense of normality to her life; she would be part of the staff and maybe have the same courage and strength, for they would all carry on as though nothing were wrong. But she was leaving. She was going back to where life was flowing on as it had been before she left; she would take her place in the stream. It would be the same and yet not the same.

She followed Karyl into her office. Karyl turned at the sound of Misty's step and smiled. Her face was pale, and yet she had the appearance of one who was confident and ready to meet the new day. "How are you this morning, Misty?"

"Karyl," Misty ignored the question, "I have something I must tell you. Have you got a few minutes?"

"Everyone's already in the chapel, Misty. Can we talk later?"

"Let me ask you this quickly. I'd like to drive up to Stillwater this afternoon. May I use the truck?"

"Of course. The fire is out; there's no danger, but what you'll see won't be pretty. Do you want someone to go with you?"

"I'd prefer going alone. It will be late when I get there, so I'll have to stay overnight, if that's all right. I'll come back early tomorrow."

"I'm sure this is something you feel you have to do. Go to the cabin, and we'll talk when you come back." Karyl opened her desk drawer. "Here's a key to the kitchen door and the keys for the truck."

"Oh, thank you, Karyl." Impulsively Misty put her arms around her cousin and held her tight for a brief moment.

Karyl returned the embrace, then stepping back said, "We'd better go."

Fred was speaking when the two women walked into the chapel.

With the ferns and mums of the night before making a backdrop for him, the man was standing informally in front of the pulpit. "We are, of course," he was saying quietly, "keeping in close touch with the Rescue Squad. But there has been no sign of anyone surviving a plane crash on the mountainside. Today is their last day. They declare neither Del nor the pilot could possibly have survived, so if they find nothing by dark, they will discontinue the search.

"We have obligations to meet no matter how hard it may be. A new group of youngsters will be arriving within the hour. Through God's grace each one of us will have the strength and courage to go on with the same enthusiasm and dedication that we had when the first group came.

"As you know, Dillon's funeral is at eleven this morning. Parents have volunteered to come stay with the children, so those of us who wish to go will be able to. Now let's join hands while we pray for the Lord's strength in this difficult time and for His guidance."

Misty found herself standing between Roy and Doris. Roy took one of her hands and Doris the other while she listened to first one person and then another as prayer rose from the circle of camp workers. And once again, instead of being torn apart, Misty knew a warm peace.

TWENTY

Misty sat next to Sadie at Dillon's funeral. She tried to relax by exhaling slowly and counting to five before she drew in another breath. In spite of her tension she could not help but notice the peace that merged with the scent of the flowers. A quiet acceptance that all was well with the little boy mingled with the assurance that the hearts of those who stayed behind would heal. Misty saw Dillon's mother looking serene even through her tears. Fred was beside his sister, and Karyl was with him. Del would have been there too, Misty allowed herself to think briefly.

She stared impassively at the back of the head in front of her, indifferent to what Pastor Rubeck was saying until his words, "Peace I leave with you—don't let your heart be troubled, neither let it be afraid," stirred her. "Dillon," he continued, "has passed through the valley of the shadow of death. Where there is a shadow there is light; in this valley Jesus is the light. Because of his faith, Dillon is safely home in heaven with Jesus."

Then the song, "Fair are the meadows, fairer still the woodlands—" came from somewhere. It was Roy's soft tenor and the same words she had heard in the chapel Friday night. Once again she was standing beside Del hearing his voice. A dry sob caught in her throat, and Sadie reached over to take her hand in her own. Misty gripped the edge of her chair with her free hand closing her eyes until the song was over.

❦❦❦

It was a little past noon when Misty turned the pickup onto the high-way that led west to the still-hazy mountains. It was good to be on the open road. She rolled down the window and let the breeze ruffle her hair that blew loose around the edges of her bandana.

A half-hour—an hour—two hours passed. Each mile brought her closer to the blackened, scarred, desolate hillsides. There was an impen-etrable loneliness, a yawning emptiness that called to Misty. As the highway wound up and up into the hills, she saw places where the fire had come to within a mile of the road. Everywhere was both horror and fascination. Piles of charred brush and grasses still smoked; black-ened trunks lay twisted in odd and bizarre shapes. Gray ash lay thick as a blanket festooning naked tree branches with eerie cob-webby strands.

Tired, the girl pulled off the highway to a parking area cut out of the side of the mountain, which no driver could see until she rounded the horseshoe curve before it. A full view of the mountains that sloped into the valley made this a favorite view stop.

Part way up the distant mountainside in the direction of the mine a grotesque shape wreathed with drifting plumes of smoke, rose from the charred hillside. Misty squinted to see it better. What was it? It looked like a fuselage. Yes, that's what it was—the remains of an air-plane. Maybe the search party had missed Del. And the pilot. Maybe they were both lying there. Misty sat perfectly still staring at the black-ened object.

A blue jay flew to a tree and a little chipmunk skittered across the road. Nothing else moved. When the silence seemed so heavy that it would break, little pinpoints of sound came softly to Misty tapping their way into the stillness. The sound became that of a motor as it drew closer, demanding her attention, drawing her away from that shape on the hillside. Turning, she saw the blue Volkswagen come around the bend.

Roy? She had spoken to him after the service, on her way to the truck while others clustered in intimate groups talking in hushed voices. She had paused and said, with the awkwardness of not knowing just what to say, "Your solo was beautiful." He had taken her hand in both of his and pressed it hard while he smiled a smile that was tremulous. But he had said nothing. Then he had let her go, and now here he was.

Had Roy been looking at his left, toward the scarred hills, he would perhaps have missed Misty. But he was intent on the road, for it was steep and the little car pulled hard. He saw the truck when he shifted to a lower gear.

"Anything wrong?" he called as he pulled into the parking area.

"No, everything's OK. I'm just looking." Misty opened the truck door as she spoke and slid to the ground. Except for the red and white pickup she could have been mistaken for one who had stepped out of the pages of history, making her way across the challenging mountains.

"Look over there, Roy. That, up on the face of the mountain. Is that the plane? See? Just a bit to our right. Maybe—" She dropped her arm from pointing and looked at Roy, her eyes shining with hope.

Roy's eyes followed to where Misty was pointing. He looked intently at the awful shape. "No," he said finally. "No, it can't be. It was farther west. I'm sure it was. I'm afraid that what you see are some burned trees." He turned back to her. "Why are you torturing yourself this way, Misty?"

"I'm not torturing myself. I want to know for sure. The men who have been searching could be mistaken."

Misty concentrated again on the blackened debris. But even as she looked, she knew that what Roy said must be so. What she saw was only trees. Had it been the wreckage of the plane, of course the searchers would have found it. Disappointment and frustration welled up inside of her. She resented that Roy had spoiled her hopes, that he had intruded on her solitude. She turned on him with an edge of anger to her voice. "Why did you follow me?" she demanded.

Taken unawares, Roy caught her anger. "I didn't follow you. I'm on my way to California. Remember? I go over Stillwater pass up here. I just happened to come along, and you just happened to be here. If there's no problem, I'll be on my way."

He turned and started for his car.

"Roy?"

"Yes?" He stopped and looked back.

"I'm sorry. I shouldn't have spoken like that. I'm sorry. Really. Everything's so—well, everything's closed in on me." She tried to smile. "You've been a truly good friend, and I wouldn't want to spoil that. Write to me? Please? When you get to where you're going? I'd really like to hear from you, about your new job and all. Here." Turning to the truck, she found a piece of paper and scribbled on it her Syracuse address. "Have a good trip." She walked up to him and putting her hands on his arms, kissed him on the cheek.

"East is East and West is West, and never the twain shall meet—" Roy thought, but he only said, "Sure, let's keep in touch." Folding the piece of paper, he tucked it into his shirt pocket as he climbed into his car. Giving a little wave and spinning his wheels, he pulled back on to the highway.

"Till Earth and Sky stand presently at God's great Judgment Seat," wondering if Misty would have understood, Roy finished to himself the words the poet Kipling had written so many years before.

✖❦✖

Misty stood watching the car until it was out of sight then climbed back into the truck and headed on up the mountain. When she saw the road that crossed a ditch and followed the gulley to the old mine, she noticed fresh tire marks and wondered vaguely about Angelo.

When she came to the access road to Stillwater National Forest, Misty drove slower, but her heart beat faster. At last she saw the log cabin. The grass was brown from the dryness, but otherwise the yard was the same. There was no flag fluttering in the breeze, but then there was no one there to raise a flag.

After a few moments she got out of the truck and walked to the back of the cabin. The dry ground and needles crunched under her feet, breaking the silence. A squirrel scolded her from high up in a tree, and a blue jay, alerted by the scolding, flew from one branch to another. Misty breathed deeply of the thin air before she fit the key into the lock and walked in.

Everything was just as she had known it would be, neat and in place. She half expected to see Del walk into the kitchen and to hear his chuckle, but all was quiet and empty. She walked into the living room and touched his big leather chair lightly. "Del?" She whispered his name then sank down on the chair and put her hands over her face. How she longed to see him—to feel his arms around her!

She dropped her hands into her lap when a cloud rolled across the sun shutting off its warmth. An easel in front of the window caught her eye, and she wondered why she had not seen it before. On it a painting of two girls by a stream, one with short brown hair, the other with long honey-colored hair. Both, with hands cupped as if drinking, were looking up and laughing.

Misty walked over to the painting and studied it carefully. Karyl's brown eyes were sparkling, and the artist had caught the blue lights in her own. A third, shadowy almost indistinguishable face—perhaps a reflection of Karyl—was between the two. Oh, Denison Elbert, she thought. You had so much to offer! What Lewis would have given to know you! Well, he will show your paintings. Maybe this will be one of them. I can't bring you back, but I can take these pieces of your loving spirit into the world.

She touched the canvas lightly then walked around the room in deep thought before she opened the door of the storage room where she had slept that night. The cot was still there. She hesitated for a brief moment. It wasn't easy for Misty to intrude, but she wanted to find more canvases. Surely they would be stored in here.

She found some where she thought she would, lying against the wall covered with an old bedspread. She drew out first one, then another, and still another until she had five lined up on the cot. Two were of the mountains and of the valley; three were of wildlife—one of an eagle, one of a mother bear and two cubs, and one of a flock of goats climbing over the rugged rocks. "I'm a mountain goat" she heard Dillon saying as she studied the intricate details of the animals. She knew she would never forget.

She studied each painting again, going over every detail. Yes, she would take them with her—take them to the camp and then, with Karyl's permission, take them to Lewis for the showing. These and the one on the easel. And somehow she would find out what had happened to the painting Del had sent to Lewis. What had happened? Why had it been tampered with? The only clue she had was the other ranger. She had been so sure "D.E." stood for Denison Elbert and that little man had not denied it. Why?

None of Del's paintings were signed with "D.E." They all had his signature, so the initials must stand for that other ranger's name. He was trying to paint like Del. That was it. Misty's thoughts became more agitated. D.E. altered Del's painting and sent it to Lewis! He is probably jealous of Del and that's his only way of getting even. Well, he will not get away with it! He has met his match. I will see to it that he is brought to court and prosecuted. Lewis will back me up, I'm sure.

Gently, she picked up the five canvases and took them to the other room where she laid them on the table. Then she tiptoed to the threshold of Del's bedroom slipping off her shoes before she put her feet on the thick bear rug. Del's slippers were under the bed; a plaid shirt lay on top of the quilt. Misty picked up the shirt and held it against her cheek. It smelled woodsy.

The clock on the table by the bed had stopped at half past one. Beside the clock lay a Bible. Curious, Misty opened it where a red ribbon hung loosely. "In Him you have been made complete." Misty read the underlined words twice noticing the word "you" was crossed out and "I" was written above it. She whispered it to herself, "In Him I have been made complete." She repeated the sentence, "In Him I have been made complete." Complete in Him? in someone else? Prescott and Angelo, even Lance—they think they are complete in themselves; all they have to do is rouse their inner selves, and they are busily working at doing just that. But Roy and Karyl—everyone at camp— seemed to be placing themselves in the control of someone who can make them complete without their doing anything. And Del—oh, Del, you trusted God to make you complete, didn't you? That's why the ribbon is placed here; it is a favorite verse of yours. Can I be like you, complete without working at it? It's a matter of God giving and my taking, isn't it? A *free* gift. "Only God can give you peace." Pastor Rubeck told me that at Maria's funeral.

After closing the book and carefully laying it down, Misty put the shirt on the bed then picked it up again. I would like to keep it, she thought. Surely no one will mind. Someone will have to come and pack all of Del's things, and one shirt will never be missed. But I'll tell Karyl. She placed the Bible with the shirt beside the paintings.

Misty looked at her watch. It was four-thirty. With nothing to eat but a few crackers and some cheese since breakfast, she was hungry. A bowl of hot soup would taste good. She crumpled some paper and carefully laid a handful of kindling in the cold kitchen stove. In seconds the fire was burning brightly, smoke rising from the chimney in homey billows. She found a can of soup in the cupboard. After emptying it into a pan, she put it on the edge of the stove. Glancing out the window, she saw the valley had grown dark from threatening clouds. The long-awaited rain was coming.

"I think," she whispered in the stillness, "I'll change into my jeans and go up to the spring before it rains. I'm sure I can find it. It's not far past the ledge of rock—Glory Rock, Del called it."

Angry at the clouds, angry again at God, she glowered at the heavens while she changed her clothes. Why didn't the rain come a week ago? Then there wouldn't have been any fire to burn through me.

Fairly running out the door, she began the difficult climb. Pulling herself up on low-hanging branches, trying not to slip on the dry grass and needles, she stopped at Glory Rock briefly to catch her breath and to take another look at the blackened hillsides that came together where mighty Saddle Stream still frothed and foamed, sending spray into the air. In time fresh new green would show, taking over what had been destroyed. There would be life after death in the valley.

For a brief moment the sun peeked through the clouds warming the girl's back. Coming to the spot where the deer trails branched off in different directions, she remembered thinking before how the animals had come from various places to meet together before they descended into the valley. She looked at each path, not sure which one Del had chosen that day she and Karyl were here. Had it been this one? or that one?

After a moment's hesitation she set off on the one that led to the right. She knew now that it was the one that led to the stream for she recognized some of the rocks along the way. Looking up she saw the big granite boulder and knew the icy stream was gurgling out from under it.

Untouched by the fire, the stream was as it would ever be; it would continue nourishing whatever it touched time without end in spite of storms and fires. Misty sat on a rock and taking a notebook out of her pocket, began to make notes on the scene and the tumultuous feelings she was experiencing in this previous, but painful place. When the fine rain began to fall, she kept on writing, feeling the cooling drops softly patting her head.

A young doe stepped out of the brush. With one foot raised, she stood watching Misty, at the same time poised to run at the first sign of danger. The two looked at one another for long seconds before Misty broke the spell. "Hi. You look like a friend of mine. His name is Sorrowful." The doe stood a moment longer then turned and gracefully sprang out of sight.

When clouds covered the sun again and the rain began in earnest, Misty stood and carefully tucked her pencil and notebook back into her pocket. Slipping and sliding she made her way down the trail, careful not to fall.

She came to Glory Rock and paused for one more look. Fog had settled in the valley making a gray shroud over the black. Oh, thought Misty, if only I can remember this! And she tried to impress the unusual scene on her memory.

As she turned to continue on down to the cabin, she heard the brush behind her crash and crackle. She knew there were bears in the woods. Del had told her so that day when the three of them had climbed to the spring. She measured the distance to the cabin with her eye. Could she make it ahead of a curious or possibly angry bear?

She began to run, but as she heard another crash and crackle mixed with something like a moan, she turned to look, then froze. She put her hands to her mouth and stared in disbelief as a man came stumbling out of the brush.

"Del!" Misty reached the figure just as he collapsed on the ground. She knelt beside him and began to lift his head in her arms then involuntarily drew back. The scratched, cut face had bristles of a beard here and there; the black hair, matted and twisted into knots with twigs and briars, was covered with a dusting of the same fine ash that lay so heavy in the valley. The man wore a heavy denim jacket, torn and burned almost beyond recognition. His trousers were in shreds as were his flight boots. He was not Del. The name Brian on his jacket identified the pilot of the plane.

Misty steeled herself to reach out a hand to the man. He appeared to be unconscious, for he lay with his eyes closed, one leg painfully doubled under him. She fought tears and shock as she said in a controlled voice, "We've got to get you down to the cabin somehow."

The pilot opened his eyes and looked at her. "Thank God!" she heard him say in a hoarse voice, then he closed his eyes again. His lips formed another word and Misty bent close to hear. "Radio," he repeated with difficulty.

"Oh, yes!" Misty scrambled to her feet. "The radio! I'll call for help. And I'll bring some blankets to cover you while we're waiting. I'll hurry." She turned and slid down to the cabin not noticing the sharp sticks and edges of rocks that cut through her sneakers. She must get help. If this man had survived, hadn't Del? Maybe even now he was lying out there in the brush. Surely the two of them had been together.

The brightly burning fire had made the cabin warm and cheery. "I'll heat the soup for him," Misty told herself and pushed the pan of soup into the middle of the stove.

"Now for the radio." She switched the transmitter to ON and began turning the dials. Static crackled and hissed back at her. "Hello? Hello? Do you hear me?" She twiddled the dials and heard only more static. "Hello? Hello?" Nothing.

She hit the radio with the palm of her hand crying "Oh!" in frantic irritation. "I'll get some blankets. And maybe there's a tarp in the garage. I'll work something out! It's going to be dark soon, and the rain is getting heavier."

Gathering all she could carry, the girl looked at the pan of soup. "I'll have to come back for it. Maybe there's a thermos. And I'll try the radio again. But he needs to be covered first."

As she began her way back to Glory Rock, Joe, high up the mountain side in the lookout tower, looked out at the swirl of clouds that hid the valley from view. He turned to his radio and checked with the Forestry Department in Frisco. "All OK," he said. "It's beginning to rain!"

It took time for Misty to cover the injured man with the blanket and tarp. "I'm going back to the cabin," she finally told him hoping he heard, "to try the radio again and bring you some soup."

The sound of an engine in the stillness startled Misty as she ran the last few steps to the cabin. At first she thought it was Karyl coming because the jeep that came up the road looked like Del's. She jumped when a man's deep voice called out, "What's going on here?"

"Oh, thank you God," Misty breathed. How did you know I needed help? she wanted to ask but instead stood speechless.

What Doug saw was bad: a truck—a woman—and the door of the cabin wide open. He felt for the gun strapped to his belt.

"I found—The pilot is here. The pilot of the plane," called Misty, relief flooding over her.

"You're kidding," said Doug striding toward her with long steps. "It's you!" He glowered as he recognized the girl. "You sure get around. What are you doing here?"

"There's a man up there and he's burned!" Misty shouted. "Don't just stand there! He needs to get to the hospital. I tried the radio but got no answer so I was going to—"

Doug didn't wait for her to finish, but brushed past her into the cabin. "I don't see anyone here," he called accusingly to Misty who was already starting toward Glory Rock. "Hey! Where do you think you're going?"

"He's up here!" she yelled, not slowing her pace.

"Show me. And he'd better be there!"

The man followed the stumbling girl. Finally, on the ledge of rock, Doug saw the mound of blanket and tarp, the quiet form underneath them. "It is Brian!" he exclaimed. "Hang in there, old man. We'll get you down and call the chopper."

Doug turned to Misty as he picked up the tarp. "We'll make a hammock out of this and the blanket. You'll have to carry one end. Can you do it?" Without waiting for an answer, he took the blanket off Brian and put it with the tarp.

Misty hesitated. She looked at Doug and then toward the dark wet brush. Surely he knew that Del might be out there, too. Surely he was concerned.

As if reading her thoughts, Doug walked to the edge of the brush. He drew a small flashlight from his belt and searched the bushes with it then shook his head. "It's too dark," he said more to himself than to Misty. "Besides," he looked Misty over from head to toe noting her wet jeans and sneakers, "I can't look by myself. Are you ready?"

Misty gritted her teeth as she seized the pilot's legs and helped Doug ease him onto the makeshift hammock. She grabbed her end in both hands, took two steps and felt the tarp slip from her grasp. She tried again, this time wrapping a corner of the tarp around each hand. It cut into her flesh, but she said nothing. They took the slow, painful descent step by slippery step, easing their weight to the ground when it got so Misty had to rest and catch her breath.

Once inside the cabin the two of them placed their burden on Del's bed and Misty fought with herself. Why does it have to be Brian, she thought furiously. Why can't it be Del? Why, God? "Oh, hurry!" she called as she heard Doug radioing for help while her thoughts darted back to the dark, wet brush.

She leaned over the inert man and asked, "Del? Where is he? Was he with you?" She watched closely for some response, but although the man opened his eyes and looked at her, he made no sound. She repeated her questions closer to his ear, careful to speak clearly. "Del? Where is he? Was he with you?"

Brian searched her face then closed his eyes again with the faintest suggestion of a shake of his head. His lips formed a word, and she bent low to catch it.

Winter? Water? They sounded so much alike and both fit the shape of his dry lips. It was hard to tell, but Misty took the logical choice. "Water?" she repeated. "You want some water?"

Without opening his eyes, Brian again tried to whisper the word.

"I'll get you some," Misty said and all but ran to the kitchen.

Hurrying so fast she almost tripped, she brought a glass of cool water. Her hand trembled as she supported Brian's head while he drank.

"How about some soup?" she said when he was finished. Without waiting for an answer, she again went to the kitchen, wanting to help and yet feeling completely incapable in the face of the suffering she sensed the pilot was enduring. She stirred the soup with one hand while she brushed the loose hair off her forehead with the other. Then she expertly checked the fire in the stove. Wood. The fire was low; it needed another piece. She gave the soup another stir and moved it to a hotter spot on the stove's surface before she hurried outside to the woodshed.

Doug switched off the radio and stepped into the bedroom. He looked anxiously at the still form on the bed. "Hang in there, fellow," he said and emphasized his words by pressing his fist gently into the injured man's shoulder. "The chopper will be here in a half hour. There's a lot of singin' and dancin' going on out there because of you! They're going to send a crew by truck at daylight, and we'll comb the woods for Del. He was with you, wasn't he? What's that?" and, like Misty, Doug leaned closer to catch the whispered word.

The ranger straightened suddenly. If what he heard was so, he must leave at once. The helicopter would be coming soon, and Brian would be taken care of. He paused on his way to the door. Where was that woman? He should tell her where he was going so she could tell the helicopter crew, but the pile of paintings on the table caught his eye.

When Misty came in with her arms full of wood, all intentions of explaining his sudden errand had left Doug. Instead he whirled on her with, "You came here to steal! Those are Quinn's paintings, and you're planning on stealing them!"

Misty dropped the wood and stuck out her chin as she glared at the ranger. Accusingly she pointed a finger at him, "You are accusing me? You're the one who ruined the painting Del sent to the Oglethorpe Museum, aren't you. You're the thief, not me. I know all about you. Don't you tell me anything. I'll have you prosecuted to the full extent of the law!" She shook with rage.

Doug's mouth dropped open at the woman's accusation and his face turned livid. Staring at her, he shut his mouth, opened it again as if to speak, then headed for the door without another word.

TWENTY-ONE

The roar of the helicopter shook the windows in the cabin while the flares, dropped to light the small field below the yard, cast weird shadows on the ceiling. Three men brushed past Misty, carefully laid Brian on a stretcher and took him away almost before she realized what was happening. She watched the chopper rise straight up into the air and turn east towards Pommel. She was alone.

She made herself a bed on the couch and lay there staring into the dark thinking of the wet woods up by Glory Rock. She thought of Brian. Could he possibly have made his way from the shape I saw on the hillside? The shape that looks so much like a fuselage? It must be the plane. How else could Brian have come to Glory Rock? If he had been where Roy said the plane crashed, so much farther west, the injured man could never have made it as far as he did. But Del? Where is he?

She thought of the other ranger, the one she knew as D.E. He has the same ideas as I did, that Del might be out there. Why else did he shine his flashlight into the woods and say what he did? He will be back. He must have gone to recruit others. Surely they will be here soon after daylight. It won't take them long to find Del. He has to be alive! I will go to the hospital with him and stay until he is able to be up and around. Then I will leave for home for just a little while—to take the paintings to Lewis. After I have seen Lewis, I will come back to be with Del as long as he needs me and wants me.

She could not sleep; the night passed restlessly. Behind her closed eyelids she saw deer trails criss-crossing one another, then car tracks going this way and that, and even a little blue VW lost in tall grass. She had visions of someone running wildly through the wet woods. It was Roy. No, Brian. Whoever it was, briars and brambles were catching him and holding him fast.

Sitting up with a start just at daybreak, she listened intently for something, anything that could be the sound of a search party. Hearing nothing, she went to the window and peered out. A cloud had wrapped itself around the cabin, leaving everything in a cloak of invisibility. She stepped out on the porch and listened again. Nothing. The hands on her watch pointed to four forty-five. She tried to see Glory Rock through the thick fog. Del must be out there suffering and hurting even worse because another day is dawning and no one has found him. The strain and agony he is enduring, of waiting and wondering, and trying to move through that brush must be devastating! There is, she decided, no more time to waste.

Her sneakers and jeans were still wet from the night before, but that was of no concern even though the jeans clung to her, cold and clammy. The path up the hill had little puddles here and there; everything was gray and dripping, but she went on determined until she came to Glory Rock. It was barely daylight as she stood staring at the spot where Brian had come out of the woods. Then she glanced at the bushes that were strangely sparse from what they had seemed in the dark. She was just above the edge of timberline where a few scrubs and some sage barely covered the ground.

Perhaps Del was down where the brush grew thicker. Slowly, she worked her way towards the trees, intent only on one thing. She stopped every few steps and called, "Del? Del? Are you in here?" But there was no answer.

She pushed past blueberry bushes, past some belated columbines, through a clump of quivering aspen and on to where the hill sloped down into a ravine. Here was a little meadow of yellow grass where she could have rested, but Misty stopped only for a minute. "Oh, Del! Where are you?" Her voice was full of exasperation and frustration as her eyes searched the meadow. "Please let me find him!" she cried out.

"The plane! If I can just make my way to it! It must be in this direction," and she forced her way through brush that was growing heavier with every step. Soaking wet and hurting, she went on, not allowing herself to think about the possibility of being lost. Surely the burned wreckage lay ahead of her while Glory Rock and the cabin were back that way. On just a bit farther. "Del? Del?"

Sure that she was going west, not thinking to watch the sun that was barely visible through the fog, and not realizing the brush grew thinner again, Misty walked in a circle. An hour after she started on her search, she ended up on the same path she had left, the one that led to the ledge, Del's Glory Rock.

"Oh!" she gave a little cry of mixed surprise and disappointment when she realized where she was. Then just as quickly she consoled herself with, "Maybe they're here!" And she headed for the cabin.

She slid down the hill not bothering to be cautious, listening for the sounds of voices, for some indication that searchers had come. But again there was nothing except the birds she would have enjoyed any other day. Maybe it was too early. It was only a little after seven. If they didn't leave Pommel until daylight, they couldn't be here quite yet. But they surely would be coming within the hour.

She should have some coffee ready. Quickly she built a fire, then changing her jeans for her skirt, she put her wet clothes near the stove to dry. She made herself a piece of toast from the end of a loaf of bread she found in the small refrigerator and wandered aimlessly about the cabin, all the time watching and listening.

The paintings. They were still lying on the table where she had put them. She should wrap them and put them in the truck. So while the coffee perked and her clothes dried, she carefully wrapped a bath towel around each picture and then, putting them all together in one large bundle, she secured them with a bed sheet.

Lifting the cumbersome bundle, she shook her head and whispered, "Too many. It's too heavy." Quickly she unwrapped her prize and took out the picture of the girls and the one of the mountains and valley. "I'll just take these," she told herself as she re-wrapped the others. "To the camp and then to Lewis if it's all right with Karyl."

She placed the plaid shirt and Bible on top of the pictures. Del would probably want the worn and finger-marked book with him when he was in the hospital, for he apparently read it a lot. She opened it again to the spot marked by the red ribbon. "In Him I have been made complete." Pursing her lips thoughtfully, she closed the book, put it back on the shirt and checked her watch.

Restless, she walked into the bedroom and straightened the bed where Brian had lain. There was mud on the quilt where his boots had been, and a bit of blood on the pillows. She brushed the loose mud off the quilt, smoothed out the wrinkles and left the rest.

By eight-fifteen the sun was beginning to cut golden swaths through the fog. Steam was rising from the grass and from the roof of the cabin. The black hillsides didn't look so black through the glistening air; here and there were little miniature rainbows caught in the folds of the remaining fog.

"Why in the world doesn't somebody come?" she cried out in the now unbearable silence. "I'm going back up there and look some more!"

Again she climbed the hill, but this time instead of heading down towards timberline, she continued on to the spring. "Del?"

It was nine forty-five when she retraced her steps to the cabin. Surely, surely—but no, there were no signs of any other life. Reluctantly, she admitted to herself that no search party was coming, not to the cabin. She might as well leave.

Refusing to admit defeat, Misty put the paintings carefully on the truck seat with the shirt and Bible on top of them. Then she climbed into the pickup and headed away from the cabin without so much as a backward glance.

❧❧

It was two o'clock when she drove through Pommel. When she came to the road to the camp, she turned in knowing she must see Karyl if only for a few minutes; she must at least ask permission to take the paintings. But Fred's car was not there; the jeep was not there.

"Karyl? Is Karyl here?" Misty called out to a gardener.

The gardener shook his head. "She and Fred should be back in two or three days," he said.

"They must be seeing about Del's things," muttered Misty. Then, "Is Sadie here?"

"In the kitchen," and the gardener jerked his head in that direction.

Misty slid out of the truck and ran across the grounds to where Sadie was busying herself rolling out dough. "Sadie, do you know anything? Isn't a search party going to the mountains to look for Del around where Brian was found? I've been waiting up there all night for them and nobody has come! Have you heard anything?"

Sadie turned at the sound of Misty's voice. "Oh, honey." Her voice was full of compassion as she looked at the young woman so pale and shaken. "Haven't you heard? They found him. They found our Del. He was in the winter cabin! They've taken him to Denver. Karyl and Fred and Roy—they've gone with him. Just pray he comes through this."

"They found him?" repeated Misty. "They found him? Oh, thank God! I'm going to go to Denver, too. I've got to hurry Sadie, or I'll miss Steve's next trip. But I'll write to you. I promise." She threw her arms around Sadie and held the woman close for a few brief moments before she turned and ran out the door.

Pressed for time, she drove up the hill faster than she ever had. She thought briefly of Angelo and after a quick check of the clearing went into the little cabin she had called home. It seemed like a strange place now. She knew she had never belonged there. Glad she was leaving, she quickly pulled off her jeans and shirt, letting them lie where they fell. After a quick wash in cold water, she carefully applied some make-up for the first time in weeks. She put on her stylish corduroy outfit and brushed her hair and let it fall loose around her face. It felt good. It felt like home. Her suitcases, typewriter, folders—she was ready to leave. After giving the cabin and clearing a final look, she turned down the hill.

Steve was about ready to leave when Misty pulled up in front of the post office. After she offered him a brief and hurried explanation, he assured her he would see that the truck was returned to Karyl.

With Pommel fast disappearing behind them, Misty shared the glorious news Sadie had given her. "They found Del Quinn," she said watching Steve for his reaction.

"Yeah. They found him about midnight. They've taken both men to Denver, to the trauma and burn center there. They may not make it, either one of them. I hear it's going to be touch and go."

They were out on the highway now, and Steve was making good time. The strong wind made further conversation impossible so Misty did not try. She scarcely dared think. It's over. They found Del. He is in bad shape, but—he will make it! He has to! Karyl and Fred and Roy are with him; I will be there in a few hours. With this thought she closed her eyes while the pent-up tears edged down her cheeks.

Glancing at his passenger, Steve called above the wind, "Everything all right?"

"Just fine," Misty yelled back wiping the tears away. "It's only the wind."

TWENTY-TWO

"I'd like to see Del Quinn, please." Misty stood in front of the information desk of the hospital, trying to sound calmer than she felt. "What is his room number?"

The volunteer behind the desk checked the list of patients. "There's a Denison Elbert Quinn," she said pleasantly.

"That's Del." Misty hitched the strap of her purse more securely on her shoulder. It had been a long, tension-filled ride from Frisco to Denver, but now she was so close to seeing Del, to seeing he was really alive.

"He's in intensive care. I'm not sure you will be able to see him, but you can go up and ask. It's on the second floor. Go down this corridor," and the volunteer motioned. "The elevators are on your right."

The corridor was long and the elevator unbearably slow. When Misty at last stood in front of the large doors marked Intensive Care Unit, she hesitated. Should she or shouldn't she push the large button on the wall that opened them? A nurse, seeing Misty's indecision, came to her rescue.

"May I help you?"

"I'd like to see Del—Denison Elbert Quinn, if I may."

"Are you family?"

"N-no—I—a friend, just a friend."

"I'm sorry. No one but family is allowed to see him. His

cousin is with him. I'll have her come out, if you would like to talk with her."

"Oh, would you please? Tell her Misty is here."

Seconds after the nurse disappeared, Karyl opened the doors from the other side. She paused, studying the young woman waiting for her who was dressed in expensive pants and sweater, hair loose around her face and just the right amount of makeup on. Misty waited for Karyl to say something.

"Misty? Misty! I hardly recognized you, but it is you. You came. Del would be so pleased."

"How is he, Karyl?" Misty blurted out. "The nurse said no one but family may see him."

"He wouldn't know you are here, Misty. He's still out of it." Karyl glanced over her shoulder towards the ward.

Straining to look past Karyl, Misty saw a row of glass-fronted cubicles; in each one lay a motionless, monitored patient. Her heart pounded as she wondered, which one is Del? The one swathed in bandages with the tubes of a ventilator and oxygen dangling from his face, an intravenous tube dripping fluid by his bed? Oh, no! Not that one! Or is he the one turned on his side partially hidden under a sheet? There were others too far away to really see. Which one is Del? Misty clutched the strap of her purse tighter.

"He's the one in the first cubicle." Karyl had noticed Misty's searching look.

"Oh no!" Misty pleaded under her breath. "Don't let that be him, please."

"The doctors say he has a fifty-fifty chance, but I know he's going to be fine. It's going to take time, but he will make it. He wasn't burned as badly as Brian. Del had on an asbestos suit and Brian didn't. Del's biggest problem is pneumonia; he breathed in so much smoke and ash. And flames, too. His right arm and leg are broken, and both legs were singed where his suit was torn. But—he's doing fine."

"He'll be all right?" Misty said out loud fighting tears, trying to smile.

"Yes, he's going to make it. We're so thankful—so very thankful." Karyl slipped an arm through Misty's. "Wouldn't you like to go down to the cafeteria for some coffee? We can talk there. Let's take the stairs."

Karyl opened a door across from the elevators. "We tried to get hold of you after they found Del," she explained as the two of them made their way to the first floor. "Joe called the cabin on the radio but couldn't get any answer so we assumed you were gone."

"What time was that?" asked Misty as they stepped out of the stairwell.

"About seven in the morning."

"I was out looking for Del. I was sure a search party was coming, but I couldn't wait—I went out alone. Oh, if only I—"

"You're here now and that's the important thing," said Karyl.

Even after they were seated at a table with their coffee, Misty's mind was on Del, but she felt compelled to open the other subject that lay heavy on her heart. "Karyl—" She paused, not knowing for sure how to begin.

"Karyl," she began again, "you know me as Misty—Misty Morrow. That is my name, that's what my folks call me, but my given name is Mary Alice—Mary Alice Morrow." Misty waited for Karyl to comprehend.

"Mary Alice Morrow?" repeated Karyl thoughtfully studying Misty's face as she spoke. "Mary Alice Morrow." She frowned slightly, trying to remember, then opened her eyes wide with surprise. "Mary—Alice—Morrow?" She repeated the name deliberately as the truth dawned on her. "You? You can't be the Mary Alice Morrow who writes 'Sketches'? Are you, Misty?"

Misty caught her lower lip between her teeth as Karyl looked at her searchingly. "Why in the world? I don't understand."

Misty lowered her eyes avoiding Karyl's troubled face as she started to explain. "I went to Pommel to write a series of stories on Martha's Camp and thought it would be great to go incognito, so—I did." She looked up at Karyl again and gave a slight shrug. "Dad, he's the editor of *The Global News,* thought I'd get better stories that way for one thing and I—I wanted to prove to myself I could do things on my own and be myself."

"Misty!" Hurt and disappointed by this revelation, Karyl made no attempt to hide her feelings. "Misty, I don't know what to say. You certainly did a good job of concealing your identity," her voice was a bit brittle, "living there in that cabin, being friends with Angelo and—"

"I wasn't friends with Angelo, Karyl. You must believe me! I was terribly afraid of him, but there was no other place to rent. I wasn't connected with him or his friends in any way. Please, please believe me, Karyl. I'm not like them."

Karyl hesitated, obviously struggling with herself, then she reached out a hand and touched Misty. "I believe you. If you'd only said something, you could have roomed with me. Oh, if we'd only known who you really are! But we would have found a place for you no matter who you are. None of us had any idea; we thought you and Angelo were friends or involved—you know—and it was your choice to live there."

"I certainly created problems for myself and for the rest of you. I'm sorry, Karyl. I should've been straight with you. I got some terrific stories, but I should have been honest; I should have been open about what I was doing. I'll see that you read them before they're printed; I won't even print them if you don't want me to. I promise you that. There's something else I must tell you."

"Another secret?" Karyl raised her eyebrows as she waited.

"My dad is Will Morrow, cousin to your mother. I didn't know that until Pastor Rubeck told me about your family."

"I remember Mother talking about her cousin Will Morrow who was playing with them when Ruby was hurt. He's your dad? My mother's cousin is your dad?" Karyl paused to think. "Then that means—"

"We're cousins," supplied Misty.

"We *are* cousins, aren't we! Can you imagine that?" and Karyl gave a little lilting laugh. "Do you know my sister Theba? Do you know about her?"

"I don't really know about her, but I know her. She's the curator at the Oglethorpe Museum of Art. I know the director there; he's very interested in Del's paintings."

"Isn't that strange—you know Theba. Does she know you're her second cousin?"

Misty shook her head. "No way," she said softly, remembering Theba's aloofness.

"She's had a hard time," Karyl went on ignoring Misty's answer. "I can't explain it all to you now. Wait a minute! What do you mean, the director of the art museum is interested in Del's paintings? How does he know about them? Surely Theba wouldn't have told him!"

"Let me get us more coffee and I'll tell you about it." After Misty had refilled their cups, she told Karyl about the painting of the eagle, how Del had entered it in the American Artists contest and how it had arrived defaced.

"Lewis, the director, was terribly disappointed. He had seen the painting at a showing here in Denver, and he was confident it would be chosen for first prize, and there it was—no good. He tried to find Denison Elbert but couldn't, so he asked me to look for him when I went to Pommel."

"Del entered a painting in that contest, and he kept it a secret all of this time? That's hard to believe! It must have been the one of an eagle with a fish, one of the best he's ever done. How was it defaced?"

"The fish has been removed," answered Misty. "You can tell from the eagle's claws that it was holding something."

"Why would someone ruin his work?" Karyl was plainly bewildered. "Poor Del! Does he know someone altered it? Who in the world would do a thing like that?"

Misty shook her head. "No, he doesn't know anything happened to his painting, I'm sure. I didn't even know he painted it; I didn't know that he was Denison Elbert until after the plane crash. Roy told me."

Misty studied her coffee cup for a moment before she went on. "When I was at his cabin and couldn't find him and no search party came, I couldn't make myself accept his probable death. I was determined to bring his art to the public, so he would win that prize and be well-known when he recovered. I found some other paintings I wanted my friend at the museum to see so I chose three to take with me. I stopped at the camp hoping to see you so I could ask you if it was OK, but since you weren't there I took the liberty of bringing them with me. I hope Lewis will want at least one to replace the eagle. There were six I wanted to bring, but I couldn't carry them all."

"I'm glad you felt free to take the ones you did," said Karyl. "Del must not miss this chance. I'll get the others for you as soon as I can. I want your director friend to see them, and I want Theba to see them, especially the one of the girls. Did you bring that one with you?"

Misty shook her head. "No, I left that one."

"I have to go back to camp tomorrow. While I'm there, I'll go to Del's cabin and take care of things and get that painting for you." She fell silent, struggling to absorb all she had heard—Misty is a journalist, she is my cousin, Del's painting has been intentionally damaged.

Finally she looked at her watch. "Fred and Roy will be coming to pick me up pretty soon. You'll want to see them too. Incidentally, Fred and I have postponed our wedding. October, maybe. Will you be here or not? I suppose you'll go back east."

"I'm not sure." Misty said nothing more for a moment then intentionally diverted Karyl's attention. "Roy's here? I thought he went to California."

"Of course, you don't know he's the one who found Del. He was on his way to California that day, but he felt he should turn in to the rangers' winter cabin. 'It was as if the Lord was drawing me to the cabin,' he said."

"The Lord?" asked Misty in wonder.

"I just know it was the Lord's leading! Otherwise Roy wouldn't have found Del. He did what he could for him and was just about to leave for help when Doug Endicott came. And Roy's stayed beside Del all this time."

"Doug Endicott!" Misty exclaimed, totally confused.

"The other ranger—the one who came to the cabin when you were there. He and Del are good friends; Del was teaching him how to paint—letting him copy some of his paintings. Brian had managed to make Doug understand that Del was in the winter cabin, so he drove down there, found Roy with Del and it all had a happy ending. I know Del will recover. We're all praying and trusting the Lord for his healing. He already has led us to excellent doctors and nurses."

"And there I was up at Del's cabin getting myself lost in the woods." Misty grimaced slightly. "I stopped at the camp and Sadie told me he'd been found, but she didn't tell me how Del got to the winter cabin. And Brian—how did he get to the rock?"

"The plane crashed not far from the mine which isn't too far from the winter cabin. Both men were able to make their way to the cabin, but Del could scarcely breathe, his lungs hurt so. He stayed there, and Brian managed to walk and crawl up the trail. He was aiming for Del's cabin, but I guess he passed it and ended up on the rock. God gave him the endurance and guts he needed."

"Was he burned badly?"

"His arms and shoulders are burned very badly and his face some. It's more lacerated. His legs are cut up pretty much, too. But he did it. And the Lord had you right there at the right time! It's too bad you can't see him too. He's isolated in the burn center."

Misty, remembering, asked softly, "Do you really think the Lord used me, Karyl?"

"Oh, yes, Misty, the Lord *did* use you. I'm positive." She looked straight into Misty's eyes when she said it. "You know, if you hadn't left the radio on when you tried to call for help, the ranger in the tower would never have known something was wrong."

Misty's eyes widened. "I left the radio on? I guess I did! I never thought about that."

"It crackled so," Karyl went on to explain, "the ranger knew someone's transmitter was on. He figured it was Del's and sent Doug to check it out. Doug found you there and—you know the rest. The Lord had you there; He arranged the whole thing."

"I wondered how come Doug showed up right when he did. Oh, Karyl, what if he hadn't?"

Both women sat silent, thinking of what might have happened, then after a moment Karyl said, "I'm sure you don't know the area around the mine caught fire. The cabin and the whole gulley were burned. It just shows who's in control—the Lord didn't want that workshop or cult there. Angelo's gone somewhere. No one knows where—not even Lillian. He and his friends probably think man really desecrated Mother Earth this time and that Gaia will have revenge."

"Gaia?" asked Misty

"She's supposed to be the earth goddess," explained Karyl, "but we know there's only one God. Everything will grow back; new life will cover the gulley in the Creator's own time. He's in control and always will be." Misty nodded, and both women fell silent for a moment. Finally Karyl asked, "How long can you stay in Denver? Do you have to get back to work?"

"I thought I'd see Del and then go on home, but I—Oh, Karyl! I can't go without seeing him; I just can't. Do you suppose that if I stay for a few days I'll be able to? I must see him! I must tell him I—"

Karyl was visibly surprised at Misty's vehemence, but she wisely asked no questions. "I think you should stay, Misty. Why don't you stay in my room while I go back to the camp? Then I can bring you the other pictures. I know it would mean a lot to Del to have you here. It will encourage him; he'll want more than ever to get well."

Misty smiled through her sudden tears. "Do you think so? I'll call Dad and explain everything to him. I know it'll be OK. And I can start on my story while I'm here. It is all right if I write a story about Del for "Sketches," isn't it?"

Karyl gave a little laugh. "Of course it's all right, but let's keep it a secret. A happy surprise will do him good." She had a mischievous twinkle in her eyes. "When he reads your story about himself, will he ever be surprised! Oh, here come Roy and Fred. I'm not going to tell them who you really are—not yet. They would tell Del and spoil our surprise. Hi, you two," she called out.

Misty watched the two men approach. Had it been but a few days since she had seen Roy? She wondered at his appearance—more subdued, perhaps even older. The memory of their encounter when she was on her way to Del's cabin flashed across her mind. She had hurt him, she knew, and even though she had made amends, she had been sure as he drove off that she would never see or hear from him again. Now here he was, subdued but with the same smile, even though he had been through so much. But then, so had she.

She returned Roy's smile but said nothing. She knew he did not recognize her and waited for Karyl to break the silence.

"What's the matter, don't you two know Misty?" Karyl laughed at the puzzled expression on the two men's faces.

"Misty, I didn't expect to see you again," said Roy obviously struggling for words. "So soon," he added rather lamely while his careful scrutiny took in every detail of her appearance. "I didn't recognize you; you—well, you look different."

"Misty's here to see Del, of course," interceded Karyl. "She's going to stay for a few days until he's able to have visitors."

"You sure don't look much like the truck driver I knew," said Fred as he sat down beside Karyl. "Will you come back to Pommel and the camp after you've seen Del?"

"I can't say right now just what I'll do, but I'd surely like to come back."

"I wish we could stay and talk some more but, Karyl," Fred turned to her, "if we're going to get back to camp before too late, we'd better go."

"I guess we had. I hate to leave Del, but—well, he's in the Lord's hands, of course. And Roy's going to be here. Misty's going to stay in my room while I'm gone, so you'd better come with us now, Misty, and find out where it is. Roy can help you with anything you might need. My bag's all packed," she reassured Fred, "so I'm ready to go just as soon as I get Misty settled.

TWENTY-THREE

Two days of sitting in the waiting room and the cafeteria, long hours broken by occasional walks around the grounds surrounding the hospital, did not help Misty to relax. The first day was bearable, even hopeful. She visited the hospital gift shop, bought herself a paperback book to read, looked over the T-shirts and other items hoping to find something she would be able to take to Del. Perhaps he, too, would like a book, she decided. She looked the titles over again more carefully, wondering if perhaps she should buy one with a religious theme or something on art. But none of the books seemed right. Flowers and balloons were out, at least for now. When he is moved out of intensive care, she thought, I can buy—Oh, Lord, he is coming out of there, isn't he? Isn't he? Panic rose in her. He won't just lie there, not moving until—until he—no, I won't think that way! I won't! Oh, I wish I had the faith Karyl has.

A collection of cross-word puzzles caught her eye. He might enjoy doing those as he convalesced. Or even a small jigsaw puzzle might be acceptable. But no, none of them appealed to her. Maybe later when he could enjoy them—when he *will* enjoy them, she told herself firmly. After choosing a get-well card that was neither gushy nor humorous, she was taking it to the cashier when a small, paperback booklet hiding under some folders caught her eye. She paged through it quickly. *Time Out* seemed to be the story of a person who had been desperately ill and who had recovered. Another slim, glossy book, *Love Your Way To*

Wellness, lay partly concealed beneath it. Misty picked up the first book. The name Lord seemed to be on many of the pages; perhaps if she took time to read the other, she would find him mentioned there, too. But she hesitated, not sure which to buy. She paid for the card and returned to the waiting room but not until after she had peeked through the doors of the ICU. Del was still lying perfectly still.

The second day she finished her book, bought several magazines and a newspaper, and toured the gift shop again. The two small books were still there. On impulse she picked them up and paid for them, looked through the glass doors of ICU at Del's still form several times, then went outside for a walk. She stopped under a tall spruce tree and gazed at the distant mountains. Was I actually up there? She marveled at the thought. How high up was I? Did I really have a rendezvous with those mountains? with those rocks? Did all those things happen to me? The camp? Angelo? Maria? The past months seem like years ago; it's almost as if it all happened to someone else, someone I just read about.

"There you are. I had a hunch I'd find you out here."

Misty turned and saw Roy coming toward her, his copper-colored hair catching the rays of sun that slanted through the tree branches. Her emotions churned; she wished that he had not found her, and yet it was good to have someone to talk to. But she said nothing.

"It's nearly 12. Don't you want some lunch?"

This was the same Roy who had asked her to go with him to eat that horrible day Del had been lost. Now he was asking her again and she was glad for his company.

"Sure. Why not?"

No more words passed between them until they sat at a table in a secluded corner of the cafeteria their lunches corralled on trays. Then Misty asked Roy the question burning in her mind. "You saw him this morning?"

Roy, carefully blowing on a spoonful of hot soup, nodded. "I did," he said seconds later.

"How come you can see him and I can't? You're no more family than I am." Angry resentment bubbled up in Misty.

Roy looked at her patiently. "No, I'm not really family, but Del and I have been like brothers for many years. I told you that. I found him, you know, and gave him first aid. No one has questioned my going in to see him. You haven't known him quite as long as I have," he chided.

"I think I'll go down to *The Denver Post* this afternoon." Misty felt the need to change the subject. "There's someone who works there I'd like to see, and I may as well go; there doesn't seem to be any change in Del. I'll be back by four. Are you going to stay here?"

"I'm going up to sit with him for a while. You never know. I'd hate not to be close by when he does wake up. There's one of his nurses just come in for lunch." Roy nodded towards the cafeteria's entrance.

Misty looked in the direction Roy indicated; Del's nurse, a slight, attractive blond, would know if he were awake or not. But the young woman showed no intention of talking to Roy. She walked to another table, so Misty stood and picked up her tray. "I'll get a cab out front. See you later," she said over her shoulder and left.

She walked quickly to the street glad to have something definite to do. She wanted to start putting together notes for the story she intended to write about Del, and going to the *Post* would be a good beginning. There might be some articles there about him that would give her information even Karyl might not be aware of. She would spend the afternoon at the paper, and this evening, after checking back at the hospital, she could start on an outline.

Purchasing a copy of the newspaper, she hailed a cab parked at the curb. "*The Denver Post,* please," she told the driver then leaned back and opened the paper. Turning to the Art section she read, "Nasby Paintings Well Received." Nasby paintings? Flora Nasby? A quick scan of the article told of the recent showing of the artist's paintings, the showing Misty had wanted to attend. A reception for the artist had been given the night before; she was leaving for the East today. "Wouldn't you know it?" muttered Misty. "I just missed her."

The afternoon went quickly. Checking with the art department, Misty inquired for Chris, the girl she had met on the plane coming west, but Chris was away for the day, so Misty searched the files by herself. There were several articles on Denison Elbert Quinn, reviews of his paintings and a brief biography of both him and his grandfather. Rather than making notes Misty made copies of the articles, and when she had exhausted that file, she turned to one on Martha Cross.

It was late when she returned to the hospital. A quick glance told her Del was as she had seen him last. Shunning the cafeteria, she returned to the hotel preferring the coffee shop there for her dinner. Once back in her room she started to read the articles she had copied then remembered the two little books she had purchased. Taking them out of her purse, she looked at first one then the other.

Time Out had an attractive shiny red paper cover with gold lettering. She opened it at random turning pages without a definite purpose. "No soldier in the Lord's army is ever 'laid aside.'" The words caught Misty's attention and she read further, "When one appears to be 'laid aside,' the Lord has only given him another commission whether it be to suffer, to fight for the Lord, or to have deeper compassion and understanding for others who are also 'laid aside.'"

The ringing of the phone startled her. "H-hello?"

"Misty, I have great news for you!" Roy's voice was filled with excitement. "Del woke up this evening! He is very much aware of his surroundings and of his injuries. He even remembers some of what happened. I checked with the doctor, and he said it's OK if you see him in the morning for a few minutes. They're going to move him to a regular room. But—but—I hope you won't be offended, but may I suggest something?"

"Oh, Roy! I'm so excited! But I'm scared." Misty gripped the phone harder. "Suggest something? Sure. What?"

"I think maybe you should sort of brush your hair back; you know, make it look more like it was in Pommel. And maybe not so much on your face?"

"You think Del might not know me?" She was suddenly very anxious.

"Oh, he'd know you all right. Don't worry about that; his mind is OK. It's just that it might be easier that way."

"All right. I understand. Thanks, Roy. I'll do it. I'll do anything to help."

Excitement surged through Misty as she hung up the phone. He's awake! Thank God! He's awake. I'll see him in the morning! He's going to be OK! She walked to a mirror and pulled her hair back tight from her face. Roy was probably right, Del would be sure to know her if she looked as she had in Pommel. She'd do her best.

It was early yet, too early to go to bed, so Misty picked up the little book and tried to continue in it. "The words 'laid aside' are not for us. We are soldiers of the King and soldiers are never shelved."

She was too excited to read. Tearing off a piece of newspaper, she placed it in the book as a marker, then stood and walked to the window. She stared down at the busy street, watching the traffic before her glance traveled over the roof tops to the brightly lit hospital. The battle between life and death was going on over there, not only for Del but for Brian and others she would never know. Was Del's room one with a light on, or was his dark and he was asleep?

Restless, Misty watched the traffic for a few more minutes, then went back to the chair where she had been reading. She picked up the second small book, *Love Your Way To Wellness*. "You are your own master," she read. "Love. Love everyone. You have love within you whoever you are, wherever you are. You can experience the power and miracle of love when you let love direct all of your mind overcoming all other thoughts. Then health and wellness will be yours. Wasn't that—? A fleeting picture of Prescott crossed Misty's mind. Wasn't that something Prescott might say? Hadn't she, all of Angelo's friends, talked much about love? But would Del like it? No, he would prefer *Time Out*. After all he was a soldier, a fighter. Hadn't he been fighting a fire, and wasn't he fighting for his life at this very moment? Tomorrow she could see him, even talk to him. She would give him his Bible and take him both little books; he could decide for himself which to read later when he felt up to it. She would like to read both of them herself, but suddenly she was much too tired to read more.

But exhausted as she was, she could not sleep. There had been other nights like this—the nights she lay awake dreading Angelo; the night in Del's cabin wondering, afraid that she would never see him again. And now as she lay awake, she tried to imagine what her meeting with him would be like. What should I say? How will he react? How does he really feel about me? Surely he will want me to stay on in Denver which is of course what I will do. I wouldn't think of leaving until he's completely out of danger. And then I couldn't stay away long. That is—if he wants me. Oh, there's so much to talk about! So much to straighten out. I must tell him who I am. And he surely wants to tell me he's Denison Elbert. And we have to talk about our feelings for each other. We didn't have a chance before the fire, but now—now anything is possible! It will all fall into place. With this happy thought she finally fell asleep.

It took more than an hour in the morning for her to shower and fix her hair as it had been in the mountains. She put some makeup on then washed it off and started over again. "A little bit," she cautioned herself, "but not too much. Maybe he won't like me with any on. But I'm in the city now. He'll understand." With this thought she brushed on a faint blush and lightly touched her lips with lipstick.

Roy was waiting for her in the lobby of the hospital when she finally walked in. She saw him watching her closely as she walked through the door and crossed the room, but she could only guess what was going on in his mind. Maybe he's wondering about me, she thought. Who I am. He never questioned my going to *The Post* yesterday, but I'll bet he wondered why. Maybe he asked me to fix my hair back this way for his own sake and not for Del's. He's probably remembering back in Pommel. I'm sure these last few days have been especially rough on him, finding Del and all. And I guess he's having to deal with his feelings for me.

"Can we go up now?" Misty didn't even bother with a greeting, as she pushed the thoughts she had been thinking to one side. She had come for one thing and one thing only. Surely Roy knew that, so why bother with social amenities? "Do I look all right?" she asked anxiously, wondering again if it were for his own sake Roy had asked her to fix her hair this way.

"You look great," said Roy simply. Impulsively he reached out a hand and smoothed back a wisp of her hair. "His new room is D511. He should be in there by now," he said as he checked his watch, "and they should be finished with what all they do in the morning. I'm sure it's fine if we go up."

He hesitated for a moment then looked at her closely. "Are you ready for this? He's not easy to look at what with all the bandages and casts and tubes. He had a tracheotomy, you know, because his lungs were so full, and he's on a ventilator as well as oxygen. I just don't want you to be upset by the way he looks. OK?"

For answer Misty began walking toward the elevator. Once inside the doors of the D ward she hesitated, clutching the strap of her purse tighter. Feeling the encouragement of Roy's hand on her elbow, she walked on to 511 where Del lay with his eyes closed. One side of his face was swathed with bandages; an unkempt beard covered the other side and his upper lip. The plastic oxygen and ventilator tubes invading his nose and throat looked dreadfully foreign and ominous. His bandaged right arm lay across his chest while an intravenous tube dripped fluid into the left. A pulley over the bed supported his right leg, encased in a heavy cast.

Putting her hands to her face in horror, Misty closed her eyes for a brief moment, then leaning over the man who looked as though he were asleep, she spoke barely above a whisper. "Hi, Del."

Del opened his eyes and looked at her. He searched her face almost hungrily, then closed his eyes again.

"It's me, Del. It's Misty. You do remember, don't you?"

He opened his eyes and again searched her face, at the same time giving a slight nod, but not even the tiniest suggestion of a smile played around his lips.

Misty put her hand over his unbandaged one, careful not to disturb the IV needle, and gently squeezed his fingers. They felt warm and strong, but there was no returning of her greeting.

Not only surprised, but hurt, she said, "Del? I came to help you get well. I'll be here as long as you need me, as long as you want me. I'm staying in a hotel nearby, so I can be here with you every day all day."

Del searched her face again, then again closed his eyes and turned his face. Misty straightened and waited. When Del continued to lie with his eyes closed, she turned questioningly to Roy, who was standing quietly to one side.

"He does know me, doesn't he?"

Roy nodded. "He knows you all right, but he's tired, Misty."

The little blond nurse Misty had seen in the cafeteria came into the room, a stethoscope draped over her shoulders, a blood pressure cuff and thermometer in her hand. "You're right," she said hearing Roy. "He's had a lot of activity this morning being moved and what all. He's worn out. I suggest you leave for now and come back later this afternoon."

Stepping closer to the bed, Roy spoke to his friend. "We're going now, fella, but we'll be back later today. Get a good rest."

Hearing Roy's voice, Del looked up into his friend's eyes. "Take care of her," he managed to whisper. "I can't." Then he closed his eyes again.

"You're going to make it, you hear?" Roy spoke over a lump in his throat. "The Lord has you in His hands. He's brought you this far; He's not going to let you go now. He has much more for you to do in this world, so He's not about to take you. You are going to make it!"

Del made an attempt to shake his head. "God doesn't care," he whispered. "He's forgotten me." And he turned his face away.

TWENTY-FOUR

Del heard Misty and Roy leave the room. He lay with his eyes closed while the nurse took his vital signs. He hurt. He hurt all over.

"If the pain gets to you," the nurse said as she smoothed his covers, "the doctor says you may have a shot. Just push the button," and she placed the call signal close to his good hand.

Perhaps when night comes, he thought, when it's dark I might ask for some relief from this terrible throbbing, but not now. I want to think for a while—think as best I can and analyze this other pain I'm having; it's deeper than any physical hurt could ever be.

He forced himself to remember: leaving Misty—the plane ride over the fire—bailing out—the jolt of impact followed by the scorching heat. Much after that was blank. Someday Roy might be able to fill him in on what he couldn't remember. All he knew was that it had been horrible beyond description. Now here he lay with seared lungs, a scarred face plus a broken leg and arm—his right arm, the one he used for painting. The doctors had put in a silver plate and two pins to hold the bones together. The nerves were so injured he might never be able to hold a pencil again, let alone a paint brush. With his good hand he hesitantly touched the hard, cold cast of the arm that lay across his chest. God! Where are You? Why?

Del did not stir when he heard Misty and Roy come back later in the afternoon as Roy had said they would do. It was easier to lie with his eyes closed, much easier than facing Misty. I can't stand to look at her, he thought, to think about what might have been. If Roy would come by himself, then I could maybe talk a bit with him—share some of the doubts and bitterness that are plaguing me. Perhaps I can ask the nurse to say something to Roy, to ask him to come alone.

When Roy came in the evening, he comforted his friend as best he could. "Don't talk that way," he said in response to Del's complaint that God had forsaken him. "Look at it this way, God brought you through all of this alive! You could have been killed right then and there; Brian could have been killed or not been able to make his way to your cabin. You don't think it was just by chance that Misty was up at your cabin and found Brian, do you? Or that Doug went to your place when he did? What if he hadn't gone? You know God works in mysterious ways. Look at the good things that happened!"

But Del only closed his eyes as he shook his head. "None of it had to happen," he said bitterly. "If God's in control, He could've stopped the plane from crashing."

Roy swallowed hard. "You know very well there are laws of nature God maintains, but He is in control," he assured his friend. "And He's going to see you through this. He's got plans for you; you'll see."

But Del only shook his head again and set his lips in a firm line.

"It's easy for you to say," he whispered and he glanced up at Roy. "You're all in one piece. No," and he closed his eyes again. "God's not with me."

✖✖

"Del?" Misty's voice was soft and her touch on his hand cool, when she came in the next morning. "Del?"

Behind his closed eyelids he saw her as she had been the night of the dedication of the camp; he saw her again standing silhouetted in the cabin doorway looking up at him when he said goodby. He heard her asking him if he really had to go. I can't look at her, he thought, I mustn't look at her. Misty, my painting, even my faith in God—they all belong to a part of my life that is past and now they're gone. Nothing, no, nothing can ever be the same again.

"I brought you some little books I thought maybe you'd like to read. When you feel better," she added. "I brought you your Bible, too." Why won't he talk to me, she worried, why? Doesn't he care for me anymore?" She forced her fear away and told herself, be sensible. Remember what he's been through. He's completely worn out and doesn't have any energy to talk.

"The title of one book is *Time Out*. It's by someone who was very sick, someone who didn't expect to live but she did. I'm sure you'll like it. There's a lot about faith in God in it." Misty paused again, panic rising in her. What's wrong with him? Del, please talk to me! "You—you don't feel like talking, do you," she said lamely. "I'll leave the two books here on your table. I'm putting a card there too."

Del heard her leave. Opening his eyes, he turned his head a trifle to catch a glimpse of her. She was standing with her back to his door watching down the hall. "You're back!" he heard her announce as Karyl and Fred came into sight, Roy beside them.

"We're back," agreed Karyl. "How is he?" She looked past Misty into the shadowy room.

"I don't know; he won't talk to me," confessed Misty her voice full of the misery she felt. "I'm sure he's not asleep; his eyelids kept kind of fluttering as if he were having a hard time keeping them closed. But he won't even look at me or say anything—not one word!"

Del caught Misty's words and her tone; he strained to hear what more she might say but it took too much effort. He turned from watching them, fighting against the deep longing within himself. It's better this way. His lips formed the words, but he made no sound. I must be strong enough to send her away.

"Give him time." Fred smiled encouragingly at Misty. "He's probably still in some shock, and maybe he just doesn't want you to see him like this."

"He's got a lot of bitterness." Roy spoke up. "He seems to have lost his faith in God. We talked some last evening, and he's—well—bitter."

"Oh, not Del!" protested Karyl looking again at the inert form in the dimly-lit room. "I can't believe that." Then, after a moment, "We'll have to pray more and harder; we'll have to pray for his spiritual healing as well as his physical. As Fred says," and she put her hand on Misty's arm, "give him time."

"It's obvious he doesn't want to see me, Karyl." Misty fought to hold back the tears that were slipping down her face. "I'll try again this afternoon and maybe—" Leaving her sentence unfinished, she shook her head and put her purse strap over her shoulder. "The nurse said there shouldn't be any more than two or three with him at once, so I'll wait in the lobby."

❧❧❧

After everyone had gone, Del watched the city's skyline light up against the darkening sky. One by one lights came on in the high-rises as the sun escaped below the cloud-flocked horizon. How different it was from his mountains; how different from the rocks he was used to climbing. While the city had a special beauty all its own, it could not compare with Glory Rock and all that lay on the mountainside around his cabin. Homesickness gripped him along with his other miseries.

The others had tried to encourage him—Karyl, Fred, and, of course, Roy—but would he ever get his old life back? How could he ever again climb those rugged peaks or live in the woods and carry on with his ranger's duties? His leg would heal, but it would not be as strong as it had been; his arm would heal—or would it? "Trust God," Karyl said. "Sure, trust God!" Del replied sarcastically.

More painful than the thought he would never be able to live in the mountains again was the thought he would have to send Misty away. A jet preparing to land caught his eye; he watched it while he continued to think of Misty. It would have been so easy to welcome her love, he thought, to give in to what I really wanted to say—so easy. He took a deep breath and set his jaw with determination. I will not give in! What do I have left to offer her now? Nothing! A scarred face, a weak body, no home, no income, no future. I can't even express what talent I might have—it's impossible with this arm. My talent's all gone. Oh, some artists have learned to paint with their mouths and their feet and they do great. But I couldn't subject Misty to the agony of my learning to do that. Besides, maybe I wouldn't have the guts to learn. No, I must let her go and get on with her life. Maybe she and Roy can make it together. It's obvious Roy cares for her; maybe she can learn to love him. Oh, who am I kidding anyway? I don't want Roy to have her—I want her. I shouldn't, but I do. I want her!

A feeling of utter desolation swept over him. Not only was Misty gone, God had really forsaken him, left him without hope. "Where are You?" he asked searching the sky now shrouded with black clouds.

"Why have You done this to me? I've tried to obey You, to do what You say to do. I've believed in You, believed You were my strength and my help. I've prayed; oh, how I've prayed, but You probably never even heard me. And I've read Your word—daily. I thought You were always with me, but what a mess You've made of my life." He was becoming accustomed to the taste of bitterness that rose in his throat.

The night nurse came in to adjust his covers and pillows. "Anything you need or want?" she asked gently. "A snack maybe?"

For answer Del shook his head. "I'm OK," he lied. "Just turn out the light, will you please?"

After she left, pulling the door partially closed behind her, muted light from the hall still pervaded a far corner of the room. But Del lay in darkness.

Sleep did not come. He stared into the night and as he stared he reviewed the times God had forsaken him. Oh, I thought then, God, that You were either teaching me something or strengthening me, that those painful experiences were for my good; would work out best for me. I relied on that verse that says "All things work together for good for them who love God," but those times didn't work out for my good. Look at me now!

As if digging for proof, he enumerated three times when he had trusted God and nothing had come of his trust. There was the time when Aunt Martha died. Since I had been praying money would be supplied so I could continue my art studies, I felt sure the answer to my prayer was in her will. But it wasn't. Most of the money went to her two girls and the camp. Oh, I got some, but I gave it to Cindy. I was sure the Lord would honor my helping her and I'd still have enough to go on with my studies. It didn't work out that way, but I kept my faith. Didn't I keep saying "The Lord will provide?" You know I did, God.

So I entered my painting of an eagle and a fish in the contest that was being sponsored by the big Oglethorpe Art Museum back in Syracuse. That was a few months ago, and I've never heard so much as a single word from them. I don't know if they even received the painting, let alone judged it. I counted on that money too for further study—prayed and trusted You, God. And what good did it do?

When I met Misty, I prayed about her, that she was the woman for me, the one You chose. What good did all those prayers do? This is what happened. He was conscious again of the heavy casts and his smarting face.

Any fool can see You have forsaken me. Why? What have I done? Or not done? I can't figure it out, but I do know this much—there's no need to pray any more or to hope any more in spite of what Karyl says. "We'll keep praying, Del. Fred and Roy and I pray together three times a day for you." Well, they may as well save their time and breath. You won't hear them, God. Maybe it would be just as well if none of them came back to see me any more. Karyl said she and Fred have to get back to camp again to get things ready for winter so that will eliminate them. Roy will still be around, but he should be with Misty. Probably he will be.

By the next morning Del's mind was made up. I will free her, he told himself, I must say whatever is necessary to force her to go on with her life. I must love her enough to let her go—to make her go.

When he heard her footsteps in the room and the sound of her voice, every fiber or his being wanted to put off the inevitable break. He wanted to pretend to be asleep; he couldn't bear to look at her and tell her to go.

"Del?" she called him gently. "I know you're awake. Please look at me, speak to me."

He forced himself to open his eyes and look into her face. Mustering all his will power, he managed to whisper, "It's better if you go on with your life, Misty."

"No!" she cried. "I want to be with you! Please just talk to me. I'll do anything to help you."

"Go on with your own life, Misty," he repeated.

"Don't you want me?" she asked, as tears ran down her cheeks. "Don't you want me at all?"

There was a hint of a sob in her voice that nearly weakened Del's resolve, but he steeled himself and said as firmly as he could, "Not anymore. Not this way. I want you to go—go now."

"I'm going," Misty took control of her voice, "but I won't just leave here and forget you. I will keep in touch with Karyl. I will not give up on you!"

She leaned closer and brushed his forehead with her lips. Then she left.

The flight home from Denver was a hurting time for Misty—she relived not only what Del had said but how he had escaped from her by closing his eyes. Why? she silently demanded of him. Why did you reject me? Is it because of your injuries? You're afraid of how you look? I don't mind; really, I don't. I love you. I'll take you as you are.

You've even turned from God; that's really a shocker to everybody. Oh, Del, I need to pray for you like Karyl and Fred and Roy are doing but—I don't know how to pray. I need help! God's help, I know, but I need a person to teach me. Jan! Jan will help me. How could I grow up in the church and not know how to pray? I mean, really pray!"

Her heart ached for Del. How lonely and deserted he must feel if he thinks God has left him! I feel lonely and deserted now that Del has left me, but how much worse he must feel now that he thinks God has left him! What a terribly desolate feeling. If he had only let me try, I might have been able to help him through this; I don't know how, I don't know God all that well, but I could have tried, I would have done anything! But he just didn't want me.

When the long trip finally ended, Misty was glad, glad to be back again in her familiar and comfortable home where life seemed to be flowing on as though nothing had ever interrupted it. She felt comforted and at ease. "Oh, there's so much to tell you," she said as she basked in the attention her parents were showering on her. "There's so much to talk about." But she knew that although she would tell them about finding Denison Elbert, the artist, it would be purely impersonal—at least for now.

Her thoughts never really left Del; she called Karyl as soon as she had a chance. "He's getting better, Misty." Karyl's voice was cheery over the miles. "But it's slow. He needs space and time. Maybe when he's up and around he'll be ready to see you."

Is there a chance he will ever be ready to see me, Misty wondered as she hung up the phone. Perhaps the short time with him I had is all that there is to be. I should be thankful he is alive and recovering, and I am thankful; thankful too I was able to bring some of his paintings home with me. If he can only win that prize, it could help him so much.

The paintings. Lewis was coming over this very evening to see them and to hear what she had to tell.

❦❦❦

She recounted her adventures to Lewis and her parents over dinner that evening. Her mother frowned when she described the cabin she lived in and a few of her less painful encounters with Angelo and Maria. They all laughed over her description of her driving the camp truck and painting cupboards, and her father exulted over her story of Martha Cross. Even though Misty had written him, hearing it from her was like hearing it for the first time. He was like a child finding a long-lost treasure.

"To think she was my cousin, my very own cousin. The one I used to play with," he said, happy the mystery had been solved.

"That makes you and Theba related, doesn't it?" Lewis asked Will.

"Well, yes, as a matter of fact it does. And Theba and Misty. And then there's Karyl whom I've never met. Mother," he said to Alice, "we've got a family!" And he continued to chuckle over this new turn of events in his life.

"You'll like Karyl," Misty promised. "She was good enough to let me bring these paintings. How do you like them, Lewis?"

"They are beautiful," he said simply. "Beautiful. I'm looking forward to meeting the artist. When he's able, I'm sure that can be arranged."

"Perhaps," said Misty softly. "There's something more I must tell you," and she told about finding the person she felt sure had defaced the eagle painting. His name was Doug Endicott. She spoke reluctantly; she had mixed feelings about Doug. He had saved Del and yet— wasn't he guilty of ruining Del's chances to win the coveted prize?

Lewis had left when Lance called to welcome her home. "I'm so anxious to see you." His words sounded genuine, and Misty felt a tiny bit of the old comfort in hearing them. "You do know about the dinner at the Applebys', don't you?"

"Yes, Mother told me." Misty gripped the phone a bit tighter in anticipation of what Lance was going to ask.

"May I pick you up? The dinner's at seven. How about if I call for you at six-thirty?"

Misty hesitated for a fraction of a second before she said, "Sure, that will be fine. I'll be ready." She hung up the phone and wondered, Can I slip back into my old life? Can I carry on as before? Of course not. But I need to talk to Lance face to face.

There was much thinking to do, so much that the night was far spent when she finally turned out her light. She thought of Lance, but Del's face kept getting in the way, and as she looked around the room where she had dreamed many dreams as a child and again as a teenager, she winced as she remembered the poverty-stricken cabin in the mountains. So many things had happened—things she had not talked about. Tomorrow she would go to her apartment, and maybe in a short time she could tell her parents about Dillon and Cindy, and some other things she was not yet ready to share like her feelings for Del.

TWENTY-FIVE

Misty was ready when Lance called for her the next evening, ready and lovely in a short black dress with a sequin-covered bodice.

"It's good you're back," and Lance kissed her almost dutifully. "Nice dress," he said matter-of-factly as he touched her shoulder.

The dinner proved to be all that Misty expected it to be. There being no Mrs. Appleby, Sharon, the senator's daughter, made a gracious hostess seeing that everything was done with exacting propriety. Misty, feeling somewhat awkward with Theba there, even though her husband kept up a lively, impersonal conversation, was no more comfortable with Lance. She was glad her parents were among the guests— glad for their support and Lewis'. Another couple completed the dinner party—the Staffords, who were new to Syracuse.

The dinner was served on delicate pink china that blended with the tiny rosebud center piece. The crystal and silver reflected the candlelight. The iced fruit cup was refreshing, and the roast duck a treat for Misty. She ate slowly taking little bites, and although she said little, she watched the others—from plump, curly-headed Sharon to her own mother, small and serene in a pale yellow sheath, with Will beside her.

"Yes, sir," Will was saying, "it's great finding out about cousin Matty. I had no idea. Theba, do you realize we're related? And you and Misty? It was your mother's money," Will went on without giving the cringing Theba a chance to answer, "that built that camp in memory of her sister Ruby. Imagine. Misty solved the whole thing. That and the mystery of who ruined the painting Lewis wanted to show. She even found the missing artist. Of course, you all know I'm not the least bit prejudiced when it comes to Misty."

They all laughed, and Misty smiled at her father then she was drawn to look across the table at Theba, who looked pasty in the candlelight. She should never wear white, thought Misty. It doesn't do a thing for her. And such a low cut neck. It shows off the blotches on her chest. Feeling Misty's eyes on her, Theba returned the look, then lowered her eyes to her plate and industriously speared a piece of asparagus.

"The canvases Misty managed to bring back are priceless." At the sound of his voice Misty turned her attention to Lewis. "Absolutely priceless."

"Then you will be showing one or two?" Senator Appleby knew little about art, but he showed a genuine interest.

"Probably two. Since I'm undecided between the one of a family of bears and the one of two girls, I think I'll show them both."

"How do they compare with that of the woman whose painting you are showing, Lewis?" asked Alice Morrow.

"Flora Nasby? She does excellent work. Her pastels are very commendable. She stands a good chance of winning the prize that is being offered. A very good chance."

"Have you met her yet?" Alice asked. "I know you hadn't last spring, but I was wondering if perhaps she had contacted you by now."

"So far I've only corresponded with her. She lives in Phoenix. I have the feeling she is handicapped in some way and prefers to leave things as they are. She did attend a recent showing of her paintings in Denver, so I'm hoping she'll come to the exhibit, but—"

Lewis was interrupted by loud gasping sounds from the other side of the table. All eyes turned to Theba who had begun to choke, the blotches on her throat and neck standing out even more against her white skin.

"Are you all right?" Hal patted his wife on the back. "Here, take a drink of water."

"I'm fine," sputtered Theba between sips.

"Put your arms up over your head," Alice instructed. "That always helps."

"I'm all right." Theba insisted, forcing a smile. "That bite went down the wrong way. Sorry, Lewis. What were you saying?"

"I believe I'd finished. I was saying what excellent work Flora Nasby does. how her paintings stand a chance—along with the bears."

A ripple of laughter went around the table.

"Bears?" Sharon's eyes were big. "Oooh, bears. Did you see any there in those mountains, Misty? Did you really enjoy all of that wilderness?"

"I loved it." Misty spoke quietly. "But no, I didn't see any bears. Just deer and mountain goats."

"How exciting it must have been," exclaimed Sharon; then she turned to Lance and began asking him about horses and what was the best day to go riding. Perhaps someday he could show her just where the stables were?

Lance and Misty drove from the senator's in almost complete silence. The crystal still dangled from the car mirror and Lance, seeing Misty watching it, broke the silence with, "Great things, those crystals. I had a bad back, real bad, and all I had to do was put a crystal on it. It's fine now."

"A crystal? On your back? Oh, come on, Lance. You sound like you believe in the same things Angelo believes in."

"It worked, I tell you. They're great. They have real healing power. Angelo? Who's he?"

"Someone I met in Pommel," answered Misty briefly. "He and his friends believe in spirits and all that goes with them."

"Well, the crystal did work," defended Lance. "And there are spirits. I'm learning quite a bit about them, how to channel and all that. I've even got a spirit guide. His name's Ralah."

A shiver went down Misty's spine. Ralah? Wasn't that the name of Prescott's spirit guide? "What about God, Lance?" she demanded.

"Oh, we worship Him too. And we worship the master Jesus."

Misty said nothing more. Lance's words disturbed her terribly. A most unsettling feeling crept over her, like when she'd been with Prescott and her group. How secure and at peace she had felt in the children's camp after being with those people. And now here at home was Lance; he *was* just like Angelo. More refined, but he had the same beliefs—like an ugly picture put in a gilded frame. Couldn't she get away from it? Her thoughts turned to Del. "We're praying for him and trusting the Lord to heal him," she heard Karyl saying.

"How do you like it?" asked Lance suddenly. He was driving past the house he and Misty had looked at that spring Sunday so long ago.

"The house?" asked Misty coming out of her reverie. "Oh, it's all finished. Is anyone living in it?"

"It's mine," said Lance, then added meaningfully, "I moved in last week. Let's go in. I had Ryan's Interiors do it. You'll love it. There's even an oriental rug in the living room."

"No, no I'd rather not go in. Thanks anyway. I'm sure it's lovely but you'd better take me home."

✹❦✹

At precisely nine o'clock the next morning Misty's little Porsche slid into its customary slot in the museum parking lot as if the routine had never been interrupted. Turning off the ignition, Misty glanced over her shoulder to make sure the carefully wrapped canvases were still on the back seat. She smiled as she remembered the exuberance Lewis had expressed over them, especially over the two Karyl had brought her from Del's cabin. Carefully lifting the large package, she walked towards the museum. Her high heels made the same clicking on the asphalt as before, and the elevator carried her up to the top floor with the same slow motion. But this time when she reached the tiled hall, she ran as fast as the cumbersome paintings would allow. Although she had talked to Jan, she had not seen her yet, and she was eager.

"Misty!" Jan left her desk and rushed to her friend, taking the package from her before catching her in a tight embrace. "Oh, it is so good to see you. Let me look at you! You look—good." Jan paused. "Thinner," she went on enthusiastically, "but wonderful! Are you really fine? You've been through so much. I prayed for you like I said I would, even more when you wrote about that character you rented from."

"I'm really fine, Jan. Your prayers—something—really kept me safe. Someone was watching over me. Oh, thanks, Jan. I've so much to tell you."

"You're all right, thank the Lord. Oh, Misty!" and Jan gave her friend another hug. Then she called, "Lewis? She's here."

The door to Lewis' office opened and the man stood smiling, looking even more handsome than ever. "Hi, there, Misty," he said with genuine affection.

Misty motioned to the canvases on Jan's desk. "There they are."

"This is great," said Lewis picking up the package. "Let's go into the office and have a look. Jan," he called, "have Theba come in and you come, too. We all want to see what's here."

"Theba?" A little cloud passed over Misty. This was Karyl's sister who was coming—Karyl's sister and her cousin, someone she should like.

"She and Hal were gone for a while," Lewis was saying. "—to Phoenix and Denver. They came home just last week. Here she comes now."

While Misty watched Theba cross the hall with Jan, she was aware of the old irritation awakened by the greeting "Misty! Darling!" She took a step behind Lewis' desk to avoid any embrace that might come.

"It's so good to see you again." Without a second look at Misty Theba turned to watch Lewis cut the twine that bound the canvases. "What have we got here? More paintings?"

Gently, Lewis unwrapped the canvases and laid them where the light was to their advantage.

"My word," said Jan softly. "Just look at those. They are beautiful!"

Theba leaned over to examine the paintings more closely. She hesitated over the one of the girls, looking at every detail. Then, putting her hand over her mouth, she took a step back. But no one noticed. "Denison Elbert!" she said finally, recovering her composure. "So you found him and you brought these home with you?" She carefully touched the corner of one canvas.

"It's pretty obvious," said Misty wishing she could be a bit more gracious.

"Well, I did think he might have sent them himself," defended Theba.

"Del couldn't send them," retorted Misty. "He's in a hospital."

"In a hospital?"

"He was injured in a forest fire."

"Injured? In a forest fire?" Theba looked at Misty. "How—"

"This is my preference," interrupted Lewis tipping the picture of the mother bear and two cubs to get a better look at it. "There's no reason in the world why it can't replace the one of the eagle and be entered in the contest. You did a great job, Misty, finding the man who ruined that painting. A great job. We'll begin proceedings against him next week. You'll have to testify and come up with more evidence, but if he's guilty, we'll make him pay."

"I knew you might want to do that," said Misty. "But—" and she thought again of how Doug had saved Del.

Her thoughts were interrupted when Theba, with a gasp, turned from the three who were still intent on examining the paintings. "I hear my phone ringing," she stammered and rushed from the office.

For a moment Misty stared after the retreating woman then she said, "I'd better get back to my desk, but I think I'll run down and look at the display room where these will be hung. Ok?"

"Of course," answered Lewis. "We hung the eagle there just to see how it would have looked, but we'll replace it with this of the bears."

"I'll go right down. Thanks, Lewis. See you later. Can I talk to you a minute, Jan?" she asked as the two of them started out the door.

"Sure." Jan quietly closed Lewis' door behind them. "Something's wrong, isn't it?" she demanded. "I could see it in your eyes. Is it Lance? Angelo? What is it, Misty?"

Misty spoke urgently. "Oh, Jan, I need your help. It's about God and prayer and this awful inadequacy I feel. I'm so mixed up! Could we get together to talk? Maybe tonight? I know it's an imposition, but—could we get together?"

"Of course. Just call me when you're home." Jan hugged her as she spoke. "I'll come right over. Remember, the Lord has you in His hands, no matter what."

Misty bit her lip and forced a smile. Then she nodded and turned towards the exhibition room.

Glad to be alone, Misty flipped on a light in the dark room. The pastel painting of Flora Nasby still hung where she remembered it. The only other was the painting of the eagle with its claw clutching the empty air. She stepped closer to the canvas to find the almost invisible outline of the fish. She wondered at the perfection and delicacy of the claw that had not been touched when the fish was removed. "That kind of tampering would take talent, I should think," she whispered to herself remembering the amateur paintings in Doug Endicott's cabin.

Looking at the eagle transported her thoughts back to the mountains and the valley, Glory Rock and the stream. Someday soon I am going back to visit Karyl and the camp. Maybe Del will be there—her thoughts went no further.

Misty shook herself out of her reverie. *The Globe* would start publishing her stories of the camp next week. This was no time to cry over what might have been if Del had let her stay. There was much to be done, much to occupy her time and thoughts. She was where she belonged for the moment. Not spiritually, she knew that, but physically.

She started up the dimly lit stairs unaware of Theba coming down until she heard her coo, "Leaving so soon? I had rather hoped you would tell me more about Del—uh, Denison Elbert and his being hurt in a fire."

Misty paused, one foot on the next step and her hand resting lightly on the stair railing. In the half light she looked intently at the tall, young woman. "What did you say?"

"That I'd like to hear more about Denison Elbert."

"You called him Del. You haven't seen him or heard from him for a long, long time have you, Theba? Whose fault is that?"

Theba's face crimsoned. She opened her mouth as if to speak then turned and left. Misty stood alone for a full minute then walked quietly out to her car.

She worked late at the newspaper, but once she was in the seclusion of her apartment, she leaned against the door and kicked off her shoes. The day had been another strain added to that of the evening before. Misty was exhausted. She changed into her sweats before fixing herself a supper of cold chicken, salad and toast. Finished, she called Jan. "I'm home," she told her friend. "Come over when you can. OK?"

Throwing herself face down across her bed, she closed her eyes. Thoughts about Lance scuttled across her mind. Remembering what he had said about crystals and spirits, she shuddered. How could he believe in those things and worship God? And there was Theba. Seeing her had been hard—knowing she was her cousin had made it doubly hard. With an effort she forced all thoughts from her mind and instead envisioned the pictures in Lewis' office. What was it Lewis had said? That he would probably show the painting of herself and Karyl, and the one of the bears? The painting of the girls was lovely, so detailed and realistic except for that shadowy portrait in the background.

Misty sat up suddenly. She wanted to see that painting again; she wanted to really look at the background. She would ask Jan to go to the museum with her the first thing in the morning before Lewis got there. Misty heard a knock on the door and opened it to find Jan.

Settling themselves comfortably the two talked of this and that for a few minutes—of the museum and of Lewis, of the paintings and of Theba and then of Del. "Why, Jan," Misty blurted out, "why do you think God let Del be injured so? Why is He letting him suffer this way? He's making a bitter man out of him!" And she went on to tell how Del had turned from God and from her and seemed so full of venom he was antagonistic to everyone. "Why?"

"I can't tell you why, Misty. It's not possible to understand why God allows some things to happen. We must remember He's a personal God, not just a principle as some believe. He's concerned about what's best for us, but what He does, and how He does it, is His business. Our part is to trust and wait. I'm sure He is working in Del's life in ways we can't imagine. There's a verse in Isaiah that says 'For as the heavens are higher than the earth, so are my ways higher than your ways and my thoughts than your thoughts.'"

"I wish I had your faith. I wish I really knew God."

"You can, Misty. Just tell Him you want to know Him and Jesus. As long as you tell God you need Him and admit that you've been separated from Him, for that's what sin is, being separated from God, He'll forgive and accept you and take you into His family. Reading your Bible and praying will help you learn and grow. The Holy Spirit will guide you."

"The Holy Spirit? Those people in the mountains I wrote you about, they believe in spirits. And so does Lance! Wait until I tell you what he told me last evening. He probably does the same things those others do—some really odd things like dancing and chanting to make vibrations—vibes, they call it—to chase away the spirits they don't want. And they channel to speak to the spirits they want to talk to. They ask the spirits for advice, and the spirits give it to them! These people think they're doing the right thing."

"Those spirits are very real, Misty. When people who believe in them channel, they do talk to a spirit. That spirit speaks through the one who is contacting him and gives advice. Yes, those spirits are real, but they are Satan's spirits. The Holy Spirit is very real too; He is from God. He lives in you the minute you believe and will be your guide. He'll never, never leave you. If you keep praying and studying the

Bible, you'll grow spiritually and understand all of this. And all will be well with Del. God may not choose what you would choose for Del, but whatever the Lord has for Del will be right. Just pray, Misty."

"Pray? I'm not so sure—"

"Just tell God what's on your heart, that's what praying is. He will listen, and He'll answer when the time is right."

"Do you think Del will ever get his faith back? Do you think he'll ever come back to God?"

"We'll keep on praying for Del and God will answer. I'm sure his faith will be stronger than ever because of this testing. You know, faith is like gold—it has to be put into a fiery furnace to get rid of the impurities."

Misty cocked her head to one side. "That's quite a thought." She remained silent for a few minutes then asked, "You will pray for Del, won't you?"

"Every day," promised Jan. She smiled, for she was fully aware of what lay hidden in Misty's heart. "We can pray together even over the phone, if we can't be in the same room."

"Oh, thank you, Jan." Misty, smiling through the tears that clouded her eyes, gave her friend a hug. "I don't know what I'd do without you."

Jan glanced at her watch. "It's late. I'd better go. Tomorrow's another busy day."

"Can you meet me at the museum early tomorrow?" asked Misty. "Would seven-thirty be too early? I want to look at that painting of the girls again without anyone else around."

Jan looked at Misty quizically. "Seven-thirty? If you can make it, I can. Sure. See you then."

It was late, but suddenly Misty was not tired; talking with Jan and the idea of really examining the painting had given her new energy. If Lewis chose to exhibit it, it might make a difference in what she wrote about Del.

Going to her desk, she took out the story she had roughed out in longhand while in Denver. Tomorrow after looking at the painting again, she would make any necessary changes in the story, then polish it when she put it on the computer at the office. It would be on its way before long.

"The world almost lost a great artist when Denison Elbert Quinn was severely injured in the mountains of Colorado while fighting a forest fire. No one else could capture the freshness of his paintings, the exquisite, true-to-life details.

"Del (she could not bring herself to refer to him as 'Quinn'), as he is known to his friends and family, uses his unusual talent to express his faith in the God of creation, even as the master Rembrandt so expressed his faith.

"Because he knew how to live, Denison Elbert, Del, faced death fearlessly so others could be safe."

Misty paused and put her hands over her face. "Oh, dear God," she whispered, "What has happened to Del? What's happened to his faith? What I've written is true: he did express his faith in You in his paintings. But what has happened? Look at Lance with his belief in crystals and spirits; nothing bad has happened to him." She paused while she sorted out her thoughts. Then, "What is the truth? If Karyl's faith is truth—and Fred's and Roy's, Jan's too, why have You let Del down? Why has he turned away? If You really are the great God, he needs You now more than ever. And so do I. All of these years, and I've never really known how to live. I'm totally confused. I've lived deceitfully, especially these last few months. I've hurt a lot of people, and I feel terrible."

A sob escaped her before she continued. "I'd rather know how to live and die than anything else. I want to know now, not wait until I'm old and crotchety. I want to know the truth about Jesus; if He's really Your Son, I want to be complete in Him because I know I'm nothing in myself."

She sat in the same position for long minutes while a peace, warm as the sun, flooded over her. "Thank you, God," she whispered, then took up her pencil again.

"Del risked his life for what he believed in. Two of his paintings will be shown at the Syracuse Oglethorpe Museum of Art in the American Artists exhibit on September 23. These and his other paintings are his heritage to America."

Tired at last, Misty went to bed and slept soundly.

TWENTY-SIX

Jan was waiting at the entrance to the museum when Misty drove into the parking lot at exactly seven-thirty the next morning.

"We're not the first ones; Theba's here." Jan motioned to another car parked several slots down the lot as she greeted Misty. "She doesn't usually come this early. And she locked the door after herself."

Unlocking the door and quietly slipping inside, the two women walked quickly to the elevator. "What was it you wanted to see?" asked Jan as she pushed the button.

"The painting of Karyl and me. Something about it has been bothering me. You know that other portrait sketched in in the background? I've never really looked at it."

"Who do you think it is?" They were at the fourth floor now, and together they clicked down the tile hall.

"I'm not sure what I think. Is it in Lewis' office?"

"It was." Jan had already opened the director's unlocked office door and turned on the overhead light. "It's not here now."

The two stood looking at the other paintings still on the table. "Do you suppose?" said Jan looking at Misty. Not waiting for an answer, she turned and started towards Theba's office.

The door stood slightly open but Theba, so intent on what she was doing, had not heard the women. When she did look up, a slow flush began to spread from her throat to her chin, continuing on to her cheeks, at last reaching her forehead. She said nothing.

"Theba, have you seen Denison Elbert's painting of the two girls?" Jan was reluctant to go all the way in.

Theba sat as if frozen, paint brush and palette in hand. The painting of Flora Nasby's was on an easel in front of her, Del's of the two girls on the floor beside it.

"What are you doing?" Misty brushed past Jan to get a better look.

"Oh. This?" Theba, coming to life, put the brush and palette down while she waved a hand at the painting on the easel. "Nothing really. I noticed a few little spots that needed re-touching. That's all. Just trying to make it better." She smiled weakly.

"You are touching up Flora Nasby's painting? The one that she is entering into the contest? You are making it better? I can't believe this!"

"It's quite all right, darling. She won't mind. Really."

"And you are going to touch up Del's a bit, too!" Misty accused.

"He won't mind because he's not able to defend himself—maybe never will be!"

The two women stared at one another, the one in fear, the other in anger. Jan stood beside Misty, waiting.

Suddenly Misty pointed an accusing finger at Theba. "You! You are the one who ruined his painting of the eagle! You are, aren't you?"

"Misty!" whispered Jan.

But Misty paid no attenition. "It wasn't that ranger at all. It was you! Why, Theba? Why did you do it? Why are you tampering with Flora Nasby's painting? What's gotten into you?"

Theba made no reply. Instead she pushed herself away from the easel and walked to the window. She stood with her back to Misty and Jan looking out at the street that was coming to life for a new day.

"Don't try to hide or deny this, Theba," advised Misty after a few minutes of silence. "I'm going to have to tell Lewis I've accused the wrong person. What Lewis will do I've no idea. It's your problem."

Picking up the painting of the two girls, Misty left with Jan following.

After placing the canvas on the table in Lewis' office with the others, Misty leaned over the one of Karyl and herself. Carefully, she inspected the faint portrait that was half hidden by the leaves of the trees—brown hair, arched brows. "Jan," asked Misty finally, "does this look like someone you know?"

"Well, yes, it looks like Theba. Maybe it's just because we're both so angry at her," said Jan.

Misty shook her head. "I assumed it was a reflection of Karyl, until I got to thinking! Jan, I'm sure I'm right."

"What in the world do you mean?"

"This," and Misty lightly tapped the faint portrait, "is Theba. She is Karyl's identical twin. Del told me that. He knew how much Karyl was hurting over her sister and he was, too. So he put her in the picture. He wants her to be part of the family."

"The Lord is working in her life just as He works in all of our lives," said Jan. "He works in ways we would never think of. He will work in your life, Misty, if you will ask Him to."

"I did, last night." And Misty told Jan how she had prayed and how peaceful she had felt.

Jan smiled. "That's it, Misty! Oh, I'm so happy for you—so happy that you have found the Truth."

"You know," Misty ran a finger along the edge of a canvas as she spoke. "If I hadn't gone to Colorado, to Pommel, I might not have come to know God. I might have gone along with Lance otherwise. I went under false pretenses; I know now I was wrong, but Karyl's forgiven me." And she looked at Jan with wide open eyes. "It's almost as if I had a rendezvous with God! I kept saying I had a rendezvous with the rocks, but it was really God I was going to meet. What are you smiling at?"

"A verse just came to my mind, something from Psalms. 'To Thee, O Lord, do I call; my rock, be not deaf to me, If Thou be silent to me, I become like those who go down into the pit.' Doesn't that fit? 'My rock,' the psalm says. God is your rock and you did have a rendezvous with Him."

"I wish you could see those mountains, Jan. How high they are." A happy smile wreathed Misty's face. "You're right, I had a rendezvous with God The Rock. And He wants Theba to know Him as I do; He's working in her life through this picture—by having Del show her she's part of the family. Oh, Jan, we'll have to pray for her too—we'll just have to! But—I still have to tell Lewis what we saw."

Lewis was visibly shocked when Misty told him how she and Jan had found Theba altering a painting of Flora Nasby's with one of Del's beside her. The implications were too obvious to ignore. "We've got to get to the bottom of this at once," he said somberly. He called Theba, and the four of them sat in a small close circle in the middle of the director's office: Lewis, Theba, Jan and Misty.

It was warm. Lewis walked to the window, opened it, then sat again. "Theba, you've been here for five years, and they have been good years. I personally do not understand what has happened, what you have done or why you did it. I'm sure you have an explanation."

Theba studied her hands resting in her lap, then she sat up tall and looked at Lewis. "I meant no harm to Del, believe me. We had painted together as children, competed in contests and done all kinds of things together. As a child I envied him; I was sure my grandfather, who was an artist, paid more attention to Del than he did to me. Del had the talent Grandfather wished my father had.

"When you came back from Denver in early spring, Lewis, and exclaimed over the painting you had seen, I vowed I would do one that was even better. I worked and worked at it. When Del's painting came, you weren't here so I opened it, which I was sure was all right— I've done that many times. I had it in my office where I could study it. I saw a few colors in it that I thought I could use on my own painting, so I put mine on the easel and took out my paints. Somehow I knocked a bottle of paint remover down and it—"

Theba paused and swallowed. "Right across the fish. I felt—well, I can't tell you how I felt. But I knew I had to fix it. So I tried, but the more I tried, the worse it became. I could not make it like it was; it was only a mess. The logical thing seemed to be to remove the fish altogether. I didn't even try to paint it in again."

The other three sat still, Lewis looking at Theba intently while Jan and Misty tried not to.

"You say you had a painting of your own in your office that you were working on. Isn't your office a pretty poor place to paint?"

Theba nodded. "The light is poor. I paint mostly in my studio at home."

"You never showed me any of your paintings."

Theba said nothing.

"Theba, you couldn't be Flora Nasby, could you?" asked Lewis.

Without looking at Lewis Theba whispered, "Could be."

The silence in the room grew heavier.

"I see," said Lewis finally and again walked to the window.

"I've done commercial art for a long time under that name," explained Theba, "and I thought it was a good way to compete in the American Artists contest."

"You didn't have to go that route, you know," Lewis said.

"I know."

"It would have saved a lot of people a lot of trouble and hurts, if you hadn't," he said.

"Yes."

"I'm not sure what to do about all of this."

"I—will withdraw."

Misty looked away. Theba was so drawn and pale. Someday maybe she would explain why she had drifted apart from her family. Had she been jealous of Del to the point of cutting all ties? She had said her grandfather paid more attention to Del than he did to her. Perhaps her father did too. And Karyl? Had Theba left because she felt rejected?

"Karyl would like to hear from you," Misty ventured gently after the silence grew unbearable.

Theba looked at Misty, and Misty realized there was no haughtiness, no longer any ridicule in the brown eyes under the arched brows. While she looked, she remembered the Honda she had seen parked in Pommel the day she drove with Del to see Dillon; she remembered the woman who had ducked to get in the car. It had been Theba. She must have come to Pommel to see the camp, maybe even to catch a glimpse of her twin and of Del.

"Someday soon I'll go to Colorado and visit her," Theba said.

"I think that's all we have to discuss right now." Lewis walked to his desk and sat down. "I see no need for you to withdraw, Theba. Your work is exceptionally good. Don't stop painting. I'm convinced you were not being malicious, and if what you say happened had not happened, we perhaps wouldn't have these other paintings of Denison Elbert's. If it's necessary to pursue this further, I'll let you know. Let's get back to work."

Theba stood tall, poised, and haughty as ever. Still sitting, Misty looked up at her. "Theba, how did you feel when you learned my dad is your mother's cousin—that we, you and I, are related? It must have been something of a shock to you."

"I've known it ever since I came here." Theba's voice was cold.

"Then why—? Why didn't you say something to Dad the other night at the Applebys'?"

"Because I didn't want to, that's why. I didn't want to have anything to do with any of my family at all, and you, your mother and dad were part of it. We came to Syracuse, Hal and I, because of his job. And I wanted to keep on with my art, so I came to the museum."

"Oh," was all that Misty could manage as a harsh realization came to her. Theba had been deceptive, but she, Misty—hadn't she been just as deceptive in what she had done? Oh, God, forgive me—forgive me for—yes, for hating Theba. I'm no better than she is. We are alike in many ways.

But I can't really understand because I have never experienced rejection like she has until—until Del sent me away. It's terribly painful. It must be because she's felt excluded that Theba has been so rude and cruel, not wanting me or any of the family to get close to her in any way; it has been her way of protecting herself from further pain. And yet her paintings at Pommel and the ranch, the portrait of her mother in the chapel, were her way of reaching out to the very ones she was pushing away. Someday, thought Misty, maybe I'll be able to understand these other destructive forces of jealousy and rejection.

For now Misty said nothing and watched Theba sail out of the office, her old confident self.

TWENTY-SEVEN

Days have a way of passing; sometimes too fast, sometimes too slowly, but they do pass. Misty's days passed slowly in spite of the fact that she plunged into her work. No matter what she was doing, part of her mind was on Del. She spoke to Karyl frequently, who reported on Del's slow progress. Misty refused to give up on his recovery, so she prayed and prayed for him. And she prayed about many other things. Now that she had learned she could talk to God about anything, she found she had a lot to say.

For Del the days passed even more slowly. The fourth day after Misty left the nurse raised the head of his bed a bit higher, shaved the unbandaged side of his face and combed his hair.

"Say, you look great," she said as she held a mirror for him to see. "Maybe I should have been a barber."

Del smiled slightly as he rubbed his left hand over his smooth cheek. "Feels good," he admitted.

"There are a couple of little books here one of your friends left for you. Maybe you'd like to read for a while." The nurse put *Time Out* and *Love Your Way To Wellness* within reach on his bedside table. "And look at the cards you've gotten! I'll pin them to the bulletin board on the wall so you can see them. But maybe you'd like to read through them first." She put the cards in a neat pile on top of his Bible beside the other books.

"See you later." And she left.

One by one Del picked up the cards and looked at them. There was the one from Misty, one from Cindy, one from Pastor and Mrs. Rubeck, one from the mayor of Frisco, several from Sadie and the others who were still at the camp. And of course, one from Doug Endicott.

Doug had written a note on a separate piece of paper that fell out of the card. Picking it up Del read: "How're you doing, Buddy? Sure miss you around here. Everything's OK at your cabin. I'll keep checking and close it up for winter, so don't worry. We're all rooting for you and counting the days until you're back at it.

"I never did have a chance to tell you that that gal who worked at Karyl's camp told me a painting you sent back east had been ruined. She thought I was you; that's why she told me. But I sure don't know who she was or what she was talking about. How come you sent a picture back east without saying anything? We'll talk more about it and her when I see you. I'll tell you how I found her rummaging around your cabin the day after the accident. Hope I can get down to Denver soon."

Del read no more. So—that was why he had never heard from the museum about his painting. It had been ruined! Ruined? His painting? How? And who in the world was the girl Doug mentioned. Someone who worked at the camp, he said. The only women who worked there were Sadie, Karyl and the nurses and—Misty. Would she know anything about his painting? Would she have been rummaging around in his cabin? Why, yes—she did bring him his Bible, didn't she? But why in the world—?

Del closed his eyes. What, oh what was Doug talking about? What did it all mean? "God, You've really done it," he breathed after several minutes. "I trusted you with that picture, and it got ruined. And Misty. You knew all the time what was going on. She had something to tell me, but You didn't let her. You broke it up; You did this to me instead. Oh, God, for the thousandth time—why?" and Del clenched the fist of his left hand.

Exhausted, he lay still, breathing deeply. Only that morning he had been freed of the ventilator, and it felt good to take even one breath on his own. His fingers explored his throat. A small bandage still covered the tracheotomy incision, but the doctor had told him it would heal quickly, that he was one step closer to recovery.

Quieter now he began to think of what he would do once he was out of the hospital, but what could he possibly do? Help out at the camp? Was he a candidate for there, to be a ward of Karyl and Fred's? Never! God had really put him on the shelf and forgotten about him.

Restless, he picked up the two little books Misty had brought. A touch of her fragrance seemed to linger with them. He looked them over casually then chose *Time Out* with its colorful cover.

The piece of newspaper Misty had placed as a marker made it easy for Del to turn to the page she had been reading. "No soldier in the Lord's army is ever 'laid aside' although when he is ill or injured it may seem that the Lord has shelved him. No, not so; the Lord has only given this one another commission whether it be to suffer, to fight for the Lord, or to have deeper compassion and understanding for others who are also 'laid aside.' Never, never is one of the Lord's shelved so he can be of no further use. Like a true soldier the one so 'laid aside' must let his Lord, his Captain, say where, and for what is his new commission."

Turning a few pages at random he read further: "If you are called to suffer, I pray you will let God's love comfort you. The Blessed Controller of all things does not allow suffering, does not bend the course of a life without His own eternal purpose in mind. He who sent His own Son to suffer and die and who Himself is love, does what He knows is best for each of His children."

The book dropped to the bed while Del lay staring at the wall ahead of him. The words "His own eternal purpose. . . what He knows is best" repeated themselves in his mind. "His own eternal purpose. . . what is best"— God, why is this Your purpose? How could it be Your purpose for me to be banged up like this? to hurt so? How could any of this possibly be best for me? I don't understand; it just doesn't seem right or fair. My life is ruined, and it's best for me? If You're there, You'll have to show me.

After a few minutes he hesitantly reached for *Love Your Way To Wellness*. "To be well you must love." The print was large; cartoons emphasized what the author had to say. "Get rid of all your fears, all your anxieties, all your resentments and love—love—love. Love everyone. Make a list of those you might have a resentment against and determine to love them. True healing and wellness come only with love. We all have it within ourselves—"

Del managed to push the book off the bed. "Love!" he snorted. " 'We all have it within ourselves—' Crazy! I don't have it in me to love. The person who wrote that doesn't know what he's talking about. God is love. Without God it's impossible to love, so since God has left me, how can I love my way to wellness? Sounds like something those way-out people in the mountains, that what's-his-name landlord of Misty's and his pals, might believe."

He picked up the first book again. "He who sent His Son to suffer and die and who Himself is love—" Del closed his eyes as the words replayed in his mind. "—who Himself is love—" Hadn't he, Del Quinn, just made the statement "God is love"—a statement that came from years of faith in a love that would not let him go? And what does love do? Bears all things in silence, has unquenchable faith, hopes in all circumstances, endures without limits.

Again Del's fingers explored the patch on his throat. He *was* recovering, but he was so tired—so torn apart. Why, oh why had God done this to him?

When he closed his eyes, the words "—who Himself is love—" appeared before him again as if on a screen. Then he slipped into a deep, deep sleep as he head his own voice saying, "God is love."

Misty had held off publishing the story of Denison Elbert, waiting until word came from Karyl that he was strong enough to read it and maybe—oh, maybe he would want to see her. She had re-written the rough penciled draft adding a short biographical sketch, as much as she knew, and telling about Del's involvement with the respite camp and his life as a ranger. It was gratifying when she saw the finished story printed in *The Globe*. The four weeks since the fire seemed an eternity to her.

"This is great, Misty," Will said when he read it. "I'm glad 'Sketches' is syndicated. It would be a shame to limit this to only our territory."

And so editors across the country were receiving "Sketches" and printing it in newspapers that were being folded and sent out by the thousands. *The Denver Post* was one such newspaper. Distributed all over the state, stacks were left in the usual places—on street corners, in newsstands, stores, apartments, business complexes, and in hospitals.

Papers for the patients were left just inside the door of the Memorial Hospital on the north side of Denver; from there they were taken to the rooms of those who requested them. The patient in Room D511 had been asking for one every day for the past week.

"How are you feeling this morning?" The nurse placed a breakfast tray on the table by Del's bed. "I brought you this morning's paper. Thought you might like to read it while you're waiting for your cousin to come. Maybe you'd prefer to sit in the chair? I'll help you. There you go. Oh, sorry. I'll get it." Leaning over she picked the little book *Time Out* off the floor from where it had fallen. "Looks like you've been reading this quite a bit."

" 'Pain,' " she read aloud from where the book was creased, " 'cannot shut the door to God, nor fatigue nor discouragement dim His shining face. No one can find peace by searching the sea or the mountains. Peace cannot be purchased with gold or silver or any fine jewels. But His word is forever: Peace I leave with you, My peace I give unto you; not as the world giveth I unto you. Let not your heart be troubled, neither let it be afraid.' That's nice, really nice. Do you believe that?"

"I would have said no two weeks ago," said Del, "but now—yes, I believe it."

"I believe you must," said the nurse. "You look so much better, and you're making much faster progress than anyone thought you could. We all need something to believe in, something to hang on to." Then placing the well-read book where he could reach it, she patted him on the shoulder. "Eat hearty!" she encouraged and was gone.

Hungry but still weak, Del leaned back to rest for a moment before taking the cover off the plate. It had taken four weeks for him to get this far; in another few days he would begin therapy for first his arm and then his leg. The doctors promised that in six months there would be nothing left to remind him of his burns on his face but some faint scars; he would be using his arm and walking and running as good as ever.

He ate what he could then pushed the table away to have more room to unfold the paper. He scanned the front page. There was more fighting in the mid-east and more starvation in the Third World. Nothing had really changed. The economy was so-so, and the comics were boring, but what he was looking for was on C3. "Sketches." He glanced over it quickly. Scarcely able to believe his eyes, he went back to the beginning and read slowly, hungrily, hardly able to comprehend what he was reading. When he had read it for the fourth time, he closed his eyes.

Mary Alice Morrow, he thought. She writes as though she knows me. But how could she? Where did we ever meet? "Mary Alice Morrow." He whispered her name this time. Then, as a sunbeam penetrating the fog, he said out loud, "Misty! Misty is Mary Alice Morrow. That's what she wanted to tell me. I don't understand, but that's who she is."

He sat looking again at the story about himself. "Lord, she knew I had turned from You, but yet she wrote this. I sent her away, refused her love because of my stupid pride! But she was faithful to me, and she was faithful to You. She believed You would heal me. But how could she have? She didn't seem to know You when she was here. Something has happened to her, something I prayed for back in the mountains when I thought she was a member of that strange bunch. I quit praying in my time of darkness, Lord, but You didn't quit. You kept working until You brought her home to Yourself. Oh, thank You! This story proves You have been working in her life. And it proves she cares for me! She really cares. And there is going to be a showing of my painting at the Oglethorpe. I don't know which painting, but You've been with me all the time and worked things out. I've been the faithless one, not You. Forgive me, and thank You. Thank You!"

After long moments of sitting, basking in the peace and joy that suffused him, he looked at the small calendar by his bed. September 23, the day the museum would present the prizes. He had a goal to work toward. Maybe he could begin his therapy sooner. But first he had to explain his plans to Karyl and Fred, and to Roy. He needed their help.

Roy listened carefully. Anyone watching him closely would have noticed the muscles in his neck and jaw tighten as he listened and as he, too, read the article. He remembered well the day he had started to drive over the pass in the mountains—the twisted, burned wreckage that lay on the side of the hill, Misty standing beside him as they both looked. He remembered, too, the sudden inspiration that had caused him to turn in on the grassy road that led up the gulley to the old Jerose Mine. He had driven as hard and fast as he could up that gulley until he had come to the mine devastated almost beyond recognition, the cabin scorched and the tumbled stacks of lumber nothing but pieces of charcoal. The old sluice was completely gone; only the boulders remained. No one was in sight.

From there he had made his way to the rangers' winter cabin where he had found his friend. What happened after that would be told and re-told many times. Doug Endicott had come, then Roy had retraced his tracks to town—fast. He had made some telephone calls that changed his personal plans, then flew with the injured men to Denver. It had been a grueling time, but they had won, and now Del was asking for one more thing. And Roy would do it.

The exhibit room at the Oglethorpe Museum was crowded. The warm, late September evening had brought out many of the city's elite to view the paintings, that after months of expectation, were ready for public viewing. There was an air of anticipation, for it was rumored that the highest award was to be given to the artist who had been severely injured trying to stop a forest fire.

Misty, wearing a simple blue silk dress, stood to one side watching the entrance. A breeze ruffled her hair which fell loosely over her shoulders. She squeezed her hands together nervously. All she could think of was Del, still fighting to regain his normal life. *If only he can win first prize,* she thought, *how encouraged he will be. Dear Lord, if it's Your will, let him win. Please! Karyl says his body is healing, please give him this award as an encouragement for his spirit.*

She looked around the room for Theba and spotted her in a far corner with her husband. To the casual observer she looked like her usual self, poised and self-confident. But to Misty she looked flushed and her smile forced; it was obvious she was nervous about the fate of her own painting, the one she had entered under the name of Flora Nasby. Misty tried to imagine how Theba must feel. *It must be hard,* thought Misty with sudden compassion. *She wants to win—needs to win. I can understand that.* Lewis was trying to make it easy for her. He had said he would introduce her as Theba Peterson who painted under the name of Flora Nasby. Nothing wrong with that. Artists could have fictitious names.

Lance was there, too, with Theba and Hal. And Sharon Appleby by his side, just as Misty had expected. She felt no regrets. All she felt about Lance was relief. The few times she had seen him since she had come home from Colorado, Lance had not been the same. Was it because he was into this cult, something Misty could not tolerate? Perhaps it had been a difficult time for him; perhaps he had not known just how to break with her. But more likely he had been undecided as to who was the more influential—Misty's dad, the editor or Sharon's father, the senator. Apparently the senator had won.

Jan stood by Misty. "The announcement of the winners should be any minute now," she encouraged. "There goes Lewis to the microphone now." Both women turned toward the front of the room.

"I'm so nervous!" Misty whispered to Jan and grabbed her hand.

"Ladies and gentlemen," Lewis began. "The suspense has gone on long enough. It is my pleasure to announce that first prize has been awarded to—Denison Elbert!"

Misty gasped, grabbed Jan and hugged her, and wiped tears of relief from her eyes. "Oh, thank God!" she cried. "Oh, if only Del could be here right now!"

Jan took her by the shoulders and gently turned her around.

Surprised by Jan's action, Misty looked at the entrance, suddenly drew in her breath and said, "Del?"

Del smiled at her, and the crinkles around his eyes deepened.

"Del, oh Del!" Misty cried as she raced to the man in a wheelchair and grabbed his outstretched hand. "You've come back like you promised," she said looking deep into his eyes.

"Like I promised," Del repeated, "my body needs more time, but thanks be to God, my spirit is healed."

"Ladies and gentlemen," Lewis announced as he pointed toward Del, "the artist, Denison Elbert."

"Thanks be to God!" Misty repeated Del's words.

Much to Misty's surprise, Karyl stepped into view and placed her hands on the back of the wheelchair, patiently waiting to propel Del to where Lewis and the judges were standing. Lewis was holding the first prize award that was to be Del's. A mischievous smile played around Misty's lips as she withdrew her hand from Del's and stood beside him. "Karyl's waiting!" she said, and they both laughed.